The Boss's

DAUGHTER

The Black Rose Series
Book One

Jennifer Bates

The Boss's Daughter

Limitless Publishing, LLC
Kailua, HI 96734
www.limitlesspublishing.com

Formatting: Limitless Publishing

ISBN-13: 978-1-64034-264-4
ISBN-10: 1-64034-264-8

DEDICATION

I read the chapter
11/9/2015

Prologue

An hour away from walking down the aisle, Renee was dressed in her gown—hair done and makeup applied—listening to her bridal party get ready because they apparently believed you could improve on perfection. Renee smiled as she looked out the window overlooking the Isle of Lilies where Christopher and she had shared their first kiss.

"This bridal suite is enormous," Alice said. "I could totally be happier living here than at the hotel."

Michelle was holding a pair of stockings in each hand, trying to decide which to wear for the day. "Don't let him hear you say that. Any hint he thinks we don't appreciate him is just trouble."

"He'll find a way to make your life worse than hell." As the words were coming out of Saffron's mouth, her friends turned to Renee, waiting for a disappointed reaction, but there was none. Renee couldn't blame her friends for thinking the way they did. Matthew Parnell was one of the most powerful and wealthy men in New England who bathed in the admiration and respect he had earned over the years, while at the same time would not hesitate to have a bullet dispatched if he felt disrespected or threatened. Renee didn't consider Alice's statement as disrespectful, but the others were right. It was best if he didn't hear it.

Renee gave a reassuring smile. "He won't ever know it was said."

Renee watched as Saffron started digging through her bag containing her wedding day essentials and smiled as she spotted the familiar packaging she knew contained at least a pound of marijuana. Drugs were one of her father's main sources of income, and just because she was getting married didn't mean organized crime in New England came to a halt.

Saffron scanned the bride for any imperfections and found a flaw. "Where are your mother's earrings?"

Renee grabbed her ears to verify the missing jewels. "They're in my bag. And before any of you say anything, the shoes wait until the last minute. I'll be standing for at least an hour during the ceremony and I would like to be comfortable before I have to put them on."

Her four friends turned back to their own primping as Renee dug through her bag to fish out her mother's emerald tear drop earrings to complete her wedding day ensemble. Then she glanced down to the side of the vanity to make sure her shoes were, in fact, still there. As she was pulling the bobbles from her bag, there was the sound like a cannon being shot into something metal coming from outside. Renee, Michelle, and Saffron froze in place as Charlotte and Alice ran to the window to see if they could find out what was going on.

"There are people running down the driveway. I don't—"

Before Alice could finish her sentence, Renee hiked up the hem of her dress and ran out of the bridal suite as fast as she could until she reached the end of the driveway, ignoring everyone and everything around her. She couldn't see through the crowd of guests encircling some kind of dilemma. All she could see was smoke, all she could smell was copper, and all she could hear were muffled voices. Renee ran toward the swarm of people and briefly noticed her father, his captain, Mr. Crescent, and three of his associates standing away from the crowd like they didn't care to get involved.

"Renee!" Charlotte yelled out as she was trying to catch up.

Hearing Charlotte's call, a few of the wedding guests and reporters turned, half-heartedly trying to reach out and stop her. Renee pushed them aside and broke through the crowd, coming to a halt as disbelief washed over her. Christopher's metallic blue truck was crushed by another truck on the passenger side. The only thing of note about the second truck that Renee could distinguish was the bloodied body folded over the steering wheel and the skull halfway through the windshield. There were men at both vehicles working desperately at what appeared to be a rescue. Renee watched as they succeeded in removing Tucker Wilson, Christopher's best man, from the truck and laying him on the ground as Dr. Seaver and Dr.

Michaelson ran from the crowd to examine him.

Renee could feel her father's eyes on her, but she couldn't look in his direction. Matthew Parnell may have been one of the most loved by everyone he rubbed elbows with, but he was also the person she fiercely loved more than anyone else in the world, and looking at him would only cause her to break down. He promised her the perfect wedding. He promised her that this would be the day she had always dreamed of. He *promised*.

Cameras flashed from all directions and chaos encircled her as Renee watched Christopher being pulled from the truck and set down for Dr. Michaelson to examine. Christopher's hair was damp and red with blood, explaining the smell of copper in her nose. His bright green emerald eyes were closed as blood ran down his face. She saw the beginnings of bruises, swelling, and the rise and fall of his chest—she knew she did—and that was all the hope she needed.

Renee ran to Christopher's side and sat next to him, staring at Dr. Michaelson, who could only look at Renee with heartbreak. "I can't promise you anything. I'm going to do what I can until the ambulance gets here."

Choking on tears that refused to fall, Renee nodded in understanding. She would not cry, because crying meant two things: weakness and finality. Renee watched Christopher's chest rise and fall like he was begging for air as she cradled his head in her lap, trying to stay out of Dr. Michaelson's way, but with a firm look, letting the doctor know she wasn't going anywhere.

"I'm here, baby. Please stay with me."

Christopher opened his eyes and looked at her with no confusion on his face; he knew it was her. All Christopher could do was gaze into her eyes and try to breathe as Renee faked a smile as best she could. "Dr. Michaelson is here and he's going to make you better."

Renee leaned down and gently kissed him. When he weakly returned her kiss, he looked in her eyes, deep and true, and the hope began to drain from her. Christopher let out a breath and a trickle of blood started from the corner of his mouth. Renee focused all of her attention on his face, willing herself to wake up from this nightmare.

Christopher reached for her hand and cupped it in his. In painful breaths he said, "Since the first time I saw you, I loved you. I always will."

Christopher's chest ceased to rise and fall. The understanding was immediately there and Renee began to shake as shock took her over. She didn't know how long she had been holding onto Christopher before she was being involuntarily lifted to her feet to look into the eyes of her father. He gave her a sorrowful look as Renee fell into the safety of his arms. She made no sound, had no emotion, and just wanted to wake up from this nightmare. After a few minutes, her father kissed her gently on the forehead and spoke softly. Seeing Charlotte and Michelle approaching, Renee turned her head back in the direction of the accident to validate what she couldn't believe to be true. Charlotte wrapped an arm around Renee, pulling her in the opposite direction, but Renee couldn't move.

"She needs to leave," Matthew said sternly.

Michelle and Charlotte helped Renee through the crowd of people, Alice and Saffron silently following behind. Heartbroken, Renee just wanted her father to hold her and tell her everything was just a bad dream. When she turned her head, everything suddenly changed when she saw it—and there was nothing subtle about it. Renee stopped walking to make sure she wasn't seeing things as she watched the expression on her father's face change. Matthew was no longer the man who had held her just minutes before; he was the man his business friends and enemies had gotten to know. He had turned away from the crowd to try to hide his expression from the cameras, the beginnings of a smile on his face. She could see the satisfaction appear on his face as he spoke, and then he did something that made Renee's heart stop once more. He laughed and turned to light a cigar.

Renee's thoughts immediately went from sorrow to complete disbelief. Matthew Parnell only smoked cigars for two reasons: to rub elbows with people in high places or when he was celebrating a job well done. Renee looked to her friends and knew they saw it too. She also knew they were smart enough to avert their eyes so they wouldn't have to speak. Renee picked up the hem of her dress and walked back to the mansion to pack her bags and go home.

Chapter 1

Twenty Years Ago

Renee had a short childhood. Her mother died bringing her into the world, leaving Matthew to raise her alone in the only manner he knew how, to the best of his abilities. For the most part, Renee was a typical, happy child who laughed and played as she began to learn how her world would work. She spent more time with nannies and women who worked for Matthew, but spent as much time as possible with her father. Always a curious and diligent child, she was loved and praised by many, either because she actually was a well-behaved child or because she was Matthew's daughter, and it was clearly obvious that she was fiercely loyal to her father.

By the time Renee was ten, she had seen and heard things that no child should ever know. She never questioned her father and was never fazed by what she witnessed; she grew stronger because of it. Renee devoted herself to her father and the Family,

7

the only exception being Evan Crescent. He was cold and contemptuous to her and she would return the feeling every chance she got. Out of respect for her father, they treated each other with polite indifference, usually shooting daggers out of their eyes when they had to speak to each other. If she never saw him again, she wouldn't care.

When she wasn't in school, she spent most of her time with Sasha Wheeler, the madam for the New England Family. Sasha was young and beautiful, generous and patient, and helped Renee grow from child to young woman. Renee would often imagine her mother when Sasha talked to her about the plethora of choices life would have to offer instead of fully committing herself to the Family. But just like her father, Renee was stubborn and dedicated to getting what she wanted. What Renee wanted most in the world was to make her father proud.

With slight reluctance from Sasha, before and after school for almost a year, Renee would meet with Sasha to discuss work and life. Renee always focused on work—whether it was preparing contracts, scheduling clients, or arranging deliveries—and was quickly accepted by the girls servicing Matthew's clientele by being understanding and direct. Just like everything else she touched, Renee took to the job she was given with focus and determination. Nobody, especially her father, would be let down.

"You seem to be enjoying your work," Sasha said over a private dinner with Renee one night. "I'm surprised. I thought with your excellence for numbers you would want to go straight to bookkeeping."

"I can do that too," Renee replied after swallowing her food. Talking with food in her mouth was the number one rule she would never break. "I already do."

"I meant for more than just what we do."

"What, you mean like for the hotel?"

"I think your father would be pleasantly surprised with the work you could do downstairs."

Renee slightly narrowed her eyes at Sasha. "Why would you want me downstairs? Am I doing something wrong?"

"No," Sasha said with a defeated sigh. "No, you're not."

"Then why would you want me downstairs?"

"Renee, you're fourteen years old. Girls your age are thinking about proms and shopping, hoping the captain of the football team wants to take them out for pizza." Sasha put her hand up before Renee could interrupt. "I am fully aware that you are not like other girls your age and I absolutely love you for who you are. But I have to wonder, do you really want to work in this hotel, upstairs, for the rest of your life?"

"I know my father has other jobs that I would be good at, but I want to be with you and the girls. I'm good at my job. You said so yourself."

"I did," Sasha agreed. "What I don't understand is why."

"Because I love you and the girls are my friends. I can't leave you guys."

There was no emotion in Renee's features or tone when she spoke. After all, she was right. All she knew was the life she had. She had no friends her own age outside of the hotel and had become closer to the girls than Sasha ever thought she would. On top of that, Renee knew Sasha loved her as much as she loved Sasha.

Sasha smiled at Renee with a mother's love and wiped her mouth with a napkin. "It's getting late and we have to get back upstairs. We have a client in less than an hour."

"Why haven't I been marked yet?"

All of the girls who worked for Matthew had a mark—a black rose tattoo that adorned the back of their right shoulder with a blood red *P* dangling from the green stem.

Curious, Sasha asked, "Why do you want one?"

Renee looked at Sasha like it was the most obvious question she had ever asked. "I'm a member of this Family and I should have my mark."

Sasha couldn't argue the logic. "Ask your father. If he says yes, I'll make the arrangements."

***

"You're a little young to get marked, Renee," Matthew said without taking his eyes off the newspaper.

"Don't you think I have earned my mark, Father?"

"The responsibility that comes with the mark is heavy, Renee. Are you sure you're ready for it?"

"I wouldn't be asking if I didn't feel I was ready for it."

Matthew cocked an eyebrow at her over his

newspaper. "I don't care. Do what you want."

The next day, Renee's back was adorned with the black rose tattoo that she wore as a symbol of pride and loyalty to her Family. Her tattoo differed from the others only in that she was marked with the letter D for daughter. Once the ink was done there was no question that she would now and forever be a permanent fixture in every aspect of the business.

Chapter 2

Renee was in a bad mood—pouty, whiny, and all around simply put out.

Sasha was going to Chicago with David, leaving Renee heartbroken and with a massive responsibility in front of her. Tonight, she would be Sasha's successor in the Family. It didn't matter that she was only sixteen years old, what mattered was proving she could do the job both publicly and privately.

Renee sat in front of the vanity with a scowl and a look of utter disdain on her face as Sasha stood behind her, smiling while she curled Renee's hair and not saying a word.

"What are you smiling at?" Renee snapped at Sasha.

Sasha continued to smile, replying innocently, "Oh, nothing."

"Ow!" Renee exclaimed, and then growled under her breath as Sasha brushed out a curl she had just put in.

"Sorry," she said. "Hold still."

"I *am* holding still." Renee crossed her arms in front of her, huffing like a three-year-old who didn't get their way, and it just made Sasha smile more as she hummed along with the radio.

"It's my birthday and I don't even want a party."

"I know," Sasha said with empathy, "but it's going to be a wonderful night and a fabulous party. You'll see."

"Fat chance," Renee scoffed, then let out a resigned sigh when Sasha raised an eyebrow in the mirror. "I love my father, but he's the one who wants this party."

Sasha rested her hands on Renee's shoulders. "You know you must do things like this from time to time. It's important that your father maintain his societal status, and you are part of it. It's not the first time, and it certainly won't be the last. Besides, whether or not you want this party, I know you would do anything to make your father happy, and this will make him happy."

Two of Renee's companions, Saffron and Michelle, entered the room dressed and ready for the party. Renee had become close with them, but wondered if that would change now that she was in charge.

"We just wanted to let you know the girls are ready," Saffron said, then added, "Wow. You are a knockout."

Renee giggled then stiffened up, completely surprised by the sound that came out of her mouth. "What the hell was that?"

"Did you just giggle?" Michelle asked, dumbfounded by the foreign sound.

"She has been acting like your typical teenager for the past three hours," Sasha said through a laugh. "It's been quite entertaining."

Embarrassed to discover she had been acting like a child, Renee decided to focus on her responsibilities for the night. "It won't happen again, that's for sure."

"You, my dear, are done," Sasha said as Renee studied herself in the mirror, completely speechless at what Sasha had transformed her into.

Renee hugged Sasha as hard as she could. "Thank you so much."

"You are so very welcome. I love you, you know."

"I love you too." All Renee could think about was that this was probably the last time she would get moments like this with Sasha.

"Your party starts in twenty minutes, birthday girl, so get dressed and we'll see you downstairs," Saffron said as she handed Renee her shoes, then quietly left the room with Michelle in tow.

Sasha smiled and held Renee at arm's length to look her over a final time. Then, like the flip of a switch, Sasha looked at her with complete seriousness as she sat Renee back down. "I have something I need discuss with you, *but* you have to promise that you will never repeat it. I cannot stress the seriousness of this conversation. So, please, listen carefully."

Renee silently, but curiously, nodded as Sasha reached into her bodice and pulled out a key. "Do not ever lose it and don't let your father know about it. In the bottom left cabinet of the credenza in the conference room there is a false wall with a lock. This is the key to that lock. There is a small metal box that your father must not know about, and I'm going to ask you not to try to open it. I can't tell you not to open it, because when you tell someone not to do something, their first instinct is to do what they're told not to. But," Sasha looked at Renee with dangerous seriousness in her eyes, "if you are as smart as I know you are, you will not open that box until the time is right."

Renee's forehead creased in confusion. "How will I know the right time?"

Sasha ran a hand gently down the side of Renee's face. "You will know."

Renee's thoughts were racing as she looked at Sasha. "How are you certain that my father doesn't know about the wall or the box?"

"Because I am still alive."

Renee felt like she had been slapped. If her father knew about this secret box, Sasha would die. "What's in the box?"

Sasha closed Renee's hands around the key and Renee instantly felt the awesome and secret responsibility that Sasha was handing her.

"Sasha? What's in the box?"

Sasha took Renee's dress off the hook, turned, and looked Renee directly in the eye. "Proof."

Chapter 3

Matthew Parnell joined the Lundy Family out of high school and quickly befriended Wyatt Lundy, son of the Family boss, David Lundy. David was a fair and well-respected businessman who owned more than one successful real estate company that he used as a legitimate cover for his illegal activities in the largest organized crime family apart from the New York Five. Matthew rose faster in the ranks than anybody before him, which allowed him to work in various arenas such as drugs, money laundering, extortion, and deliverance of the consequences. It wasn't long before David tested Matthew's abilities by handing both him and Wyatt the Boston territory. Elated that he was quickly on his way to the power he dreamed of, Matthew stepped away from getting blood on his hands and relied heavily on Evan Crescent to take care of whatever business Matthew felt appropriate.

One year after arriving in Boston, Matthew met Elise when she checked into his hotel for a weekend vacation. He fell madly in love with her, and they married only a few months later. He was both surprised and elated when she returned his love after he made it painfully clear to her that he would not accept a child in his life. So when she announced she was unexpectedly pregnant, it was a betrayal that cut him deep and would never be forgiven. Matthew resented Elise for forcing him to play the happy, undeniably in love couple for the public, but he had no choice—he would do what he must if he wanted to maintain his social standing and gain the power that had been his goal since joining the Family.

Matthew's problems were only exacerbated by the fact that Wyatt felt he didn't need to work as hard, feeling entitled because he was David's son. Matthew never said a word about Wyatt's gambling or drug use, but he did put a stop to Wyatt's time with their girls when it was discovered that one had gotten pregnant. The pregnancy was quietly terminated and, fortunately, Matthew's problems with Wyatt didn't last much longer. Wyatt had decided to spend his birthday in Las Vegas and was supposed to be gone for five days. It was six months later when his body was found decomposing in the hot desert sun with two gunshots in his head.

***

Dressed in a tuxedo, one hand in his pocket like he didn't have a care in the world, Matthew met Renee when the elevator doors opened. Looking at his daughter reminded him of Elise, and when he thought of Elise, it took everything he had not to be disappointed, hurt, and angry. A camera flash out of the corner of his eye broke his train of thought and he straightened his posture as Renee stepped forward with all the grace and poise expected of her. It was time to play the happy father for the crowds.

Checking to make sure the media was watching, Matthew held her at arm's length to look her over, forcing a smile and giving his daughter a firm look. "Appearances, Renee. You're the daughter of Boston's Man of the Year."

Renee nodded her head and took her father's arm as they entered the ballroom to greet their guests. There was applause and greetings from every angle of the room as Matthew and Renee smiled and waved, Matthew internally toasting himself just for being him with his daughter next to him, boasting with pride. Guests approached to give their hugs and handshakes for what seemed like an eternity until a familiar face entered the room. Matthew knew the effect David being here would have on Renee.

Matthew took David's hand with a smile. "I'm glad you could make it."

"I wouldn't have missed this," David replied with a jubilant grin.

"David!" Overly excited to see him, Renee stopped herself from jumping into his arms to hug him.

"You didn't think I would miss this party, did you?" David laughed playfully at her as he broke the hug and planted a loving kiss on her cheek. "You and I will dance later."

***

Renee counted eight scarlet lapel pins shaped like teardrops attached to each of the eight men she had met with earlier. Each pin represented proof of payment for the pleasure of going upstairs with their companion after the party. She received varied reactions from each of them, from disgust to humor, as she knew she would. Even she knew that any full-grown man would be more than slightly offended at the fact that he now had to transact business with a teenager, but not one of them made a derogatory comment to her as they accepted their pin.

Renee played her part as she mingled with guests who were pretending to listen to the governor-elect's wife prattle on about one thing or another of no import when, out of the corner of her eye, she saw one of her girls in the process of being cornered by a man who had apparently already started raiding the open bar. She saw Kristin slowly backing away from her client, trying to keep from making a scene as he continued to try to close the gap between them. Renee briefly locked eyes with Kristin, who was clearly giving the damsel in distress look.

Gracefully as she could, Renee interrupted her guest's story. "I'm sorry to intrude, but I need to say hello to someone before they leave for the evening. Thank you so much for coming. We will have to try to find each other later on so you can finish your story." It was a lie, of course, but it was time to go to work.

Renee wrapped her arms around Kristin in a

welcoming embrace, while at the same time nonchalantly placing her foot on top of the offender's, her floor-length gown covering the fact she was digging her one-inch heel into his foot. The more he tried to dislodge his foot, the more weight she put down. The look she gave was daring and cold, and she spoke to him with authority through a forced smile. "Judge Middleton, are you forgetting there is an expected etiquette for tonight that you have agreed to follow?"

Judge Middleton, a middle-aged and arrogant man, knew they were being watched and didn't appreciate a child digging her heel into his foot. Through teeth clenched and a smile he responded, "Get off my foot, bitch."

Renee applied more pressure and he sucked in a breath of pain. "Am I correct that you were told it is still early in the party and that you would have to be patient for your pleasure?"

He could only nod.

"Would it be fair to say that you will be more than happy to wait at least another hour before casually and discretely leaving with her?"

"Yes," he said, sucking in a hard breath, thinking her heel would go through the top of his foot.

Renee drastically applied more pressure and leaned into him, her ear close to his mouth. "I'm sorry, I didn't quite hear you."

"Yes," he said forcefully through the pain.

Renee smoothed the front of his jacket and straightened his pin. "I'm so happy this misunderstanding has been cleared up. I sincerely hope you enjoy the rest of your evening, but I would advise avoiding the bar for a little while. For future reference, you will address me as Ms. Parnell."

The wide-eyed judge nodded and Renee removed her foot from the top of his. As Renee crossed the room to greet another guest, she locked eyes with Sasha, who was smiling and raising her glass in a silent toast to a job well done.

Chapter 4

Matthew wasn't happy that Sasha was leaving. Standing in the back of the ballroom discussing business of their own, Matthew and David quietly watched Renee make a federal judge feel like a horse's ass with tact and decorum.

Nodding in the direction of where Kristin and the judge were standing, David said, "You've done well with her. If Elise were here—"

"Elise isn't here," Matthew interrupted with an abhorrent tone.

David ignored Matthew's tone and felt the need to point out the obvious. "Don't underestimate her. She's a smart one, and determined at that. She will go far in the Family."

"If Sasha wasn't leaving, we wouldn't even be having this conversation."

Matthew knew David didn't care how he felt about Sasha's relocation. David took a draw of his cigar and caught a woman watching them from across the room. She looked to be just a few years younger than Matthew and was striking in her red evening gown, sitting decorously while patiently waiting for the moment to do whatever she was planning.

"Do you know the remarkable woman in the red dress?"

Matthew looked in the direction David was and froze in irritation. Matthew inhaled deeply and spoke in a tone that told David he wasn't happy seeing her. "Her name is Madeline Frost. She was an acquaintance of Wyatt's for a time. She is also a bit of competition. Her specialty is loans and laundry, but I hear she is trying her hand at the funny money trade. No confirmation on that yet."

David showed slight concern on his face. "You're sure about that?"

"She has been trying to get into bed with us for a few years, but we have no interest in coupling with her."

"Why not?"

"She's more of a black widow than a trusting business partner."

Matthew very much disapproved of Madeline's presence and made a mental note to speak to his daughter to find out how Madeline Frost had received an invitation to this celebration. Madeline took extreme pleasure in testing his desire for her, and while Matthew did find her beautiful and secretly admired her determination, he couldn't deny that he often thought about fulfilling the fantasies that sometimes slipped into his thoughts. Sex was her weapon of choice, but sleeping with the enemy was dangerous and he wouldn't risk everything he had worked for just for the pleasure of her company.

"She's very beautiful," David noted with a smile.

"Do not be taken in by her siren song. It can sometimes take considerable effort to resist her charms. She's very persistent when she chooses to be." David gave Matthew a questioning look. "Rest at ease, David. I have resisted every time."

The band slowed the music down and David clapped his hands in front of him, rubbing them together in anticipation, and handed Matthew his cigar. "Ah, it's time to dance with the birthday girl."

As David walked away, Madeline floated toward Matthew, the epitome of sophistication and grace. Matthew turned to the table behind him to both extinguish David's cigar and take a moment to compose himself. Up until he saw Madeline, he was enjoying himself.

"Good evening, Matthew." She had a honeyed quality to her voice that made it hard for Matthew to think of her as only an acquaintance.

With an unfettered tone he replied, "Madeline."

"It's a lovely party," she said as she scanned him from head to toe with an approving grin.

It was, Matthew thought to himself, casting an eye over Madeline. Instead of saying what he was thinking, he simply nodded to acknowledge that she had spoken.

"I was invited to accompany Mr. Jamison tonight. My feelings were hurt, Matthew. Then I assumed that my invitation must have been lost in the mail."

Matthew took a deep breath through his nose to try to calm his agitation. "That's must be it."

"Your daughter is lovely tonight. You must be very proud of her."

Matthew turned to stub out his own cigar, knowing Madeline had that sly smile working overtime. David and Renee glided across the dance floor, amused to watch Matthew have to gather his composure before addressing Madeline.

"Is there something in particular you wanted, Madeline?"

She seductively smiled at him as he turned his head to look at her. Not since Elise had he wanted a woman this badly, but he was not about to give in.

Innocently, she gently rested a hand on his arm. "I wanted to come over and say hello and let you know I have been thinking about you."

Matthew had to put a stop to this conversation. She frustrated him in more ways than one.

He gently removed her hand from his arm. "What is it you really want, Madeline?"

She gave him a defining look. "The casino being built in Atlantic City."

"What about it?"

"You know my business would benefit yours."

A smile formed at the corner of his mouth. "Is business that bad, Madeline?"

"Bad? No. I want the percentage for my own reasons."

"What's in it for me? More importantly, why would you think I would agree to this?"

The sly smile came back to her as she sidled up close to him, this time resting a hand on his chest and looking up at him with those eyes that made him want to throw her into the nearest closet and have his way with her. Though his posture slightly stiffened at her touch, his expression was blank and unreadable as he bent his head and met her gaze. He couldn't help but sweep his eyes across her chest, giving him a clear and deliberate view of the curve of her breasts and how they rested nicely behind her dress.

This woman is the devil.

"I'll tell you what. Why don't you think about it and let me know what it is you would like in exchange? I'm sure I can accommodate your request, within reason, of course."

Matthew cleared his throat and regained his composure. "I'm sure. Excuse me, Madeline."

He knew he would have to relay this conversation to David later so he took the opportunity to discretely slip out of room and go outside to get some air.

Chapter 5

Renee was elated to spend whatever time she could with David, even if it was a short time. She thought of him like a grandfather and he was always there for her no matter what, whether to give advice, a hug, or to sit quietly and enjoy a movie together. Dancing with him was something she always enjoyed; after all, he was the one who had taught her.

"I was watching you earlier," David said, nodding in the judge's direction. "You did very well. I'm proud of you."

Renee smiled. "He was just eager to start his own party. Many of our clients are going to rebel against having a sixteen-year-old taking over their services, and I have to put that rebellion to rest quickly. Give it a few months and everything will be just fine."

David placed a kiss on her forehead. "You never cease to amaze me."

In her peripheral vision, Renee caught a glimpse of a young man with dark hair weaving through the multitude of guests, eventually making his way behind them and slowly continuing around the room. She tried to get a better look but suddenly he was gone, like he had vanished into thin air. She turned back to David, obviously having missed a question. "I'm sorry?"

David had followed her line of sight, knowing what distracted her. "I asked if you have already moved into the hotel."

"Oh, yes. Last night."

"And you're okay not living in the same house as your father?"

"I'm perfectly fine with it."

Renee saw the mystery guest moving along the back of the room again. Snapping her head around to try to look at him, she found he was still obscured by guests.

"Everything okay?"

Renee shook her head as if to clear it from a bad dream. "Yes. I just thought I saw someone."

As they continued dancing in silence, Renee was scanning the room, looking for her girls, Sasha, and that unknown figure in the crowd. She noticed Michelle sitting at a table talking to Sasha, and wondered why Michelle wasn't with her client.

When the song ended, Renee kissed David on the cheek. "Thank you so much for the dance. I have to go talk to Sasha but we will see each other later." She said it in the form of a question.

"We will definitely see each other again before Sasha and I leave tomorrow. In the meantime, have fun."

"Are you having fun?" Sasha asked, tapping her

feet to the music as Renee approached their table.

"I'm tired." Renee turned to Michelle. "Did something happen with your client?"

Michelle and Sasha laughed lightly then Michelle answered while handing Renee the man's lapel pin. "He couldn't stay. His wife called."

To Renee, Sasha said, "You are going to be spending weeks opening all your gifts."

"Well, on the sixteenth birthday, there's only one gift that truly matters," Michelle said. Renee looked at her, confused, and Michelle laughed. "A kiss, of course."

Sasha nodded in agreement. "Definitely. Every girl should be kissed on their sweet sixteen."

Renee didn't know the first thing about boys, dating, or kissing, and had no idea how to respond to the statement. Michelle nudged Renee with her elbow. "Hey. When you meet the guy, you'll never want him to stop kissing you."

Renee was rescued from the conversation as the lights went down and the band changed songs while her cake was being wheeled into the room. Cameras flashed and threatened to blind her as she began walking toward the cake cart, when she caught sight of the mystery guest once more. This time, he didn't disappear. He was standing next to the stage and staring directly at her, making her stop in her tracks. Her breathing seemed to stop and she stared back in stupefied silence. He was the most stunning human being she had ever seen; his eyes sparkled in the light, as green as the emeralds she wore. He was smiling at *her*. She was so transfixed on him that she had no idea if she was smiling back. As she stared at this handsome stranger, her stomach turned, her mouth went dry, and her palms suddenly got clammy.

Did the room just go silent, or am I going deaf?

The flash of cameras reminded Renee of what she was supposed to do as she approached her destination, forcing herself to focus on the crowd. She cast a quick glance over her shoulder to make sure this man wasn't a figment of her imagination— he was still there, still watching her. He made a gesture like a cowboy tipping his hat and she smiled stupidly at him, like in a daydream.

Turning her focus to Matthew as he proudly approached, she couldn't understand why she was anxious. She casually turned her head back to the stage and felt her heart crush. The mystery man was gone.

When the show was over, Renee made her way back to the table, disappointment written all over her face.

"It's okay, honey," Sasha said.

Exasperated and confused, Renee turned to Sasha. "You don't know that. If I don't know what's wrong with me, how would you?"

Sasha gave Renee a motherly smile. "He's a very attractive boy."

Renee let out a sigh. This was a foreign feeling to her and she wasn't sure how to handle it, but she knew she had to control it. Logic above all else, emotion just got in the way.

Sasha spoke with softness and complete understanding. "His name is Christopher Reynolds, and as of the day before yesterday, he is in your father's employ. And believe me when I tell you that he was watching you more than you were watching him."

Chapter 6

For the first few months in her new responsibilities, Renee often thought of her last conversation with Sasha.

"The most important thing to remember is that these girls are human beings with feelings and emotions just like anyone else," Sasha had told her. "Trust and respect are earned, not given freely just because you're daddy's little girl. You are no better than they are, and don't you forget that. Watch out for Mr. Crescent." Sasha had certainty in her eyes that told Renee this was one of the most important points in their conversation. "He is unpredictable, as well as the eyes and ears for your father. Be watchful of him. That little bastard can be sneaky."

Trying to hide and control the enormous amount of loss she was feeling was physically causing Renee pain. She couldn't let the hurt show because, in this life, people came and went, and that's just the way it was. Sasha, however, leaned in and hugged Renee, not ashamed to let a few tears run down her face. "I love you."

Renee hugged Sasha harder, almost willing her not to walk out the door, but still she would not allow herself to cry. "I love you too."

Renee's eyes were rimmed in red, waiting for the dam to break as Sasha stepped into the hallway. As the door closed, Renee was left feeling unquestionably and completely alone for the first time in her life.

***

Renee stayed in her room with the door open to wait for the girls to check in after their clients left. While reviewing upcoming appointments, her head snapped up when she heard the sound of heavy footsteps as Kristin ran into the room, out of breath and full of panic.

"Help!" Kristin yelled, trying to catch her breath.

Renee bolted down the hall toward the girls crowding the open door of Saffron's suite with Kristin on her heels. Before she was close enough to cross the threshold, she heard the crack of a fist making contact with flesh, then a muffled cry of pain coming from the far end of the room. Renee knew she couldn't waste a second as she burst into the room, in no way prepared for what she saw.

Saffron, naked except for the shreds of fabric clinging to her that used to be a silk robe, was cowering against the far wall of the room in unquestionable terror. Her face colored red and black from the fresh bruises forming at the hands of her attacker; her hands and ankles bound so she couldn't defend herself. All she could do was try to scream, but her lips were swelling too fast to let any sound escape.

On the bed, Mr. Escalona, an attaché to a visiting diplomat from Columbia, was out cold.

Her attacker was Evan Crescent. Renee never considered a confrontation like this as he hunched over Saffron, his right arm poised above his head, ready to strike. Even though he was taller, stronger, and older, Renee didn't have time to think things through. Crescent was able to bring his fist down to connect with Saffron's face one last time before Renee jumped on his back, wrapping her legs around his waist and locking her ankles together for balance. As he raised his right fist for another strike, she hooked her arm through his and pulled with all her strength, willing him not to swing again, and put her face between his head and right shoulder, biting down as hard as she could. Within seconds she tasted blood as Crescent's head snapped up, connecting with Renee's, forcing her head back and loosening her dental grip on his shoulder. He gave a grunt of pain as he violently twisted his body, trying to dislodge her, finally deciding to slam Renee up against the wall. The back of her head connected with the wall with a painful thud, but she wouldn't budge. He slammed her against the wall a second time, knocking the wind out of her as her body slacked and she slid to the floor while trying to catch her breath.

Kristin, Michelle, and Charlotte succeeded in helping a barely conscious Saffron out of the way as Crescent focused on Renee, his face speaking nothing but rage and death with blood spilling from the bite on his neck. He lifted his leg and kicked. Renee had been able to react fast enough to turn to her side and take the blow in her arm. She could have sworn she heard bone crack but didn't have time to think about it. As he readied for another kick, she rammed a fist into his groin, lunging around him as he doubled over. She quickly crawled over to the bed and lifted herself off the floor, using the bedpost for leverage. The bedpost snapped off in her hand and she saw an opportunity, watching Crescent advance on her and knowing it was her last chance to try to stop him. She choked her hands around the bedpost, bent her knees, planted her weight on her left leg, and swung the broken post as hard as she could. Her eyes widened and loud gasps of surprise came from behind her as Crescent collapsed on the floor in front of her, blood not only dripping from his right shoulder, but now also from his left ear.

Renee stood where she was, momentarily stunned. She heard the cries coming from behind her and turned to see Saffron, also unconscious, being protectively held by Kristin, and the crowd of girls all staring in awe. Renee's legs felt weak as she dropped the broken bedpost on the floor. She sat on the floor and leaned against the bed, her head tilted as she stared at the ceiling.

The drama wasn't over. She still had to deal with her father.

Chapter 7

Renee sat straight and silent, staring at her father with anger and defiance burning in her eyes, holding her arm where Crescent had kicked her. Matthew stood in the middle of the room while taking inventory of the disarray in silent fury. Crescent sat in his chair stoically with no remorse, applying pressure to his shoulder with a towel. Her arm wasn't broken and the cuts and bruises would heal in a matter of days, but she knew the patch of Crescent's blood on her chin made her father cringe. Standing quietly in the doorway were her girls, curious as to what would happen next.

Matthew took a deep breath, keeping his anger in check. "Let's start with who is responsible for the damage to the room."

"You would need to ask Mr. Escalona," Renee said while glaring at Crescent, "or Saffron if she could open her mouth to talk."

When Crescent locked eyes with Renee, even she knew the girls watching from the hallway could see the absolute and unquestionable hate between the two of them. Matthew shot Renee a significant glare that told her she was skating to the edge of his tolerance. Renee returned his icy stare, letting him know she didn't really care.

Renee turned to Crescent and asked the obvious. "Why don't you start with what you were doing on this floor in the first place?"

"Mr. Escalona's employer called and asked me to immediately deliver a message."

"Anything that has to do with the girls goes through me and you damn well know it."

"Apparently, he doesn't like working with children."

It took everything she had not to jump out of her chair and bite him on the other shoulder, but she refused to give in to her anger. "These girls are my responsibility. I have a telephone in my room and I know you not only have the number, you also know how to use one."

"Enough!" Matthew's voice boomed through the room. "Just because one of you is a child doesn't mean either of you will act like it." Matthew focused on Crescent. "What prompted you to believe you had to discipline…"

Renee stared at him with incredulity. He didn't even know her name. "Saffron," she said through clenched teeth.

Matthew, in his rising irritation, ignored Renee and addressed Crescent. "Saffron."

"When I got to the door, I could hear her yelling at him and calling him vulgar names. At first, I thought it was roleplaying. Then I heard her scream '9-1-1.' I entered the room and found her leaning over him on the bed, hysterically screaming at him."

What else was she going to do, asshole? She was bound hand and foot, Renee thought.

"His face was pale, his lips were blue, and had what looked like foam coming out of his mouth. When I tried to question her, she wouldn't talk." Crescent turned to Renee to emphasize his next point. "Her client was dying from a drug overdose and she wasn't doing anything about it. I hit her in an attempt to snap her out of her stupor and she lunged at me with a syringe in her hand. I was defending myself."

Are you kidding me? Renee knew if she said it out loud, the interrogation would be over and she would reap all of the consequences. What Renee knew from Dr. Michaelson, and what Crescent failed to mention, was that Saffron was holding a needle in an effort to show Crescent what her client had been using; she didn't stick it in his arm or cause the overdose to happen. What he also didn't mention was that when she lunged at him, it was an attempt to beg him for help. Apparently, he felt it would be best to leave that part out.

"Hitting her once is defending yourself. Breaking her jaw is something completely different," Renee pointed out.

Matthew turned on Renee, his patience almost gone. "That's enough out of you." He turned back to Crescent. "And Renee?"

Crescent lifted the towel off his shoulder, trying to hold back a grimace of pain. The bite wound was deep, and the surrounding skin was red and tender. Renee lowered her head and smiled to herself.

"Again, defending myself."

Don't let emotions get in the way, and, if at all possible, be smarter than your challenger. Matthew had instilled these words into Renee from a young age, and she repeated the phrase in her head as Matthew turned to her for her version of the story. She could see he was angry with her for the damage she caused to his captain.

Matthew examined the broken bedpost before addressing Renee. "And why did you feel that you had to play Babe Ruth with Mr. Crescent's skull?"

Renee turned to Crescent with a smirk on her face and in a mocking tone replied, "I was defending myself. Correct me if I'm wrong, but wasn't it you who brought Mr. Escalona here tonight? Did you know that he had a heroin problem when you did? Because I certainly didn't when I questioned his credentials, and he never said a word when he and his employer signed our contracts."

Crescent addressed Matthew. "I didn't know he had a needle problem, sir."

It didn't happen often, but Renee had seen that look on her father's face before when he didn't know what to do. If it had been anybody other than his captain and his daughter, one or both of them would not be breathing in the morning, but circumstances were different in this case. The bottom line was that he had to do something, or at least pretend to do something. One of his employees was in the hospital and there was no telling how long she would be there or how the atmosphere on this floor would change when she came back. She would come back because she had no choice and no place else to go. Renee knew Matthew's biggest problem was Mr. Escalona's employer and other clients who might have witnessed the fight. He would have to hope that Ambassador Sanchez would know about his attaché's drug problem and want to keep this as quiet as possible, while at the same time not jeopardizing their current business arrangements. That was, of course, if Mr. Escalona lived.

Matthew turned to Renee. "Were any other clients here tonight who may have witnessed this?"

"No. Mr. Escalona was the last of the evening."

"And the paramedics?"

"Service elevator."

"Renee, I have to wonder if I made a mistake by allowing you step in when Sasha left." Matthew quickly put up his hand to stop her from interrupting. "However, it's obvious you will still maintain our business arrangements, so I'm willing to give you the benefit of the doubt and let you continue your current responsibilities. But from now on, you will make sure that we never again have a recurrence of tonight's events."

Renee nodded. "I agree."

"And you will need to find a new girl to take…" Matthew searched for the name Renee had spit out just seconds ago. He looked to her for a clue, but she narrowed her eyes at him as if daring him to ask. "…her place. Once she's out of the hospital, she will be recovering for quite some time."

Matthew turned to Crescent. Now was the time for the show, the moment the girls in the hallway had been waiting for. "Mr. Crescent, you are more than aware that I have a strict, absolute, and unbreakable rule when it comes to my daughter. You and I will talk in my office immediately."

Matthew pinched the bridge of his nose with his thumb and forefinger as if he were dealing with fighting children. "From now on, Mr. Crescent will stay off this floor unless it's imperative that he speak with Renee. Otherwise, you will keep away from each other, only sharing the same space when required."

So far as Matthew was concerned, the issue was closed and the show was over. He signaled Crescent out of the room and, without casting a glance in Renee's direction, left as well. Renee watched him leave as the girls slowly filtered in to surround her with condolences for her pain and thankfulness for her defense of Saffron.

When Renee heard the elevator doors open, she knew two things for certain: she had undoubtedly proven herself to the girls, and there would be no consequences for Mr. Crescent. Instead, he and her father would go to Matthew's office and share a cigar.

Chapter 8

Dr. Elias Michaelson sat across the table from Renee, facing a wall entirely of windows so that he could watch the sun set over the Boston skyline. Renee was focusing on the papers in front of her, reading intently.

Dr. Michaelson was the one who had delivered her and who couldn't keep her mother alive. The guilt over losing Elise ate at him every day and damn near killed him each time he looked Renee in the eye. Over the years he had watched Renee grow up, hoping she would be like the mother she would never know. Her mother was kind, beautiful, gentle, and caring. Dr. Michaelson often wondered what kind of person Renee would be had her mother lived.

At this moment, Elias saw Renee as a typical teenage girl, comfortably seated cross-legged in her chair, wearing a pair of faded jeans, a sweatshirt that was probably two sizes too big for her, and no shoes. Her long hair pulled up, her head bowed down, studying the papers that lay in front of her on the table while chewing on the end of a pencil and occasionally taking notes. She was calm and relaxed, soft and beautiful. Then, without looking up from the task in front of her, she spoke.

"You seem restless tonight, Doctor."

Her tone was indifferent, the same as her father, which meant at the moment she didn't care whether or not everything was okay, but he had obviously done something without speaking to let her know something was on his mind while they waited for Elias's patient to join them. He couldn't stand the pain of looking at Renee for much longer so he crossed the room to the bar to help himself to a finger or two, or three, of scotch. He kept his tone as casual as he could, keeping his focus on pouring his drink so he wouldn't have to look her in the face. "I'm beginning to wonder what is taking her so long."

Renee glanced at her watch, gathered her papers into one stack, then began tapping them together on the table to make them neat and orderly. She set the papers down and looked at her friend with a smile. The smile told him that she did care he was in the room and she was happy to see him.

He took a sip of his drink and held it up in front of him. "Can I get you anything?"

She stretched her arms out behind her. "No, thank you. I feel like I haven't seen you in so long. You're doing well?"

Drink in hand, Elias sat across from Renee and relaxed. This was the Renee he loved, those rare and tiny moments when her mother shone through. "Life is fine. How's school going?"

"Ugh. Midterms." Like that was the only explanation to answer his question.

He smiled over his drink. "I'm sure you'll do well. You are an excellent student."

"I've been taking summer classes which will allow me to graduate a year early."

He raised his eyebrows in surprise. He had not heard. "Really? And after graduation?"

Like stating the obvious, she said, "I'm staying here, of course."

Keeping his face stoic, his heart deflated. He had been hoping she would have a life of her own. She had such a bright future ahead of her, but would never see it unless she got away from her father. He said the only thing he could say, even if it was a lie. "I'm glad to hear it. Things just wouldn't be the same without you."

"So," Renee picked up the stack of papers, "she's good?"

Elias changed gears from personal to professional and nodded. "She's good. She may have the capacity to develop an addiction, but I say that because she's a smoker."

Renee raised an eyebrow at him. "Not for long."

"That's why I say she *may* have the capacity."

Renee nodded in understanding as the conference room door opened and a thin, freckled girl poked her head through the door, her eyes searching the room. Elias knew what Renee was thinking as he walked the girl over to the table to stand in front of Renee, who simply stared at her, taking inventory of her possible new employee. Renee gave an accepting smile to Elias. He nodded to both Renee and Alice, and quietly left the room.

***

Renee knew her name was Alice Jenkins, barely eighteen years old. At first glance, Alice was acceptable—her skin wasn't pocked or scared, and she seemed to be well nourished. Alice kept brushing her hair behind her ears, probably a nervous habit because, try as she might, Alice could not hide the fact that her legs were shaking. Dressed in a pair of denim cutoff shorts with a midriff t-shirt, Alice chewed on her lips and bit her nails. That would have to stop.

Renee tried to relax Alice with a smile and extended her arm in invitation. "Please. Come sit."

Alice let out a nervous breath and slowly took the chair next to Renee. Renee, deciding she was uncomfortable, stretched out her legs, sat up in her chair, and straightened her back.

"Alice Jenkins?"

Alice nodded. When Renee raised an eyebrow at her, Alice spoke. "Yes, ma'am."

Scanning the papers in front of her, Renee spoke as if she were talking to herself. "Eighteen, grew up in Boston, and of good health. Except for the smoking. The women who work for us do not smoke."

"Yes, ma'am." Alice shifted uncomfortably in her chair and cleared her throat. "Sorry. I guess I'm a little nervous."

"There's nothing to be nervous about. You either take the job or you don't. You can relax." Renee sat back in her chair and decided that sitting cross-legged was more comfortable. "Why don't you start by telling me what your understanding of this job is."

"I need money and a place to live. I have no place else to go. I'd basically be a prostitute."

"No."

Alice was confused. "But that's how he made it sound. The guy, the one I met at the club."

"Miss Jenkins, let me be blunt. This job is client companionship, not prostitution. While both professions exchange money for sex, our clients are men, and sometimes women, who require prudence and secrecy. We provide them with both, along with clean, healthy, and discrete young women. In exchange, you will be paid generously and provided a room of your own in this hotel where you will live and work. You will do what is asked of you without question."

"What if I don't want this job?"

Renee asked a question she already knew the answer to. "Miss Jenkins, if you were under the impression that this job is that of a common prostitute, why are you here? There are ten other girls here who joined us for the exact same reason. Money."

Alice's eyes widened. "Ten? But how do they do it?"

"You mean emotionally?"

Alice nodded. "Well, yeah."

Renee didn't have the personal experience to correctly answer the question so she gave the speech she rehearsed after Sasha left. "Sex is not just physical. Take the emotion out of it and you'll be fine. This job is a choice. However, if you choose not to accept this job, when you leave here tonight you will be expected to keep this interview secret. The best way to ensure that is to remember that not only do you know who we are, we know who you are and we have the resources to make sure you understand that fact. Should you choose to stay, you will have rules that must be followed or there will be consequences. You will report to me because I am your boss. My boss, and believe me when I tell you this, is not the person you want doling out punishment for breaking the rules."

Alice's eyes opened wide in both fear and curiosity. "Who is your boss?"

"My boss will be known to you should you accept the job. You will always be clean and presentable. What you're wearing now," Renee gestured at Alice's outfit, "would be worn in your room, on your own time. When you are outside of your room, you are representing a Family and behaving accordingly. You will not drink alcohol to excess. You absolutely will not smoke. If a client asks you to do something that makes you uncomfortable, you immediately, and I do mean immediately, come to me."

"What I find uncomfortable could be different for someone else."

Smart girl after all. Alice pulled herself together quickly and Renee was beginning to like her. "Let's start with drugs. If you are entertaining someone who smokes marijuana and they would like you to join them, you have a choice, but nothing will be to excess. You must be in control of your faculties at all times. If you are not comfortable and don't want to do it, then you politely excuse yourself and you come to me. If you have a client who likes bondage, but that's not your thing, you politely excuse yourself and you come to me. But most importantly, if you have a client who raises a hand to you, you immediately come and find me. Do not give them an opportunity to raise that hand twice. Understand?"

Alice nodded and Renee continued. "The clients have rules as well. One point that is made clear to them is that should their particular choice of recreation involve needles, that choice will not include you. Just like you, they receive consequences if they break the rules. You will not act like a giddy pre-teen child. You will be courteous and respectful. You will have a checkup with Dr. Michaelson once a month, but anytime you feel you need to see him, all you have to do is let me know. He is not a client, nor will he ever be, so you can be assured he will treat you with kindness and respect. Lastly, you will receive a tattoo."

Alice furrowed her eyebrows. "A tattoo?"

"All of the people who work for us receive a tattoo. This is to let certain people know whom you work for. Yours will be on the back of your right shoulder. Some part of the tattoo must always be showing with the exception of certain social events that will require the tattoo to be covered. Do you have any questions?"

Renee watched Alice as she contemplatively nodded her head.

"What happens if I get pregnant?"

"We take measures to make sure you don't. However, if you do, we have a doctor on staff. Something very important you should know is that there is no quitting this job. Should you accept and receive your mark, you will never be allowed to voluntarily leave."

Chapter 9

She hadn't seen him since her birthday party, so when Renee walked into Matthew's office and saw him casually leaning against the wall by the door to the adjoining room, known as the Red Room for the amount of blood spilled on the floor over the years, she stopped dead in her tracks. She hadn't stopped thinking about him since her birthday, but after searching the hotel relentlessly and not being able to find him, she had given up on ever seeing him again.

He smiled at her as she entered the room and all she could do was stare at him, hypnotized. *What the hell is wrong with me?* She didn't understand why her heart beat a little faster and her breathing quickened when she saw him. She made a mental note to talk to the girls; one of them must have the answers because Renee was completely at a loss.

They stared at each other for a minute before he extended his hand. "Christopher Reynolds."

She could swear an electric shock bolted up her arm as she took his hand. "Renee Parnell."

"I know who you are. It's nice to finally meet you."

He grinned and she could feel her face begin to flush. She tried to push the unfamiliar emotions aside, which was easily done when she heard a pained grunt come from the other side of the door.

"You found him?" She knew the answer when Christopher smiled at her. Renee heard something hard make contact with the man who owned the excruciating grunt that was instantly followed by a more pronounced howl of distress. Mr. Sweeny was in the process of learning his lesson for disrespecting her father with an ill-timed comment.

Christopher was beginning to make her nervous as he continued to stare at her in silence. She sat in one of the chairs across from Matthew's desk, setting the folder she was carrying on her lap and trying her best not to turn her head to look back at him.

"How's the eye?"

She had completely forgotten about her fading black eye. "Better."

"I'm guessing you're a baseball fan?"

She couldn't help but smile at his question and gave a shallow nod.

"Red Sox?"

She could feel the blush rising in her cheeks again and desperately wished she knew both why she was blushing and how to stop it. "I just like the game. I've never played but I've spent some time at the batting cages."

"Obviously," Christopher replied with a laugh.

"What about you?"

"Hockey," he said, as if it were the only acceptable answer.

"Ah," she replied. "I've never watched it before."

"You should check it out."

With you? she thought, but instead said, "I will." And she would.

They locked eyes for a few heartbeats until the guarded door opened and Matthew entered his office while wiping his hands. Before the door closed behind him, Renee saw a lifeless Mr. Sweeny lying on the floor and a pool of blood slowly beginning to surround him from the knife protruding from the back of his neck. She thought nothing of it.

Matthew was clearly agitated by Renee's presence, casting a suspicious glance from Christopher to Renee, narrowing his eyes at her. "What do you want? I'm in the middle of a meeting."

"My apologies. I wasn't aware you had visitors."

Matthew gave her a cold, hard stare, implying that he did not approve of the schoolgirl crush behavior he had just witnessed, nor did he appreciate the casual dress and the tired eyes. Renee returned the stare and waited; he would either dismiss her or he wouldn't.

"We have a new employee," she said as he snatched the file out of her hand. Clearly her interruption would not be presently forgiven, but after the episode in Saffron's room, and the fact that he had told her to find someone else while Saffron recovered, she didn't care whether or not she had interrupted a meeting.

As Matthew gave the file's contents a passing glance, Renee was daring herself not to turn her head to the left. She did not, however, dare herself not to move her eyes, and she did so carefully and slowly, catching a glimpse of Christopher in her peripheral vision. He was staring directly at her, very still and very patient, not minding the interruption of their earlier conversation. Other than that, she couldn't read anything in his expression that might give away what he was thinking.

Matthew thrust the file back at Renee. "She smokes."

"Not anymore."

Renee stood her ground. Alice was her first recruit since Sasha had left and she was going to stand by her decision. The tension between father and daughter had grown considerably since she took Sasha's job—he was trying to break her and she was trying to prove there was nothing he could do to stop her.

Finally, Matthew conceded. "She'll do."

Renee gave a small, victorious smile and turned to leave the room, casting a quick glance at Christopher. The door to the Red Room opened once more and Renee's smile turned to a scowl as Crescent and another new face exited the room. She immediately didn't like Crescent's young associate. Her gut sent out intense warning signals that he would eventually be trouble, and she would do well to pay close attention to those warnings. She and Crescent gave each other hateful stares before she decided to leave the room, but Matthew stopped her with a hand on her shoulder.

"Gentlemen, this is Renee, our resident madam." Matthew gently squeezed Renee's shoulder. "This is Christopher Reynolds and Tucker Wilson, new members of the Family. Gentlemen, out of everything you take away from this meeting tonight, what I say next will be the most important. It's best to remember it, because you will only be told once. I'm sure you already know Renee is my daughter. My daughter," he focused his stare on Christopher, "is not to be touched. Should I find out anybody has harmed her, they will answer to me. Should I find out anyone has touched her without permission or injured her in any way, they will answer to me. If you know of anyone who has hurt or attempted to hurt her, you will let me know immediately."

Matthew had been repeating these words for years to everybody who came to work for him. Two men decided to test the warning and quickly disappeared. The only one it didn't apply to was Mr. Crescent.

Renee nodded at each of them and said, "Gentlemen, it's nice to meet you."

"Nice to meet you." Just as he had done at the party, Christopher tipped his invisible hat with an attentive smile and she had the sudden urge to giggle and blush. It was difficult to suppress the giggle and all she could do to respond was nod in acknowledgement, one corner of her closed mouth turned up into a thin smile.

Tucker stood before her with complete indifference and made no attempt to greet her. Her smile instantly faded as she gave him a hard stare of concentrated disapproval. Young, cocky, overly confident Tucker Wilson was in desperate need of a quick lesson in etiquette. Standing next to Tucker, Crescent merely watched with a thin smile on his lips.

Renee slowly approached Tucker like a cat on the hunt. "I know you're new, but I know for a fact you have been informed of the established propriety that is required of everybody in this Family. Contrary to what you may believe, Mr. Wilson, you are no better than anybody else in this Family, least of all me. I wasn't simply born into this Family, I have worked to earn my place and don't appreciate being ignored when simple courtesy is all that is required."

Tucker's attitude and tough exterior quickly crumbled as he realized that challenging the rules was a mistake. "I didn't mean…it won't happen again."

Faster than a whip, Renee's knee met his groin and Tucker doubled over in pain, trying not to vomit. Matthew and Crescent had no reaction while Christopher silently winced.

Renee leaned over and whispered in Tucker's ear, "You are correct, Mr. Wilson. It won't happen again."

She left the room quietly, closing the door behind her. She slid across the door to lean against the wall, hugging the file to her chest, and smiled, once again breathing easier as a wave of relief washed over her. Then, suddenly, relief was replaced by inexplicable excitement. She knew she would see Christopher again, and when she did, there would be an actual conversation involved. The only problem was that she had no idea what to say, how to say it, or how to feel. She pushed herself off of the wall and walked through the glass doors separating the hallway from the executive offices. Once in the hallway, she looked left and right to make sure nobody was around, then ran down the hall to the elevator. She had to find a female counterpart to talk to and she had to find them fast.

***

"What did you expect?" Christopher asked as he took a drink of his beer. The hotel bar was quiet. After his day of finding and bringing in Mr. Sweeny, then having to dispose of him in the next county, it was late and he just wanted to unwind.

Tucker snubbed out his cigarette and looked at Christopher. "Well, I wasn't expecting her to kick me in the balls."

Christopher laughed as the bartender approached with a questioning look. "He was rude to the boss's daughter." The bartender made a sucks-to-be-you look at Tucker as he exchanged Christopher's empty beer for a full one. "It was a knee, not a foot."

"Whatever," Tucker said, taking a long pull off his own beer. "I still feel like throwing up."

"Don't let her age deceive you," the bartender said. "She may be young, but she knows how to make a point. She's a good girl, though. She's got a good heart."

Tucker let out a huff of contention and

Christopher smiled into his beer before asking, "Are you going to do that again?"

"Fuck no," Tucker said into his beer. "Lesson learned."

"Look," said Christopher, "I know you think you're a big badass here, but, dude, I don't think you understand what you've done. All you had to do was say hello to her. You disrespected her and got kneed for it. I would say you're lucky that it came from her rather than Crescent or Parnell himself."

Tucker didn't appreciate the disciplinary lecture. Then, like a switch had been flipped, he gave Christopher a questioning look and slowly shook his head. "Oh, man. Don't tell me...you like her, don't you?"

Christopher took a drink of his beer to give himself a minute to think about a careful answer. "I only talked to her for a few minutes, but, yeah, I think she's likable as long as you don't piss her off."

"He's never going to let you date her," Tucker pointed out.

Christopher's head snapped back in surprise. "Who said anything about dating her? I just said she seemed likable."

Tucker turned to the bartender, who was listening with rapt attention. "You should have seen the way she was gawking at him."

"She was not gawking at me," Christopher corrected.

"And," Tucker continued, "the smirk on his face wasn't telling her not to."

57

"I was being nice." Christopher felt the need to defend himself because he knew Tucker was right. Since he saw her at her birthday party, he did want to take her out, and he knew Parnell would never allow it.

"Whatever. Gotta piss," Tucker said as he walked to the back of the bar.

When Tucker was out of earshot, the bartender looked at Christopher with all seriousness and lowered his voice. "Just between you and me, there were others who attempted to make an uninvited move on her. Neither are alive and neither are missed."

"I never said—"

"Wait for Mr. Lundy to get here and ask when they're both in the room. Lundy adores that girl and will do anything for her. Look, I've been working this bar as eyes and ears for seven years. Normally, I wouldn't say anything and let you figure it out for yourself, but I like you, so I'm just putting in my two cents. Keep it to yourself."

Christopher nodded in understanding and realized how much he had underestimated some of the people he had met since he joined the Family. He made a mental note to take all advice, whether good or bad, seriously. After all, nobody gave it without a reason.

"Now get out of here," the bartender said. "I want to go home."

Chapter 10

A few weeks later, Christopher had been called into Matthew's office to deliver a collection. When he saw David sitting with Matthew, he decided to take the bartender's advice and simply ask.

"Absolutely not," Matthew said with forced denial.

Christopher stood across from Matthew's desk with calm understanding on his face. "I understand, sir. The subject won't come up again."

Matthew gave a sharp nod of his head in agreement, closing the conversation, but not before David asked, "Why not?"

Matthew turned on David. "What do you mean, why not? She's sixteen years old; he's twenty. That's reason enough."

Christopher stood completely still, hands behind his back, his face impassive, not giving away the internal smile and knowledge that with David's blessing he would be taking Renee on at least one date.

David gave a short laugh. "Jesus, Matthew, it's

just a hockey game. You've got to let her have some kind of life outside this hotel, and if you don't do it now, the next guy won't ask your permission. She's old enough to drive a car, she's old enough to go on a date." David turned to Christopher. "Take her to dinner before the game. Hell, spend the whole day with her. She deserves a chance to feel like a normal girl for once."

Matthew turned to Christopher while trying to contain his obvious anger with David. "Does she know that you've come to me about this?"

"No, sir."

Matthew leaned forward on his desk and spoke to Christopher in a stern voice. "You will be a gentleman. If I hear otherwise, you will be in that room," he pointed toward the guarded door, "and won't be coming out. Do I make myself clear?"

Still with respectful indifference on his face, and in an even tone of voice, Christopher replied, "Absolutely, sir. Thank you, sir."

Chapter 11

Renee's friends said to just be herself, reminding her that when he saw her for the first time she wasn't putting on an act or behaving like a child.

She met him in the lobby, both of them smiling and eager to start their day. She was nervous and trying to calm herself as they got in his car and he started the engine, stealing looks at him from the corner of her eye. *Stop acting like a love-struck teenager, for god's sake.* She quickly knocked the immature emotions away and took a breath, but remained internally giddy at the thought of spending the day with Christopher.

"So aside from the hockey game, I really didn't have any plans for today. I was thinking we could get lunch, if you're hungry, and then play it by ear. Unless you have something you'd like to do."

This wasn't something she had been warned might happen and she didn't know what to do. They hadn't even made it out of the parking garage and the only thing she knew for sure was that she couldn't eat without the fear of her nerves making her throw up on his shoes. She said, "I'm not really hungry right now."

"Too nervous to eat?" he teased.

A little embarrassed, Renee again pushed the unwanted juvenile emotions away and cleared her throat, remembering that he already knew what kind of person she was. "Being alone with you makes me nervous. I don't know why, but it does."

Christopher turned to her with a smile and held out his hand. She trusted the sincerity she saw in his eyes and cautiously took his hand, her jumpiness slowly receding, but her lips apparently couldn't decide whether to smile or not. He leaned into her, his face so close to hers that she could feel his warm breath on her lips as he whispered, "I'm a little nervous myself."

***

Their day began with spending time at a small amusement park where they played miniature golf, which she wasn't very good at and obviously didn't enjoy, but she played with a smile on her face and focus in her eyes. They raced each other in the go-karts and afterward headed over to the batting cages, where Renee astonished Christopher with her accuracy and tenacity when it came to making the baseballs fly across the cage. She hit every ball that came at her, each one categorically being hit harder and faster than the previous. He must have spent fifty dollars at the cages just to stare in awe at her persistence.

Afterward, they found a small diner on the

outskirts of the city where they ate lunch and began getting to know each other. Because she felt completely comfortable with him, and because he was the only one she could really talk to about the world she grew up in, she told him everything she could possibly think of. When Christopher spoke, she was very much interested, locking eyes with him and intently listening to every word he had to say.

"You don't have the life of a typical sixteen-year-old," Christopher noted.

"I'm not your typical sixteen-year-old," Renee replied.

Hiding a smile behind his glass, Christopher asked, "Where did you learn to hit a ball like that?"

"David is a huge baseball fan. He introduced me to batting cages and the rest is what you saw me do. David has always been a big believer in me being able to defend myself. You should see my right hook." She smiled and he couldn't help but laugh.

By the time lunch was over, the conversation was flowing freely and she never wanted to leave his side. As they drove away from the restaurant, Christopher questioned her on what she wanted to do next. The answer came to her instantly: her favorite place in the world.

They walked through the botanical gardens as Renee narrated its history, pointing out different features and educating him on everything they saw. They entered the Isle of Lilies—her sanctuary—and she stopped walking to watch Christopher take it all in, the hopeful smile never leaving her face. The lilies were caged by a tall hedge with only one entrance and exit; the circumference comparable to that of a grain silo with a circling path just big enough for two to walk side by side. It was filled with lilies of different colors, and a fountain of marble in the middle of it all, adding to the relaxation and peace a person could find just standing there for a few minutes.

He smiled and turned to her with awe. "It's really beautiful."

Her smile grew bigger as her eyes focused on the bench situated in an alcove—the best place to get the full aroma of the flowers and just secluded enough to hide someone from the world. She nodded at the bench and they sat in silence for a few minutes, taking in the garden and wondering what he was thinking.

Finally, Christopher broke the silence. "I wanted to meet you the night of your party but I didn't think it would be right since we work together. I watched you though. You were very beautiful that night." Her cheeks were quickly warming as he gently took her hand in his. "You're beautiful right now. I'd like to spend more time with you and am wondering how you feel about that."

Her heart was racing and she felt an electric shock running through her body just from him holding her hand. She knew what she wanted as she looked him in the eye with complete certainty. "I would like that very much."

Christopher slowly leaned in, kissing her gently, which she happily returned. When the kiss ended, they locked eyes with each other and Renee felt a twitching smile coming forward.

"Do that again," she said, and he did. The kiss began slowly until Renee leaned into him and parted her lips, the tip of her tongue brushing his upper lip and giving him permission to kiss her however he wanted. He placed his hand on the back of her head in an attempt to pull her closer to him and she began to tremble. She placed her hands on either side of his face as their tongues explored each other's mouths for the first time. Renee could think of nothing else in the world except kissing Christopher as often as she could. She now knew what she had been told about a first kiss was true, except that she never imaged she would feel the electric sparks run through her body and want to be with him forever.

She couldn't say how long she felt like she was floating before Christopher broke the kiss and gazed into her eyes. Her breathing was rapid, her face was flush, her smile was still twitching, and the look in her eye couldn't have been anything but bliss. He wrapped his arms around her and inhaled the scent of her hair while she rested her head on his chest, listening to his heartbeat. There were no words either of them could say so they stayed where they were until they heard someone approaching the sanctuary of the lilies. Quietly, they left hand in hand, and from that moment on, would forever belong to each other.

Chapter 12

"I don't recall giving permission for a second date," Matthew said as he stared at his desk, reading the contracts in front of him.

"I'm not asking your permission," Renee answered definitively.

Matthew slowly raised his head to gaze at his daughter, who was returning his look of disapproval with one of unabashed defiance. "Is that so?"

"Just because you don't want me to do something doesn't mean that it can't happen."

"And if Christopher should be discharged from my service?"

Renee slightly shook her head and tried not to roll her eyes. "You would dismiss him just to prevent me from dating him? That's rather petty of you, don't you think? In answer to your question, if Christopher wasn't here, I would still find a way to be with him."

Fury burst out of Matthew as he rose from his desk. "Who do you think you are? You do not simply walk into my office, disrespect me, and tell me how it's going to be. I am the parent, you are the child, and you will do as I say until I decide otherwise."

Unaffected by Matthew's anger, Renee replied, "I'm old enough to arrange sexual entertainment, witness punishments, supervise deliveries and shipments, but I'm not allowed to choose the person I want to date? I don't understand. What is it about Christopher that you object to?"

Taking his seat, Matthew replied, "I don't have to explain myself to you."

Renee let out an exasperated breath. "Don't you ever get tired of the animosity between us? Why is it that you and I can't have a civilized conversation without it turning into some kind of argument?"

Matthew knew the fighting between the two of them had to stop. It wasn't because it was bad for business, it was because his plans for the future wouldn't come to fruition without Renee at his side as his loving daughter.

Matthew sighed and held up his hands in resignation. "No more fighting. Everybody else in this Family is expected to behave with respect and tolerance toward each other, and from this point forward, we shall do the same."

"And Christopher?"

"You won't have anything to be concerned about unless I am forced to step in for any reason."

"What about Mr. Crescent?" Her tone suggested she didn't quite trust what he was saying.

"I will speak with him."

"Thank you," she said as she stood, nodding her head at the stack of papers on his desk. "Let me know when you're done reviewing the contracts and I'll come get them from you."

Matthew nodded in acknowledgement and Renee left the room. Pushing himself back from his desk, he stared out the window with his hands clasped in his lap and, for the first time in years, thought of Elise. He thought about the first time he saw her and the first time he realized how much he loved her. He was going to spend the rest of his life with her until she betrayed him and took everything he ever loved and crushed it in an instant.

Mr. Crescent entered Matthew's office from the adjoining room. He stood in front of Matthew's desk, still as a statue and just as silent as Matthew turned to face him.

"Keep a close eye on them and let me know anything of consequence. She's young and doesn't know any better. Love is an illusion, Mr. Crescent."

"Yes, sir."

"She will fall and she will get hurt." Matthew's eyes hardened. "I will make sure of it."

Chapter 13

Present Day

Doormen with guns, Renee thought as she approached three men standing outside the restaurant who were casually surveying their surroundings. She only knew one of them, the oldest of the three, a man named Schedler who was in his late twenties, and if the rumors were true, he was one of Carl Tempest's newly appointed captains. His two associates saw Schedler's posture rise to guarded threat and watched as Renee stopped and smiled.

"Mr. Schedler," she said.

He gently took her hand and laid a soft kiss on top. "Ms. Parnell. What brings you to this part of Philly?"

"I understand Mr. Tempest is dining here this evening. I was wondering if I might be able to take a few minutes of his time."

Matthew Parnell and Carl Tempest were both successful underbosses in David's family who openly disliked each other. Renee wasn't judged on who her father was, but if one wanted to avoid a blood war, courtesy and respect was to be shown to all Family members, even if they weren't likeable. Just because her father didn't like Tempest didn't mean she felt the same.

Schedler motioned his two associates over for introductions while Renee removed the wrap covering her back. Both sets of eyes slightly widened and they looked back to Schedler, who gave a slight nod to indicate she was who they thought.

Renee smiled at the two young men. "Gentlemen."

Schedler excused himself and went inside the restaurant, leaving Renee with his two associates, who could only stare in awe at Renee and wonder. She knew she had a reputation built on truth and rumor, but didn't care how those two perceived her, so long as she was seen as confidant, which she knew she had to be.

Schedler returned and escorted Renee to a table, where Carl Tempest greeted her with a smile and a welcoming hug. Schedler held out a chair for Renee across from his boss, then took a seat himself.

Carl Tempest was as Renee remembered him. Unlike her father, he didn't crave admiration, but his demeanor demanded respect. As a child, he had been kind, quick to make her laugh, and would never leave her company without a kiss on the cheek and a promise to do well in school. Now she sat in front of him as an adult on a mission— coming to the one man she knew she could trust to ask for help in moving on with her life.

"Would you like something to drink?" Tempest asked, gesturing at the champagne bottle chilling next to the table.

"No, thank you."

He nodded as he poured himself a glass. "I was dining with business associates when I heard you were here."

"I apologize if I interrupted," she said with sincerity.

He waved his hand like shooing away a fly. "Them I can speak with at any time. You are a rare exception where an interruption is welcome."

"I won't keep you."

"It's no bother," he said as he turned back to the meal on his plate. "I understand condolences are in order. Please allow me to extend mine. It's a tragedy to become a wife and a widow on the same day."

Her hands were shaking in her lap, but her face was serene. "While I appreciate and accept your condolences, I was neither wife nor widow. Christopher died before the ceremony." Tempest's eyebrows shot up and she continued with the obvious assumption. "You heard differently."

Tempest nodded, utensils poised over his plate as he considered what she had told him. "I hear many things. Does your father know where you are?"

"I would ask your discretion in keeping this meeting between us."

She could see curiosity and questions spinning behind his eyes. She sat before him, poised and confident, boldly striking out on her own in search of something she thought Tempest could help her obtain.

Tempest set his utensils down and gave her his full attention. "Well, you certainly have me curious; however, I have to surmise, because you have come here without permission or acknowledgement, that what you seek is very important. So, please, Ms. Parnell, satisfy my curiosity."

She looked Tempest solidly in the eye. "Was Christopher's death ordered, and if so, why and by whom?"

Tempest's eyes snapped wide in surprise at her bluntness but his eyes never left Renee's, taking his time to consider his retort. Renee sat patiently, her hands still trembling in her lap, waiting for him to respond.

Tempest cast a quick glance at Schedler, then back at Renee. "What makes you think I would know anything about it?"

"There is no accusation in my purpose for coming here tonight, Mr. Tempest. I am only here to get answers to my questions."

"And you think I have those answers?"

"I hope so, sir." She took a deep breath and brought steady hands above the table, resting them in front of her. "You see, Mr. Tempest, I came here because if Christopher's death was contracted, there is a chance you would have heard about it. I came here because if you do have the answers to any of my questions, I believe you to be a man who would be honest with me no matter what the truth may be. I came here tonight because no matter how you and my father feel about each other, it is important you know with absolute certainty that I do not, nor have I ever, shared my father's feelings. I came here tonight because I need to be able to move ahead with my life. If you don't have the answers I seek, then I go home empty-handed. But at least I go home knowing I wasn't too much of a coward to ask the questions in the first place."

The reaction from Tempest and Schedler was both curiosity and respect. Schedler was silent as he raised his eyebrows at Tempest, encouraging him to continue the conversation.

Tempest reached across the table and cupped Renee's hands in his own, sympathy in his voice and caring in his eyes. "Your honesty is appreciated, so allow me to return the favor. Do I know the circumstances surrounding your loss? I'm sorry to say I do not. Do I think it was an ordered hit? Yes, I do. There is nothing tangible I can give you to prove or disprove your suspicions, and I think you know you didn't need to come to me to find your answers. What I do know is that you are a strong, capable, and confident young woman who will get through this in your own way and at your own pace, and I don't believe it will last too much longer simply because it's not in your nature to dwell. But when your grieving is complete, the Renee Parnell everyone has always known will come back to them, and you will come back stronger than you ever thought possible, and god help anyone who stands in your way." Tempest let out a hearty laugh. "I sincerely hope I am there when that day comes."

It was rare she heard praise or admiration from

anybody other than David. She knew Tempest meant what he said, yet all she could do was look at him with heartbreak in her eyes. "Do you think my father ordered Christopher's death?"

Tempest gave her hands a quick squeeze. "My dear, sweet girl, I think you already knew the answer before you came here."

She let out a deep breath and stood, clutching her purse in her hands. "Thank you for taking the time to speak with me, Mr. Tempest."

Tempest stood and held her face in his hands, searching her eyes for any sign of life. When he couldn't find one, he gently kissed her on the forehead. "If you need anything, you know where to find me. Mr. Schedler will see you safely to your vehicle."

***

It had been two weeks since Christopher's funeral. Renee attended to business and behaved as if her world had never been shattered, but the suppressed emotions made it difficult to concentrate. She still hadn't cried, couldn't even begin to force tears to well in her eyes. She couldn't get over that devastating feeling and didn't know how to go back to the person she was supposed to be and move on with her life.

She loved Christopher with a ferocity she never knew existed and now he was gone, leaving her alone and her world crushed. Because of four blissful years with him, she had experienced a part of life she didn't know even existed, and when she thought about private moments with him, she shuddered. He made her heartbeat quicken and her spirit soar and she would never feel that again. The thought of feeling pain like that was too much. She couldn't, and wouldn't, go through that again.

Renee was deep in thought and didn't hear Alice enter the room. As Alice took a seat next to her, Renee wanted the world to go away and leave her be. But she knew why Alice was there and didn't really care.

"Renee, your father—"

"I'm doing my job and still making him money."

"You missed a lunch the other day. Renee, I'm not discounting the pain you're in, but missing things like lunches with councilmen isn't something you can just blow off. And then you were gone for almost two days without a word to anybody."

Renee's face was completely devoid of emotion. "I went to Philadelphia."

Alice's face drained of all color. "You *what*?"

Renee told Alice—the only person she truly trusted—about her visit with Tempest. "He did it, Alice." There was no doubt in her voice.

Alice took a deep, shaky breath. "What are you going to do? You can't say anything. It's too dangerous…"

"I know that. I don't know what I'm going to do."

Alice held Renee's hands tightly in her own and gave a definitive look. "You have to let this go for now. You have responsibilities that you are neglecting and your behavior is affecting everyone around you. A few days ago, Michelle had a problem and couldn't find you, so she went to the first person she could find: the biggest asshole here."

This news surprised Renee out of her stupor. "Did he touch her?"

"We had to call Dr. Michaelson because we couldn't find you."

The thought of Crescent touching one of her girls made her lips tighten in growing fury. "Where is Crescent?"

"I don't know," Alice said as she stood, "but I'm sure you'll find him. I'm going to get you a wet cloth for your face and give you a few minutes to clean yourself up."

As Alice made her way to the bathroom, Renee's thoughts were interrupted by a knock at the door. She found her father standing on the other side, looking at her with dissatisfaction and distaste, a look she returned equally. This was the first time Renee had seen her father since the funeral and the look on his face told her he wanted to be anywhere but here.

Matthew stepped into the room and closed the door. "How are you doing?"

She couldn't help but feel heartbroken as she looked at him, knowing he was the one responsible for her grief. "How long did it take you not to feel pain when my mother died?"

Matthew narrowed his eyes at her and answered in a dismissive tone. "Death, as you know, is a part of life."

"You didn't answer my question."

Matthew paced over to the window and looked

out at the evening skyline. "As it turned out, your mother was not the person she led me to believe she was when we married. I fell out of love with her long before her death. The details are not important, but the fact of the matter is I wasn't overly upset when she passed away."

This revelation surprised Renee. "If you weren't in love with her anymore, why didn't you divorce her?"

"I have a reputation and a standard to live up to. Her dying was much better for me than a divorce would ever be." He turned to face her with absolute hatred, making Renee take a step back even though they were across the room from each other. "And then she had you."

The pit of her stomach dropped and she felt like she had just been slapped hard enough to knock her across the state of Massachusetts. She was rapidly trying to comprehend what she had just heard. Surely, she must have misunderstood, but the look on his face told her she hadn't.

"What?"

The expression on his face was deadly as Matthew withdrew a pistol from his jacket and pointed it at her, taking one step forward, and Renee taking one step back in complete terror. "I told your mother I never wanted children. When she got pregnant, there was nothing I could do. Just like a divorce, if word got out that your mother had an abortion, my standing in this community would have ended. Then she died bringing you into this world. I wanted nothing to do with you. I still want nothing to do with you, but I have been stuck with you since the day you were born and forced to pretend to love you."

Renee stood frozen in disbelief. Even though she and her father had their differences, she thought he loved her. Here he was telling her with seething disgust how wrong she was. All reason and logic was thrown out the window as the flood of emotions she couldn't explain began to consume her. She tried to ignore the gun pointed at her head.

"I had no choice but to give you a privileged life. Having you in my life just made things more complicated and I had to deal with the humiliation of parading you around. The only upside was that it made me more presentable. The poor, young widower raising a child by himself, and I played the part well."

Matthew walked closer to Renee, and by the time he was less than a foot in front of her, she was trapped against the door, terrified the gun would be fired. She wanted to run but knew she couldn't leave. What scared her even more was the smile on his face saying he was enjoying this.

Matthew leaned in, resting the barrel of the gun on her forehead, venom dripping from his words as he spoke. "I have had enough of playing father to you, but, unfortunately, I have to do what I must so I don't tarnish the reputation I have worked hard to achieve. I have plans for my future and you are a necessary means to achieving those plans, so here is what's going to happen from now on. *Nothing* changes except that the only time we will be in the same room is when necessity calls for it. You will, as always, play your part of the societal princess of an ever-loving father. *Nobody* will *ever* know how much I abhor you."

For the first time in her life, Renee was genuinely afraid of her father. How could he do this knowing how much she loved him? How could she live the rest of her life knowing how he truly felt about her? She thought of all of the years she believed he loved her, and absolute certainty hit her.

"You killed Christopher." The malevolence in the smile that appeared on Matthew's face made her gasp and she began to shake so hard she thought she would have a seizure. "Why?"

"To hurt you. To make sure all hope for happiness would leave you. To make you suffer. You have been a burden to me for the past twenty years and I intend to take every opportunity open to me to make your life as excruciating and miserable as you have made mine. It was my golden opportunity. And make no mistake, my dear daughter, I will keep hurting you every chance I get. There is no escape and nothing you can do about it. When I have achieved my goal and finally had enough of you, I will personally be there to make sure you join Christopher and your mother in hell, where all of you belong." Matthew cocked the gun and his smile widened as Renee let loose a gasp of terror. "Make no mistake, if you cross me, I will end you and nobody will be there to save you. Not your so-called friends. Not David. *Nobody.*"

Renee began to feel the life and energy slowly drain out of her body and suddenly wondered if Matthew pulling the trigger wouldn't be the best thing for her. "David wouldn't do that."

"David won't ever know. I promise you now that if you breathe one word of this conversation to David—to anybody—I will not hesitate to kill you where you stand and find another way to get what I want," Matthew assured her as he un-cocked the gun and forcefully pushed her away, watching her stumble across the room to finally fall on the floor as he silently closed the door behind him.

Stunned and taken over by absolute fear, Renee knew what her father was capable of and knew what he said was true. He would make her feel his hate with every twist of the knife that he was sure to bury in her chest. He was going to make her suffer in every possible way for the rest of her life and she had nowhere to go and nobody to turn to.

Out of the corner of her eye, Renee saw movement and jumped in terror. Completely forgotten about, she looked up to see Alice walk out of the bathroom with disbelief and unabashed fear on her face.

Chapter 14

Renee frantically threw what possessions she could in one of the two suitcases and duffel bag she had open on the bed. By pure dumb luck, David had called Matthew to Chicago, and this was Renee's only chance to get away. She had no idea if she was being watched, but she had no choice—if she was going to get away, it had to be tonight.

"You can't leave!" Alice exclaimed.

"He's all but put a contract out on me. And when the time comes to collect on that contract, he'll happily watch while Crescent makes sure I suffer."

"What about us? What's going to happen to us? How can you be so selfish?"

She had never been called selfish before, but she suddenly felt it; she was the one who had the means and opportunity to get away while the only people she had known as friends didn't. It wasn't that she didn't care about those she was leaving behind, but she would rather take the opportunity to save her own life before her father had the chance to take it.

"You're not the one who had her own father put

a gun to her head," Renee said. "Alice, you know what he did."

"What am I going to tell the others?"

Renee stopped packing, turned to Alice, and grasped her shoulders. "Tell them I'm devastated by Christopher's death and needed to get away. That's partly the truth."

Resigned, all Alice could do was nod in understanding, but the fear on her face didn't go unnoticed by Renee. At the same time, Renee had no time to console Alice; the longer she stayed, the more her resolve might keep her from escaping.

Renee scanned the bags to make sure she had everything she needed, then turned to Alice, handing her a fully stuffed large envelope and a key. "I have something for you, something that I can only trust you with. In this envelope is enough cash to get you out of here if you choose to go. You can keep it all for yourself or you can divide it between the girls if they want to leave too. But keep in mind, Alice, if you—any of you—choose to leave, you have to stay gone. Do whatever you have to do, but *do not* let him find you. Do you understand me? Stay gone."

Disbelief in her voice, Alice said, "Where did you…"

Renee put the key Sasha had given her in Alice's hand and quickly relayed the speech Sasha gave when the key became her responsibility. Alice gave Renee a puzzled look and considered Renee's instructions for a moment, then gave a firm nod. Renee embraced Alice as hard as she could, guilt washing over her.

"I'm so sorry." It was all Renee could say as she slung the duffel bag over her shoulder and took a suitcase in each hand.

Alice cracked open the door and stuck her head out, making sure nobody was there to see Renee leave. Without a word or a backward glance, Renee stepped out into the hallway and quickly made her way to the elevator.

Chapter 15

Renee was exhausted when she pulled into a car dealership off the interstate in Roanoke, Virginia that she knew was owned by the man she was coming to see. His name was Nicholas and they hadn't seen each other for at least ten years, but she knew he would cooperate in the end. She was, after all, her father's daughter.

***

Renee was ten years old when she watched Nicholas being escorted into the Red Room. Sitting in the chair opposite Matthew's desk, she gave her father a determined look. "I want to go in with you."

"That room is no place for a child."

She squared her shoulders and lifted her chin. "You said you would teach me how business works. You didn't say how old I had to be when you did."

Matthew took a minute to consider, then gave a

sharp warning. "Not a word."

She nodded in firm understanding and followed Matthew into the room, taking a seat in the chair by the window, her expression completely void of any emotion. Matthew ignored Crescent's questioning look and casually stood in front of a trembling Nicholas. Renee knew from her father's posture and facial expression that he was angry, disappointed, and ready to make a point. Renee saw a wet spot beginning to form on the front of Nicholas's pants as he watched Matthew, his eyes begging for mercy.

"Please, Mr. Parnell." Nicholas's voice cracked with fear. "I'm sorry. I'm so fucking sorry."

"Do you know how much money I lost because you wanted to get laid, Nicholas? In fact, if I am to understand correctly, you were so focused on this barmaid that you kept your back to the door the entire time. You gave her *your attention, so there was no way you would have been watching for anybody to walk through the door."*

"The girl...they came in while I was talking to her. I'm so fucking sorry."

Matthew leaned over to put his face inches from Nicholas's. "I certainly hope she was worth it."

Matthew sniffed, smelling the urine on Nicholas, and wrinkled his nose. He stepped back and regarded the man with an eerie calm, his gaze running over Nicholas's face and savoring the fear he invoked. He glanced at Renee, who was silently staring at Nicholas with guarded hate that, because of him, her father was unhappy.

"You cost me millions, Nicholas, and put it directly in the hands of Carl Tempest."

Nicholas opened his mouth to speak and Crescent dealt him a slap to the back of his head hard enough to snap his head forward. There was a trickle of blood from the corner of his mouth and Renee knew he had bitten his tongue.

Crescent crossed the room to the table beside Renee, each of them too focused on the matter at hand to exchange hate-filled looks. She and Nicholas watched as Crescent lifted a pair of garden shears from the table, squeezing the blades together to check the tension. Nicholas's eyes widened. Renee didn't so much as blink as Crescent stood behind Nicholas as casually as anyone would while waiting for a bus.

"As it turns out, today is your lucky day. By order of Mr. Lundy, and only by his order, you are to live." Matthew gave Nicholas a minute to comprehend what he had just heard and Renee could see relief overcoming the man, until Crescent grabbed Nicholas's left ear and pulled. Nicholas gritted his teeth to hold back a cry of pain as Matthew continued. "However, punishment must be dealt. So, since you are both my eyes and my ears, you have a choice on which one you would like to lose."

Nicholas's eyes couldn't widen any further no matter how hard he tried, and his whimper was something Renee couldn't find a comparison for. Nicholas quickly shifted his gaze between Matthew and Renee, both of whom were watching him with curiosity and expectation. Crescent pulled on his ear again and the whimper turned into a yelp.

Nicholas stammered through blood and spittle,

begging Matthew to let him go. Finally, Matthew made the choice for him. "Mr. Crescent, you've already got hold of his ear. Don't get any blood on my daughter."

Renee sat impassively in her chair as she watched Crescent take extreme pleasure in slowly and methodically snipping off Nicholas's ear, unfazed by the blood-curdling screams that filled the room. Never once did she stop to consider that most ten-year-olds would look away, have nightmares, or possibly throw up where they sat. Renee watched as the blood pooled underneath Nicholas's chair until Crescent dropped the ear on the floor and Nicholas passed out from the pain.

***

Renee checked her face in the rearview mirror. Her eyes were red and puffy but otherwise she was presentable. She had one shot to get what she wanted and she needed to be in the perfect frame of mind to get it. Her father's words came to her then: *"If they don't already know that the grave is a possible consequence of crossing a Parnell, you'd damn well better let them know it with what you bring with you. You don't have to believe it, but they do."*

She was approached by a salesman before she opened the front door. He looked to be close to her age, with the cockiness of youth and white teeth that sparkled. He probably thought all he had to do was flash a smile to win her over. *He obviously has never met a Parnell before.* She was there to see someone and would not be distracted.

"Good morning," the young man said cheerfully while flashing a smile. "How can I help?"

Her face was solid impatience and her tone let him know she wasn't there to see him. "I'm looking for the owner of this dealership."

"Is there a problem? Maybe I can help."

"There will be a problem if you don't get me the owner of this dealership."

The salesman took a few seconds to stammer to himself, trying to figure out how to fix the situation. "Maybe my sales manager can help."

"I didn't ask for the sales manager. I want to see the owner of this dealership." The deadly glare in her eyes sent a chill up the young man's spine as she leaned in and whispered in his ear. "I will not ask again."

After the young man broke into a run toward the back of the dealership, she helped herself to a cup of coffee, her breathing even and her confidence solid. She was tough, she was fierce, and she would get what she wanted. Her face contorted in disgust after her first sip of coffee, and as she threw it in the garbage, she saw who she came to see approaching her with a confused look on his face. Renee cracked a thin smile when she noticed the scar tissue had been replaced with a prosthetic ear.

Nicolas offered his hand with a smile, seemingly cheerful and ready to resolve whatever problem there was. "How can I help you, ma'am?"

Renee took the extended hand, not intending to let go until he answered her question. "Was she worth it?"

She knew she had him. His grip slightly tightened on hers, then dropped to his side, immediately understanding that he had to start playing a game he hadn't had to play in years. Nicholas dismissed the young salesman and waved his arm in an invitation for Renee to follow him. When they entered his office, he slowly lowered himself in the chair behind his desk while she stood, surveying the décor, her eyes immediately going to the framed picture of him with a beautiful blonde-haired woman draped on his arm, sitting in a restaurant, celebrating something. Both of their smiles screamed happy and she was momentarily glad for him.

She could see he was nervous, but couldn't afford to put him at ease quite yet. What she did next would solidify the risk she was taking. She would either succeed or fail, and she couldn't afford to fail. As she turned her back to Nicholas, she slowly removed her jacket. His eyes widened as her mark came into view, the letter D falling like a teardrop.

"Holy Christ," Nicholas muttered under his breath. Renee knew she was the last visitor he expected and could see his mind scrambling, trying to think of what he might have recently done to have Matthew Parnell's daughter before him. Renee casually took her seat opposite him, ready to get to work on her new life.

"The ear looks good, Nicholas."

Nicholas swallowed the lump in this throat and asked, "How did you find me?"

"People talk. I listen." She had found him

through a rumor.

"I haven't done anything," he said, trying to keep the shaking out of his voice.

Renee gestured to the photo on his desk. "Wife?"

Nicholas glanced at the picture with a pang of sadness but looked at Renee with growing curiosity. "Ex."

"Ahh." She stared him down for a few heartbeats, allowing him to frantically try to figure out the reason for her visit.

Nicholas nervously lit a cigarette and offered one to Renee. When she waved his invitation away, he asked, "Why did he send you? I haven't done anything."

"Nicholas, I'm exhausted so I'm going to get to the point. I need papers."

"Papers?"

She leaned forward and glared at him, wishing she could shoot fire out of her baby blues. "Don't try to play me for a fool, Nicholas. I know what you do. *I* need papers."

Nicholas had a smile that was ever widening by the time he finally spoke. His anxiety was gone and his appearance told her that he was going to try to use this information to his benefit as best as he could. "Why do *you* need papers?"

Renee didn't flinch and her face never gave away her desperation. "Not important."

"Oh?" He was beginning to get a sparkle in his eyes, and his smile stayed where it was. "Did you and Daddy have a fight?"

Renee stared silently at him. Her stone face told him, without question, he was not going to get an answer.

"Why come to me? Parnell has people of his own who would fall over each other to give you papers."

"Exactly the reason I am sitting here in front of you."

"And you don't think he'll figure out you came to me?"

"He wouldn't even consider it as an option. He could never imagine anyone not engaging the fine services he has to offer." The tone in her voice, disgust mixed with hurt, told Nicholas she had indeed had a falling out with her father.

"He always was a self-righteous bastard," Nicholas said.

"Don't forget yourself, Nicholas. He may be a bastard, but he is still my father. My father is many things, but he underestimates one very important strength of mine."

"And what's that?"

"I'm smarter than he is." She said it with the irrefutability of nothing less than the truth.

Nicholas sat back in his chair, deciding how to stretch this out and think about what his return for her request would be. After everything her father had put him through, she knew Nicholas had to tread carefully. It was obvious he wasn't overly comfortable having his former employer's daughter sitting in front of him, demanding his services with no explanations.

"I might be able to help you. But first, let me ask—"

She gave him a direct look that said she was not leaving until she got what she wanted. "Here's all you need to know: I need papers, I'm going to get papers, and I'm going to get them from you. You're not going to argue, you're not going to get what you want, and you're not going to turn me away."

Nicholas had to at least try to get something out of it. "And what's in it for me?"

"You get to keep both your ears and continue breathing." She had to make sure Nicholas would have no doubt that she could be as cold and heartless as her father and make him question the consequences of denying her request. She inclined her head toward the photograph on his desk. "You and your ex."

"What do you need?"

"Everything. Identification, passport, birth certificate. Your full custom package of what you do so well." She flashed him a quick smile in hopes that he would interpret it as a gesture of appreciation for the fine quality of his work.

He nodded his head. This was a serious request from a rather important person and he would be a fool to pass it up. "It will cost you."

Renee reached into her purse and tossed a tightly packed envelope on his desk. He thumbed through it, casually trying to estimate the amount of cash she had brought with her. Keeping his head slightly bent, he looked up at her through his eyelashes and shook his head. "Sorry, lass. Prices have gone up."

"Don't think for one second that you will attempt to take advantage of me. There is more than enough in that envelope to cover your expenses in addition to securing your discretion and absolute, eternal silence." She paused, then asked him the obvious question. "You wouldn't pass up an opportunity to take Parnell money, would you?"

She was full of surprises and he couldn't help but be impressed. "You took this from him?"

"And," she continued, ignoring his question, "keep one thing in mind before you decide whether or not to grant my request."

"What's that?"

"I'm smarter than you too."

The blood drained from his face and he slowly leaned back in his chair, slapping the envelope against the palm of his hand, considering. Reconciled, he let out a sigh. "Identification and the like are doable. I can also provide credit cards, bank accounts, and credit reports."

"I need a career as well," she stated as she suppressed the victorious smile that threatened to escape. "Something that will keep me moving."

"Anything in particular?"

"I've been in business management for the past five years. Be creative."

"I can do that. It will take some time to get this done."

She didn't have time. "Twenty-four hours."

His jaw dropped at the impossibility of her demand and he shook his head. "Twenty-four hours? Can't be done."

"Make it happen," she said with fiery eyes and an uncaring voice.

He looked out the window and she could see the contemplation on his face. She knew she would get what she wanted, but she also knew, for his own safety and peace of mind, he would do it just to find a way to get her away from him.

Nicholas turned back to Renee. "Anything else?"

"I'll need to trade in my car. Give the commission to the young man who tried to help me when I got here. He earned it and didn't piss himself in the process."

***

Less than eighteen hours later, Renee merged her new vehicle onto the interstate, heading west with her new identity in an envelope on the passenger seat. Her destination was unknown, but she only had one thought in her head. *Goodbye, Renee Parnell. Hello, Chloe Riggs.*

Chapter 16

After twenty-four straight hours of driving, Chloe Riggs checked into the Holiday Inn off Interstate 94 in Bismarck, North Dakota. By the time she locked the door behind her, she was drained. She dropped her bags on the floor and fell backward on the bed, staring at the ceiling. Everything had happened so fast, but here she was, safe for now.

She thought about the girls, her only friends. Her father was surely back from Chicago and she tried not to think about what he might be doing to them now that she was gone. Whatever punishment he was dealing was undoubtedly her fault.

For the first time, she was completely on her own and anonymous to anyone she met. She was sure that nobody knew where she was, but had no idea how long it would stay that way. She knew Nicholas wouldn't say anything; she had paid him well and given him a good enough scare to pretend he never knew she ever existed.

Chloe tried to sit comfortably on the bed as she

kicked her shoes to the floor and noticed the clock beside the bed read just after midnight. She had never been this afraid before and had to suppress all her fear and anxiety if she was going to attempt to have a normal life, if it could be called normal. Reaching into one of her bags, she removed two envelopes. One contained the cash she had taken from her father. What she kept for herself she thought of as remuneration for five years of services rendered managing his companions, twenty years of venomous hatred, and a little extra for murdering Christopher. The other envelope had been provided by Nicholas, which she dumped upside down and watched as her new life tumbled onto the bed.

Her driver's license listed her as a resident of Minnesota. She made a mental note to go online in the next few days and study up so she would at least sound like she was familiar with the Land of Ten Thousand Lakes. She flipped through her new passport and discovered she had already been a tourist in Spain and Norway within the past three years. She had new credit cards, a bank account, social security number, and phone number. Nicholas gave her business organization papers, all filed and legal, making her the sole proprietor of a small consulting firm that helped businesses with strategies and techniques to create success and think smarter about their goals. He also provided her with a more than impressive resume and a stack of referrals from companies she had "consulted" for. She would have to come up with some creative explanations for those companies when the time came but she liked the idea of her new profession, and Nicholas told her to be expecting a call in a few days from her first client. She didn't bother to ask what happened to her true identity. The less she knew, the better.

She put her new life back in its envelope, lay back on the bed, and made a mental list of everything she would need to accomplish if this telephone call for her first job was actually coming her way. She tried desperately to shut her brain off, not wanting to think about Christopher, her father, or her desertion anymore. After a few minutes of staring at the ceiling, it finally happened, and there was nothing she could do about it.

She clutched a pillow, curled up in a ball, and wept uncontrollably until sleep finally claimed her.

Chapter 17

Eight Years Later

"Thirty-year-old Michelle Stephenson of Boulder, Colorado was hit by a car while walking to the field to watch her son's game. She died at the scene before paramedics arrived. The driver of the vehicle fled the scene and police are currently investigating. Police are asking if anyone has information about the vehicle or any information that may assist with the investigation to please call the police non-emergency number. In other news…"

A picture of Michelle Stephenson of Boulder, Colorado—formerly of Boston, Massachusetts—flashed on the screen during the news report. She looked exactly the same as she had eight years ago, except for the fact that she was smiling and sickeningly happy. The balloons and streamers in the background, as well as the children and jubilant adults in the foreground, gave away that the picture had been most likely taken at a child's birthday party, most likely her own child's.

The television went black with the click of the remote and Chloe took a few deep breaths, trying not to let the pain stab her in the heart too much.

Thanks to Nicholas and his choice of career for her, she drove all over the country for work, never staying in one place for too long. Her routine was the same wherever she went. She rented a furnished home or apartment to temporarily live, secluded herself when she wasn't working, and watched the national news every morning, hoping not to see a story of her father looking for her, as well as another story about a murdered woman who had a black rose tattoo. While the news never mentioned the mark, she, of course, knew they had one because she recognized who the women were from the pictures the news flashed on the screen. The first news report she saw had been six years ago. Thinking about that first murder still hurt just as much as all of the others that followed. No matter what city she was in, she knew one undeniable truth: it was her fault they were dead.

When she felt she could breathe again, Chloe went back into the bathroom to finish getting ready for her day.

Chapter 18

Stopping for coffee at Ma and Pop's Java had been a Monday through Friday morning routine for Hunter Lawton since his wife died. Amy had been with friends enjoying Mardi Gras parades and catching all the beads she possibly could when someone described as a tall, bald man with an unkempt beard and yellow teeth bumped into her, almost pushing her off the sidewalk. He caught her by the arm to stop her from falling and stabbed her in the neck, instantly killing her. Her friends and parade enthusiasts watched in horror as a group of men took chase after the bald man, only to lose him in the crowd, leaving Amy's death unsolved. Hunter blamed himself every day. If he hadn't been so tired, he would have gone to the parade with his wife and she would still be with him today.

Just opening the front door of the coffee shop gave Hunter's sense of smell the burst of coffee and fresh baked pastries that he had become accustomed to over the years. It was a small but prosperous place, owned by Mr. and Mrs. Davidson, a couple who had decided to leave their high stress, overworked jobs in their late forties and open a coffee house. Hunter had developed a taste for his wife's favorite coffee and was one of his daily routines in an attempt to keep a piece of her alive. Besides his coffee and his job, there wasn't much else.

Mrs. Davidson's smile as he walked in said she had been waiting for him all morning. She was more like a mother to him, always giving advice, trying to make sure he was happy, and relentlessly trying to find the perfect woman for him. He wasn't interested in meeting the perfect woman, but her heart was in the right place.

"Good morning, Agent Lawton," she said as she handed him his coffee.

He took a sip and she watched with anticipation. "Good as always."

Satisfied with his happiness, she leaned on the counter for their brief morning chat, leaving her husband to tend to the customers. After five minutes of filling Hunter in on their weekend activities, she began her predictable matchmaking routine, starting with, "And that nice young lady came in over the weekend."

Hunter wasn't interested in meeting anybody or getting into any kind of relationship. He had gone on a few dates since Amy's death, but never had a second date with any of them. He didn't want to hurt Mrs. Davidson's feelings, so he spoke in a slightly uninterested tone, hoping she would take the hint. "Oh yeah?"

She tried so hard to pick out the perfect woman

for Hunter and apparently believed she had finally found *the one*. The "nice young lady" had been a regular customer over the past few months, but only on the weekends. He had been repeatedly told she was attractive, obviously worked hard, and, most importantly, was single. Mrs. Davidson gave him that motherly look that said it was time he settled down again.

"She sat in that corner for a few hours working on her computer." She raised her eyebrows at him to question whether or not he had been listening to her over the weeks of telling him about this nice young lady.

He smiled and tried to find the conversation amusing. "Her name is Tricia. She's a realtor."

"One day, your paths will cross."

"Mrs. Davidson, I would think you, of all people, would agree that if we were meant to cross paths, it would have happened by now."

Mrs. Davidson let out a *humph* and crossed her arms. From behind the espresso machine, Mr. Davidson attempted to save Hunter from his wife by giving his playful, "Woman! Let the man get to work. You can worry about his love life later."

Mrs. Davidson shushed her husband with the wave of her hand. Mr. Davidson shrugged his shoulders at Hunter, apologizing for the failed rescue attempt.

"Ignore him," Mrs. Davidson remarked.

Hunter chuckled but took this opportunity to step out. Raising his cup to her, he said, "It's getting busy in here and I really do need to get going. I'll see you tomorrow."

Mrs. Davidson came out from behind the counter and gave Hunter a quick hug. "This conversation isn't over, you know."

Pulling back from the hug and smiling down at her, his only reply was the obvious. "I know."

Mrs. Davidson patted him on the shoulder and began to straighten his tie. It was a habit she'd picked up since he started coming in every morning, and Hunter found that he didn't mind. To him, it was a gesture that she cared about him, and it felt good to have someone who cared, even if it meant putting up with mothering and matchmaking.

Satisfied he was presentable, Mrs. Davidson gave Hunter a quick kiss on the cheek and smiled. "You got yourself a new suit. Looks good on you. Now, you go and catch bad guys. We'll talk about Tricia later."

Chapter 19

Chloe sat in the reception area of Keller and Keller law firm, waiting to meet with the managing partner. All those years ago, and before her first client had called as foretold by Nicholas, she did all the research she could on small business consulting—she had to know what she was talking about. Of course, it didn't hurt that she was raised to be a ruthless, cold-hearted businesswoman. She knew how to get what she wanted, how to twist conditions to her favor, how to shake down the corruptible, and how to make the results her clients wanted happen. She was pleasant when she needed to be, and vicious when she wanted to be. It was safe to say that she loved her career.

She left New Hampshire three days ago after helping a medical office climb out of possible bankruptcy and made her way to Lafayette, Louisiana. She liked going to Louisiana, but each time she did she was sure to avoid New Orleans like the plague. Last she heard, Jack Lawrence was still underboss in New Orleans and he had a steadfast loyalty to David that would never be compromised. Chloe had always liked Jack—he never gave her any reason not to—but the fact that David favored her father, and Jack favored David, gave her enough reason to keep a wide berth around New Orleans. Lafayette was at least two hours away, which fell just within her comfort zone.

Her first impression was that the Keller brothers should have spent more money on the aesthetics of the office; white tile floors, white walls, and a few pieces of modest yet dark and dreary furniture. The multi-colored earth tones of the heavily worn area rug underneath the sofa and matching chairs was the only place for someone to walk without making noise in the lobby. The decorator was obviously going for a distinguished and smart impression on anyone who walked in, but to Chloe it felt like a morgue—very sterile and very boring. The receptionist had a large, semi-enclosed workstation facing the waiting room. There was a door to one side of the lobby that led to, Chloe assumed, the work area. She took comfort in the fact that with the tile floors, and nothing to absorb the noise, nobody would be able to sneak up behind her.

She and the receptionist eyeballed each other a few times, making their own mental first impression judgments. Chloe hadn't been to one business where someone, or various someones, didn't go to the receptionist for the daily news. It didn't matter what the issue was, the gossiping receptionist was one of the main problems her clients complained about. In the world Chloe grew up in, the receptionist would have been referred to as a rat. A squealer. The one who loved to talk and then would deny everything if confronted. In the end, however, rats always ended up in a trap with their necks snapped.

Chloe studied the young woman leaning against the desk, focusing intently on the device in her hand, either playing a game or texting. She was maybe nineteen and definitely not dressed the part of what a client might expect from a law firm. Although Chloe couldn't see the receptionist from the waist down, the top half showed that this young woman had a nice figure and she was intent on showing it off in an almost transparent tight shirt, foolishly assuming that adding a colorful scarf to her ensemble would hide this fact. When the phone rang, she was irritated at having to set her own phone aside, so she didn't. She simply answered the phone with the look of someone who was interrupted from something more important, still concentrating on her own device.

"Keller and Keller. How may I direct your call? Sure. Hang on, please."

Chloe mentally winced at the drone and uncaring of her voice. *Well, at least she said please.*

The young girl pushed a few buttons, dropped the receiver into its cradle as if it were acid burning her hands, and turned her attention back to her phone. Chloe slit her eyes at her, considering how best to deal with this particular problem, and knew two things that would be a certainty: within a week this girl would no longer be a receptionist, and within a half hour of meeting with Walter Keller, Chloe would become the latest gossip at the reception desk.

Walter Keller, a middle-aged, portly man with salt and pepper hair, bags under his eyes, and a jovial disposition entered the reception area from the side door. The young receptionist put her phone away and looked like she cared.

"Ms. Riggs?" He held out his hand to shake hers.

"Mr. Keller." She accepted his hand as she stood. "It's nice to meet you."

"Please," he said, extending his arm in an invitation to accompany him to one of the staff doors, "follow me."

"Thank you." Chloe picked up her purse and briefcase from the floor and didn't miss the fact that curious eyeballs from the receptionist desk were watching as she did.

Chloe followed Walter through the staff area where The Cubicle People lived. She picked up the distinct clicking of fingers on a keyboard, a few people on the telephone, and a group of three women standing around another cubicle whispering and talking about nothing work related.

"I've asked my brother, Arthur, to join us," Walter said as they entered a small conference room containing a small circular table with four chairs and what looked like a bedside table in the corner with a telephone on it. This room was dull, desperately needing paint and maybe a picture or two hung on the walls. At the table sat Arthur Keller, who obviously, unlike his brother, had no desire to be in on this meeting.

As Chloe took her seat, Arthur overtly scanned and studied her as if she was a conundrum in quantum physics that he would never be able to solve. He reminded Chloe of her father—a man who felt superior to anyone else and would get what he wanted no matter how many people he had to trample along the way. Thankfully, she had been ingrained with the skills to handle people like Arthur.

Chloe extended a hand to Arthur. "Good morning, Mr. Keller. It's a pleasure to meet you."

Arthur ignored her greeting. She smiled at him in challenge as she reached into her briefcase and pulled a stack of papers out, sliding them across the table.

Ignoring his brother's rebuff, Walter was happily optimistic as he spoke. "You came highly recommended by Gordon Mackey. He said you turned his firm around in less than a month."

"That's very kind of Mr. Mackey." She had been contracted by Gordon at the beginning of the year and had flipped the firm into the black, with a surplus in his budget, in less than a month without losing any employees.

"So, what is it exactly that you can do for us?" Walter asked.

"That would depend on what you expect from me. I need to know the exact circumstance of what it is you need me to accomplish for you. I can help you increase your revenue and profits, and help you reach and find new clients."

Arthur looked at Chloe over the contract with a scowl on his face. "How can you improve staff issues when it's a morale problem? You can encourage, but can't force someone to be motivated."

"You can if they fear losing their job," she said evenly.

Walter smiled as he perused the contract. "Is there anything you don't do? Financial management, organizational structure, budgeting, staff morale."

She gave him an appreciative smile then told a little white lie. "I didn't go through all those years of business school for nothing, Mr. Keller." Okay, a big white lie.

Arthur flipped a page of the contract and looked at her with surprise. "This is your fee?"

"For the first month. If, within the first month, you decide that my services are no longer needed, the full amount is due. If my services are required after the first month, then my wage continues, pro-rated, until I'm done. The longest I have been contracted is six weeks. However, the time I spend at one particular location is solely dependent on the work I am asked to perform."

Arthur set the contract on the table and looked at Chloe in challenge. "If there was one thing you could recommend to me, what would it be? Give me an example, if you will."

She decided to give him what he wanted with the first thing that came to mind. "Your receptionist is atrocious. She is unprofessional, rude, and irritable. She is getting paid to play on her phone and she knows it. *You* know it. My recommendation? My example to you? Kick the bitch to the curb."

Walter's head snapped back in surprise and Arthur simply stared at her. He obviously wasn't used to being spoken to by somebody, and more than likely a woman, so brazenly and unapologetically.

Walter smiled and set the papers on the table in front of him. "I appreciate your straight forwardness, although I must tell you that Kimberly is not our receptionist. She is filling in while our receptionist is on vacation. Luckily, she'll be back on Monday."

"So what is Kimberly's position in the firm?" she asked Walter.

"She's a file clerk and backup receptionist."

"And her performance and attitude as a file clerk?" Chloe could tell by the look on his face that he honestly didn't know. "Don't you think you should find out?"

"When it comes to personnel, we have an office manager to handle employee issues." Arthur had a cold tone to his voice.

Chloe cocked an eyebrow at Arthur. "Whether or not she is sitting at the front desk or filing, during work hours she is a reflection of this firm. Mr. Keller, I have been to medical offices, law firms, warehouses, food processing plants, and even an amusement park. It's pretty much the same anywhere you go. People in your position always say, 'I hired someone else to take care of it.' Nine times out of ten, the problem *is* the people they hire to take care of it. You already know you have a problem. You called me."

She leaned back in her chair to let the brothers take a moment to comprehend what she was saying. They gave each other a look of approval, but Arthur still wasn't won over.

"Tell us more about yourself," he cautiously demanded. "Your education and background, for instance."

"Those questions can be answered by reading my resume, Mr. Keller."

Arthur clearly wasn't accustomed to being told to mind his own business, and before he could respond, Walter stepped in.

"We have a plan to expand the firm and open another location. You can put together a business plan and help set up the new location?"

Before she could answer, Arthur decided to try to rattle her once again. "Your fee—"

She interrupted with a cold certainty in her voice. "Is non-negotiable."

Arthur scoffed. "Everything is negotiable, Ms. Riggs."

"Neither I nor my fee would be included in that statement," she replied, and added for the sake of making it clear to him that the game he was attempting to play was over, "contrary to your belief, Mr. Keller."

"You are very determined to get what you want when you want it, aren't you, Ms. Riggs?" Arthur asked.

"Blame it on my nature, Mr. Keller."

"Your nature," Arthur repeated skeptically. "Should I take that to mean you had a strict, yet strong upbringing?"

"You could say that."

"And where did you grow up, Ms. Riggs?"

Like it matters, she thought. "In the mob, Mr.

Keller. We always get what we want."

Walter's eyes widened in surprise and Arthur laughed at the ridiculousness of her response. Chloe simply gave a thin-lipped smile and waited.

Arthur took a pen from his jacket and reluctantly signed Chloe's contract. "When can you start?"

"Monday morning. I will need my own workspace, copies of complete personnel files, employee manuals, and firm procedures. If I could get this information by Friday so I can review it over the weekend, that would be appreciated."

Walter rubbed his index finger along his chin, considering. "I'll have everything you need ready by noon on Friday. Would you like to pick them up or have them delivered to you?"

"I'll be out and about taking care of a few personal errands. I can pick them up. Make sure Kimberly's file is on top of the pile."

She indicated their meeting was over as she stood with satisfaction, again extending her hand to Arthur. Silently and still scrutinizing her, Arthur accepted this time.

Walter stood and gave her the *ladies first* gesture. "I'll show you out, then. We appreciate your time, Ms. Riggs."

She smiled in satisfaction. "Please, call me Chloe."

Chapter 20

Hunter entered his office and realized one cup of coffee wasn't going to be enough. He hung his coat on the rack behind his door, grabbed the slightly deformed coffee mug Amy had made him when she decided to try pottery, and walked toward the breakroom where fresh, warm coffee would be waiting for him. He smiled as he looked at the mug decorated with a red heart and a yellow arrow through it, the mug splashed with every color of the rainbow around it. Some of the paint had run before it went in the kiln and it came out looking like something a second grader would make and give to their mother for Christmas. He loved it.

As he approached the breakroom, there stood two other agents blocking his path to the coffee pot. Dennis Hall had worked with the Bureau for almost fifteen years. When he took a bullet in the leg, he was given two options: retire or learn how to type. He took the desk job.

The other was Judd Fowler, a twenty-something hothead three months out of the academy, full of ideas with no clue what unexpected surprises his career would throw at him. But just like Hunter, Judd would figure it out on his own.

Dennis was leaning casually against the wall, sipping on his coffee, showing absolutely no interest in talking or listening to Judd, but pretending for the sake of killing time. Hunter had no idea, and didn't care, what Judd was boasting about this time. Judd just wanted to fit in and be one of the guys, but there were many times when Hunter wanted to jab him in the face, just to deflate Judd's puffed up head. Unfortunately, Hunter drew the proverbial short straw and was Judd's supervisor and partner.

"No coffee," Dennis said, interrupting Judd's story as Hunter reached for the coffee pot.

Hunter stared at Dennis with incredulity. "What the hell do you mean, no coffee?"

Dennis let out a short but steady laugh. "It's out. Make it yourself, you lazy bastard. You got two hands."

Hunter glanced at the full cup in Dennis's hand. "The mystery of who emptied the pot will baffle us for years."

Dennis smiled and took another sip, just to rub it in.

"It's times like these I bet you wish you had a secretary to do that kind of stuff for you, huh?" Judd asked in an effort to be included.

Hunter smiled and put a friendly hand on Judd's shoulder, casting a sideways glance at Dennis, who was also smiling. "You know, you're right, Fowler. A secretary to make my coffee sure would be nice.

Then again, that's what we have you for."

Dennis quickly drained his cup and handed it to Judd. "Black, two sugars."

Hunter handed Judd his empty mug. "If you don't know how I like my coffee, then you clearly haven't been kissing my ass. *Do not* break my mug."

Hunter and Dennis cleared the breakroom, leaving Judd holding two empty coffee mugs and wondering what the hell just happened.

***

His coffee fix fulfilled, Hunter sat in his office reviewing case files, notes, coroner reports, and everything else available in preparation for testimony he would soon be giving, provided everything for the trial went as planned. He was the agent who pursued and arrested Mack Finley for the double murder of two Louisiana state policemen who pulled him over for a broken tail light. They were killed due to Mack's fear of them finding the suitcase of drugs he had in the trunk of his car. Hunter was nothing if not meticulous, and he was going to make sure Mack Finley suffered the consequences.

"How's it going in here?" Dennis asked from the doorway of Hunter's office, watching the focused determination on Hunter's face.

Hunter started rifling through the files on his desk. "I could swear I'm missing something. Part of the coroner's report."

Dennis let Hunter do his search and destroy for

the missing document. It only took about a minute before Hunter pulled a sheet of paper out from under the keyboard, then he lifted his eyebrows to Dennis with a what-can-I-do-for-you expression. Dennis pushed himself out of the doorway and took a chair in front of Hunter's desk. Hunter didn't like the look on Dennis's face; it was the look that said he didn't want to have to be the one to talk to Hunter about something, but he was the only one who could. It was the look Hunter received when Dennis told him about Amy. No, he did not like this look.

"So?" Hunter asked, trying not to sound put out or impatient. "Spit it out, man."

"You been watching the news lately?"

"I catch a piece here or there when I think about it. Why?"

Dennis lightly tossed a file on Hunter's desk, upsetting his organized chaos. Dennis sat silently as Hunter apprehensively picked up the file folder and cracked it open. The first thing he saw was a police report completed and submitted by the State of Colorado, County of Boulder. It was obvious that it was a homicide report; there would be no reason for Hunter to receive any other kind. The report cited a hit and run, and witness accounts said that nobody saw anything except some kind of car, maybe a truck, maybe a sedan. It could have been a moped for as much as these so-called witnesses paid attention. There were photographs that made him catch his breath and threw him back in time. Unfortunately, this was not the first time photographs like this had opened up old wounds that he couldn't seem to close.

Hunter looked at Dennis, desperately trying not to take his anger out on him. "How long have you had this?"

"Came in about an hour ago. Boss gave it to me to look through before showing it to you."

"How does it feel always having to be the one breaking news like this to me?" Hunter asked.

"Sucks ass, man, but I'm the only one who can give you bad news." Dennis cracked a smile. "Everyone else thinks you're a dick."

Hunter shook his head and let a chuckle escape under his breath, thankful for Dennis trying to make him smile while simultaneously hitting him with another Black Rose Murder. He picked through the photos and sucked in his breath when he found the one he was looking for. The picture was exactly what he expected and told him everything he needed to know. It was, of course, the black rose with the letter P on the victim's back—the same tattoo that showed up in six other files that had come across his desk over the past six years. The same tattoo his wife had.

"This is the seventh," Dennis pointed out, and received a look that said Hunter already knew that piece of information.

The first murder known to law enforcement occurred at a home improvement store in Indiana where a woman bearing the tattoo was gunned down while standing in line to pay for her painting supplies. Then Amy was murdered, followed by two in California who were found hanging from the second story balcony of a shopping mall at

Christmastime. Next was a home invasion in Ohio, and another in New Jersey who had been shot while standing in line at the ATM outside her bank during a lunch break by somebody who knew exactly how to avoid all the security cameras. Finally, this soccer mom from Colorado. Seven women in the past six years, all with the same tattoo, all very public deaths, and all with witnesses who had given useless statements. All with no leads.

It was no secret that these cases were taken personally by Hunter.

"The profilers…" Dennis began, but was cut off by the look Hunter gave him.

Not bothering to hide the anger, Hunter let out a disgusted scoff. "Profilers. In six goddamn years the profilers don't have anything fresh to say. They're as clueless as the rest of us. Every time we think we have a lead, every time we think we have a name, every time we think we have *something*, we come up empty. And it pisses me off!" With rage running through his veins, Hunter forcefully swept his arm across his desk, upsetting everything on it. Papers and pictures floated in the air until they landed softly on the floor. His nameplate and pencil holder hit the wall. His keyboard hit the floor. His computer monitor wobbled on its stand.

Judd happened to walk into Hunter's office at the same time that Hunter kicked his desk and yelled to nobody in particular, "Fuck!"

Stunned, Judd looked from Hunter to Dennis. Dennis shrugged and gave Judd the look that said everything would be okay, but it would be best to turn around and leave the room immediately.

Fortunately for Judd, he took the hint and left as quickly as he had arrived.

Hunter let out a calming breath. "I'm good."

Dennis stood to leave and nodded his head in understanding, looking at the papers and desk supplies strewn on the floor. "You know I'm not helping you clean any of this shit up, right?"

Hunter looked around his office, hands on his hips. "Maybe I should call Fowler back in here. Have him clean it up."

Dennis left Hunter's office knowing Hunter would eventually be fine until the next file landed on his desk. Then it would start all over again.

Chapter 21

The Pawtucket Falls, a mile-long set of rapids, were located in Lowell, Massachusetts and just happened to be one of Matthew's favorite places. The University of Massachusetts was also located in Lowell and was the venue of choice for where the governor decided to honor Matthew Parnell, once again, for his generous humanitarian services to the community and the state.

The city purchased ten acres with the intention of building a new community recreation center for after school programs and a place for children of university students to go while their parents attended classes. Once the land had been purchased, however, the anticipated funding for the project had been canceled. The city had no idea why the funding had been withdrawn, but Matthew did—he had heard about the project, pulled a few strings, and called in a few favors. Within two months of the project being put on hold, Matthew swooped in like a super hero to save the day and donated three-quarters of the funds needed to make the center happen. Finally, it was time to celebrate the opening. Giving a humble smile, Matthew put the scissors to the ribbon, flashed a glimmering smile at the crowd, and said, "It is my privilege to admit you entrance into your new kingdom."

Children cheered as they ran for the playground, parents merged toward the food, and politicians puffed out their chests for photographs as Matthew graciously excused himself and made his way over to Mr. Crescent, who had been patiently waiting in the background with Tucker.

"He's here, sir."

He being someone who owed Matthew either an explanation or payment for a very large shipment of casino money to be washed that had not yet reached its destination. Either way, the man was going to bleed.

"Excellent, Mr. Crescent," Matthew said as he lit a cigar. "Find me at the reception at the boathouse when you're done. I think the falls are a particularly wonderful sight to see. Not a required point of interest, just a suggestion."

Crescent and Tucker left for their errand while Matthew stood alone with his thoughts. Matthew was very good at what he did and won every battle he undertook. Had Wyatt still been with him, Matthew probably wouldn't even be halfway to where he was today. Wyatt Lundy was selfish, entitled, and useless as a business partner. He knew he was better off with Wyatt gone these many years.

Even though Matthew had met most of his current goals, he had one goal that he was running out of patience to attain. The more he thought about it, the more he planned. The more he planned, the more obsessed he got. He knew the only way he would get what he wanted was for David to step down and pass the scepter to him, but he also knew there was only one way David would do that. His daughter would have to come back into the fold. She was the key to get to David. Matthew had been looking for her for eight years, with no luck and no leads.

And it infuriated him.

***

Matthew was surrounded by a small circle of admirers when he caught a glimpse of Madeline exiting the main room of the boathouse. Before disappearing from view, she turned her head, locked eyes with him, and offered an inviting grin. Always suspicious of her, Matthew politely took his leave from his company and followed her outside.

The light of the setting sun glistened on the water and, for a brief moment, Matthew smiled inwardly, enjoying one of the few places that brought him contentment. But his bliss was shattered when he saw Madeline at the far end of the deck, casually leaning against the railing, holding a glass of champagne, watching him with that smile on her face. Her hair hung loosely over her shoulders, shimmering with gold flakes from the reflection of the sun on the water.

No matter how many times he had suppressed his desire for her, it still surprised him how she could draw him near her with just a look. He also instinctively knew that behind those sly eyes and seductive smile she had something else in mind, which was her ulterior motive for being there and luring him outside. Her close-lipped smile widened slightly as he stopped in front of her, took her right hand, and softly planted a kiss.

"Always the gentleman, Mr. Parnell."

He straightened and smiled back. "When necessity calls for it, Ms. Frost."

Ignoring his rebuff, Madeline took a sip of her champagne. "It was a lovely ceremony, Matthew."

"Mmm," he replied suspiciously.

"Don't worry. Nobody took your spotlight away. We others were simply thanked with a letter and a cursory acknowledgment."

Matthew cast a casual glance at his watch as if his time were being wasted, knowing his indifference made Madeline's blood boil. It amused him to watch her push her irritation aside in order to keep her composure. While she always experienced unexplained delight in rattling him and knowing she was tempting to him, she was there for a specific purpose, which was obvious with her sudden mood change as she angrily turned on him.

"You have broken a promise to me, Matthew. We have mutually benefited from each other over the years—*you* more than I. Because of my help when you were in need, you promised that my share in Atlantic City would increase forty percent. That was eight years ago, and my share has only risen twenty-seven percent. *Twenty-seven percent*, Matthew. And then, yesterday, I receive a call from Atlantic City saying that my services won't be needed any longer because you," she quickly jabbed him in the chest with her index finger, the tip of her nail slightly digging into his chest, "apparently changed our arrangement without discussing it with me."

Matthew couldn't help but form an amused smile on his face, further infuriating Madeline, which only made his smile widen. He didn't think it was possible, but she was actually becoming more beautiful the angrier she was getting, and the angrier she got, the more he wanted her. Under normal circumstances, Matthew's reaction to her outburst would have made her try to tease and titillate him to no end. His silence, however, just made it more difficult for her to calm down.

"I have helped you more than once over the years, Matthew. I have always kept my word and my promises. It's time you do the same."

Matthew carefully contemplated his response. At one point he had intended she receive her forty percent slowly, over time, simply as a courtesy for her help in the past. If it wasn't for her, he would have suffered a severe temporary loss of business. On the other hand, he never would have even had to consider engaging her services had it not been for his runaway daughter.

Matthew saw Crescent soberly standing by the entrance to the boathouse, nodding to indicate his errand was complete. Matthew took the opportunity to take his leave and said, "I will speak to my associates in Atlantic City."

As he turned to walk away, Madeline grabbed him by his arm. "That's it?"

Matthew turned back to Madeline and gave her a chaste kiss on the cheek. It wasn't the kind of kiss he often thought about giving her, but it was the only one that would ever do with this woman. "Get home safely."

Leaving Madeline to stew in her spurned rage, Matthew got comfortable in the back of his car, where Crescent and Tucker waited. "My money, Mr. Crescent?"

"Recovered, sir."

Matthew quickly looked between his two men, Tucker smiling like he'd just won the lottery and Crescent obviously proud of a job well done. After a heartbeat, Matthew asked, "And Mr. Wells?"

Crescent let out a contented sigh. "The falls are quite a sight to see, although I got the distinct impression Mr. Wells wasn't as enthusiastic about them as I was."

"Well," Matthew said while lighting a cigar, "one can't truly appreciate the beauty of the falls while having their head held under them."

Chapter 22

On her first day of work, Chloe was in no way prepared for the cosmic bitch slap that would gut punch her when the elevator doors opened and she locked eyes with the Kellers's full-time receptionist back from vacation. The blood drained from the receptionist's face like she was looking at a ghost. Chloe was speechless as she intently locked eyes with this woman—one with an innocent and carefree smile, sun-washed blonde hair, and hazel eyes she had known so well, and shared secrets with, a lifetime ago. A woman she once considered to be her best friend, who had come to her a scared and confused girl of eighteen years that Chloe had protected, cared for, and loved. A woman she had implicitly trusted and then selfishly abandoned, leaving her to the cruelty of Matthew Parnell. Chloe had thrown this woman to the wolves in order to save herself and now she was being forced to face her past.

"Fucker bitch." Realizing what she had said, Alice Jenkins looked around the lobby to make sure nobody heard her, then turned back to Chloe, the shock slowly being replaced with cautious elation at seeing each other again. "What the hell are you doing here?"

The wrecking ball in her gut was loosening its grip on Chloe as she responded. "I could ask the same of you."

"I work here."

"So do I."

Alice opened her mouth to respond when Walter entered the room and changed the atmosphere between the two old friends. From the look on Alice's face, Chloe knew she and Alice were on the same page to temporarily pretend it was just another typical Monday morning.

"Ms. Riggs," Walter said, shaking Chloe's hand.

In her peripheral view, Chloe saw Alice shoot her a questioning look. *Riggs?*

"Mr. Keller." Chloe had always been able to act for the appropriate moment and she was doing it exceptionally well at that moment.

Walter started laughing. "I bet you're glad to know that our Ms. Morris is back from vacation."

It was now Chloe's turn at a silent question. *Morris?*

Chloe had to get out of the lobby and away from Alice for the time being in order to focus her attention on Walter. "I look forward to spending time with Ms. Morris. In the meantime, shall we get started?"

***

127

It wasn't until after the lunch hour that Chloe was face to face with Alice, staring in disbelief. The next thing Chloe knew, Alice was crossing the room and fiercely embracing her. Chloe returned the hug and realized how much she had missed Alice. Chloe broke the hug and they sat across the table from each other with a mix of emotions that included suspicion, happiness, and confusion.

Chloe finally spoke. "When did you leave?"

"About a year after you," Alice said. "I saw a produce delivery truck in the back alley behind the kitchen and I thought to myself, 'I would love to hide in that truck and just disappear.' A few days later, I was gone."

Alice continued her story of how she had sworn Michelle and Saffron to secrecy, telling them Renee was gone and giving them all the means to escape if they wanted to. Chloe could tell by the look on Alice's face, and the way she spoke, that Alice was talking about emotional demons she had never talked about before and would rather leave untouched and locked away. Matthew was apparently furious when he came home and found his daughter gone, turning to her friends for answers. When he didn't get the information he wanted, it was Crescent's turn to interrogate her friends.

The thought of Crescent being let loose on the girls left Chloe choking for air. She wanted to tell Alice to stop talking, that she didn't want hear about the hell they had gone through because of her sudden and selfish desertion. She never imagined her father would take it as far as he did and it made her want to throw up.

Alice's voice was somber and distant, the pain of memories written all over her face. "We would get called into his office one at a time, and every time, both Crescent and Tucker were waiting for us. When we wouldn't tell them anything…what Crescent and Tucker did wasn't just a consequence of you leaving, it was also a consequence of me keeping my mouth shut. I could have told them everything I knew, but I didn't. I never did."

They sat in silence for a few moments. The shock of unexpectedly seeing Alice again and learning of the aftermath of her disappearance bounced through Chloe's mind like rocks skipping on the water. She couldn't even begin to imagine how Alice was feeling, but Chloe now knew one thing for sure—her friends all suffered more than they should have because she left.

Chloe didn't know what she could say that would ever take Alice's pain away and her gut painfully churned when she heard Alice's next words. "Charlotte died."

Chloe's mouth dropped open in disbelief, her chest tightening with every intake of breath, and Alice tried to hold back tears but failed. "They tortured her, Renee. They burned her, and cut her, and forced her to…I'll never forget her screams. Your father just watched and let them torture her with every unanswered question. We were told to let it be a lesson to us, and if he found out we were keeping secrets from him, what happened to Charlotte would happen to us. He paid the mortician at Carter's and she was cremated that night. He literally made her disappear from the face of the earth."

Chloe never considered that her leaving would lead to her friends being beaten, tortured, or murdered. "I killed her."

"And I helped by keeping my mouth shut. Now I have to wonder, who are you and why are you here?"

Chloe propped her elbow up on the table and rested her forehead in her hand, feeling sick and light headed. Once she got home, she would deal with the emotions, but for the time being she was trapped. Chloe lifted her head to lock eyes with Alice. Even with what she had just been told, Chloe couldn't let her guard down. She only revealed information she thought she could trust Alice with, vaguely explaining how Renee Parnell disappeared and Chloe Riggs was born. Alice listened and didn't press for more; Chloe would give whatever information she wanted and the rest would have to wait.

In an effort to sweep the gloom out of the room, Chloe let Alice catch her up on what her life had been like after leaving Boston. Alice stopped in Mississippi and got a job as a data entry clerk at a trucking company where she met her husband, Reggie, and within a year they married and moved to Louisiana after Reggie was offered a job working in the oil field. They had six-year-old twin boys, Charlie and Samuel, who were obviously the center of her world.

"Do you still have the key?" Chloe asked.

"Well, not the original key you gave me, but *a*

key. I was actually moving the box last week. That's why I wasn't here. I just get a pang in my gut that tells me it shouldn't be kept in one place for too long."

"Can I ask where it is?"

"Rockford, Alabama. Box number eighteen."

Chloe knew where Rockford was and was relieved that Alice would hide the box somewhere so remote nobody would ever think to look for it. "And the key?"

"The key is in the light." At Chloe's confused look, Alice added, "You know. You just don't know you know. Because I don't have a signature card at the bank for you, if you ever need to get to the box without me, ask for Mr. Wilkins and tell him the key is in the light. He is being well compensated, so only talk to him."

Chloe shook her head in disbelief. "My father's keeping his promise. He knows that each one he kills stabs me with unforgivable guilt every time."

"Don't think for a second that I don't feel the same way," Alice said. "If I hadn't kept my mouth shut—"

"Then it would have been you instead of Charlotte and you wouldn't have Charlie and Samuel. You didn't know—couldn't have known—what he would do to Charlotte. Even I didn't see it coming."

"Enough about that," Alice said to change the subject. "You should come over for dinner."

"Alice, we have to be careful. I mean, Jack Lawrence is in New Orleans, and he probably has people here."

"Do you honestly think that any of Jack's boys, or even Jack himself, would know who we were?" Chloe gave her a stern look. "Okay. Jack might know it if he saw you, but how long has it been?"

"It's not only that. I'm the one who is theoretically deciding the fate of your employment. Speaking of which…"

Taking the hint, Alice nodded and they both stood up. "I understand. But you *are* coming over for dinner. You can think of it as a receptionist extending southern hospitality. You'll come for dinner tonight, and after the boys go to bed and Reggie starts watching *Sports Center*, I'll tell you what happened when David found out you were gone."

Chloe didn't want to hear it. Her heart hurt just thinking about David. She still loved and missed him so much that she had to fight tears when she thought of him. He was her family, and with a few choice words, her father made it clear to her that David wouldn't be there to stop him from hurting her. Every time she thought about David, she wanted to break down.

Alice must have seen the despair on Chloe's face because she smiled and said, "You have no idea how happy I am to see you."

Alice and Chloe embraced once more and Alice left the room with a smile on her face, leaving Chloe with too many thoughts going through her head and wondering if there were more surprises waiting for her in Louisiana.

Chapter 23

It was after five o'clock on a Friday night and Chloe had been in Louisiana for almost four weeks. She was done with her employee assessments, had moved on to the business plan for the new office, and was optimistic that if she pushed herself, she could be out of Louisiana in less than ten days.

From the conference room on the tenth floor Chloe could hear music, varying in style from rock to what sounded like African tribal drums celebrating the hunt. She turned toward the only window in the room, closed her eyes, and let herself be distracted by the sound of the drums until a knock at the door broke her peace.

She had expected Alice or Walter to be on the other side of the door, but instead it was an older woman with skin the color of burnt caramel, her hair almost completely gray, and piercing dark eyes. She was dressed in bright pink scrubs and held an unfolded plastic garbage bag in her hand. As she opened the door wider, Chloe noticed a rolling cart behind her stocked with cleaning supplies. When she spoke, her Cajun accent was so thick, Chloe focused intently to make sure she understood what was being said.

"My apologies, chérie," the woman said as she pointed to the garbage can against the wall next to Chloe.

Chloe began gathering the papers in front of her. "I can leave the room if—"

The woman gave a *tsk* and waved her hand at Chloe. As the woman walked in the direction of the garbage can, Chloe asked, "Where is all that music coming from?"

"Why, the festival, o'course," she replied with a laugh. "You not from here."

Chloe smiled at the woman. "No, ma'am."

The woman forgot about her own work and sat at the table next to Chloe. "Willetta Boudreaux."

Chloe prepared herself for the game of twenty questions she knew was coming. "Chloe Riggs."

"Where you from, Ms. Chloe?"

"Michigan," she lied.

Willetta looked at her with curiosity and gestured with her chin to the stacks of files and papers on the desk. "What is it you do?"

"I'm a consultant." Giving the shortest description she could, Chloe explained what she did for a living, and while she listened, Willetta would nod in understanding.

"Well, now. That sounds like a good job. Are you happy, child?"

Chloe felt bad that she had to lie to Willetta again. "Of course."

"Hmm," Willetta said with a doubtful tone.

"What about your family?"

"My mother passed away and my father and I don't spend a lot of time together."

"Well, maybe if the Lord smiling down, you be able to see your father again soon. Nothing more important than family." Chloe faked the best smile she could as Willetta patted Chloe's hand. "Well, enough about that. Back to your question. The Festival International is what's being celebrated outside. It's quite a celebration, it is. People from all over the world come to this festival, it's true." Willetta stood up and changed out the garbage liners in the can. "You need to go to that festival, chérie."

Chloe had been captivated by the music and had a feeling Willetta was right. "I might be able to spare some time tomorrow."

"You be sure and do that."

After Willetta left the room, Chloe looked at her watch, realizing she had an hour before she had to be at Alice's for dinner and wondered if the music could be heard from that far away.

***

"I most certainly did too tell you about the festival," Alice said, setting a cup of coffee in front of Chloe, and sat down at the table. "Sometimes I wonder if you hear half the things I say to you."

Chloe had been spending a majority of her free time outside of the office with Alice and her family. Reggie was good for Alice and obviously loved her unconditionally. Charlie and Samuel—who could be heard playing together in the other room, either video games or pretending they were warriors hunting down dragons and bad guys—were the center of their world. Chloe instantly fell in love with the boys and they took to her as if they had known her since the day they were born. Occasionally she would read them a story before bed, knowing it was just an excuse to get to stay awake for an extra ten minutes, but she didn't mind. There was a part of her that was jealous Alice was able to achieve her dream of a family and being happy, so she took what she could get until she had to leave Louisiana.

Alice took a sip of her own coffee, glancing at the clock, counting the minutes until she would force the boys to go to sleep. "Ms. Willetta actually lives two houses down across the street. Her granddaughter lives with her, but I've never met her. From what I've been told, she is in a wheelchair and prefers not to leave the house."

"That's too bad." Chloe decided it was time to ask the question that had been burning in her mind since she first saw Alice. "Do you think it's a coincidence that we're both in the same place at the same time?"

"I did for a little while, but not anymore."

"Why?"

"Because we're still here." From the other room she heard the boys howl with laughter and Alice smiled. "And because I think we have been careful to make sure nobody knows who we are."

"Reggie knows about your tattoo," Chloe pointed out.

"True, but he doesn't know who I used to be." Alice let out a sigh. "Reggie knows I am keeping secrets from him. Every once in a while he asks questions about my past and I am either vague or make something up because I can't tell him. I know he gets frustrated sometimes but he doesn't press me for information. He says when I'm ready, I'll tell him."

Chloe stared into her coffee cup and silently wondered if the day came when she met someone she was willing to give a relationship a chance with, would she would keep all of her secrets or trust them enough to tell the truth and not be afraid anymore.

"Besides," Alice said, "we won't be hiding forever. Maybe, if we're lucky, your father will get sick again and won't have the energy to go on."

Chloe's head snapped up. "What do you mean, sick?"

"I told you about that," Alice said defensively, then thought about it. "Didn't I?"

"Trust me, I would have remembered."

Alice shrugged her shoulders. "I don't know if he's still sick, but about a year after you left, your dad got sick. Nobody knew for sure, but all of the girls agreed it must have been a heart attack. He was in the hospital a few days. David came out to check on things and Dr. Michaelson was there every day for weeks."

Chloe took a drink of her coffee, taking her time to think about it. Her father was sick or had been. If something were to happen to him, as his daughter, she would be the beneficiary of his kingdom. But if she wasn't there to claim the crown, who would it go to? The next question she had to ask herself was, if—not if, when—she inherited the throne, would she even want it? She was surprised to admit to herself that she didn't know the answer.

Alice interrupted Chloe's thoughts. "So, the festival. You should go and at least check it out."

"I'm not too crazy about hanging out in crowds for very long."

"So take a once-around just to say you've been and go home. Seriously, blow off work for one weekend and go have fun." Alice looked at the clock then turned her head down the hall. "Boys! Ten minutes!"

Within seconds, Charlie and Samuel, came running in, both dressed in old Halloween costumes—Charlie in an almost too-small Spiderman costume and Samuel wearing Superman, complete with cape whipping out behind him as he ran. They both rushed Alice with hugs, begging to stay up longer.

"Just a few more minutes," Charlie said.

"We love you, Mommy," Samuel added in the sweetest voice he could muster.

Then both at the same time, with puppy dog eyes, "Pleeease?"

Chloe smiled into her coffee cup. Those boys were fantastic.

Alice had to hide a laugh and smile. "We have to get up early in the morning to go see Granny and Papa. Go get ready for bed. I'll be in in a few minutes."

Both boys turned on Chloe, still with the puppy

dog eyes, looking for some kind of savior to let them stay up just a little while longer. All Chloe could do was press her mouth shut so she wouldn't smile or laugh, and gave them a look that told them they'd better listen to their mother. Defeated, both boys slumped and turned back toward the bedroom. The disappointment was abruptly forgotten as Charlie turned to Samuel.

"Race you!" Charlie ran down the hallway with Samuel on his heels.

It was confirmed. Chloe was jealous.

Chapter 24

Chloe's senses were bombarded all at once by the different smells of various foods wafting throughout the air, at least six different bands playing six different styles of music from six different corners of the festival, and the enormous crowd of people filling the streets. There was music, food, and purchases to be made from all corners of the globe, and Chloe inspected every one of them. Cautious that such a large festival might bring Jack Lawrence up from New Orleans, or any associates who might recognize her, she was able to let herself get lost in the festivities, while at the same time paying close attention to her surroundings. That was a habit she would never be able to break, and it was also how she knew she was being followed.

She'd noticed him earlier in the day when she had stopped at one of the stages to listen to a band. While standing in the crowd, she glanced around the people surrounding her and saw him staring at her with his knee-melting smile. Both his hands were full, a drink of some kind in one and food in

140

the other. Instantly attracted, she wanted to return the smile, but didn't want him to take it as an invitation to approach her, so she turned around and left. Not paranoid, but not completely comfortable, she decided to take another walk around the festival to test herself and make sure that every warning of possible danger was all in her head. She strolled through the various rows of vendors and stopped at one for a few minutes, leaving with a pair of earrings and matching necklace. As she continued to walk past local businesses whose doors were open and happily welcomed customers during the festival weekend, she could see his reflection in the windows. He was still following her, and, surprisingly, she was okay with it. Realizing her need to be overly cautious was all in her head, she stopped and calmly turned around to confront him. When he stopped in front of her, he smiled and the pit of her stomach tightened.

"Hello, strange man who has been following me for the past forty-five minutes," she said coolly with curiosity filling her thoughts.

She could see that he was obviously trying to think of something to say so she waited for him to speak again. She would give him thirty more seconds and if he didn't speak, cute or not, she was going home.

His smile widened. "I guess there are some people I can't follow without being caught. I'm Hunter."

"I'm Chloe. You know, you're not very good at following someone."

He threw his head back and laughed. "Don't let

my boss hear you say that." She raised an inquisitive eyebrow at him. "I'm an FBI agent."

Her eyes widened and panic struck her momentarily. *FBI?* This was the perfect time to make an excuse to get away from him, go home, and pack her bags to leave town, but she didn't feel any threat.

"You're not wanted, are you?" he asked in a joking manner.

Involuntarily, she looked at him with all seriousness in her eyes and slowly shook her head. "Not by the FBI."

She could tell he was trying to determine if she was kidding or not, but he laughed all the same. They stood across from each other in silence for a few minutes, each taking the time to look the other over carefully. He was beautiful, with a square jaw, straight nose, perfectly shaped ears, broad shoulders, and eyes that seemed to pierce through her. He was dressed in a pair of jeans and a long-sleeved button-down shirt. There was no way the conversation, or the fantasies, would continue until she knew something for sure.

She cleared her throat, not believing what she was about to ask and hoping he didn't think she was some crazy lady with a fetish. "Can I ask you a favor without having to give an explanation? Would you mind rolling up your shirt sleeves? Just to the elbows will be fine."

He seemingly found her request amusing as he threw his beer in the garbage can, rolled up his sleeves, and rotated his lower arms with no clue what she did or didn't want to see. She felt absolutely foolish, but had to make sure there was no indication he was part of the Family.

He began to roll his sleeves back to their previous position. "Got a thing for arms?"

"Sorry. It's just..." *Stupid*, she thought to herself. She waved her hand in front of her in an effort to make the cloud of idiocy forming around her vanish.

Neither of them seemed to notice hundreds of festival visitors passing by them in all directions while they stood across from each other. The more he smiled at her, the more her stomach fluttered. She knew this was simply lust at first sight and nothing more. The fact that he had no tattoo on his arm made her want to talk to him, but her wall wasn't coming down.

"So," he said in an effort to keep the conversation going, "are you enjoying the festival?"

"It's quite an event with so much to see."

His eyebrows shot up with realization. "This is your first time."

She nodded. "I was told, by more than one person, that the festival was one thing I absolutely had to experience."

"There's a restaurant down the street," Hunter said. "We could get a table. While we walk, we can have our awkward silence while we try to think of things to talk about."

Oh, she liked him, and showed it with the smile she gave him. He extended a chivalrous arm in the direction of the restaurant to let her take the lead, but she stood still. He looked at her, a little confused.

She gave a slight laugh. "While I appreciate the *ladies first* gesture, I don't know where we're going. I'll follow you this time."

***

They sat across from each other in the back of the restaurant with a half-eaten plate of appetizers between them that had been sitting there for at least four hours. Surprised at how comfortable she was talking with him, Chloe caught herself starting to be a little too honest about who she was and had to stop herself. She could tell Hunter was nervous by the way he would clear his throat and run a hand though his hair when he wasn't sure what to do or say next.

They started with easy topics like where they grew up and their families. Hunter was the oldest of three boys, born and raised in New Orleans. One of his brothers, two years younger than Hunter, was career military and currently stationed in Germany. The other brother, five years younger, was a professional burden on society, happy to feel the world owed him and mooch off whoever he could to avoid taking on any real responsibility of his own. His dad took off when he was eight and had no idea where he was. He briefly told her about Amy but didn't go into too much detail.

Chloe had made up a somewhat imaginary world about her past, some false information mixed with a little bit of carefully worded truth—dead mother, only child, privileged childhood, Michigan winters were cold and she didn't miss them, business school, she and her father didn't see each other often but she would try to get together with him when she was in the area. She told him about her friends growing up, omitting that they were her employees, who were paid for giving sexual favors to the elite, as well as acting as couriers of illegal contraband and whatever else they were ordered to do. It wasn't exactly like she could come out with the truth that she had run away from a sadistic father, changed her identity, and paid for a new life.

"I like the puzzles," he told her when she asked what he liked best about his job.

"Puzzles?"

"You know, every story has clues. Like the first time I go to a crime scene. It's not all neat and orderly. I go in, look at the clues, and try to piece everything together." The way he smiled and sat up straighter when he started his explanation showed this was obviously a subject he was passionate about and she found it endearing. "See, the thing is nobody ever tells the whole story. Everybody lies. It's like there are six different jigsaw puzzles scattered all over the floor and I have to try to sort them out and put them all together in a few hours. I'm good at filling in those holes."

"So you're the type of guy who always believes everyone is hiding something and you're going to be the one to find out what it is."

"I am sorry to say that I am that guy."

Chloe nodded and looked out the window, noticing the sun would be going down soon and the swarm of people participating in the celebration outside was getting bigger. "So, you come to the festival every year?"

"Every year."

"To stalk women?" she teased.

"Naturally." He smiled at her and she knew the attraction was definitely mutual. "We have festivals in New Orleans too, but every year I take the opportunity to get out of the city for a few days."

His smile made her want to reach across the table and touch him just to make sure he was real. He made her feel the same way Christopher once did and she wasn't sure what to do because that was the feeling she had been wanting and dreading for too many years. Her stomach was in knots—she wanted him, knew he would be temporary, and she was okay with that.

"I'm sorry," the waitress they didn't see approach said, a little embarrassed, "but my manager says he needs the table because you guys have been here for hours and haven't ordered..." The glare Chloe was beginning to give made the waitress forget what she was trying to say.

Hunter watched silently, surprised curiosity on his face. The daggers in Chloe's eyes were gone as fast as they appeared and she pursed her lips together and smiled. The waitress started shifting uncomfortably from foot to foot, waiting for some kind of response—either for them to order something or leave the restaurant. Something in Chloe's mind clicked and she decided she didn't like being asked to leave, especially by a man who was too much of a coward to come over and do it himself.

Her features once again hardened, but her voice

was casual as she reached into her purse, producing a hundred-dollar bill and holding it out to the waitress. "Who's the manager?"

The waitress looked over her shoulder at a group of coworkers and one middle-aged, overworked, and underpaid manager staring back at her, curiosity steaming off their heads like water over hot coals. Chloe locked eyes with the manager, narrowing her eyes and daring him to come over to their table. Hunter watched in awe as the manager stood paralyzed in Chloe's glare. The waitress was obviously confused and looked to Hunter for some kind of clarification, but all he could do was shrug his shoulders and wait to see what happened.

"If you wouldn't mind," Chloe said to the waitress, "would you please tell your manager we're not ready to leave yet? This will cover our bill, and your tip, until we do."

Hunter looked on with rabid curiosity as the waitress locked eyes with Chloe, debating what to do, until Chloe raised her eyebrows to indicate she needed to make a choice quickly.

The waitress snatched the money out of her hand and smiled. "Let me know if you need anything else."

The waitress walked away and Chloe smiled as she reached for her glass, catching Hunter watching her out of the corner of her eye, his mouth slightly agape with surprise and approval.

"Wow," was all he could say.

One side of her mouth curled in a grin. "I know we'll probably be leaving soon, but that was fun. Don't you think?"

"I have to say you certainly seemed to enjoy that. What now?"

"We both know the answer to that question but you need to know this isn't the beginning of anything."

She studied the reaction on his face and saw that he not only understood what she was saying, but he also wasn't a one-night stand kind of guy and the decision he would make in the next few minutes wasn't easy for him. She needed to let him know that whatever his decision, she wouldn't hold it against him.

"You don't seem like a casual sex kind of guy to me," she stated.

"Not usually, no," he confessed.

She smiled and thought, *Not only a gentleman, but a gentleman with morals. If I fall for him, I'm completely screwed.* Whether it was passion or lust, she wasn't prepared to break any of her rules and poke a hole in the protective bubble she had built around herself.

Hunter forced the final decision. "Your place or mine?"

"You paid for a hotel room," she said with a flirtatious smile. "Wasting money is a terrible thing."

Chapter 25

Before the door could close behind them, Hunter had Chloe pinned against the wall, his body crushing hers, holding her hands above her head, wanting to take complete control of her. They kissed each other hard and deep, tongues hungrily exploring with want for more from each other. He let go of her hands to wrap his arms around her and Chloe took the opportunity to embrace him, pulling him into her, grinding her hips against his.

Through the partially opened curtains, the lights of the city, in conjunction with the moon, were their only illumination. They kicked their shoes off and tugged at each other's clothes, desperate for what they had been waiting hours for. When Hunter reached for the light switch, Chloe instinctively batted his hand away, gave him a mischievous smile, then let out a soft moan as Hunter lightly circled her breast with the palm of his hand.

Sparks seemed to shoot from every nerve in their bodies. Hunter lifted Chloe's arms above her head to remove her shirt and threw it on the floor behind him. The half second they had to part lips was a half second too long for Chloe. Once the shirt was clear of her head, she took Hunter's face between her hands to kiss him deeper.

Hunter broke the kiss only to move his lips across her body, slowly savoring every bit of her— her face, neck, shoulders, the curve of her breasts. His hands stroked over her at the same time, and with each touch she would release a moan, letting him know she didn't want him to stop. Permission had been granted to taste every inch of her that he chose to.

Gooseflesh rose all over her body as he very slowly and softly ran his hands down the side of her body, almost like a feather being lightly brushed across her skin. His hands moved up and his fingers traced the swell of her breasts, round, full, and wanting. She let him take control of her, desperately wanting him to take in all of her. Her eyes jerked open, suddenly aware that she could no longer feel his tongue caressing her skin, but instead felt his arms wrap around her, his hands working the clasp on her bra.

She pulled his shirt over his head and threw it on the floor to accompany hers. Her palms glided over his chest, hard and muscular, rippling with every trace of her fingers. She buried her head in the curve of his neck, inhaling deeply to capture the scent of him, a mixture of musk and sweat radiating off his skin. She kissed his neck and moved her tongue toward his jaw, tasting him and taking him into her senses.

He was staring at her, hunger and wanting

dominating every feature. His stare penetrated her like the fire of a thousand suns. Her breathing was shallow and her eyes begged him to finish whatever he intended to start. He kissed her hard and deep, rough with wanting, as she reached down and took hold of his jeans, unbuttoning them and taking them off with her feet. He kicked his jeans behind him and threw her bra across the room, once again crushing her against the wall, locking her in place with his hands on her wrists and his mouth over hers.

She could feel him harden against her stomach and her body instantaneously responded with a jolt of lightning shooting through every nerve. She gently took him in her hand, and with each stroke, the harder and deeper he kissed her, his grip tightening on her wrists. She liked it and he knew it. A moan escaped his throat and she shivered, feeling like her legs would give any instant.

Hunter finally pulled her away from the wall and they managed to take three steps closer to the bed before Hunter took Chloe to the floor where they were. Protected underneath him, Hunter reached up and hooked a corner of the bedspread in his fist, then pulled. The bedspread billowed as it caught air, bringing a pillow with it that landed at their feet. Once they had somehow managed to maneuver themselves on top of the bedspread, Hunter pinned her arms above her head, holding her down as he hovered over her, staring intently into her eyes. She wrapped her legs around his back, urging him to enter as her lips met his once more. He bent his head and kissed her, this time softly, slowly moving his tongue around the shape of her lips, letting her know he would be taking his time to make her remember this night.

She greedily returned his kiss as she reached down to take him in her hand once more, but he began to slide down her body to show her that he had other plans. He traced kisses down her neck and chest until he took one of her breasts in his mouth, her nipples hard in anticipation of his warm breath bringing them to life. He was taking his time and her body was screaming for release. She sucked in a shuddering breath and held his head to her as he made her feel tingling in places she didn't know she had.

Arching her back in response, he wrapped one hand around her back while his other hand began to caress the length of her body, only to stop between her legs. She opened her legs, granting him access, inviting him—begging him—to take her. He teased her with his fingers until she couldn't hold back a scream of pleasure.

He let go of her breast and moved down her body, replacing his hand with his tongue. She arched her back as much as she could in need, her hands pressing against the back of his head to keep him where he was, begging him not to stop. He was slow and meticulous, making sure she remembered every area he touched. She moved her hips to his rhythm, and it wasn't long before she could feel the wonder of release, then suddenly he had her, and her body shuddered with every contraction of her muscles, moaning while whispering his name at the same time.

As he kissed his way back up her body to meet her mouth, she flipped him onto his back, letting him know it was now her turn to be in control. Chloe took her time, savoring his body, tasting every inch of him with insistent kisses on his inner thighs, using her tongue to trace the way to her destination, teasing him until she lowered her head, her mouth enveloping him slowly, savoring every second, making sure to give him the same exotic pleasure he had just given her. He collected her hair in his fists, and as he pulled, guiding her, showing her what he liked and what he wanted, he quietly moaned with desire.

He stopped her and lifted her head, wanting to take her the way he had been dreaming of since he first saw her. She straddled him and gently lowered herself onto him, moving to his rhythm. His grip was fierce as he held her in place, guiding her hips with his until they moved together as one, each thrust progressively stronger and harder, burying himself deeper, knowing each other's exact desire with every moan of pleasure. One final thrust and his grip on her hips tightened, forcefully holding her in place as he spilled into her. Slowly, she slid off of him and stretched out next to him, taking his hands in hers and smiling with the knowledge that she had been right about the correlation of his hands and passion at first glance.

The light of the moon illuminated them as they lay facing each other, both trying to catch their breath, smiling at each other with awe. After a few minutes, and completely out of habit, Chloe pulled the comforter around her, twisting her body until her tattoo was covered.

Energy and stamina were quickly leaving their bodies and Chloe closed her eyes. She couldn't stop the thoughts running through her mind about how she was not just physically, but emotionally feeling. There was a definite emotional connection with this man that she had never felt with anyone except Christopher. There were no warning bells and she quickly began to realize that with Hunter, she might be willing to run the risk of those intense feelings once again. She also knew that with those feelings came the possibility of loss, and she refused to let herself be exposed to that kind of tragedy ever again. *That's completely ridiculous. We've known each other less than twelve hours*, she thought in an attempt to move away from any emotions except tired and content. *You don't know what you're feeling. Just enjoy the moment while it lasts.*

He had a deep, gravelly tone to his voice. "What are you thinking?"

She slowly opened her eyes and gave a satisfied chuckle. "I'm having a hard time thinking of anything right now."

He pulled her closer and gave her a gentle kiss. When he pulled back, he looked deep in her eyes, brushing her hair out of her face. "You are so beautiful."

She knew he meant it and the butterflies in her stomach started fluttering again. She didn't know how to respond so she said the first thing that came to her mind. "Thank you for stalking me."

***

Hunter woke up on the floor, where they started and finished their night together, as the sunlight burst through the window, threatening to blind him if he didn't move out of the way. He rolled over, expecting—hoping—Chloe would be next to him, sleeping or watching him, waiting and wanting to have him one more time as much as he wanted her. Instead, he found himself alone. He propped himself up on one elbow and looked toward the door. Her things were gone and so was she.

Disappointed, he lay back down, scooting over an inch or two so the sun wouldn't be hitting him directly in the face. He had fallen asleep foolishly confident she would still be with him when he woke up. He let out a sigh knowing that Chloe was gone, and he doubted he would see her again.

Chapter 26

Hunter almost felt like he was betraying Amy by having feelings for Chloe, a woman he would probably never see again but hoped he would. He often thought if he were able to solve Amy's murder, he would be able to get some closure and allow himself to pursue another woman, guilt free. The only problem was that he had been trying to solve the Black Rose Murders for years and was no closer to finding the suspect than he was on the first case.

Hunter had files and photographs strewn on his desk, trying to put the puzzle pieces together, trying to find the meaning behind the black rose tattoo. Dennis walked into Hunter's office and took a seat in front of his desk, sipping coffee and watching him with curiosity. Hunter let out a frustrated sigh, leaned back in his chair, and ran his hands though his hair.

"How was your weekend?" Hunter asked. "Did the missus finally get you to the farmer's market?"

"Hell no," Dennis said. "I'll tell you, this

gardening thing is starting to drive me a little batty. She came home from the market and asked me if I would help build her a greenhouse. Can you believe that?"

Hunter smiled, knowing that Dennis would build that greenhouse on the moon if his wife asked him to. "Her honey-do list is going to be enormous when you retire."

"Tell me about it. I would rather buy an RV and drive across the country. Alone. *That's* enjoying retirement." He was joking, of course, and let out a laugh. "So, did you go to the festival?"

Hunter nodded as he thought about Chloe's piercing blue eyes and the way they drilled a hole right through his gut. He quickly shook off the thought and cleared his throat. "Yeah, I went."

Dennis glanced over Hunter's shoulder then gave Hunter a suspicious look. "What's going on?"

"What?"

Dennis pointed to Amy's coffee cup sitting empty on the file cabinet. For the first time since Amy died, the coffee cup was not being used. "That's what."

Hunter looked at the plain white coffee mug with *FBI* in bold black letters in front of him and knew Dennis was the only one he trusted to tell. "I met someone at the festival." Dennis's eyes widened with intrigue and he gave Hunter a look that said *It's about time* and *Who is she?* "Don't get too excited. She loved me and left me."

"At least you got laid," Dennis joked.

Hunter shrugged his shoulders. "She told me that it would be a one-night stand and I was okay with that at the time. But this girl…" He let out an aggravated growl. "I don't know. I just have to let it go."

The conversation went no further as Judd was walked in with a somber look on his face, taking the seat next to Dennis. Hunter suspiciously looked from one to the other, knowing something was wrong and neither one of them wanted to be the one to speak first.

"What the hell is going on?" Hunter demanded.

The way Judd nervously shifted in his seat, trying to get into a comfortable position, reminded Hunter of how he had reacted the first time the job required him to break bad news to somebody, hoping like hell they wouldn't throw something heavy at him. Dennis didn't say a word.

Before Hunter could ask again, Judd cleared his throat and spoke with a hint of nerves in his voice. "So, something's come up. Two somethings, actually. First, Mack Finley is trying to turn state's evidence."

Hunter looked at Dennis in disbelief. Dennis's expression of irritation, along with the sharp nod of his head, confirmed what Judd was telling him.

Hunter let the words sink in for a moment, then said, "You know what will happen, don't you? He'll ask for witness protection."

"Probably," Judd confirmed. "But, apparently, he's only willing to give his story if you're in the room with him and his lawyer."

"Why?"

"Finley said he thought you would be interested to hear what he has to say."

"How long have you known about this?" Hunter asked, curious as to why both Dennis and Judd would keep this kind of information a secret.

Dennis jumped in then. "The paperwork came across my desk about an hour ago and I had to prep Fowler on how to break the news to you. You have a tendency to not take bad news very well."

Knowing this was true, Hunter looked to Judd. "Second?"

The younger man let out a deep breath and gestured with his chin to the files on Hunter's desk. "There have been two more. One was a missing hiker in Idaho they're calling an accident. The other one is staying out of the news and as far away from the public as possible. I haven't seen the file or any photos yet but Vegas PD says we will have a full copy of the file as soon she's identified. She was found in the basement of an abandoned car repair shop. Vegas said she had been down there at least a month, maybe longer." Judd's body gave an involuntary shudder.

Hunter considered what he was hearing. He could understand the authorities wanting to keep something like this out of the news, but Judd was omitting something.

"How soon until we have identification?"

"We don't know yet. Her fingerprints were burned off so Vegas will try to use DNA."

"DNA? That takes too long. What about a picture to match to DMV records?"

Judd forcefully shook his head and Hunter could see he was struggling with what he had left to say. Hunter couldn't imagine what could be so terrible that Judd had to look to Dennis for some kind of reassurance, but after Dennis silently nodded his head, Judd composed himself and looked Hunter directly in the eye. "In order to do that, they'll need to find her head first."

Dennis didn't say a word and Judd let out a breath he didn't know he'd been holding as they watched Hunter accept what he had just been told. Hunter slowly stood up and paced the room, Dennis's and Judd's eyes following his every step, trying to anticipate his reaction. This was the worst murder so far and Hunter didn't know what to think. He was shocked and appalled. He was angry at the fact that he hadn't been able to stop it from happening. He was tired of chasing a ghost. He wanted—he needed—to stop the bastard responsible so he could finally stop blaming himself for Amy's death.

After three laps around his office, Hunter went to his desk, took out his gun, then casually walked out to the shooting range.

***

"You did good, kid," Dennis said. "You're going to do just fine." He patted Judd on the shoulder and left the office.

Left alone, Judd stared at the wall in front of him, glancing over Hunter's newspaper clippings and handwritten notes stuck to it. He then let his eyes wander over the open files on Hunter's desk and realized that this was the first Black Rose Murder that Judd would be involved in from beginning to end. The second he found out about this recent death he had resolved himself to put forth everything he had to help solve the case. Not only to put a stop to the killing, but also to help give Hunter a little relief.

By the end of the week, Judd got the report from Las Vegas, studying every word and every picture, making sure to miss nothing. He was going to become intimate with the case and would forever wonder what Sasha Wheeler had ever done to deserve losing her head.

Chapter 27

Four Months Earlier

When it came to doling out consequences, Matthew thought of it as teaching a lesson. With Sasha, however, he was simply covering his ass.

James and Lawrence Garafola were both captains in Las Vegas, brought in substantial money for the Family, and followed orders without hesitation. When the brothers called and asked if they would be able to partake in Matthew's fine hospitality in Atlantic City, he immediately granted their request and decided to meet with them for dinner over the weekend. It was during this dinner that Matthew found out Sasha had recently been seen in Las Vegas. Lawrence's comment made every fiber of Matthew's being feel like it had been hit with a jolt of electricity. Stunned and shaken by what he'd just heard, he decided he needed to hear it again.

Lawrence was trying to swallow a hunk of steak he had just shoved in his mouth so James repeated it for him. "He said he recognized her because they hooked up a few years after we took care of your problem. She worked for you back then, right?"

"She did."

James nudged Lawrence with his elbow, a grin on his face. "If this guy can remember a hook-up from that long ago, she must have done something right."

Matthew attempted a smile to show he found the humor in the comment, but it just wasn't coming out right. He wiped his mouth with his napkin in an attempt to gather his thoughts, and realized that if he wanted to get more information about Sasha's secret visit to Las Vegas all those years ago, he would have to feign interest.

"Well," Matthew said, "Sasha did have a knack for putting a smile on men's faces long after they had parted company. It's too bad you only got one night of her expertise."

Lawrence shook his head, his fork poised in front of his mouth. "We didn't leave the room for three days." He gave himself a congratulatory smile and shoved the fork in his mouth.

Matthew quickly tried to recall how long Sasha usually went away on business trips and calculated the longest he could remember her being gone was no more than five days, and never recalled her visiting Las Vegas.

Lawrence had a smile and a thoughtful look on his face. "Yeah. I wouldn't mind getting together with her again. It would be nice to get another video."

Matthew's head snapped up and he stared at

Lawrence. "Video?"

"He likes to watch," James clarified.

Lawrence shrugged his shoulders. "Eh. It's just a hobby."

Matthew was getting impatient. "What video?"

"Oh, I have a digital camera set up at the foot of the bed." Lawrence let go a proud laugh. "We had plenty of footage. Three days is a long time."

"Do you remember any of the conversation you shared over the course of three days?" Both James and Lawrence looked confused and Matthew let out a frustrated sigh. "Did you happen to mention anything about our business arrangement?"

Lawrence gave an uncaring shrug of his shoulders as he scooped up another forkful of food. "I don't know. Damn, now that I think about it, I wish I could go back and watch the video again but she took it with her when she left. Or, I guess she did. It was gone when I tried to find it a few days after she left."

***

Matthew was in Las Vegas within a week, Crescent and Tucker in tow, to hunt down Sasha. Matthew was hoping to find her quickly; they were in somebody else's territory, unannounced, and had to tread carefully. While Matthew convinced Neil Parsons, underboss of Vegas, that he was there for pleasure, he sent Crescent and Tucker in search of Sasha. Within twenty-four hours, she was found.

In the basement of an abandoned auto repair shop, Matthew sat down in front of Sasha, full of sorrow and disappointment. Sasha was one of the few women he trusted and was genuinely hurt when she left Boston. It pained him to see her tied to a chair, shaking and scared to death, taking in her surroundings and most likely knowing any one of the numerous auto parts and tools would probably be used to inflict a lot of pain. Crescent and Tucker stood on either side of Sasha while Matthew calmly assessed her, trying to decide the best tack to take. He could see was desperately trying to be courageous and unafraid of the inevitable.

Matthew's tone matched the look on his face—he would get what he wanted from her. "I understand there is a video. Tell me where it is."

Matthew could see from the way Sasha's eyes popped wide open that he had learned a secret she never wanted him to know. Sasha spoke through the tears choking her speech. "I don't have it."

Crescent's hand flashed out and his fist violently cracked Sasha's face, blood spraying from her nose as the force jerked her head from one side to the other. Matthew patiently waited a few moments to let her regain her senses before asking again. Sasha, though taken with white-hot pain, straightened herself in the chair, tried to control the tears, and looked at Matthew with angry defiance in her eyes.

"Who else knows about it?"

"Nobody!"

"If nobody else knows about the video, then where did it go?"

When Sasha didn't answer, Tucker put his full force behind swinging a torque wrench across her left thigh. Matthew knew the pain was immediate and excruciating, and Sasha let out a wailing cry of pain as another blow hit her leg with enough force to break her tibia. She quickly sucked in shuddering breaths, closing her eyes against the pain, her tears freely falling. When she looked at Matthew once more, the fire in her eyes was still there, but there was something else. Something that told Matthew she had information he never wanted her to have. Suspicious, he asked her, "How much do you know?"

Sasha barred her teeth against the pain and gave a pained smile. "Everything."

***

When Sasha learned Matthew's secret, the first thing she wanted to do was tell David, but she wouldn't be able to go to him without proof. Her opportunity came when a delivery of compromising photographs needed to be made in Arizona and Matthew sent Sasha to personally deliver them. Once her errand was completed, she snuck over to Las Vegas. It didn't take long to find the Garafola brothers. Hastily seducing Lawrence and suffering three days in his company got her the information she needed.

"Your boss didn't like this guy he was partners with. I mean he really didn't like him. Apparently, he had been stuck with him because he's the son of someone important and your boss was sick of his friend fucking everything up." Lawrence undoubtedly got a rush of excitement from telling the story, and an even bigger rush from being the person responsible for taking care of the problem. Sasha could see the enthusiasm both in his face and between his legs. "So, your boss paid us a little extra—two hundred and fifty thousand each—to take this guy out to the desert and make him disappear. We roughed him up a little bit but I got bored, so I put two shots in him. Afterward, we went to the casino and I won a grand at the blackjack table."

Lawrence shrugged to indicate his indifference, then reached for Sasha and quickly replaced the conversation with his excitement. She didn't expect to be able to get physical proof, but Lawrence's fetish for making videos of sexual encounters was simply an added bonus. On the third day, after Lawrence finally left the room to meet his brother, she showered and gathered her things, including the digital footage, and boarded a plane for home.

***

"If you have had this information all these years, why haven't you told anyone?" Matthew asked.

"Because even though you are an arrogant, selfish, murdering son of a bitch, I couldn't let her grow up without a father."

Sasha had succeeded in infuriating Matthew. He shot a commanding look and Tucker dealt another blow to Sasha's face. This time her head snapped backward, her neck threatening to break. She bit her tongue and blood dripped out of her mouth. Another fist connected with her face before Matthew held up a hand and gave Tucker a look that said to wait for further punishment until instructed.

"Where is the video, Sasha?"

"I locked it away," she said through clenched teeth.

His exasperation was beginning to show. "And where is the key to its hiding place?"

A cracked smile formed on her face through the blood and the pain. She definitely had another secret, and Matthew was determined to know everything she knew. Instead, she left him curious.

"I passed down one key when I left Boston."

Surprised, Matthew asked, "There is more than one key?"

Sasha glared at Matthew with a hardened look that informed him she was done talking. Instinctively, Matthew knew Renee would have one of the keys, and he had one more reason to find her and force her to come back. After he had used Renee to get what he wanted, he could dispose of her and never look back.

Matthew gave Sasha a disappointed look, then turned to Crescent. It actually hurt him to cause Sasha pain, but he wouldn't let that deter him from his quest. "Find out where those keys are and then make sure she will never be able to repeat that story. I'll meet you at the airport in a few hours."

Matthew turned and walked out of the basement, leaving Sasha alone with Crescent and Tucker, where begging for her life would be completely pointless.

Chapter 28

Present Day

Chloe sat in the conference room, staring at her computer screen, and tried to concentrate on work, but her thoughts kept drifting to how desperately she wanted to see Hunter again. The more she thought about Hunter, the more she was reminded of the tragedy of her previous relationship. She made no apologies for leaving after he had fallen asleep. She had made many rules for herself over the years, which she adamantly followed, and when it came to sex, sleeping over was never an option.

Arthur entered the room, breaking her out of her thoughts, and took a seat across from her. "Good afternoon, Arthur."

He got right to the point. "Expansion for the future is a very immediate goal. I would like you to assist us with opening and setting up a second location, which means we would need two business plans: one for this office and one for the new location."

She didn't like being in one place for too long, but gave consideration to what he was saying. If she did stay, she would have more time with Alice. She would also have the possibility of seeing Hunter again, which excited her. She quickly shook off the thought; she couldn't allow herself to risk feeling the pain of loss again.

"I would also like to extend an invitation for you to join Walter and myself at dinner next weekend in New Orleans with other colleagues in the area, as well as some friends from other professions. I thought it might be an excellent opportunity for you to network your services." His tone suddenly changed to indicate the power he intended to exude. "With my supporting recommendation, of course."

Just like her father, Arthur was used to getting what he wanted, and his means of getting it was threats and intimidation. Arthur's flaw, however, was in underestimating Chloe. The animosity she felt toward Arthur at the moment was only one issue. New Orleans was a completely different issue. Jack Lawrence was there, and in a room full of strangers, she didn't want to risk being spotted. She had no idea if Jack, or any of his associates, would even attend a function such as this, but she certainly didn't want to take the chance of finding out.

Chloe narrowed her eyes at Arthur, revulsion in her gaze. "Of course."

Arthur must have taken her response as acceptance to his invitation and stood to leave. He spoke to her in an almost demanding tone, once again reminding her of Matthew. "Next Saturday.

The reception starts at three, dinner is at five. Formal dress. I'll have my secretary get you the location and directions."

"I'll let you know if I can make it," she said.

Arthur cocked an eyebrow at her, ready to do battle in an effort to get his way, but the hard stare he was receiving said to bring it on.

"I carry quite a bit of weight in many circles. While at this dinner, I could help you immeasurably." He shrugged his shoulders in an attempt to challenge her. "Or not."

She leaned forward and replied in an icy tone, "My career has done just fine over the years. I doubt your recommendation, or not, would change that."

"Well, maybe that's something we should put to the test."

"You don't want to test me, Arthur."

If Chloe was ever able to unnerve a man with a single look, it showed on Arthur's face. The outcome of the conversation obviously wasn't what he expected. He simply nodded and left the room. For the first time in years, Chloe's temper got the best of her and before she knew what she was doing, her half-empty coffee mug was sailing across the room, then shattering against the door.

"Dick."

The conversation with Arthur solidified the answer to the question she had been contemplating earlier. She needed to finish her work and get the hell out of Louisiana.

***

"Is there any reason to believe Arthur or Walter might have connections to Jack?" Chloe asked Alice a little while later when Alice came to check on her.

If Chloe decided to go to New Orleans, she had to be as sure as she could be. In all reality, there was only one reason she was even considering going, and that reason had woken up alone.

Alice's jaw almost hit the floor. "You're not going to go, are you?"

"I'm just asking."

Alice leaned forward, crossing her arms on the table. "If you go, although I can't even begin to wonder why you would, even if you do see Jack or anyone who works for him, he's not like your father and never has been. True, there is a chance he would call Matthew, or even David. But after eight years, Jack might be curious enough to try to get you in a room alone and hear your side of the story."

Chloe thought of the possibilities if she did come face to face with Jack. "It's still dangerous."

"I'm not disagreeing with you."

Their conversation was interrupted by a knock at the door and a smile beamed on Alice's face as Willetta entered the room, rolling a vacuum cleaner behind her.

"I hear there some broken glass."

"I'm so sorry," Chloe said. "It's my fault. If you want to leave the vacuum, I can clean it up."

Willetta waved a hand at Chloe while surveying the broken coffee mug, then gave Chloe a look of understanding. "Mr. Arthur?"

Chloe smiled, a little embarrassed. "Mr. Arthur."

"Mm-hmm." That was all Willetta had to say as she plugged in the vacuum and was done seemingly before she started. When she was finished, Chloe and Alice said their goodbyes as Willetta left the room, softly closing the door behind her.

Chloe leaned over in her chair, picked up the newspaper from the floor, and set it on the table. "Did you see this?"

Kristin was the latest victim, missing for more than two weeks and found at the bottom of a ravine by a group of college students out enjoying a weekend of camping and not worrying about homework.

"You and I both know it wasn't an accident."

Alice's voice shook. "I'm going to be next, aren't I?"

Chloe reached for her friend's hands and held them tightly. "No. Nobody else is going to die."

"How do you know? I have kids, Chloe."

Chloe tightened her grip on Alice's hands. "Alice, listen to me. Your kids are not going to grow up without you."

Alice's voice was choked with tears. "How do you know?"

"Because I'm going back."

Chloe thought about all of the women she had once known, and a few she hadn't, who had been dying over the years because her father wanted to punish her for running out on him. She thought of Alice and her boys and realized that he would eventually find her, and when he did, her boys would grow up without a mother. The thought made

Chloe sick to her stomach.

"He's doing this to hurt me and it's working. He's killing me, Alice. If I go back, I think he'll stop. He's doing this to get me back. I can only hope that once I'm back, he won't feel the need to continue. We don't know how many more are out there for him to hunt down. I have to try to stop him. It's my fault this is happening. I sacrificed you guys when I selfishly ran away. It's my turn to sacrifice myself so that you and your children are safe."

Chloe could see the relief for her children's safety slowly wash over Alice, but when she looked up at Chloe, there were questions in her eyes.

"There's something else bothering you," Alice said. "And I don't think it's just about being face to face with your father again."

Chloe decided not to tell Alice about Hunter. Her weekend with him and subsequent feelings she couldn't understand were more than she wanted to think about. All Chloe knew was that she was going to miss him and didn't want to talk about it. "I'm just distracted. I have a lot to do before I leave."

"Is there anything I can do?"

"No," Chloe said. "This is all me."

Chapter 29

Hunter decided to take the weekend off and try not to think about work, Mack Finley, or black rose tattoos. For the first time in years he was distracted by a woman he wanted to get to know better, a woman he craved to see again. He left work early on Friday and drove to Lafayette, going to the only place he knew where to start looking for her—the restaurant where they had spent most of the festival together. The only thing he knew for sure was that she worked in the building across the street but had no idea what floor she was on.

The manager who had tried to remove them from the restaurant during the festival recognized Hunter when he walked in and took a seat at the window. Hunter met the manager's eye, smiled, and inclined his head in greeting. The manager gave him an uncaring look and turned away. It only took a few minutes for the same young waitress to approach his table with a bounce in her step and a smile on her face. He could only conclude that if she was that happy to see him, she was hoping for another hundred-dollar tip.

"Hey there!" she said, setting a drink napkin on the table in front of him. "Welcome back. Are you meeting anyone in particular today?"

"I hope so. In the meantime, I'll have a beer."

Hunter was trying to be optimistic, but as the hours passed, the odds of finding her weren't looking good. It was almost seven o'clock on a Friday night; the daylight was beginning to fade, the restaurant was getting crowded, and people had stopped coming out of the building an hour ago.

It was about the time that Hunter decided to give up that the bartender approached him. "The woman you were here with at the festival—a couple people at the table back there know her. Tenth floor."

Tossing a few bills on the table, Hunter faced the bartender and shook the man's hand with a glimpse of hope in his eye. "Thanks, man."

As Hunter crossed the street, his body slightly stiffened, then relaxed in what could only be relief as Chloe slowly stepped out of the building to meet Hunter with a smile. Hunter felt like the wind had been knocked out of him. Tired as she looked, she was beautiful as she stood across from him with a look of surprise and a rush of unanticipated elation on her face. The bags hanging over her shoulder had slipped down her arms and Hunter took them, hefting them over his shoulder, wondering what to do next.

"What are you doing here?" she asked, wary but happy to see him.

He never thought it would be possible for him to be breathless without exerting himself beyond his bodily limits, but there he was trying to catch his breath, stepping closer to her as he spoke. "I knew there was a possibility that we wouldn't see each other again, but I haven't stopped thinking about you and I wanted to see you."

He leaned in and kissed her softly. Even though the kiss was brief, it seemed to last for hours and the taste of her lingered in every nerve of his body.

***

Chloe had never imagined she would find so much contentment and peace with another man. Hunter and Chloe lay tangled together in the sheets of her bed, facing each other, Hunter slowly running his fingers through her hair and she trying desperately to keep her eyes open.

"What are you grinning at?" Her words were slightly slurred with exhaustion.

"I always thought it was the guy who fell asleep right after sex."

She let out a soft moan and snuggled closer to him. "It's not my fault. You wore me out."

Her stomach growled loudly, clearly telling her to tend to something important like feeding it, and her eyes popped open, suddenly awake.

"Was that your stomach?" Hunter asked with a laugh.

"Apparently missing lunch and dinner, combined with post-sex munchies, is catching up with me. I'm sure there's the possibility that I have something deliciously unhealthy in the kitchen, I just don't feel like getting up to go get it." She snuggled closer, holding him tighter. "And, no, you're not allowed to leave this bed either."

Hunter kissed the top of her head and let out a deep breath. "I couldn't stop thinking about you."

Chloe could have said the same thing but decided to keep quiet. She couldn't let herself get swept away by the emotion of everything because she knew she would be gone in a few days. At the same time, the longer he held her, the more she considered changing her mind about leaving. After Christopher died, she vowed to never fall in love again, so what scared her the most was that she was falling in love with Hunter. And she couldn't control it. She didn't know how it happened, and she certainly wasn't expecting it. They hardly knew each other. Just like when she was sixteen years old, she didn't believe it could be possible to have happened this fast.

With just one look, with one word, he could try to keep her in Louisiana and she would want to stay. But she couldn't go to New Orleans or stay in one place for the rest of her life without feeling like she constantly had to look over her shoulder. She also knew that so long as she was living this life, there could be no possibility for a relationship. Just like Alice and Reggie, there would be too many secrets, and she couldn't do that to Hunter. He was a good man and he deserved better, but she wanted to know if what she was instinctively feeling about him was true. Did he feel the same way about her? Her gut was telling her without a doubt that he did.

"You okay?"

"Yeah," she said with a sigh. "I'm just thinking."

"Are you sorry that I came to see you?"

She lifted her head and looked at him with glistening eyes. "Absolutely not. In fact, I was invited to New Orleans next weekend for a dinner and have been debating on whether or not to go."

He smiled up at the ceiling. "Oh yeah?"

Chloe covered a yawn and her belly growled at her again. "It's a work thing. I don't want to go to the dinner, but thought if I were able to find you—you know, stalk you outside *your* office building…"

He laughed and held her tighter as she melted into his body. He grabbed the sheets and fluffed them, letting some air in. She grabbed for the sheets, trying to cover her back.

"Hey!" she playfully exclaimed.

"Jesus, it's a thousand degrees in here. Aren't you hot?"

She settled the sheet back where it was and gave him a sly, flirtatious look. "It's only hot because I've got you in my bed."

Hunter stretched like a cat just waking from a nap. He was right about the bedroom being hot, yet he seemed to be happy and content. Chloe watched him, propped up on an elbow. He suddenly got a very serious look on his face.

"What's wrong?"

"The last few weeks have been a bitch, and I do mean bitch," he said, rubbing his hands over his face. "The thought of what I have to deal with next week just jumped into my brain."

"So tell me. If you talk about it, you'll get it out of your mind."

She was genuinely concerned about what was

bothering him. He rubbed his palms over his face again and put an arm under his head.

"There's this guy I busted my ass to arrest and now he wants to turn state's evidence. But here's the kicker. He won't give any kind of statement or confession unless I'm in the room with him and his lawyer."

"Yikes," she said in a flat tone.

"Yeah. So now I have to go meet with this asshole and his lawyer next week."

"Why does he want you there?"

"Because, apparently, he thinks I'll be interested in what he has to say. On top of that, there are other murder cases that I've been working on for *years*. And just when I think I'll finally find the piece of the puzzle to put them all together, another one falls in my lap and it starts all over again. This sick bastard gets worse with every one, and it's never the same way twice. I know—I *know*—there is something I'm missing that's right in front of my face."

"It's like a puzzle piece was left out of the box," Chloe said.

Hunter threw his arms in the air. "Exactly!"

Chloe lay next to him, giving him the silence he needed before he was ready to speak again. Finally, he let out a frustrated growl and turned to Chloe, kissing her soundly. "I'm sorry. I shouldn't even be thinking about work right now."

She smiled at him. "It's okay."

The eruption that came from Chloe's stomach could have woken the dead two states over. Hunter threw the sheets off, got out of bed, and began searching for his pants.

"That's it," he said as he pulled his boxers over his hips. "Let's go find something deliciously unhealthy to feed you."

***

After opening and closing every cupboard and the refrigerator, Hunter turned to Chloe and stared at her in disbelief.

"Shall I start calling you Old Mother Hubbard?"

She laughed and gave him a crooked grin as she stood in her living room wrapped in the bed sheet, watching as he investigated the nakedness of her kitchen. "I work a lot, so I don't cook very often."

Hunter asked in a teasing tone, "Do you know how to cook?"

She gave him a look of playful indignation. "I can burn water, if that's what you mean." He was smiling at her as she pointed to the smoke detector above the front door. "And I'm pretty sure that is the oven timer."

Hunter burst out laughing, shaking his head at her most probable honesty. Then he said it before he knew it was coming out of his mouth. "Oh my god, I love you."

Smiles immediately left both their faces as silent tension filled the room.

After a moment, she cocked her head toward him and asked, "What?"

"What?" he parroted.

Hunter saw the fight or flight look in her eye. She was frozen in place as he walked over and stood in front of her, neither one reaching for the other. He didn't mean to say it, but he did. As he studied her face, the realization hit him—ridiculous and unbelievable as it was after only knowing each other for one night, he absolutely meant what he said and she felt the same way.

He stepped closer to her and she didn't move. "I love you."

She took in a shuddering breath, terror in her features. He took one more step closer to her, silently searching her face. "Why are you afraid?"

She pulled the sheet tighter around her like a cocoon and spoke softly. "Because I'm leaving soon, and if I don't say it, then only one of us would be in pain."

Hunter took a step closer so they were close enough to feel their breath on each other's faces. "Chloe, that's not true and you know it. For the past few weeks I have done nothing but think about you. I woke up this morning and did something I have never done before. I blew off work to come find you. Even if I didn't find you today, I would have hated myself for not trying. I know you're leaving after your work is done. I get that, but it's a choice. You don't have to leave if you don't want to, and I don't think you do. I think you're letting whatever it is you're afraid of dictate your decisions. But I'm not going to pressure you. I will take whatever I can get, whether it's just for tonight or longer. I just want to be with you. I just want to spend time with you. I want to remember you."

He leaned in and kissed her softly, waiting for her to respond. When she returned the kiss, she told him she loved him without words. He wrapped his arms around her as she placed a hand on each side of his face, the bed sheet slipping down her body and resting on her breasts that were crushed against his body. He could feel the warmth of her tears as they slowly slid down her face and he could taste the salt of them as he kissed her. This was not a kiss that said goodbye; this was a kiss that said the possibility of forever was real as long as he had time, understanding, and patience—which he would happily give if it meant having Chloe for the rest of his life.

Hunter broke the kiss and held her to him, staring deep into her eyes. *She's not just afraid. She is haunted—tormented—by something that won't let her love. She wants to, but she can't.*

As if perfect timing to break the emotional tension in the room, Chloe's stomach reminded them that she hadn't eaten in almost twenty hours. They both gave a nervous laugh.

"We need to get you some food," he said, "and since you don't have any food, there must be a twenty-four-hour place around here somewhere."

Chloe let out a breath, smiling at him. "Thank you for not pressuring me."

"When the time is right," he said with a shrug, meaning to cut some of the anxiety out of the room. "I meant what I said. I just want to spend time with you. Come on. Food. I may not be as hungry as you are, but I could stand to eat."

"Okay, you win." As she started to walk to the bedroom, she stepped on the sheet and, too late, tried to wrap it around her before it slid down her back. Hunter momentarily froze in place. He was dumbfounded. He felt like he had just been gut punched.

"What the hell is that?" His voice roared throughout the room.

Startled, she turned back to him. "What is what?"

"You have a black rose tattoo."

In an instant, Chloe's demeanor went from happy and playful to almost icy, coldly staring him down. "Is it a problem?"

"Is it a problem? Yeah, it's a problem. It's a big fucking problem! *You* are my goddamn missing puzzle piece!"

Chapter 30

The atmosphere of the room was now filled with anger, tension, unanswered questions, and defiance. The shouting of questions and demanding of answers from Hunter had gotten him nowhere. Hunter paced the living room, stopping every few minutes to stare out the window, fists clenched in tight balls. Chloe got dressed and found some coffee hidden in the back of her cupboard. She set one cup on the coffee table for Hunter, the other one she held onto as she curled up in the corner of the couch. She would worry about the fact that she had lost Hunter's love as fast as he gave it later. She was too busy berating herself for not seeing this coming. If her guard hadn't been down, she would have.

Hunter tried to avoid looking at her while he paced, but she caught him looking out of the corner of his eye a few times. He stood silently for a few moments, unclenching his fists and relaxing his breathing. "For years I have been working on these murders. I know every word, every name, every date, and every detail. I have talked to experts, professors, doctors, and profilers. Months can go by without another file coming across my desk, but eventually I do get another one and it starts all over again. I've never been able to find the clue. And now, all of a sudden, I have a real, live, walking, breathing, talking clue sitting in the same room as me who I'm in love with! I have seven, soon to be eight, possibly nine, files on my desk. Every single one of those files belongs to a woman who has the exact same tattoo as you."

She sat like a stone, unmoving and seemingly uncaring, while inwardly she felt like she was being repeatedly stabbed. The guilt of being the person responsible for those deaths took its time eating her alive. She had to assume that number nine was Charlotte, although, if what Alice told her was correct, that would be impossible unless the mortician gave a deathbed confession. The only other possible conclusion would be that someone else was dead because of her and it hadn't been made public yet.

Hunter sat next to her on the couch, almost reaching out for her hand, but he stopped himself. "These murders are getting worse by the count and I don't think they're ever going to stop. I need answers. Chloe, I need closure."

She slowly turned her head to look at him, captured by the last words he spoke. "Why do you need closure?"

When he looked at her, her heart instantly cracked down the middle. He had the look of a lost and defeated man as he spoke with a slight tremble in his voice. "This case is personal to me, Chloe.

My wife had that tattoo."

Her jaw slacked open and her muscles went weak as the sudden realization of his confession hit her. The coffee cup shook between her hands. He said his wife's name was Amy. The names of her former employees raced through her mind and she came up blank. Chloe quickly did the math in her head. She had been gone eight years. Amy died four years ago. They had been married for two and dated for a short time before getting married. The only thing Chloe could determine was that Amy arrived after she had left and then departed shortly thereafter. Hunter went to the bedroom and returned, digging in his wallet. He produced a small, worn snapshot that had been looked at often, always resting next to him.

The blood rushed from her face as she sucked in a shaky breath. A beautiful young woman in her wedding gown, standing under an oak tree banked on the edge of a bayou holding a bouquet of pink roses in front of her and a smile that said nothing but rampant happiness. Her eyes—her arresting hazel eyes with flecks of gold sparking in the sun—said she had finally found her Prince Charming and her happily ever after.

Chloe was going to hyperventilate if she didn't calm herself down. Her hands trembled as she handed the picture back to Hunter, who had been watching her reaction and trying his best to patiently wait for whatever Chloe had to say. One thing he knew for sure was that she definitely knew his wife.

"You knew Amy?"

She slowly nodded her head. "I did know her, but I didn't know her as Amy. Her name was Saffron."

***

"The mob?" Hunter asked with skepticism.

She had no idea why, but Chloe decided to tell Hunter as much truth about her past as she could. If she told her story carefully and convincingly, there was the possibility she could help him get what he needed to have closure.

"I know it sounds fantastical, but try to be patient with me. I've never told anybody what I'm going to tell you. I met Saff—I mean, Amy—when I was fourteen years old. I spent a lot of time with her; she was one of my best friends and a bridesmaid at my wedding." She saw the look on his face and responded with, "I'll tell you that part later."

All Hunter wanted to hear was information pertaining to his wife, and she would tell him what she could and what he needed to hear. She decided to be as forthcoming as she could without crossing her own comfort zone. When she told her story, she would have no embarrassment or apologies in her voice, only truth for what she chose to tell him.

"Saff was such a good person and a very close friend. We all lived on the top floor of a hotel so we saw each other every day. We spent a lot of time together at meals or just talking. The man we worked for..." She paused, thinking of a way to make it not sound as bad as she knew Hunter would interpret it. "The man we worked for is a very

188

wealthy, very powerful, and very influential man. The thing is, choosing to work for him is voluntary, and once anybody agreed to work for him, they couldn't leave without his express consent. Once she said yes, she got her tattoo and belonged to him."

"She belonged to him? What did y'all do for this man?" Hunter asked warily, as if he really didn't want to know the answer to his question.

"Client entertainment."

He snapped his head up. "*What* was client entertainment?"

"His clients were prominent people who required extreme discretion. She—"

"She was a prostitute?" he shouted.

"No!" Chloe exclaimed, then in a quiet voice said, "She wasn't a prostitute."

"What was client entertainment?"

"It wasn't dirty and random. Our clients were people of standing in the community, in many different communities. If they wanted dinner, they got dinner. If they just wanted someone to talk to, she would do that. If they wanted to sleep with her, she did."

Hunter looked at her like she was four years old. "She had sex for money, the definition of prostitute."

She knew on some level he believed her, but desperately didn't want it to be true. "She was a good person, Hunter, but she knew exactly what her job description was and she chose to do it. Jesus, she almost died and still came back to work after she healed."

Chloe told him the story of what had happened with Mr. Crescent and watched him mentally lock the name away. She told him about Dr. Michaelson and everything he had done for Saffron to keep her alive.

"How old were you at the time?"

"Sixteen."

Complete disbelief washed over him. "Were you a client entertainer too?"

"By definition, I was the boss."

She explained what her role in the Family was as Hunter looked out the window and absorbed everything he had heard so far. She knew he felt like the wind had been knocked out of him, not knowing what to think or what to believe. The Amy he knew, the one he fell in love with and promised forever to, would never have done any of the things he was hearing. He needed more information, but didn't want to necessarily hear the answers.

"Who is this man? The man you worked for."

Chloe knew that no matter what she told Hunter about her father, he would have a difficult time making any substantial charges against him. She selfishly thought that maybe if she helped Hunter, he wouldn't hate her as much as he probably did right now. At the same time, he had been trying to solve these cases for years and deserved whatever help she would be able to give him. But it felt good to tell her story, and she wasn't as nervous as she was a few minutes ago. Her tone was very straightforward with no fear, only absolute certainty that she wanted to tell him.

"His name is Matthew Parnell."

"Where is he?"

"Massachusetts," she said, and quickly added, "but you can't stop him, Hunter. You would never be able to prove that he's responsible. He doesn't do any of the dirty work himself. He orders, his soldiers obey. Unless you can get solid, rock-hard, undeniable testimony from someone, or irrefutable evidence, it will be more difficult than you think."

"Would you testify?"

The question caught her off guard. She hadn't considered it and knew that Matthew had friends in high places, an extremely good attorney, and testifying against him would be the same as signing her own death warrant.

Hunter saw the expression on her face. "You're terrified of him."

She didn't quite know how to make Hunter understand what kind of man he would be dealing with if he was able to convict her father. "Hunter, he is the most powerful underboss in a very large, very dominant crime organization. He is tremendously protective about his position and loves the power he has over people. If he feels threatened, disrespected, or betrayed, he doesn't hesitate to give an order. He sometimes kills just to cause pain and watch someone suffer."

"How did you come to be in his employment?"

"My mother married into the Family."

"Do you know why Amy died?"

She really didn't want to answer that question, but she would. Hunter would never understand the immense weight of blame she had put on herself that never went away, and the agony she felt every time she saw the news and how it reinforced Matthew's threat to her that he would do anything to hurt her.

"Remember I told you we weren't allowed to leave without his permission? Well, I did. I packed a bag and ran away in the middle of the night. I disrespected him, embarrassed him, and betrayed him. He knows that every time someone dies, I blame myself, and the guilt is eating me alive. She died—all of these women have died—because of me."

Hunter most certainly was not prepared for that admission and it showed on his face. "What was it that drove you to sneak out in the middle of the night?"

"He murdered my fiancé on our wedding day, put a gun to my head, and told me that unless I did exactly what he said, that I would be next."

Chloe went into the bedroom and came back with the only picture of her and Christopher that she had held on to for all these years. The picture was taken at the governor's birthday party and just happened to be the same night Christopher asked her to marry him. "I was nineteen when that picture was taken. His name was Christopher and he is the reason that I couldn't tell you how I feel earlier. The thought of losing you and the pain that would follow if Matthew found out would kill me if I had to go through it all a second time."

Chloe's body was slowly shutting down from hunger and exhaustion, as well as being emotionally drained by having to relive a part of her life that took her so long to get over.

"Why did Parnell have him killed?"

"I didn't know it at the time, but he did it because he despised me and wanted nothing more than to simply destroy me."

A crease appeared between Hunter's eyes. "Why does he hate you so much? What did you do?"

She gave a small chuckle and failed at trying to stifle a yawn. "I breathe. That's what I do."

"What if I could get you witness protection? Would you agree to testify?"

"I paid someone to change my life for me and put myself in self-proclaimed witness protection eight years ago." He gave her a questioning look. "Yes, obviously, not everything I told you about myself was the truth, but most of it was. If you recall, I scraped over my childhood when we were swapping stories, but I don't blame you for hating and distrusting me. It's understandable."

"I'm angry, confused, tired, and have too many questions. But if you're willing to tell me all of this, why wouldn't you be willing to take it a step further and testify?"

"Because I would never make it to the courthouse." Chloe gave Hunter a few examples of her father's wrath, then told him about Alice and how fate, karma, or whatever it was, threw them together. "*If* she agrees to testify, would you be able to promise her and her family witness protection?"

"I promise I will see what I can do for your friend."

"And her family," Chloe added.

"And her family," Hunter confirmed as he covered a yawn of his own. "I have one more question. If you think I can't get him, then who do you think can?"

She and David were the only two people who could stop him. Obviously, since her father was still alive, David wasn't doing anything about it. As for herself, she had made up her mind to try, but didn't know what she was going to do yet. She hated to admit that she was still afraid of her father and it pissed her off that the task fell to her.

"Me."

"You?"

"I'm the one he's punishing, the one he wants to punish." Her eyes were sagging with fatigue and she felt like she was going to collapse any second. "I'm going back to Boston to try. I'm so tired, Hunter. Tired of being afraid and tired of running. I thought I was okay being alone and moving from place to place, but then I saw Alice and the life she was able to make for herself after she left. The more time I spend with her, the more she proves to me that I deserve that chance at happiness too. And then I met you, and the more I thought about you and the short time we spent together, the more I wanted to try to find that happiness, even if only for a little while. If I can stop him from killing other women by going back, I will. He can do whatever he wants to me, but he took away so much from these girls for so long. He shouldn't be allowed to take anymore."

Chloe had been running from, and afraid of, Matthew Parnell for the past eight years, and was now planning on throwing herself in front of the gun, hoping not to take a bullet too soon. She knew

194

there was too much information rattling around in Hunter's head to process all at once. He was just as tired as she was. As they sat quietly, Chloe's body began to relax and her eyes began to droop slowly shut until, after a few minutes, they were simply not going to open. She felt a blanket gently cover her, a soft kiss on the forehead, and then heard the front door quietly shut behind Hunter as he left.

Chapter 31

For the past three years, every Sunday morning after breakfast and a conversation with her granddaughter, Bernadette, Willetta Boudreaux would go into her kitchen and prepare herself a hot cup of tea, then meander into her living room to get comfortable in her favorite chair and make a telephone call. The calls would never last long and the conversation usually revolved around Bernadette's health and mental wellbeing. Had it not been for this particular acquaintance, Bernadette and Willetta would be using food stamps just to avoid starving to death.

Bernadette had lived with her grandmother for the past twelve years. Due to an unfortunate consequence of an impulse decision she had made, she was paralyzed from the waist down. She was known as Bennie all those years ago and worked for Matthew Parnell for almost a year before she decided she was unappreciated in her work and wanted more from life, so she decided to take a chance. While her client was in the bathroom,

Bennie fished in his pants for his wallet and found two thousand dollars in cash. He caught her and went directly to Renee, whose first duty was to do everything in her power to retain the client's future business. She had eventually been able to calm the client, giving every assurance there would be consequences for such unacceptable behavior. Renee would have been the one to deal with Bennie, but the client happened to run into Matthew in the lobby of the hotel and decided to explain what had happened.

Bennie told her grandmother that her fate was determined when Mr. Crescent walked her to the bus stop four blocks from the hotel. The next thing Bennie knew, she was being forcefully pushed in front of the bus, the driver unable to stop in time before hitting her. Crescent had disappeared and Bennie, lucky to still have the ability to breathe, lay in the middle of a rain soaked road with broken bones, internal bleeding, and massive contusions. While she survived the accident, her life was changed forever.

A few years ago, a chance encounter with someone from Bennie's past life changed everything and a bargain was struck when that chance encounter brought an unexpected opportunity for their benefactor. Bernadette and Willetta would keep an eye on Alice and report back anything they thought might be of interest. In return, Bernadette and Willetta would live a financially comfortable life.

After Willetta vacuumed up the broken coffee mug in the conference room, she had to make a decision—should she or shouldn't she tell her benefactor what she had discovered? After conferring with Bennie on the matter, the answer came down to the simple fact that they had no choice. Their supporter had kept their end of the bargain and there was no way around it. The phone call had to be made, and it only took three rings before the call was answered.

"How are you today? I got something to say that you gonna wanna hear. You know that little girl we been keeping an eye on all these years? Well, she got herself a friend. The one you been looking for."

Chapter 32

Matthew woke with unbearable chest pain and had no choice but to call Dr. Michaelson. While he was waiting for the doctor to arrive, Matthew sat in his office to try to get some work done. David had secured a deal with a certain congressman who had promised to see things David's way regarding the upcoming vote on corporate bailouts and pay raises for public servants who didn't do much for the public. In exchange, the congressman wouldn't have to worry about exposure to the public, and his wife, of his addiction to and particular fetish with Matthew's girls. Since this had been taking place in Matthew's territory, it was up to him to get everything in order and prepare for a meeting with the congressman later in the week. He wasn't going to let a little bit of chest pain stop him from anything.

When Matthew's phone rang, he was surprised to hear Jack Lawrence's voice on the other end. Jack didn't like Matthew and wouldn't call if it could be avoided. "You have a problem, Matthew.

Mack Finley."

Matthew had completely forgotten about Finley since his arrest. "What about him?"

"He's talking about turning state's evidence. He's scheduled to talk with the FBI later this week." To Matthew's ears, it almost sounded like Jack was laughing. "I'll also trust you to mention it to David, if and when the time comes that you need to."

With that, Jack hung up, leaving Matthew to listen to dead air. Matthew had to take care of Finley and he had to do it in a hurry. The pain in his chest started to increase and he sat back in his chair, taking deep breaths, trying to calm down.

"Where the hell is Michaelson?" he said to nobody in particular just as Crescent walked into the office.

Crescent took one look at Matthew and knew something was wrong. "What is it?"

"We have a problem."

Crescent listened closely as Matthew relayed his conversation with Jack. "I'll call and get the plane ready. After the doctor clears you for flight, we will leave."

"Matthew," Elias approached the underboss and began digging his stethoscope out of his bag, "how long were you having dizziness and pain before you called me?"

"What took you so long?" Matthew asked.

Ignoring the question, Elias gave Matthew a quick examination and packed his instruments back in his bag. He then gave Matthew a stern look. "Are you taking your medication regularly?"

Matthew gave an irritated nod. "Yes."

"Are you doing your best to keep your stress levels low?"

"Well, I was," Matthew said with irritation, "but I just got a phone call that wasn't good news. Don't look at me like that. Either of you. I'm not too old to forget how to take care of myself. I take my medication and have been trying to keep my blood from boiling. Today just isn't a good day."

Crescent turned to the doctor. "Can he fly?"

Dr. Michaelson let out a scoffing laugh. "You're not serious, are you? No, he can't fly. Not right now, anyway. I will need to run some tests. I'm not going to let him get on a plane and risk a heart attack or worse."

Crescent turned to Matthew, who wasn't doing a very good job at hiding his anger and frustration. "I'll make sure the problem is taken care of."

Matthew didn't have a choice. He would not be going to New Orleans to see Mack Finley, but he trusted Crescent to do what needed to be done.

Dr. Michaelson interrupted Matthew's thoughts. "If you want to join Mr. Crescent on his errand, you will need to get the tests done right now."

When Elias discovered that Matthew hadn't eaten a substantial meal since yesterday morning, he told Matthew that he would be coming back to the office with a tray of food. "If you won't eat it voluntarily, I'll force it down your throat."

With Crescent off arranging the flight and the doctor getting him food, Matthew was enjoying the peace and quiet of a brief babysitting reprieve until he heard the door to the office lobby open and footsteps approaching. He groaned in exasperation.

Madeline leaned against the door, affecting disappointment. "Matthew, you hurt me when you don't seem happy to see me."

He had to wonder if his day could get any worse as she floated into his office with a flirtatious, teasing grin on her face. She took a seat in front of his desk, slowly crossed her legs in a skirt that wasn't too short, but showed a lot of leg, and smiled at him.

A plane ride may not give me a heart attack, he thought, *but she might.*

They stared at each other in silence for a few moments, the grin never leaving her face, and the scowl never leaving his.

"What do you want, Madeline?"

Her temperament went from flirty to serious, her face hard and determined. "The contract in Atlantic City. My patience has thinned and it's time we discussed it again. You promised me forty percent and I haven't heard a word. You stole business from me, Matthew, and I won't stand for it. You said you would make a phone call. I'm here to make sure that phone call is made."

Matthew gave her a look of surprise. She had never been demanding like this with him before and he didn't like it. "You want me to call right now?"

"Yes, because I'm not going anywhere until you do. Besides, you wouldn't be losing much. Only sixty percent."

His eyes widened in surprise and he let out a laugh. "Sixty percent? Are you out of your mind? What makes you think I would give you sixty percent?"

She rose from her chair and stood behind him, hands on his shoulders, gently massaging them. Her touch sent electricity through him and he tried to ignore it, yet he didn't make any move to avoid her touch.

"Oh, Matthew," she said sweetly. "Why do we do this? Don't you ever get tired of the cat and mouse game that we play? It's tiresome, don't you think? The sexual tension between us is so thick you couldn't cut it with a chainsaw. But we have done nothing over the years to relieve that tension, instead, we banter back and forth—me making blatant advances on you and you pretending you're not interested. While I do enjoy the game, I can tell you don't quite know what to do about it, so I have an alternate offer for you to consider."

Matthew was having a hard time ignoring her touch, and tried to keep an even voice. "An alternate offer?"

"We each have something the other wants. You call the casino and revise the contract and we will both get what we want. In fact, now that I think about it, sixty percent really isn't acceptable." She tightened her grip on his shoulders. "I want the whole thing."

Matthew shifted in his seat to break Madeline's touch, and would have jumped out of his chair if he wasn't currently burdened with sexual desire and a painful ticker in his chest. He turned and stared at her with disbelief. "You are out of your mind! Who in the hell do you think you are?"

Madeline kneeled in front of Matthew, put her hands on his thighs, and slowly moved them up his legs as she spoke, her voice silky. "I think you'll do it, Matthew. In fact, I know you'll do it."

Matthew grabbed Madeline's wrists and squeezed, forcibly stopping her hands from advancing further up his legs. His desire was gone and he glared at her, his anger reaching its peak as he stood and raised her off the floor. "I don't want what you have to offer, Madeline."

"Oh, I think you do."

Matthew scoffed. "What could you possibly have that I would want?"

"I received an interesting telephone call last night, Matthew." Madeline leaned in close enough to kiss him, her grin never disappearing. In a satisfied, triumphant tone, she looked him in the eye and told him, "I know where your daughter is."

***

Outside the door, Dr. Michaelson, carrying Matthew's tray of food, held his breath and prayed nobody else came in the room.

Chapter 33

Judd looked as frantic as Hunter expected after having been woken up before seven on a Saturday morning with a direct command to get to Dennis's house as soon as possible, and not to forget his laptop under threat of bodily harm.

"I'm here," he said, setting the laptop on the table, then looked to Dennis with questioning eyes. Dennis was relaxed and calm as he raised his coffee cup to Judd in welcome.

Hunter had a spectrum of anger, frustration, confusion, and determination to get something accomplished flashing through him, and now that Judd was here, he might be able to finally get a few more answers.

Judd took a seat next to Dennis and said to Hunter, "Dude, you look like shit."

Hunter gave Judd a hard, tired stare. "Yeah, I've had quite a night."

Dennis turned to Judd. "Go get yourself a cup of coffee. My guess is that we're in for quite a story."

After Judd returned from the kitchen with his

coffee, and Dennis's wife had excused herself to her garden, Hunter told the whole story from the day he met Chloe until he left her apartment early this morning. He went into detail about his late wife and who she apparently was in a previous life—a woman named Saffron, working for the mob, who sold herself for money in exchange for food in her stomach and a roof over her head.

Dennis scratched the stubble on his cheeks and gave a quiet whistle. "Damn, boy. That's a blow to the balls, isn't it?"

Hunter gave an agreeing laugh. "A goddamn crippling one. I still feel like I'm going to puke."

"Well, I'm sure lack of food and sleep might have something to do with that too." Dennis took a drink of his coffee and gave Hunter a sympathetic look. "I'm sorry, man. I know you were pretty nuts about this girl."

"The drive back home was torture, man. I shouldn't still care. She lied to me, but at the same time, she spent hours giving me some of what I've been looking for to solve these cases. But she still didn't tell me everything. There's more to the story that she's holding back."

"There's a lot in here," Judd said as he stared at his computer screen.

Dennis's eyebrows lifted, impressed, as he leaned over to glance at the computer screen. "That didn't take long."

"If you'd get a damn computer in your house, we would have been able to find him an hour ago, you cheap bastard," Hunter said as he reached for Judd's laptop to see what was found. "You're lucky your neighbors don't have a password on their wireless or I would have dragged you to the office instead."

Hunter clicked on the most recent link that mentioned Matthew's name. It was a newspaper article from the *Boston Herald* about the groundbreaking ceremonies, held two days ago, for a new wing at a children's hospital. Hunter scanned the story, but that wasn't what he was interested in. He was interested in the picture featuring the joyous members of the hospital administrators and board of directors, the president of the board shaking hands with the man of the hour—the generous benefactor to the ailing and terminal children of Massachusetts. Hunter clicked on the picture, enlarging it so he could get a better look at Matthew Parnell. He wasn't as old as he imagined; he was a handsome man, clean-cut, very tightly composed, with a generous smile on his face that said, *Oh, it's nothing. Really.*

After a few minutes, Judd broke the silence. "What exactly are you looking at?"

Hunter turned the laptop around so Dennis and Judd could see the picture of Matthew, both of them with questioning looks on their faces, but Hunter didn't allow them long to study the picture. "The Black Rose Murderer."

Judd's head snapped up in instant understanding. "That's him?" Hunter nodded, but the look on Judd's face said their work would be cut out for them. "If this guy is who she says he is...I gotta be honest, guys. Going up against the mob..."

Dennis gave Judd a slap on the back of the head like a scolding parent. "Don't even finish that thought. Besides, the mob is Italian. This is just a well-organized, yet slightly dysfunctional organized crime family." As Judd rubbed the back of his head, Dennis turned to Hunter. "Do you think she'll help us?"

"I don't know. She's afraid." Hunter stared at the picture of the man responsible for the Black Rose Murders with a hard and determined look. "I can tell you this. Chloe is right about this man's power, ego, and reputation being everything to him. Just look at the smug smile on his face and the pat on the back he's giving himself."

"When is she planning on leaving for Boston?" Dennis asked.

"We didn't get that far in the conversation before she fell asleep. I'm going to call her in a couple days," Hunter said. At Judd's look of impatience, he added, "I *need* to give her a few days. She has to think about what she wants to do, and she will probably want time to talk to this friend of hers. Which reminds me, you need to get ahold of the Marshals and have them meet with me ASAP. I need to be able to tell her what they're willing to offer if her friend testifies."

"If you can get him to trial," Dennis reminded Hunter.

"Oh, I'll get him to trial," Hunter said assuredly. "But if the Marshals don't offer anything, I can guarantee that her friend won't talk, and Chloe will walk away. I know it."

Dennis turned to Hunter. "Is that it?" he asked.

"That's it," Hunter affirmed.

"Okay." Dennis stood and approached Hunter,

speaking with a stern tone. "The guest room is upstairs, first door on the left. You're going to go up there and sleep the sleep of the dead." Hunter was about to argue but Dennis put his hands up. "Don't even think of arguing with me, boy. I'll drag you upstairs by your ears if that's how you want to play this out. Or, if you prefer, I'll go get the missus and you can hear it from her. Your choice."

Judd covered a smile with his coffee cup while Hunter looked at Dennis like a child being punished for setting ants on fire.

"While you're sleeping," Dennis motioned to Judd, "*we* will start by getting all the information we can on Parnell and let you know all about it when you're awake and fed again."

Dennis and Hunter had a stare down that lasted no longer than ten seconds before Hunter gave in with a sigh and stood up.

"First door on the left?" Hunter asked with a grin.

"Smart ass," Dennis replied. "Get up there."

Hunter went upstairs, took off his shoes, and was asleep before his head hit the pillow. He dreamed of the faces of the women in his files, each one of them looking to him for the chance to finally bring them peace.

Chapter 34

The time had come for Chloe to talk to Alice. The two friends sat in Chloe's living room as she confessed everything to her friend, from the second she first saw Hunter to the last time.

"Witness protection?" Alice said with awe. "For all of us?"

"Nothing is set in stone yet. He made no promises."

"Reggie," Alice whispered. "Would Reggie understand? Maybe. Would he come with me? I don't know. Would he let the boys come with me? Of course he wouldn't. Would the boys want to come with me without him? No, they wouldn't."

"You can ask and answer questions all day, Alice. The bottom line is that you have a difficult decision to make. Whether or not you agree to protection, if and when Hunter does get proof against my father, he will have the power to make you testify." She let out an apologetic sigh. "Look, I know your choices suck, but what if I fail? Hunter's the only one who can help you."

"Do you think you will fail?"

The unknown crossed Chloe's features. "It's a definite possibility."

"Do you know what you're going to do yet?"

"Not yet, but I will figure something out. If I can get some kind of evidence while I'm there and get it to Hunter…"

Alice looked at Chloe like she was an idiot. "Do you really think that's going to happen? When you walk through those doors, Matthew will have you locked down so tight you'll need permission to go to the bathroom. How do you expect to get any evidence?"

Chloe's voice exploded as she threw her hands above her head in exasperation. "I don't know! Look, this is the best I can come up with right now. I can't make any promises or guarantees."

Alice nodded in understanding. "When are you leaving for Boston?"

"I've got to prepare myself to be fed to the lions. I'm leaving Friday."

"Well, then," Alice said with decisiveness in her voice, "I need to have a chat with my husband."

Chapter 35

After three days of searching, the only thing that Hunter, Judd, and Dennis could find out about Matthew Parnell was that he was one hell of a swell guy in New England. They had no probable cause, so obtaining any kind of warrant for deeper investigation was out of the question. There was nothing found on Evan Crescent, which didn't surprise any of them since he stayed in the shadows and only came out when called, and very little learned about Dr. Elias Michaelson.

Hunter and Judd had met with, and told the story to, the assistant director of the FBI, the US Marshals, and the federal prosecutor. They wouldn't have to prove that Parnell personally committed any kind of illegal activity, all they would have to prove was that he owned or managed a criminal organization that performed specific illegal activity, which was what Parnell was doing when he paid people to erase problems. Witness protection would absolutely be available to Alice and her family, as well as Chloe or anybody else, should they choose to testify against him. If what Chloe had told Hunter was true, that Parnell had his hands in many powerful pockets, and if he chose to name names while in custody, the situation could get stickier than fresh pulled taffy, and the publicity would only make it worse.

But before any promises of witness protection could be made or any deals struck, an investigation of the threat or potential for danger had to be conducted. If the potential threats were deemed credible, and Hunter was certain they would be, then the final decision for protection would be made.

The same would be said for Mack Finley.

Hunter stood behind his desk, inventorying all of the files that had to do with the Black Rose Murders. His stack of files had grown to nine; he had handwritten notes and two folders full of printouts, photos, and all of the information they were able to find on Matthew Parnell, Evan Crescent, and Dr. Elias Michaelson. Unfortunately, neither folder was as thick as he had been hoping. His puzzle pieces were in neat stacks on his desk and all he had to do was put them together, then find the missing few.

Judd knocked on the door to Hunter's office and leaned in. "They're here."

***

Hunter exchanged a good-to-see-you nod with Finley's lawyer as he and Judd entered the conference room and took their seats with their backs facing the partially shaded glass doors. Mack Finley sat next to his lawyer, his hands resting on the table in front of him, handcuffs firmly in place. Finley's lawyer, Doug Comeaux, was a good guy and a fair man, a criminal lawyer for twenty years who obviously didn't like working with criminals anymore.

"Agent Lawton," Doug said in greeting.

"Doug," Hunter replied, getting comfortable in his chair without looking at Finley.

"Who the hell is this?" Finley asked, indicating Judd.

Judd was silent and observed the interviewee. Mack Finley was twenty-seven years old and cocky. His orange jumpsuit had a smell to it that suggested it probably hadn't been washed in a few days, his jet-black hair was slicked back with what smelled like grease and shit, and he wore a smug grin that showed teeth that occasionally had a passing acquaintance with a toothbrush.

"This is Agent Fowler," Hunter flatly replied as he helped himself to a cup of coffee from the tray on the table.

Finley gave Judd a look of repugnance, his eyes slanted and his mouth drawn tight. "I don't want him here."

"Too damn bad," Hunter said.

Finley's face tightened in avid disappointment and he slumped in his chair, crossing his arms in front of him as Hunter sat back, sipping his coffee.

Finley gave his lawyer a glare, then turned to Hunter, who was looking back at Finley casually and uncaring. The lack of importance and urgency they were showing wasn't what Finley was expecting or wanting.

Hunter smiled into his coffee cup as he pictured Dennis sitting behind the glass, feet propped up, reading the newspaper.

"Let's start with why we're here," Doug said in an attempt to move things along.

Finley gave a wide smile like he had a secret he was dying to tell but waiting for the right time. "Okay, I only did what I did because I was told to. It was my job to deliver from point A to point B and make sure the delivery got there on time and in one piece. When I got pulled over, the cops started asking me all kinds of questions about what I had in the car and why was I acting all twitchy, walking around my car all suspicious like I was hiding something. If that delivery wouldn't have been made, my ass would have been in the ground long before you got to me. The only reason you caught me was because I got sent down here again and was stupid enough to drive from Atlantic City on the same route."

"Stupid is one way of saying it," Hunter said.

Finley leaned forward, resting his arms on the table. The sleeves of his jumpsuit slid up, revealing a simple tattoo on his right inner forearm. His tattoo was nothing special, just a badly faded and indeterminable letter of the alphabet in black outline, three inches long and one inch wide.

Finley said with a hard look, "You don't fuck with this guy I work for. He says and you do. You don't and you die. It's that simple. I did what I was told. I'd rather be in jail than on the receiving end of

215

him being pissed off, that's for sure."

"And you don't think testifying against him will piss him off?" Judd asked, and was answered with a hard glare from Finley.

"I get witness protection, then I won't have to worry about that. Will I?"

"You traveled a lot to make your deliveries, right?" Judd asked.

"Sure."

"All over the country or just specific places?"

"East Coast, man. All up and down the East Coast."

"So you delivered to multiple locations and dealt with a lot of different people. What about the people you delivered to for the first time? How did they know you were the guy to deal with?"

"They just did."

Judd sat back and inclined his head, indicating Finley's tattoo. "I just thought maybe they knew who you were because of your tattoo."

Finley immediately tensed as Hunter leaned forward and grabbed his arm to get a closer look at the tattoo.

"Hey!" Finley shouted.

Doug reached over and pulled Hunter's grip off Finley's arm. "Come on, Agent. You know better than that. Let him go."

Finley rubbed his arm. "What the fuck, man? It's just a tattoo."

Hunter wisely kept his mouth shut in an effort to calm down before speaking again.

"So he's the bad cop and you're the good cop?" Finley asked Judd.

"Let's just move this along," Doug said, then turned to Hunter. "You good?"

Keeping his focus on Finley, Hunter nodded.

"Okay," Judd said. "So, just for clarification—and you've already admitted this—you did what you did because you would rather face federal prison than piss off your boss?"

"So?" Finley said with a scoff.

"Then I guess I'm confused," Judd said. "If you're so afraid of this man, why are you willing to turn on him now?"

"Because I don't *want* to go to federal prison, and if I talk to you, Uncle Sam will take care of me. I'd rather be alive in witness protection than dead anywhere else."

Hunter spoke, his irritation rapidly growing. "So what does this have to do with me? Why did you want me here when you could just have your attorney deal with it?"

Finley leaned forward as far as he could and spoke in a cool voice. "Because I know something you don't know, and if I tell you, I'm pretty sure you'll help me." Finley leaned back and shrugged his shoulders. "Then again, you never know."

Doug caught both Hunter's and Judd's eye and gave a slight, solemn nod. Yes, Hunter would find the information interesting after all.

Hunter looked back to Finley. "Yeah? And what do you know that I don't?"

Finley's grin widened enough so the corners of his mouth reached the bottom of his eyes. Relaxing in his chair, Finley spoke like he had the winning lottery numbers in his pocket. "The guy I work for, he's a big mucky-muck on the East Coast, owns a bunch of hotels and casinos. He has a lot of business going through there, if you know what I mean. I tell you, man, Atlantic City would shut down if this guy goes down." Finley was obviously hoping for some kind of reaction and got nothing, so he continued. "Anyway, I'm in Atlantic City and his guy comes up to me and says the man wants to see me. So, I go up there, he gives me a couple suitcases and says to take them down here. So, I do."

"We know all this, Finley. Get to the point," Hunter interrupted impatiently.

Finley raised his hands. "Okay, okay. Jesus, man. I'm getting to it. So anyway, I'm down here now, what? Two years? Guys in prison, they like to talk, and they talk about all kinds of stuff. But what caught my ear was that a few of the guys in there know you—well, hate you is more like it. Anyway, they were talking, trading stories and shit, and I heard about your wife."

Hunter's eyes widened in surprise, then quickly squinted, staring at Finley with dangerous curiosity.

Judd cast a cautious sideways glance at Hunter. Doug sat silently and gave Hunter an apologetic look. Finley gave a satisfied and cruel grin.

Hunter hardened his face and spoke in a calm, yet demanding tone. "What about my wife?"

"I know who killed her," Mack said smugly as he wiped his nose with his sleeve, "and I know who ordered it. The good news is that you don't have to worry about it anymore. The guy who did it got shanked a few years back, so there's that."

Hunter was breathing deeply through his nose, glaring at Finley with the full intention of throwing him through the window behind him.

Finley leaned forward again. "I hear she was a real beauty, that wife of yours. I also hear she had herself a tattoo on her back. A flower, right? A rose?"

Hunter continued his hard stare. "What about it?"

Finley was starting to twitch in his seat, excited by the reaction he got from the FBI agent. "There's a bunch of other women with the same tattoo who are ending up in the morgue too."

Hunter's mind raced to the only logical thing Mack could say next. It would be the same thing he heard the other night with Chloe.

Finley leaned back in his chair, resting his hands across his chest with a satisfied grin. "Well, now, seems your wife and these other dead girls with that tattoo all work for the same guy. The same guy I work for. The same guy who ordered the hit on your wife and the same guy I am willing to tell you about for protection."

Hunter desperately wanted to lunge across the table and strangle Mack Finley where he sat. Judd saw it and turned to Finley, asking the question he already knew the answer to. "Who's your boss, Mack?"

Hunter could see from the look on his face that Finley was having second thoughts. "Hey, you came to us."

Finley let out a heavy sigh. "His name is Parnell."

Furious, Hunter silently shook his head while berating himself for letting his distractions get the best of him and not figuring it out sooner.

"Matthew Parnell?" Judd asked. "The mob boss in Boston? That Matthew Parnell?"

Amused, Finley replied, "You know him, huh?"

The animosity in Finley's eyes that he was directing at Hunter as he turned his head changed to sudden and uncontrollable fear as a figure casually passed in front of the doors. His face had gone slack and the pit of his stomach dropped to his feet. The three other men in the room exchanged confused looks at this sudden onset of fear and change of behavior. Finley was looking past Hunter through the glass doors of the room, his eyes focused and unwavering. He went from twitching excitedly to near wetting himself in a matter of seconds, and his hands were trembling, like he was getting ready to jump out of a plane at ten thousand feet with no guarantee that the chute would open. The others watched in cautious curiosity as Finley slowly stood and apprehensively walked to the door, cocking his head to get a better view. He muttered a few words under his breath and definitively spun around.

Finley adamantly shook his head and his voice shook with fear. "Nope. I'm done. You assholes set me up."

"What the hell are you talking about?" Hunter asked. "Sit down."

"You know what he does when he wants to deal with someone who's a problem? He sends someone to get you. You set me up, called him, and told him that I was coming to talk to you guys."

"He sends someone?" Judd asked, confused. "What the hell—"

"He sends someone! Someone to take you back to him! And if you can't get back to him, then they just kill you where you stand! And if you think I'm going to say another word while *she's* out there, you can think again! Ain't fucking happening!"

Doug led Finley back to his seat as Hunter peeked out the door. Surprised by what he saw, and further confused by Finley's reaction to it, Hunter lifted the blinds on the doors, giving everyone in the room a clear view of the lobby where a woman sat patiently. Hunter was the only one who knew it was Chloe, sitting casually and minding her own business, flipping through the pages of a magazine, completely oblivious to the panic she had stirred up in Finley. Although the timing was bad, for a second or two he was happy to see her, and then suddenly wondered what she was doing there and why Finley was so afraid of her. Doug and Judd looked to Hunter for some kind of explanation, but he didn't have one.

Hunter turned back to Finley. "Who is she?"

Finley gave Hunter an exasperated look. "Are you kidding me? If he sent *her*, then it's over! I'm a dead man!" He threw his hands in front of him, motioning at Chloe. "Who is she, he asks. She's his goddamn daughter!"

***

In the observation room, Dennis sat up in his chair, leaning forward with his elbows on his thighs and his hands dangling between his knees, paying close attention. Even though Dennis couldn't see her, he knew who Finley was talking about. Dennis's jaw gaped open and he said out loud, "I'll be goddamned."

Sitting behind Dennis in the last free chair, the assistant director of the FBI was quietly observing the interview with concentrated interest. He and Dennis were of the same age, but unlike Dennis, this man wasn't planning on retiring any time soon. The only way he would ever retire from the Bureau was by death. His name was Jack Lawrence and he had a phone call to make.

Chapter 36

To say Chloe was confused was an understatement. One minute she was sitting in the lobby, quietly reading a magazine, and the next Hunter had a fierce grip on her arm, yanking her into his office. Judd and Dennis followed, leaving a terrified Finley and a confused lawyer alone with an agent standing outside the door.

Not even a second after Judd closed the office door behind him, Hunter let go of Chloe's arm and stood behind his desk, glaring at her, overwhelming rage in his eyes. Chloe looked at the other men, waiting for someone to explain.

Chloe rubbed her arm where Hunter had grabbed her. "Could somebody please explain?"

"You're his daughter?" Hunter shouted the question.

Chloe naturally assumed that he would put two and two together when he eventually came across a photograph from one of the many public events she attended with her father. She squared her shoulders and steeled herself, defiance in her eyes. "Yes."

"And you didn't think that might have been important to tell me the other night?"

"No, not at the time," she replied. "And if you don't stop shouting at me, you won't hear any more from me. You'll be civil or I'll be silent."

Hunter picked up the first thing closest to him and threw it. Dennis and Judd watched in amazement as Amy's coffee cup hit the wall and shattered.

Dennis stepped forward and stood between Hunter and Chloe. "Okay, let's all calm down." He gave a pointed look to Hunter, silently telling him to get his shit together. Hunter turned toward the wall and started at the broken mug on the floor while Dennis made his introductions and took a seat on the corner of Hunter's desk.

Hunter turned on Chloe. "You told me that you paid someone to give you a new life. What's your name? We already know your last name is Parnell."

Chloe's defenses were strengthening by the second and her eyes began to harden against Hunter, glaring back at him, daring him to challenge her. Hunter cocked his head and raised his eyebrows as if to say, *Well?*

"Renee," she said.

Before Hunter could speak again, Dennis once again stepped in. "Okay, let's just try—"

"Is there anything else you didn't think was important enough to tell me?" Hunter asked Chloe.

"Yes," she replied, unrepentant.

Hunter slammed his hand on his desk. "Goddammit! You lied to me!"

"I didn't lie! And don't you dare say the phrase

'lying by omission' to me."

"All right, that's enough!" Dennis gave Hunter a hard enough stare that Hunter let out a disgusted breath and threw himself down in his chair. Dennis then gestured to the chair in front of Hunter's desk and lightly placed a hand on Chloe's back. She got the hint and sat down.

Judd brought in another chair for him and placed it on the side of Hunter's desk so they could all face each other. When everyone was as comfortable as they were going to get, Dennis addressed Chloe.

"Okay. Let's start with why you're here."

The only person in the room Chloe had any hostility toward was Hunter, so she looked directly at Dennis and spoke to him with respect, like she had been raised to do. "I'm sure he told you what happened over the weekend. I came down here—risked my life to come down here—to talk about my friend who has agreed to testify, but only if she and her family would be guaranteed witness protection. I thought talking to him in person about this would be the best course of action." She looked at Hunter with slanted eyes. "Apparently, I was wrong."

Hunter was about to say something, but Dennis stopped him with a firm stare, and then turned back to Chloe. "What do you mean you risked your life to come down here?"

Chloe made no attempt to answer Dennis's question. Judd cleared his throat and Chloe gave him her attention. "The reason for all this…um, the tattoo. We know that the girls who work for your…for Parnell…they all had this tattoo on their back." Chloe nodded in confirmation. "Do the men who work for him have a tattoo as well?"

"They do."

"Is it on the inside of their forearm? A letter of the alphabet in Old English script?"

"Yes." She explained the significance of the tattoo, and the letter associated with it, was meant as identification to anyone who knew about Parnell's secret life. "All of the tattoos, except for mine, have the letter P."

Hunter snapped his head up at her, his eyes calling her a liar. "I saw your tattoo. You have the same letter."

Chloe turned to Hunter, the hard, angry look back in her eyes. "Actually, mine is a D. I guess you didn't look close enough."

Judd jumped in before Hunter could retort. "And the D stands for?"

"Daughter," Dennis said, understanding coming over him. Chloe nodded. "I'm guessing your tattoo carried a lot more weight and significance than the others."

Hunter began to pace in slow circles. His fists were clenched in tight fists at his sides and his face was rapidly turning from red to purple. It was killing Chloe that with every word she spoke she was hurting Hunter, but if she was going to suggest helping each other in their quest to capture Matthew, she had to fill in as many blanks as she could.

Chloe looked at Dennis and continued. "My father's captain, Evan Crescent, thoroughly enjoys inflicting pain and carrying out the orders that he is given, and he does it without question and with complete loyalty."

Judd let out a long whistle. "Well, that explains Finley's freak out."

"I was watching from the other room and it seems to me he was more than a little terrified of her," Dennis said to Judd, tilting his head in Chloe's direction.

At Chloe's look of confusion, Judd said, "Mack Finley. He shot and killed two state troopers."

Understanding instantly crossed Chloe's face and she looked at Hunter. His face was no longer red with anger, but still he was frustrated. He nodded to confirm that this was the man he had told her about, the one who wanted to turn state's evidence against his boss, who just happened to be her father.

Judd continued. "I asked you about the tattoo because Finley has one on his arm. When he asked for witness protection, he offered to give up Parnell, and Parnell's boss, in exchange. He took one look at you and freaked out. He said you were sent here for him."

Painfully aware her past had officially come back to haunt her, Chloe wore a slight grin as she closed her eyes and gave a small shake of her head. It wasn't a grin that would indicate any kind of happiness, it was a grin that said she wasn't at all surprised that the thought of crossing her would be as bad as crossing her father. Because she was his daughter, and had once been known for abruptly and sternly putting people in their place when the need arose, people automatically knew that if and when Matthew sent her anywhere, it was worse than sending Crescent, even though she never had to, and never would, physically harm anyone.

Dennis turned to Chloe. "What about the other guy? Parnell's boss?"

David. She felt like a thousand daggers had just been thrown into her chest. The thought of David being pursued and investigated by anyone made Chloe sick to her stomach and furious at Finley for even attempting to say his name aloud simply for something as selfish as trying to get away with murder. There was no way she would allow David's name to slip through Finley's lips and into the FBI's hands.

"My father is the boss," Chloe stated with a scoffing laugh, avoiding the truth while not quite telling a lie. Her voice, her posture, and her eyes said it was an undeniable, undisputable fact, and she knew everyone in the room believed her.

Clearly frustrated and defeated, Hunter hit the back of his chair and it spun at a forceful velocity. It took him a few minutes, but he had finally cooled down. When he turned to Dennis, Chloe ached at the desperation and silent pleas he was giving his oldest friend, who could offer no comfort at the present moment. It was obvious Hunter wanted both Matthew Parnell and Mack Finley in custody and both with a lethal injection in their arms. The desperation came from the fact that Hunter knew there was no way he would get both. It would be one or the other.

"Sorry, man." It was all Dennis could say.

"There has to be more than that," Hunter said. "Finley could have seen her and decided that she would be the perfect excuse to change his mind. Don't look at me like that! There *has* to be more! The only thing we have on Parnell is her story. It's not even testimony. We have these files in front of us, but we have *no evidence* to point to Parnell. He cut off someone's head and we have no fucking evidence!"

Chloe's head snapped up and she stared at Hunter in silent shock.

Judd cleared his throat and told her, "There was a woman identified as Sasha Wheeler recently found in Vegas."

The immediate recognition on Chloe's face and the slow nod of her head at the mention of Sasha's name didn't go unnoticed by anyone in the room. Every nerve in her body seized up and she froze in horror, imagining the torture that Sasha must have gone through. What could Sasha have done to make him cut her head off? Very slowly, the fear she had felt about confronting her father was replaced with disgust and eager determination to see him rot in his own filth.

"I will get you proof," she said quietly.

Nobody heard her over Hunter's rant to Dennis. "Other than her," Hunter waved his arm at Chloe, "all we have is Alice's testimony. We'll need more than that, and Finley won't talk now because he's afraid of her! And she can't make up her mind whether or not she'll testify against him."

Chloe raised her voice as she stood and leaned against Hunter's desk. "I will get you your goddamn proof!" Hunter looked at her like he was just noticing her for the first time and she lowered

229

her voice. "I told you that I was going back to Boston. I will get you whatever you need to convict him and every other man responsible. I know what RICO is, and I know that all you need is proof he was responsible, not just for the murders, but for all of his activities in the Family. All he did was give the order, but he *did* give the order. I know it, Alice knows it, and that jackass in the other room knows it." She gave Hunter a hard, sincere look. She wanted her father stopped just as much as he did. "I *will* get you what you need."

The room fell silent as everyone focused their eyes on Hunter.

"I will get you what you need." She was trying to assure him, but she knew she was failing.

Hunter turned to Dennis. "Finley will get protection."

Dennis shrugged his shoulders. "If he testifies, more than likely."

"Ugh," Chloe said with disgust. "This Finley guy is irrelevant. I can promise you right now that if my father knows Finley has even thought about talking to you, he won't be breathing long enough to even see trial."

All eyes in the room set on Chloe, each one of them with curious and suspicious expressions, which she wasn't deterred by at all. She let out an exasperated sigh. "Oh, come on. With everything you know so far, do you honestly think my father will let anyone mention his name under oath?"

"What about this other guy Finley told Doug about?" Dennis asked. "Finley said Parnell has someone he reports to."

"I told you..." Chloe began as she whipped around on Dennis, but then abruptly stopped. Her blood turned to ice and her breath caught in her throat as she saw Jack Lawrence casually leaning against the doorframe, listening to the entire exchange.

Jack gave Chloe a stern look that told her, in no uncertain terms, they did not now, nor ever, know each other, and casually said, "Please, continue."

Chloe poised herself and turned back to Dennis. "I told you, he *is* the boss."

"Says you," Hunter sharply said.

Chloe whirled on Hunter, fury in her eyes. "You know what? Fuck you!" She thrust her arm out behind her, pointing in the direction of the conference room. "He will tell you the exact same thing. And before you ask, I don't know what his reasons are."

"I bet she can get him to tell us what we want to know," Jack said. Chloe looked at Jack with widening eyes and he returned her stare with a look that said, *Trust me.* "And my guess is that she can do it without saying a word."

"Seriously?" Judd asked, doubt in his voice.

Jack walked into the room, addressing everyone. "My money is on her that she can get him to tell the truth about whether or not this Parnell guy reports to a higher power. Everything that you know so far, you only know it from this woman. From what you've been told, does it sound like Parnell tolerates any kind of insolence? Including lying?"

"Jack," Dennis said, "you were sitting behind the glass. You saw how he reacted when he saw her."

"I did, but there is something that you all seem to be forgetting. Mack Finley worked for Parnell, who is apparently the boss of a very powerful organized crime family. Because of that, I also see that Finley knows the consequences of lying to a Parnell." He cocked his head in Chloe's direction. "And it seems to me that Finley is more afraid of the daughter than the father. Look at her. She's not going to threaten his safety or his life. She won't even be in the room. If you want to know whether or not Finley is telling the truth about this other guy, then she's the only one who will get it out of him. He has no idea why she's here, but if he's terrified of her just by being in the same building, then let him think she's going back with news that won't get him killed."

Judd, Dennis, and Hunter all exchanged questioning looks as they considered what Jack was saying. Chloe sat back down in an effort to stop her knees from shaking.

"Lawton and Fowler will be in the room with Finley and Doug." Jack turned to Chloe, giving her a look she knew all too well—the look that said she already knew what to do no matter what he said next. "She will stay here."

"And do what?" Hunter asked, looking between Jack and Chloe.

"Nothing," Jack replied simply.

Knowing what Jack was expecting of her, Chloe was back in her old life. Her body language and expression didn't give away any emotions and she had a tight rein on her composure.

There were no other options available. Judd and Dennis nodded as Hunter stood in disbelief. Finally,

Hunter threw his arms in the air in defeat.

"Excellent!" Jack said with a smile, giving everyone in the room a satisfied look, then locked eyes with Chloe. She was poised and ready, her eyes telling him that she understood. Jack gave her a sincere smile, almost like he had missed her over the years and it was good to see her again. He rested a hand on her shoulder and said, "Five minutes."

As he walked out of the room, Jack gave her shoulder a light squeeze to confirm the smile did, indeed, mean that he was happy to see her healthy and whole, and that they would definitely be speaking later.

***

Mack Finley didn't trust the confidence Hunter and Judd seemed to exude as they entered the room and took their respective seats at the table. Finley had stopped trembling, but was still nervous, his eyes roaming toward the door every few seconds.

"Where do we go from here, gentlemen?" Doug asked.

"Is your client going to continue with any kind of statement?" Hunter asked. "We can't go to the Marshals with what he's given us so far."

Doug turned to Finley for the answer to that question, but Finley's eyes were focused on the door looking out into the lobby, which was currently empty.

"What about her?" Finley asked, gesturing toward the lobby with his chin.

"Who?" Judd asked, looking behind him to

verify she wasn't there, then turning back to Finley. "The woman from before? She's nobody."

"Bullshit she's nobody!" Finley said. "I know who she is!"

"Is he right about who she is?" Doug asked Hunter.

"I can tell you with absolute certainty that the name on her identification is not Parnell," Hunter said. "So, do we continue or call it a day?"

They were all looking at Finley, waiting for an answer, while he stared straight ahead into the lobby. Within seconds his muscles began to tense and his eyes began to widen, but he was able to keep his hands from shaking. Chloe walked through the lobby toward the elevators and glanced in Finley's direction as she casually pushed the button to call the lift. Finley's eyes were frozen on Chloe. She had a hard and malicious stare burning into the back of his eyes that said if he had one working brain cell swimming in that head of his, he would keep his mouth shut, go back to his cell, and cut out his tongue.

Without much enthusiasm, Doug looked through the door into the lobby, but only saw the elevator doors close.

Doug turned back to his client. "What do you want to do?"

"I'm done," Finley spat out.

Doug started to pack up his pens and pads of paper into his briefcase. "All right."

"And what about the man you claimed to be Parnell's boss?" Judd asked.

Finley wasn't completely stupid. "I said I'm

234

done."

Chapter 37

Kimberly manned the reception area while Alice took a long lunch so she and Reggie could take Charlie and Samuel to the dentist. When the elevator doors on the tenth floor opened, Evan Crescent and Tucker Wilson stepped into the lobby of Keller and Keller and were greeted with warm eyes, a wide smile, and a conservatively dressed young woman who was the epitome of what Chloe called "first impression professionalism."

"Can I help you?" Kimberly asked, a little too perky, while she looked Tucker up and down and thought to herself, *Wow.*

"Good afternoon," Crescent replied in a pleasant voice. "I was wondering if it would be possible to see Ms. Renee for a few minutes."

"I'm sorry, we don't have anyone here by that name."

Crescent and Tucker exchanged a look, then Crescent turned back to Kimberly. "You're sure? Average height, late twenties, red hair, blue eyes..."

"Drop dead smile," Tucker added with a flirtatious grin.

Kimberly returned Tucker's flirtatious grin and addressed him. "Um, I'm sorry, there's no Renee here. Maybe she's on another floor of the building?"

Tucker leaned against the partition boxing in the reception area, his eyes quickly scanning the work area of basic office necessities and personal photographs, all the while flashing his gleaming white teeth at Kimberly. "She told a friend of ours that she just started here a few weeks ago. We very well could be on the wrong floor. We probably should have tried calling first. You know how attorneys are with their schedules. They never know when they might have a free minute for someone to just stop by. I'm really sorry that we wasted your time."

Tucker winked at Kimberly and she turned to a puddle of goo, her cheeks flushing and her grin threatening to become permanently fixed to her face the way it was. "Oh, no," she said like a schoolgirl being hit on by the high school quarterback. "You're not wasting *my* time."

"We should go check another floor," Tucker said, reaching forward and placing a hand over Kimberly's, "but I really appreciate your time."

Kimberly was desperately trying to think of something that might keep Tucker in front of her just a few more minutes, and that thought came to her just as Crescent pressed the elevator call button.

"The only person I can think of would be Ms. Riggs. She's only been here for a few weeks, but she's not an attorney and, sadly, not here today."

Tucker's gave Kimberly a slight bow from the

waist. "We must be on the wrong floor, but thank you for your courtesies."

As the elevator doors opened, Tucker gave his winning smile to Kimberly and winked at her. "Thank you, ma'am. For future reference, I'll remember what floor you work on."

Kimberly's schoolgirl smile and blushing face were permanent as the elevator doors closed behind them.

***

Crescent stared at the mirrored walls of the elevator as Tucker took his cell phone out of his pocket, dialed a number, and waited. It took two heartbeats for someone to answer. "It's me. We don't have her yet; however, we did find someone else. She's a receptionist at a law firm."

He hung up the phone and said to Crescent, "He's on his way."

Chapter 38

At Jack's insistence, Chloe checked into the hotel suite he had reserved for her. She took advantage of the balcony, sitting outside as the sun went down, admiring the city and thankful for a breeze. Unexpectedly, she wasn't as worried as she thought she would be. Besides, the more she thought about it, she was sure that Alice was right and Jack wanted her side of the story before deciding whether or not he would be placing a phone call. Jack didn't particularly like her father, and she thought, maybe, there was a chance he might be able to help her in her quest to stop him. Then again, he might not.

She felt absolutely nothing; no fear, no joy, no anger, no guilt, no pain, no confusion. At that moment, she was just simply there, unfeeling and emotionally drained. She didn't want to think anymore, she just wanted to sleep. There were three things she knew absolutely had to happen: she had to get to Boston, she had to make sure Alice and her family were safe, and she had to say goodbye to

Hunter. But before she could do any of those things, she had to talk to Jack.

A few hours later, she showered, made herself as presentable as she could, and took the elevator to the top floor. Jack opened the door to his suite with a warm and welcoming smile, embracing her tightly. He broke the hug and escorted her into the room with a hand on the small of her back.

"It is so good to see you, Renee, although, I will admit you were the last person I expected to see when I woke up this morning."

She undoubtedly knew Jack was being sincere; she could see it in his eyes, hear it in his voice, and feel it in his touch. Her wall of safety had been reinforcing itself around her all afternoon, and as much as she wanted to let go of everything and enjoy spending time with an old friend, she couldn't get too comfortable. Just because she wasn't afraid didn't mean she wouldn't be careful. Their night together had just begun, and she was sure it would be spent as an intense question and answer period.

"Well," she replied with the same smile, "I came close to wetting myself when I saw you, so we can call the surprise even. It's good to see you too."

"How has it been for you all these years? You're doing okay?"

Aside from adding eight years and a few pounds, physically, she was fine. Chloe kept telling herself that there was nothing to be nervous about, but she could feel the prick of an ominous feeling between her shoulder blades. Something was up, but if Jack had any malicious intent, she would have felt that warning run through every nerve in her body.

"I've been doing what I've had to. Thank you for asking."

Jack stopped just before entering the dining room and turned to Chloe, gently placing both hands on her shoulders. "Renee, it's no secret I detest your father and would do everything in my power to not help him find you." She tried to suppress a smile, which didn't go unnoticed by Jack. "I want you to know that I have not called, nor do I intend to call, Matthew."

Relief seeped out of every pore in her body and she gave Jack a thankful smile. "I appreciate that."

"That being said," Jack smiled as he turned her toward the dining area, "there is one person in particular I couldn't wait to call, and I don't think you will be disappointed."

Chloe froze and her eyes widened in shock and elation as the room went dark around her and she stared into the eyes of David Lundy. She didn't know how to react as David stood up from the head of the table and approached her with a wide, toothy smile and open arms, laughing with happiness, ecstatic to see her. He was still a few years away from eighty, but he moved like he was twenty, almost running toward her. His hair had greyed slightly, and he had a slight pouch to his gut, but otherwise the years had been good to him.

David grabbed hold of Chloe and pulled her into him, his arms wrapping tightly around her, almost squeezing the breath out of her. It took her all of five seconds to realize how much she had missed David over the years and wondered if she had been wrong about not going to see him all along. Tears threatened to fall, but she forced them down, melting into David's embrace and returning the hug with mixed feelings of suspicion, relief, and love.

David broke the hug and held her at arm's length, a beaming smile on his face and laughter in his voice. "Oh, baby girl, we found you. Look at you! You look wonderful! I have missed you so very much, and now here you are!"

Chloe was stunned, but at the same time she shared the feelings with David, with the exception that she also felt shame. She had been wrong all these years—she could have gone to him at any time. David would have protected her, but instead, she foolishly believed what her father had told her. She didn't know what to say; instead, she embraced David again, still trying to fight back the emotions that were threatening to spill out.

"Oh, David," she said into his shoulder. "I am so sorry. I should have come to you, but he told me…I have missed you more than you know."

David laughed to let her know there was nothing to be forgiven. "It's okay. I knew we would see each other again."

A thought suddenly stabbed her. If Jack called David that morning after discovering her in the lobby of the FBI building, how did David get from Chicago so fast? Was he already in New Orleans and was this all one big karmic coincidence? Chloe pulled back with the question in her eyes, but no accusation in her voice. "How long have you been in New Orleans?"

"Two days," David said.

The timing made no sense. "Two days? But…"

"We heard you were here and got here as fast as we could."

"We?" Chloe asked, suddenly tense again.

David let out a reassuring laugh as he turned Chloe to see Dr. Michaelson resting his hands on the back of a chair, both excited and relieved to see her. She was just as happy to see Elias as she was David, albeit mildly curious. She had never known Elias to be outside of her father's beck and call radius, but then again, if David wanted or needed the doctor with him, who was Matthew to say no?

Chloe gave a questioning look first to David, then to Jack, asking whether or not she was safe. David laughed and Jack smiled, both seemingly amused by her uncertainty. David gave her a kiss on the cheek. "Everything is fine."

"It just feels…" She was going to say *wrong. Something is wrong and this isn't the happy reunion it's supposed to be.* She didn't want to believe her words, so she didn't say them out loud.

As if reading her mind, David cupped her chin in his hands, giving her a consoling look. "Everything is fine and is going to be fine. We have much to discuss that will hopefully make your feelings of unease go away, but for now, please know that you're in no danger here. We are here only to help you."

Chloe raised a suspicious eyebrow. "Help me, how?"

David nodded his head from side to side, contemplating his answer. "It has been too many years and we have a lot to talk about. I suspect we will all have a surprise or two to reveal along the

243

way, but for now go say hello to an old friend who has missed you as much as, I suspect, you have missed him."

All at once the tension left her body and comfort, warmth, and family surrounded her. She hugged Elias tightly and he did the same as he stroked the back of her hair.

After a few minutes, Chloe's embrace instantaneously slackened as all the blood rushed out of her body, the pit of her stomach dropped, and she took three steps back from Elias in trembling and terrified shock. She looked over the doctor's shoulders, trying to breathe and shuddering with every intake of air. She thought it must be a trick of her mind; what she was seeing was not real, but her logical and rational mind knew it was no apparition she was looking at. But how could it be?

She was hypnotized by the sparking, smiling emerald green eyes staring back at her. Then he bowed at the waist, tipped his invisible hat, and spoke a single word. "M'lady."

The room went black. It was the first time she had ever passed out.

Chapter 39

Chloe regained consciousness on one of the sofas, slowly opening her eyes and staring at the ceiling. She didn't care how long she had been out, didn't try to hide the fact that she was awake, and didn't have to ask herself where she was or what had happened; she clearly remembered.

She could sense herself being watched and knew that David, Dr. Michaelson, and Christopher were all seated around her, waiting for her to compose herself and sit up. She no longer felt overjoyed; the ominous stab between her shoulder blades had been replaced with curiosity and dread.

Chloe owed it to David to listen to what he had to say. The fact that her back-from-the-dead bridegroom was sitting next to her didn't help either. She took a deep breath and sat up, making herself as comfortable as she could, curled up in the corner of the sofa. She took another breath before forcing herself to look at Christopher sitting in the chair next to her and looking at her like he always had since the day they first met—a crooked grin and eyes that still seemed to be able to read her mind. Her stomach did an unexpected little flip, but she wrote that off as memories of the past coming back to the surface and the shock of finding out that he was not, in fact, dead.

"I asked Jack to leave so we could have privacy. Shall we start with the obvious question?" David asked, looking at Christopher.

When Chloe spoke, it was cold and deliberate—she refused to let any emotion get in the way and muddle up her thought process. "I think that would be best."

"The short story is that I found out about Matthew's plan to kill Christopher on your wedding day," David said. "We found out who he had chosen to cause the accident and got to him before he could carry out his order."

"Who caused the accident?"

David waved his hand like he was swatting a fly away. "He was nobody important until he tried to kill Mr. Crescent during a collection. Unfortunately for this particular gentleman, his gun misfired and Crescent wasn't alone when it happened. Instead of killing him, Matthew decided to use this man to his benefit. We found this man and directed him on how the accident would actually occur."

That's how he's here, living and breathing, sitting next to me, close enough to reach out and touch. Chloe had so many questions and she was trying desperately to organize her thoughts. She looked at Christopher, still having a hard time believing he was real. "And you?"

Christopher looked back at her with ache in his

eyes. "I've missed you."

"That's not what I meant," she said sharply.

"I gave him an anesthetic and put him to sleep," the doctor said. "The man who hit them was told where to hit the truck so that Christopher would be a little broken and bruised, but not in any serious danger. Because of the chaos with people trying to help and getting in the way, nobody noticed me giving him the injection. I put him to sleep and made sure to put him in the first ambulance to get there."

"Why?" she asked David. "Why didn't you stop the whole thing from happening?"

"Renee, you must understand. I couldn't stop it. For one thing, this man who caused the accident earned his death. For another, I couldn't let Matthew know that I had found out about his plan. Believe me when I tell you that I knew it would devastate you, but I couldn't stop it. Matthew has been very good for business and I needed him." He put up his hand before she could say anything. "It's selfish, I know. But I needed him and I never would have thought he would tell you the truth of what happened or his reasons. I never thought you would leave. I'm sure he didn't either."

"He honestly thought I'd stay after he did what he did and said what he said?"

David got up and made himself a drink. "Nobody is allowed to leave without permission. And you did stay. Granted, only for a few weeks, but you stayed. I am curious though. What finally made you decide to leave?"

She gave them a brief recount of what happened,

the whole time feeling like a knife was being plunged in her chest. "He had already destroyed and terrified me. I wouldn't have been able to stand anymore pain because of him. And when he was done hurting me, there is no doubt in my mind that he would kill me."

David raised his eyebrows at her. "He told you that?"

"Did you hear anything I just told you?" Chloe asked, exasperated.

David nodded in the doctor's direction. "Elias told me that Matthew took his anger out on the girls."

Chloe took a deep breath, remembering what Alice had told her about the aftermath of her disappearance. "I heard."

David sat back down and said, "I know about the girl who died after you left."

"Do you know what he did to Sasha?"

David's face turned to silent fury for a moment. "Jack told me."

"Then you also know about the ten other women he has murdered over the past eight years." Chloe did not say this as a question, but more like an accusation. "Why haven't you done anything about *that*?"

"Because of you," David stated like it was the most obvious answer.

"Me?" she asked, surprised.

"Matthew's ultimate goal is to overthrow me. He loves the power a little too much. The more power he has, the happier he is and believes himself better than anyone else. I have not done anything about this for many reasons." David gave an amused chuckle. "One of those reasons is that I am rather enjoying the game and I haven't lost yet, so I must be better at it than I thought. Another reason is that Matthew has been very good for business, and replacing him would set me back quite a bit. However, he has also instigated and followed through with many activities that have gone against my explicit instructions. Matthew believes himself to be invincible and immune to consequences. The penalties for some of his decisions will be his own ruination and I will be there to see it, if not make it happen myself." David held up a hand to stop Chloe from interrupting. "I know the reason Matthew is murdering these women is to get you back to Boston, which, I understand, you plan on doing. He has always wanted the ultimate power, and in his mind, the only way he can do that is to use you to get to me. Unfortunately, we both need you. He needs you to get to me and I need to you to finally stop him."

"You both need me." Chloe said the words as if she was debating whether or not to believe what David was telling her. "I don't understand why *you* would need me. You are the end all, be all of final decisions. If you want to stop my father and remove him from power, it could be done at the snap of your fingers. Hell, Crescent would probably do it for you."

David leaned forward, his eyes saying he agreed with her. "I need you, Renee, because when the time comes—if you are going back, that time will be soon—it's important that you are there. You are, after all, next in line."

Unlike other Families in organized crime, in David's Family, there were three ways to become the boss: whoever has permission to justifiably kill the current "king," the oldest child if the person in charge dies in a manner other than murder, or by stepping down and David appointing a successor. *David is going to kill my father*, she thought. *And when he does, he wants me to take over because I'm his daughter.*

"Renee…" David started.

"My name is Chloe," she snapped. "You make it sound like I would want to take his place, that I should be honored to step into his shoes. Granted, I would be much better at it than he ever was, but who's to say I even want it? Have you considered that? You've told me why you need me. Why does my father need me?"

"Since the day you were born I have always known how he has felt about you. While you were growing up, I did everything in my power to make him behave properly when it came to you. He played the role as well as he could, but he still resented the fact that he was forced to do it. He did it, in part, because he knows how I feel about you— how much I love you and cherish you. The bottom line is he would use you against me. He has already proven that he can hurt me by hurting you. I can only assume that once he has you back, he will not only continue to make your life miserable, but he will try to make every attempt worse than the one before. Once he believes he has me cornered to where I will agree to step down and appoint him in an effort to stop hurting you, he will have achieved his goal. He wants the power, but with his sense of self, he has no idea the harm he will cause. His only saving grace is that he's not dumb enough to try to kill me himself or ask someone else to do it for him."

"Because if someone else did it for him, he wouldn't succeed you." David nodded and Chloe continued trying not to show the impatience in her voice. "You're avoiding answering my question, David. *Why* does he need me? How can he hope to win his prize by using me against you?"

David took a drink and exchanged a confirming look with both Dr. Michaelson and Christopher. "Because you are my granddaughter."

Her face was twisted in confusion as she tried to process what she heard. "What was that?"

"You are my granddaughter. Matthew is not your biological father. My late son, Wyatt, is. *You* are the reason Matthew has not been removed from his post. *You* are the reason Matthew treads lightly around me." David let go a compassionate sigh. "You are, and have always been, the reason for many of the decisions the two of us make."

Chloe gave all three men a dumbfounded look, and their faces all told her the same thing: David was telling her the truth. Her shock was quickly being replaced by white-hot anger, and for the first time she could ever recall, she glared at David with abhorrence in her eyes and spoke with hardness in her voice. "Has my entire life been a lie?"

"I'm sorry, baby girl."

Chloe was angry enough to cry and she knew she

had to get out of the room. Slowly, she stood to leave and David put up a hand to stop her, which she swatted away. "I need a few minutes to think. I just found out that my entire life has been a lie, and, apparently, my sole purpose in life is to be a pawn for both you and my—"

She abruptly cut herself off and walked to the dining room where, maybe, it would give her some time to absorb the blows that were flying at her. She had calmed herself down to the point where she knew she had her emotions in check enough for her to think clearly, but the problem was she had too much to think about. The fact that her life had been nothing but a lie for the past twenty-eight years was irrelevant. The important thing was that her life over the past eight years had been her own and she wasn't about to give it up so that the two men she had loved since childhood could use her to pit themselves against each other.

She could hear quiet talking from the other room and didn't bother to try to eavesdrop. Whatever they were discussing, she would hear about it eventually. After a few minutes, she felt composed enough to go back and sat back down on the sofa. She had decided that no matter what else she was told, the wall she had built around herself would not crumble. She thought about when Nicholas had lost his ear. She didn't flinch, she didn't cower in terror, and she never had nightmares about it. If she could stomach that kind of brutality at ten years old, she could certainly deal with learning her entire life had been a lie.

Chapter 40

"When your mother first suspected she was pregnant, she came to me," Dr. Michaelson began. "She told me that she was apprehensive to tell Matthew about the pregnancy for many reasons, but mostly because she knew he didn't want any children. So, naturally, I tried to reassure her that everything would be fine. I had no idea Matthew was furious with Elise and swore he would have nothing to do with fatherhood. She probably would have been okay with his reaction to her pregnancy had it not been for the fact that the baby was fathered by somebody else. Because Matthew couldn't produce children of his own, there was no question that you did not belong to him. Matthew had apparently been spending a lot of time traveling for work and she was lonely. She told me that she and Wyatt began spending more and more time together when Matthew was out of town, and the affair inevitably happened. Don't misunderstand, that doesn't make what she did right or acceptable, but she made her choice and accepted responsibility for the consequences." Dr. Michaelson strongly emphasized his point.

"Was she in love with Wyatt?" Chloe asked.

"I don't know, but she did tell me that while she regretted what she had done, she never stopped loving your father and never would."

Chloe narrowed her eyes at the phrase "your father."

Dr. Michaelson gave her an apologetic look and continued. "Your mother died in childbirth, but she wouldn't have if I were a stronger person."

He could see Chloe come to the instant realization of the truth—he was responsible for her mother's death. "Matthew made it undeniably and painfully clear to me that neither you nor your mother were to survive the birth."

Chloe looked at him in absolute disbelief. "How could you do that? First do no harm. Ring a bell?"

"Because you lived, my wife died." There was no blame in his voice as he looked at Chloe with grief in his eyes that showed the years of guilt and horror he had been carrying with him all this time. "But first he tortured her until I made my choice: my wife, or you and your mother. Helen died in a fire. The official report was that she had drunk herself into a stupor and passed out, leaving candles burning as she slept. The unofficial report—the truth—was that she had been bloodied, bruised, and broken. She had been lain out on the bed while Matthew's men spread accelerant throughout the house and lit a dozen candles, tipping them over as they left the house, and burned her alive."

Chloe didn't think it was possible to feel

someone else's pain the way she was now. Her heart was aching. She couldn't fathom what her friend had gone through and the pain he had been enduring all these years because of her father and his absolute abhorrence of her mother and her. She wanted to be angry with Elias, wanted to hate him and resent him for the rest of her life for causing her mother's death. But, in his mind, he'd done the right thing, he'd saved an innocent life that he felt had the right to experience life, fully aware of the consequences of his decision.

"You..." Chloe couldn't bring herself to say it out loud. "Why?"

A tear slowly ran down the doctor's face. "How could I not? Helen wanted me to choose what I believed was right, which told me that she was willing to sacrifice herself if it meant saving another life. That's what kind of woman she was and I have to believe she understands and forgives me. After the funeral, I had no choice but to sell my practice and go to work for Matthew, where he repeatedly reminds me of the two reasons I wasn't with my wife when the house caught fire. One was because I could be used to his benefit, the other is to make me live with the consequences of my choices. He always has, and always will, blame me for forcing him to play father to you."

Chloe turned to David. "Is Wyatt dead because of my father as well?"

David's features softened as the memory of his son saddened him. "If I had tangible, undeniable proof that Matthew murdered my son—or ordered him murdered in Las Vegas—I would have no reservations whatsoever in doling out the consequences to him personally."

"And he has no idea that you are here with David?" Chloe asked Elias.

"He knows I'm with David, but he doesn't know where we are."

"How do you know?"

David chimed in. "If he did, I would know it. The doctor comes to Chicago at least once a year to see me and that's what Matthew believes now. When we found out where you were, the doctor was able to detain him for a few days so that we could try to get to you first."

"How did you find out where I was, Elias?"

Dr. Michaelson told her the story of how she had been located and how he had overheard the conversation in Matthew's office.

"Madeline?" Chloe asked, surprised. "Who does Madeline know in Louisiana?"

"She didn't say," Elias explained, "but she was adamant that her source was telling the truth."

"Do you know there is another one here with me, another with the tattoo?" Chloe asked David.

He nodded. "We heard, but don't know who she is."

"It's Alice." Chloe turned to Christopher, whose silence throughout the evening had been bothering her. Chloe saw out of the corner of her eye that David was about to say something, and she held up a finger to stop him as she addressed Christopher. "You've been quiet so far. Other than being alive, do you have anything to contribute to the plethora of weight being thrown on me this week? Was I just someone for you to use as leverage too?"

"I put Christopher to work in Boston," David said in Christopher's defense. "When Sasha asked me about leaving Boston and recommended that you take her place, my concern for your safety grew. Without telling Matthew my reasons, I put Christopher in Boston solely to keep an eye on you, make sure that Matthew didn't abuse his power or fail my expectations when it came to you and your new responsibilities." David smiled and glanced between Christopher and Chloe. "The fact that you two fell in love just happened to be a happy bonus."

Chloe had heard enough. She couldn't seem to pick an emotion, although disgust and anger were the easiest to feel at the moment. In a matter of hours, she had learned she was a bastard child who was supposed to be murdered instead of born, both her mother and biological father had been murdered, the man she had once desperately loved and mourned was alive, and the man behind it all was who she believed to be her father. And in the midst of it all, she had two things on her mind that she couldn't shake, and she had to deal with them sooner or later—she had to talk to Hunter and she had to find Alice.

"Renee," David said as she stood to leave. She shot him a dangerous look and he corrected himself. "I apologize. Chloe, I know this is a lot of information to take in, but it is past time that you learned the truth. It's also time that Matthew is stopped before the next one dead is you."

"In an effort to get to you," she clarified, and David nodded.

Chloe understood everything that had been said, and had to admit that while she wasn't prepared for what she'd heard, she was grateful that it was David who'd found her first. Her features softened as she sat back down and faced David.

"Are you going to kill him?"

"Once I have an undisputable reason to, yes."

Chloe wasn't surprised by his abrupt honesty and wasn't sure how to feel about David's plans. There was a large part of her that understood David's reasoning. "And you need my help?"

"Not as much as he needs you to get to me," David replied. "I need you to not let Matthew use you as he intends to. I don't care what happens to me, but if he decides he has no further use for you...well, let's just say that his consequences will be swift and severe. He didn't give a second thought to murdering your mother and father, and he wouldn't think twice about putting you in the ground either."

Chloe felt a chill run down her back at the truthfulness of David's words. "I know this is a redundant question, but I'm going to ask it anyway. I have heard stories that Wyatt was more of a partier and playboy than he was interested in running the business. Not that I'm trying to defend Matthew, but is it possible that he didn't have anything to do with Wyatt's death?"

"Anything is possible." David removed something from his coat pocket and held it in his fist. "Then one day, maybe a year or so after she left Boston, Sasha came to me. She was troubled and wouldn't tell me exactly what it was that was bothering her, but she did say the reason she couldn't tell me was because she was afraid of hurting you. Then she gave me this."

David leaned forward and placed the item in Chloe's hand. Her breath caught in her throat and her heart skipped a beat. Chloe held a small key, only about an inch and a half long, with three jagged teeth on one side. Not a key big enough for a big lock or a door, but a key just the right size for a small box. A box she had seen before. A box she had handled before. A small metal box that she wouldn't open until she knew it was the right time.

Chloe stared at the key as David continued. "She never told me what the key represents and she never told me what they key fits. All she told me was that you would have the answers."

Chloe looked at David from under her lashes, the weight of awareness of the key threatening to pull her arm to the floor. "I don't have *all* of the answers you're looking for, David."

"Does that key have anything to do with Wyatt's death?" David asked, hopeful.

"I don't know that answer, but I do know what the key fits. Sasha gave me the key to the hiding place of a small metal lockbox the night of my sixteenth birthday and asked me not to try to open it. She said if I was as smart as she knew I was, I would know when to open it."

"Did she tell you what is in the box?"

"Proof."

"Where is the box now?"

"Alabama," she stated. "I'll leave tomorrow. I can be there and back in one day."

David nodded in both satisfaction and gratitude. "You know what will happen if this box contains anything to do with my son's death."

The fact that she knew Matthew's death warrant was signed didn't bother her. "I'll be leaving for Boston after I return with the box."

Chapter 41

As the night went on, Chloe wasn't really interested in small talk and it bothered her that Christopher hardly said a word. When she left Jack's suite to go back to her room, he didn't try to approach her or say anything other than good night.

She was able to sleep for a few hours before checking out of the hotel and getting ready to drive back to Lafayette in the early morning hours. Her first priority was to get to Alice and the key. Second would be getting the box and delivering it to David. Lastly, she would try to find Hunter and talk to him, even if it meant saying goodbye for good.

It was still dark as she walked through the parking lot toward her car and was not surprised to see Dr. Michaelson waiting for her. She had a feeling somebody would be waiting for her, but she thought it would be Christopher. She approached the doctor with a tired smile and saw he had coffee in his hands.

"I had a feeling you would be sneaking out in the middle of the night," he said lightly, handing her a cup.

"Follow me to my car?" she asked in a tired voice. "You need to know that I'm not angry with you for the choice you made. If what I was told tonight was true, and I believe it was, it was the most difficult choice you have ever had to make."

Elias waited until Chloe put her bags in her car to answer. "How could you not be angry with me after what I've done and what I should have told you years ago?"

She needed to find a way to reassure him that she forgave him. "If I had known her and grown up with her, I might feel differently. I don't know if I could have made the same choice. You sacrificed everything for what you thought was right and I can only thank you for saving me. I cannot even begin to imagine the suffering he has put you through over the years."

"I was hoping he would kill me too." The doctor had a far-off look, like he was studying the world around him. "But after a few years, I was glad he didn't because I had the opportunity to be with you and try to reassure myself that I did the right thing after all. You never disappointed me, but you constantly surprised me."

Chloe gave him a sincere smile. "This may very well be over soon. It's time you forgive yourself, Elias."

He raised his eyebrows and gave a thin smile to say he would think about it, and softly hugged her. "Thank you," he said in choked words. "I don't deserve it, but thank you."

When the hug broke, she said, "I was told he is

sick."

"That's correct."

"What's wrong with him?"

"He's got what's called Long HQ Syndrome. It's a rare heart condition. He could have inherited it and been born with it, or he could have simply developed it as he got older. It's a delayed repolarization of the heart following a heartbeat that increases the risk of irregular heartbeats that originate from the ventricles, which could lead to palpitations, fainting, or even death. I've been giving him beta blockers to help blunt the surges of adrenaline that trigger episodes of arrhythmia, but it's no guarantee that it will work."

"What would cause a surge of adrenaline that might cause him to have an episode?"

"It could be anything from stress to a sudden loud noise taking him by surprise. There is actually a case study where a little girl died from her teacher yelling at her. That's why it's important he take his medication and try to avoid as much stress as he can."

"Then it would behoove him not to miss a dosage. Is David aware of the seriousness of his condition?"

Dr. Michaelson slowly nodded and smiled. "I will stop talking now and let you get done what you need to. I am flying back to Boston later this morning. I will be sure to act happily surprised to see you in a few days."

Both she and Elias turned to see Christopher walking toward them, Elias with an unsurprised smile on his face while Chloe's expression showed skepticism and distrust.

"I'm coming with you." Christopher's tone said he was not taking no for an answer and there was no use arguing with him. She gave a resigned sigh and waved toward the car, indicating that he should get in before she left without him. Christopher stood where he was for a moment as Chloe stared into his eyes with uncertainty of how she should feel at that exact moment.

Irritation, mixed with being commanded, momentarily got the best of her. "Unless you have developed teleportation powers over the past eight years, you need to get in the car if you're coming with me."

Christopher was amused by her reaction and it showed in the smile he gave her as he got in the passenger seat.

Chloe turned and gave Elias a strong hug and a kiss on the cheek. "Now it's time for you to forgive yourself. I'll see you in a few days."

"Be patient with him," Elias said, clearly talking about Christopher. "If you think the years have been hard on you, don't think for a second he doesn't have regrets. He punished himself for years. I suspect he still does."

Chloe nodded in understanding and got into the car, preparing herself for what was to come and feeling better about not being alone anymore.

Chapter 42

Alice pulled into her parking space across the street from the office building, hoping Chloe would be there and anxious to know if there were any answers to unresolved questions. Alice hadn't seen Chloe for almost two days and didn't have the first clue where she was. All she knew was that Chloe had promised to get more information for her, and all Alice could do was wait. Alice thought about never again having to live in fear. She thought about her boys, who wouldn't understand why their lives were being turned upside down, but she knew they would be strong enough to handle it, each in their own way.

Alice was so preoccupied with her thoughts of a possible future and planning her day that she never saw them coming. One second she was turning from her car to walk to her office building, and the next thing she knew she was waking up in the back of a limousine, slowly sitting up in the leather seat, confusion filling her head. As she batted her eyes open and they began to focus, she found herself staring into the hard, spiteful eyes of Matthew Parnell.

"Where is my daughter?" Matthew, sitting in the seat across from her, spoke severely with concentrated aggression in his expression. Crescent was sitting beside Matthew in his ever-stoic manner, silent and observant, always ready to pounce at the snap of Matthew's fingers. They were both still as intimidating as she had always known them to be, but this time there was a difference—in addition to their icy stares, there was also fury running through them both.

The partition that separated driver from passengers was raised and she wondered two things: who was driving and where they were going. Alice became immediately hysterical, uncontrollably shaking and tears free-falling down her face as she stared into Crescent's black, piercing eyes that warned her if she misbehaved, he would take the necessary steps to remedy her behavior. She tried to inhale deep breaths through her nose to compose herself, but was failing miserably.

"I know she's here and I know you two have been spending time together. Where is she?"

Alice tried to control the terror in her voice as she answered. "I don't know. Please, Matthew! I promise you, I don't know!"

Matthew narrowed his eyes at her, as if trying to decide if she was telling the truth. "When was the last time you saw her?"

Alice was trying to breath in between stifled sobs. "A…few…days…ago."

"When do you expect to see her again?"

"I don't know," Alice said, still shaking but otherwise gaining control of her thoughts. "I was hoping she would be back to work today but she makes her own schedule."

"I see." Matthew cocked his head and studied her for a few moments, watching as she tried to control her breathing through the intense fear, yet unable to stop the flow of tears streaming down her face. "I'm curious why you left me, Alice. I haven't had an opportunity to ask any of the other girls except Sasha, and I didn't like what she had to say."

There was no sense in lying. No matter what she said or did, she already knew she would not see tomorrow. Alice momentarily caught her breath and answered simply, "I felt like a prisoner."

"So you ran away like she did. I don't understand. I treated all of you better than anyone else ever could. I gave you food, shelter, and opportunities you would never have had otherwise. You traveled, you spent time with powerful and influential people, and you were paid extraordinarily well for your work. You were safe and always had my protection. I just don't understand why so many of you felt the need to leave."

Matthew's arrogance was enough to make Alice nauseous. She had no idea how to respond so she sat silently, the tears beginning to lessen and her breathing beginning to even. She looked out the window, watching the scenery go by, realizing they were on the interstate and heading east. The tears began to flow again as she thought of Charlie and Samuel, and everything she was going to miss as they grew up.

I won't get to say goodbye.

Matthew gave her a mixed look of anger and amusement. "You ran away from me. You humiliated and embarrassed me." Matthew leaned forward, his face inches away from Alice's terrified and slightly ashamed gaze. "You stole from me."

Alice turned her head to stare out the window, noting that they were approaching Baton Rouge, the limousine preparing to exit and continue on to places unknown to her. There was no point in pleading with him. Matthew would do what he would do and there was nothing she could do to stop it. "Renee took the money and gave it to us."

"So you used *my* money to get away from me." When Alice didn't answer, Matthew gave a quiet, disappointed sigh and turned to Crescent. "Go ahead."

Crescent retrieved a laptop computer from a bag next to him, opened the lid, punched a few keys, and handed it to Matthew.

"Today's technology always amazes me. There are so many things a person can accomplish just with a push of a button or the download of software. I like that it can make a person's life—my life—so much easier." He turned the computer screen for Alice to see. "What you're looking at is a live feed. Do you recognize the location?"

Matthew sat quietly, watching Alice with a cruel grin on his face as her eyes widened in horror, everything in her replaced by absolute knowledge, agonizing grief, and ultimate fear. Of course she recognized what she was looking at. The camera was in an elevated position and aimed at the recess yard of the boys' school. Children began running into the yard for their morning playtime. In Alice's mind, it was too early for morning recess; she had just dropped the boys off at school minutes ago. *How long have we been driving? Who is on the other end of this feed?* Instinctively she knew it was Tucker as she looked from the computer screen to Matthew with pleading eyes. "No! Please don't hurt them! They haven't done anything! Do whatever you want to me, but please, I'm begging you, don't hurt them!"

Matthew gave her a cruel stare. "Where is she?"

"I don't know!" Her gaze flickered between Crescent and Matthew, looking for any sign that would indicate her children would be left alone. She would say and do anything to save Charlie and Samuel, but would Matthew leave them alone today only to come back to them if Chloe wasn't where Alice said she might be?

"Think hard," Matthew said. "Mr. Crescent has a text message prepared for the person on the other side of this feed. All he has to do is press send."

"Boston!" Alice shouted, and Matthew raised his eyebrows in surprise and exchanged a minor glance with a similarly surprised Crescent. "She told me that she was going back to Boston!"

"When?"

Hysteria rose in Alice's voice. "She said in the next couple of days, but she could have already left. I haven't seen her."

"But you don't know for sure," Matthew stated.

The trembling that took Alice over grew so

strong her tensed muscles ached and she slowly shook her head, defeated. She knew there was nothing she could say to keep herself alive, but she had to do everything she could to save her boys.

He wouldn't, Alice thought. *He's only threatening Charlie and Samuel to find Chloe. Goddammit! I don't* know *where she is!*

"And what do you know about a key?"

Alice's gaze snapped between Crescent and Matthew, and she felt all the color drain from her face. The fact that Crescent hadn't said a word and had hardly moved was scaring her more than Matthew was, solely due to the fact that Crescent was in charge of the deadly text and literally had his finger on the button. Matthew waited five heartbeats, and when she didn't respond, his face hardened and he asked again.

Please forgive me, but I have to try to save my family. "Before she left, Renee gave me a key to a safe deposit box. There was a lock box inside, but I don't have a key to it. I don't know where the key is and I don't know what's in it. I took the box with me when I left Boston." Even though Alice had no idea what was in the lock box, she knew it was important enough to keep hidden. She knew Chloe would immediately go for the box once she found out Alice was missing and she needed to give Chloe a chance to get to the box before Matthew could. "It's in New Mexico and the key to the safe deposit box is in the glove box of my car."

Alice proceeded to tell Matthew the name of the bank she had used almost three years ago in Albuquerque. They key to the safe deposit box actually was in her car; she hadn't closed the account with the New Mexico bank just in case she decided to move the box back there one day. Her hope was that since he knew Chloe was going to Boston, Matthew would return and send someone else to Albuquerque to try to find the box. She was counting on the fact that once her body was discovered, just as all of the others had been, Reggie would know to get the boys and himself out of town as quickly as possible.

"Please, Matthew," Alice begged. "Please don't hurt my boys. I swear I told you everything I know."

Matthew raised an inquisitive eyebrow at her, while at the same time Crescent took his gun from his jacket pocket, attached a silencer to the barrel, and pointed it at her. Her eyes locked with Crescent's, cold and unforgiving, then moved to the computer screen, watching her boys on the playground. Charlie was throwing a football with one of his friends, and Samuel playing tag with a group of other kids, happy and having fun. She froze with terror, her breath labored, and all she could think of was saving her boys.

Alice forced herself to look at Matthew. "I swear, Matthew. That's all I know about where she might be and that's all I know about the key."

She flashed her eyes back to Crescent, waiting for the inevitable pull of the trigger, then back to the computer screen just as Samuel gained ground on a running friend, tagging him with the tip of his fingers. She knew morning recess lasted fifteen minutes, and thought if she kept talking long enough, her boys would be back inside before Tucker could pull the trigger.

"I was in the bathroom when you came to her room and told her why Christopher died. But I swear I have never told a soul what happened that night. She was devastated and terrified. That's why she left."

She could see Matthew wasn't prepared for her confession. "Is that everything?"

Alice looked from Crescent to the computer screen. "Why are you doing this? Please don't hurt them."

"I want Renee back and will do whatever it takes to meet that end," Matthew said in a cold voice. "And I think you're lying to me. I think you do know where she is. Do you know how it makes her feel every time she learns that another one of her friends has died because of her? I do. Unlike me, she actually has a conscience and empathy. She knows it's her fault they are dying, and as you apparently know, I told her that I would take every opportunity I could to make her suffer."

Alice suddenly felt a surge of confidence come over her. She knew she would soon be joining her dead friends and decided to take the opportunity to be bold. She sat up straight and defiantly looked at Matthew. "You're not wrong about how she feels every time she finds out someone died, but she won't go down without a fight and you know it. No matter how much power and charm and strength you think you have, she has more. She's stronger than you give her credit for. She will be the one to break you and make you hate yourself for ever underestimating her."

Matthew gave her a hard stare and an uncaring smile that suddenly turned foul. "Maybe she'll get to Boston faster when she finds out about you. After all, you two were the closest all those years ago and I know the loss of you would overwhelm her. The loss of a child would probably kill her." Matthew gave a slight nod to Crescent.

"No!" she screamed, and jumped up from her seat to reach the phone, forgetting about the gun Crescent had pointed at her. Matthew pushed Alice back in her seat as Crescent's thumb descended on the send button for the text. Once that was done, Crescent was hovering over Alice, his knees weighing down on her thighs to keep her legs from moving, one hand on her shoulder, the other hand pushing the gun to the side of her head as he forced her to watch the computer screen in agony.

"And," Matthew said calmly, "I'm sure the knowledge that she is responsible for the death of a child will get her back to me faster."

Suddenly the world was moving in slow motion for Alice as she had no choice but to watch, tears streaming down her face like a waterfall. She jerked under Crescent's weight when she heard the sound of a crack come from the speakers of the laptop. The next thing she knew she was watching as Samuel, laughing and having fun playing tag with his friends, stopped running and stood frozen in place for a few seconds before his legs buckled and he collapsed on the ground, a cloud of dirt billowing around him.

Matthew leaned in close to lock unapologetic

eyes with a mother in sudden and grieving disbelief, her body shaking so fiercely her anguish could easily be mistaken for a seizure.

Speaking in a sharp, clipped tone he whispered, "Not forgetting you have another son, I'm going to ask again. Where is my daughter?"

Chapter 43

Chloe sat on the bed in Alice's bedroom, defeated, as she met Christopher's eyes. "I don't know. I even took the covers off the light switches."

"You're sure it's here? She wouldn't have hidden it anywhere else? Her car, maybe? Or the office?"

Chloe lay back, palms covering her eyes as she let out a sigh. "No. It's here." She saw it as she moved her hands. Her forehead crinkled and she stared at the ceiling. A dark spot on the inside of the light cover in the shape of something that wouldn't normally be there. She let out a small laugh. "They key is in the light."

As soon as Christopher recovered the key from the light cover, they were on their way to retrieve the box. They barely spoke on the drive from New Orleans to Lafayette, until Chloe told herself that she should take Elias's advice and try not to let her emotions get the best of her. The drive to Alabama would be a long one, and they couldn't ignore each other the entire trip. The only sound filling the silence was music, and, thankfully, Chloe had plenty of music stored on her phone.

She couldn't help but think about Hunter, and with Christopher sitting next to her, she involuntarily began to compare the way she thought she felt about each of them. She wouldn't deny that seeing Christopher again confused her, but there was a part of her that also wanted to make sure he was real, hoping she was waking up from an agonizing eight-year dream.

To her surprise, she had fallen in love with Hunter in a matter of hours. Somehow, Hunter had shattered her armor, and the thought of never seeing him again crushed her. She tried, and was failing, to convince herself that she didn't have time to worry about Hunter; after all, now that he knew the truth about who she really was, why would he want anything to do with her? But he was taking up permanent residence in her thoughts and she just wasn't ready to let him go. No matter what happened to her once she returned to Boston, she would never forget him. She didn't want to.

"Stop that," she snapped.

Christopher smiled at her. "Stop what?"

"Staring at me," she replied, but he continued staring and smiling until she spoke again in a soft voice. "I have no idea what to say and your eerie silence is unnerving."

"I'm sorry." The remorse in his voice was sincere. "I know that probably doesn't mean much, but I am sorry. Seeing you again wasn't supposed to happen this way. Nothing went the way it was supposed to."

"Then tell me how it was supposed to go and I'll tell you how much 'I'm sorry' means."

When he didn't answer, she let herself get lost in the music, trying to relax, until she saw Christopher reach for her phone and she slapped his hand away.

Rubbing his hand and trying not to laugh, he said, "I just wanted to look at your playlist."

"Did you consider asking me? And stop staring at me."

Christopher couldn't hide his smile. "I haven't seen you in eight years. I'm going to look at you more than occasionally."

"Yeah, well, whose fault is that?"

"We missed you by two hours in Cleveland a few years back, and then about a year before that we heard you were in Washington, but all we could find out was you were there and gone. Nobody knew where. We were going to tell you. The plan was that after a month, David would have you come to Chicago and we would tell you everything. Then you were gone and the plans changed. I know that Matthew didn't expect you to take off, and for a while, Matthew was nervous when it came to David. You being David's granddaughter is the *only* reason Matthew still has his position and his life."

"Had I known this information," Chloe said with irritation, "I might not have left."

"Considering the circumstances, everyone involved, including your mother, knew it was best that Matthew played the role of your father and that you didn't know about it."

"Best for whom? Matthew? David? The Family? Me?"

"Yes."

"With me as leverage."

"When Elise and Wyatt died, David knew Matthew had something to do with their deaths, but you know David. He won't do anything until he has solid proof. Michaelson gave the proof for your mother's death but he wants the details of his son's death before he does anything. So David used whatever he had to in order to make sure you were protected. He knew how Matthew felt, so when Sasha asked to leave, David didn't have anyone to watch over you. He hired me and sent me to Boston."

"So you knew?"

"Not everything at first. I mean, I knew the reasons why I was there. I knew that Matthew wasn't your father and I knew David's version of how Matthew felt about you."

"Was it real? How you felt about me, I mean."

"I didn't plan on dating you, much less falling in love with you, but it happened and I have never regretted a single moment we had together. Even though your father didn't approve our being together, David did. When I went to David and told him how I felt, he knew I would love you and protect you. I still love you and I always will."

"I used to think it was all a dream and that I would wake up with you next to me," she confessed. "After getting over the shock of seeing you again, I thought my first instinct would be to run to you and make sure you were real. Now I just don't know how I feel."

"Jack told us that you met someone else," he

said, sounding disappointed, and let out a sigh. "I couldn't expect you to pine away for me forever. Especially since we didn't know how long it would take to find you. Does he feel the same about you?"

She focused on the road and scorned herself for bringing up the topic. "It's complicated."

"I bet," he said in agreement.

"You know what? You're supposed to be dead, so I built up this wall and keep myself guarded so that I never have to feel the pain I felt when you died. Then I meet someone who breaks through that wall, someone I think about a future with, and then you come back to life and throw a wrench into everything. I've lied to him, deceived him, and betrayed him all for the sake of protecting myself. So, yeah, it's complicated."

Christopher nodded. "Fair enough. So tell me about him. All Jack said about this guy—"

"Hunter," she interrupted.

"Hunter," he repeated, "is that he's an agent at the Bureau. Widowed, a good man, and completely distracted by you."

She smiled at the last part, then asked, "Did he tell you that Saffron was Hunter's wife?"

Christopher groaned. "Shit. Really?"

Chloe let out a long breath. "I just found out a couple days ago, so you can understand why Hunter went a little ballistic when he found out the truth about his wife."

"How'd you meet him?" Christopher asked.

She gave Christopher a brief recollection of her short time with Hunter, all the while not knowing she was smiling.

"Why didn't you think you would see him again?"

"I made it a point to keep my distance from others when it came to my personal life. I mean, it's not like I could tell the story of my life to anyone."

"And the other men you have dated? I mean, I'm assuming you have dated other men since you left."

"Dated? No."

Christopher raised curious eyebrows.

"Well, it's not like I became a nun after you died."

"And then you met Hunter."

Chloe let out a heavy sigh. "And then I met Hunter."

Chapter 44

Chloe was grateful they spent the rest of the drive talking and reminiscing, taking it slow and getting to know each other again. The subject of how they felt about each other, and how she felt about Hunter, wasn't brought up again. She told him as much as she was willing to about her life over the years, and he told about his time in Chicago with David. Christopher spent most of his time in charge of the collections, working out of David's offices, but if someone didn't come through on their debts, he had to enforce the consequences.

"Unlike Matthew, murder isn't the answer to everything."

"Did you ever kill for him?" When Chloe turned to look at Christopher, she clearly saw the shame on his face. "How did I never know?"

"I had to play the game. Doesn't mean I liked it. The first time I did it, I never told you because I knew how much it would hurt you. Before that, I was just the schmuck who had to clean up the mess. Tucker was the one who got his rocks off when it came to punishments."

"Unsurprising," she replied.

"So what happens when we get to the bank?" Christopher asked, changing the subject.

"I go inside and get the box."

"But how are you going to get the box? Doesn't the bank have identification rules and signature cards and stuff like that?"

"Alice took care of it," she said, trying to put him at ease. "It shouldn't be a problem."

"How can you be so sure?"

"Because," she said, "contrary to popular belief, anyone can be bought for the right price."

***

Within an hour, Chloe parked in front of the bank and turned off the car, taking in their surroundings for a few minutes. Well off of the highway and seeming to be engulfed with trees, Rockford was not only remote, it was one place Alice knew nobody would think of looking for the box. Still, in a population of less than five hundred, Chloe couldn't imagine staying longer than they had to.

"How did she find this place?" Christopher asked. "It's in the middle of nowhere."

"I don't know. She probably took a road trip and drove around until she found the right place. That's what I'd do."

"Are you sure this is the place?"

"I'm guessing this is the only bank in town," she said as she opened the car door.

"Wait," he said as he reached for her, resting his hand on her arm.

She thought his touch might ignite some kind of feeling she hadn't felt in a long time, but it didn't. The only thought that momentarily ran through her head at his touch was her wish that it was Hunter's touch.

"Are you afraid to stay in the car by yourself?" she asked jokingly. "Just sit back and take in the…" she paused trying to find the right word, "…nostalgia. Seems like this place is stuck in the sixties, although it's a small enough town that I wouldn't be surprised if we are being watched from behind closed shutters. I'm leaving the keys so you have air conditioning and music. *Do not* leave me here."

Christopher held up the index and middle fingers of his right hand. "Scout's honor. I won't go anywhere."

Chloe scoffed with amusement. "Like you were ever a Boy Scout."

They exchanged a quick smile as Chloe grabbed her purse and approached the front door of the bank.

***

Mr. Wilkins, the bank manager, was a handsome man of middle years and a little more than curious about the stranger standing before him. Chloe guessed that the last time a stranger came into the bank was when Alice had been there a few months ago. She knew that if she didn't cut his curiosity off at the knees, she would be there longer than she wanted to.

"How can I help you, Ms. Riggs?"

"A friend of mine was here a few months ago to obtain a safe deposit box. Number eighteen."

He raised a suspicious eyebrow. "I'm sorry. Box eighteen?"

Chloe held up the key. "Box eighteen."

"Do you have identification?" he asked suspiciously.

She could see she would have to revert to intimidation tactics with Mr. Wilkins just as she had done with others in the past. She got a flutter in the pit of her stomach because she knew she was good at it, and part of her enjoyed this game—after all, she had learned it from Matthew, a cold-hearted, malevolent man who enjoyed watching her make others twitch. "You will always get your way if you can remember this," he told her once. "Knowing how to read your opponent will determine whether or not you win or lose, and I am not raising a loser."

She cracked a small but caustic smile and leaned forward, almost whispering in his ear. "The key is in the light."

He jerked his head back and his eyes were wide with surprise. Chloe's tone was demanding and impatient, but she kept her body language calm enough so as not to arouse suspicion from anyone else in the bank. She raised her eyebrows to indicate she was waiting for an answer.

With a shaky voice Wilkins replied, "Please, follow me."

She followed him into a separate and secure room lined with safe deposit boxes and a long table in the middle. Mr. Wilkins inserted his key into one of the locks of box eighteen then silently indicated to Chloe to insert her key as well. They both turned their keys at the same time and the door opened. Wilkins pulled the medium-sized metal box out of the wall and placed it on the table. He then took another key and opened the box, revealing the lock box stored inside, and turned to leave.

"Please stay, Mr. Wilkins," Chloe said as she removed the lock box and inspected it carefully, Mr. Wilkins watching her in wonder the whole time. The box was exactly the same as it had always been and there was no evidence that anyone had tried to unlock it. Alice had taken great care with it. Satisfied, Chloe put the lock box in her purse and turned to Mr. Wilkins. She had demands, and like it or not, he would follow them.

"Has anyone else been here to try to claim this box?"

"No, ma'am."

She slightly narrowed her eyes at him to make him think she was deciding whether or not to believe him. "You may not be aware of this, Mr. Wilkins, but there are people who would have no reservations to cause considerable pain to get this box. I sincerely hope you are a fabulous liar, because *if* someone else comes looking for this box, you know nothing about it. You have never heard of anyone in possession of the box and you have no idea what you are being questioned for. There is a chance that you will experience pain you never thought possible if whomever you talk to doesn't believe you. I'm not telling you this because it will happen, I'm telling you this because it might. I wouldn't be too concerned about it, but I thought you should be warned either way. You have been paid well to watch over this box, but there will be no further payments now that I have it. There is no amount of money to protect you should someone be told that I have this box. I assume you understand what I'm saying."

Mr. Wilkins's eyes were wide with fear as he slowly nodded his head.

"Have a pleasant day, Mr. Wilkins."

Leaving Mr. Wilkins in a petrified stupor, Chloe walked out of the bank to go back to Louisiana, pack her bags, and meet her destiny.

Chapter 45

The crime scene in front of the courthouse was flooded with paramedics, fire trucks, and police trying to keep the crowd of people surrounding it out of the way. When Hunter approached, he saw a body covered by a dark blanket to keep the onlookers from seeing anything they shouldn't, and couldn't help but notice splashes of what could only be brain and blood surrounding the body. Even though it was almost full dark, the crowd of spectators was growing and the media was excited and arguing with police to try to get their stories.

Hunter and Judd had been given the details on the drive from New Orleans—a woman in her early thirties, most likely drunk or high, jumped off the roof of the courthouse, which was an equivalent of eight stories. Construction equipment from repairs to the building were how she got to the roof. Nobody saw her go up, but someone saw her come down and called 911. Unfortunately, the mystery caller either wasn't there anymore or was standing somewhere in the crowd, protecting their anonymity.

Hunter and Judd were called to the crime scene for one specific reason—the victim had a black rose tattoo on her back. When the paramedics lifted the blanket to reveal her face, Hunter couldn't give a positive identification, but from what Chloe had told him, and because of the tattoo, he knew exactly who she was.

Judd stepped away to talk to an officer in an attempt to get more information and give Hunter a little space. Hunter's gaze focused on the roof and the construction equipment, then back to the woman, and wondered if Chloe knew and where she was. She might have heard the sirens and noticed the commotion from her apartment since it was only a few blocks away, but knowing Chloe, she would ignore the drama because she would assume it wouldn't have any effect on her life. He decided that when he was done, he would go to her apartment and let her know. It was better she heard it from him than somebody else.

He turned and walked toward Judd and the police officer. "Who's that?"

The officer pointed in the direction of a man being questioned by another uniform, grief and torment written all over his face. "That's her husband. And the boy who was killed in the school yard this morning?" The officer pointed back to the body. "That's his mother. Maybe she threw herself off the building because she felt guilty for killing her kid."

"Collect evidence and photos," Hunter said with ice in his voice, "then we'll find out why."

Hunter went over to Reggie, who was sitting on the sidewalk. From what he understood from Chloe's description of him, Reggie was a strong man with the resolve of a brick wall—nothing would ever make him fall. A good man with a great sense of humor and a fierce protection of everything and everyone he loved. Now he sat with his head in his hands and his body limp with grief. Hunter motioned for the officers to leave, and as they did, Hunter sat next to him.

"She didn't do it," Hunter said quietly.

Reggie slowly raised his head and looked at Hunter in a daze. "Who are you?"

"Hunter Lawton. I'm an acquaintance of Chloe's."

Reggie nodded his head. "I know who you are."

"Your son, she didn't do it."

Reggie looked at Hunter with questions in his eyes.

"Alice told you about her past, right?"

"Yeah."

"I don't know for sure, and this is just between you and me, but my guess is that the past has come back to haunt her, and I'm so sorry to say your son got caught in the crossfire. She's not the only woman with the same tattoo who has been murdered; my wife had the same tattoo and was killed a few years ago. There is no way Alice would harm her children or throw herself off a building. There's no way."

"You think this Parnell guy is here?" Reggie asked. "You think he did this?"

"I do," Hunter said. "But I need to talk to Chloe.

I need more information."

"Are you going to talk to her as a friend or a cop? Because I get the feeling she'll only talk to the one who doesn't look like a threat to her."

"She came to see me in New Orleans a few days ago about protection for your family, which is going to be granted," Hunter said, still upset with himself that he didn't mention that fact to Chloe in all the distraction surrounding her confessions. "The more she told me about herself, the more betrayed and hurt I felt, and I'm still trying to process all the information, you know? But I have to talk to her because she is the only one who might be able to provide the answers *you* need right now."

Reggie looked off into the distance in contemplation. "I didn't know what to think when Alice told me who she used to be. But the more I listened, the more I realized that she lied and kept secrets because it was what she had to do to protect herself. She didn't do it to hurt me or the boys; she did it because she had to." Reggie faced Hunter. "She did the right thing and I knew that one day, when she was ready, she would tell me. Go talk to Chloe and find out what you need to so my son and wife can be buried in peace, so that my other son and I can have some peace."

"She's going back to Boston," Hunter said. "She said she was going to help me get evidence to put him away."

"She'll fail," Reggie said with certainty as Hunter gave him a questioning look. "She'll try, but then he'll probably kill her too. But I have a feeling she already knows that. No, she won't get any evidence for you. You'll have a corpse before you get any evidence."

From the look in Reggie's eyes, Hunter knew he was probably right. "Do you need anything?"

"He killed my boy and my wife. I want *his* corpse."

There was nothing else to say. All Hunter could do was nod in sad understanding and stand up to leave.

As Hunter turned, Reggie asked, "Do you love her?"

Hunter ran a hand through his hair and let out a deep sigh. "Yeah, I do."

"Then all you have to do is understand and accept, and hope he doesn't get to her before it's too late."

Chapter 46

Hunter went straight to Chloe's apartment from the crime scene. After ten minutes of waiting for her to acknowledge his unrelenting ringing of the security bell, he tracked down the landlord, who was willing to let him into the building after being reassured that his tenant wasn't a criminal.

When there was no answer to his knocking, he tried the door to find it was unlocked. Drawing his gun, he slowly and quietly opened the door and entered the apartment, immediately seeing the silhouette of someone in the living room. As he entered the room, he saw an older man with rimless glasses sitting on the couch, casually reading through the papers and files Chloe had left on the coffee table. Hunter guessed the man was in his mid-seventies and was surprised this stranger was comfortable enough in this place not to react to Hunter's entrance.

David looked up, casting a warm smile at him. Hunter froze in his tracks, immediately recognizing the man on the couch, gun still poised as he tried to discern what the smile actually meant.

"You must be Agent Lawton," David said casually.

"You're David Lundy," Hunter said as it all clicked into place. "You're the mystery boss Finley and Chloe didn't want us to know about. Parnell works for you."

David slowly rose from the couch, replacing the papers on the coffee table, and approached Hunter. "Now that we know each other, you can put that away. There is no danger here tonight. I'm simply waiting for my granddaughter to get home."

"Granddaughter?" *I'm so sick of surprises.* "What do you mean, granddaughter? Where is she?" Hunter's eyes scanned the apartment for any sign of Chloe.

"She'll be back soon."

A voice in the back of Hunter's mind kept telling him to relax, that there really was no danger here, but Chloe had not told him about David Lundy, much less the fact that he was her grandfather.

"Are you Parnell's father?"

David smiled at the assumption. "No. Please, Agent Lawton, you can put the gun away."

Holstering his gun, Hunter asked, "How did you get in here?"

David took the key out of his pocket and held it up for Hunter's inspection. Hunter remained suspicious as he moved into the living room, taking a seat across from David.

"Please call me David."

"Chloe didn't mention you were in town. In fact, she didn't mention you at all."

"I just got in a few days ago," David replied, ignoring Hunter's second statement. "I haven't seen her in years."

"Eight?" Hunter asked, already knowing the answer.

David nodded, a look of remembrance on his face. "To be exact. Sadly, she didn't tell anyone when she left Boston. She was misguidedly devoted to her father from the time she was born, although, to be honest, at times I couldn't figure out why."

"You knew what she did?" Hunter was surprised that a grandfather who obviously adored his granddaughter would condone the work her father had done and allow her to start following in his footsteps.

"Of course I knew," David said as if the answer was obvious. "I insisted she do the job. Renee—I mean, Chloe—was a stubborn girl, and fierce in proving to everyone she was going to do what she wanted and was going to do it her way. She and her father had their battles, but she more often than not got what she wanted if for one simple reason. She knows how to play the game better than Matthew. She learned at a young age and Matthew is too foolish to realize he's the one who taught her."

The more David spoke, the more Hunter's intrigue was piqued. "How do you mean?"

"She studies people. She has this instinct for being able to read people and find both their strengths and weaknesses that she can lock away for future use. She knows how to diffuse a hostile situation faster and with more efficiency than Matthew could ever conceive of doing. If Matthew felt betrayed, he would send Mr. Crescent to deal with it; if she felt betrayed, she would deal with it herself. Not so much with force, but with words and intimidation." David let go a small sigh of amusement. "She was very good at it, and, I'm guessing, still is."

Hunter shared David's smile as he thought back to the first night they spent together in the restaurant and the brief, but effective, way she dealt with the manager wanting to take their table. "You're not wrong about that."

They sat in silence a few minutes, studying each other. It was Hunter's nature to be suspicious, but he found that he was comfortable with David despite the fact that he was a reputable mob boss in Chicago. He had questions, but part of him wanted Chloe with him when he got the answers. The other part of him thought taking advantage of the situation wouldn't be a bad idea.

"Do you usually come to see her this late at night?" David asked.

"Uh, no," Hunter replied. "I came over tonight because I need to talk to her about something that can't wait."

"From the look on your face I would guess that whatever you have to say is something she's not going to like."

"No, she's not." Hunter was supposed to protect this friend of Chloe's and he'd failed. "A woman by the name of Allison Morris was killed tonight. You might know her as Alice Jenkins."

Hunter saw recognition on David's face. "Yes. The two of them were very close when Renee was growing up. You'll have to pardon me, Mr. Lawton. It will take me some time to get used to saying her new name. She's going to be devastated."

"That's not the worst of it," Hunter said. "Alice's son was murdered this morning as well; a six-year-old boy."

David's head snapped up with hard curiosity in his eyes. It was obvious he wanted more information, so Hunter told him every detail he knew about both murders and his unconfirmed suspicion that Matthew had something to do with it. When he was done, there was no other way to describe David's reaction than pure rage, and Hunter instinctively knew David was trying to suppress it. He also knew that David didn't think Matthew was behind it, he knew it. Hunter watched David walk over to the window, back straight, shoulders tense, breathing even, knowing he was looking at nothing in particular while trying to keep his anger inside.

He murdered a child to hurt her just so she'll go back, Hunter thought to himself. *Why do I get the feeling he has no idea the consequences he will suffer?*

David turned to Hunter, his face somber. "My granddaughter has had her heart broken too many times during her lifetime. She's always been strong-willed when it comes to quashing her emotions. She was raised with the understanding that emotions were a problem and showed weakness. She was raised to always be logical and rational. If emotions needed to be vented, it would be done in privacy where no one could be a witness. I tell you this because what you have to tell her will shatter her. If you love her—and I believe you do—after you tell her, be there for her. Without saying a word, I know she feels the same for you and I think you may be the only person she will show her true self to."

Hunter doubted that. "You mean since Christopher?"

"I mean ever," David said, giving Hunter a poignant look. David let Hunter absorb that for a few heartbeats before clapping his hands and rubbing them together with a smile on his face, all anger seemingly forgotten. "Now, why don't you and I play question and answer while we wait?"

Chapter 47

Christopher parked in front of Chloe's apartment building and turned to her with the intention of waking her up, but instead watched her sleep for a few minutes. He wanted to reach out and stroke her hair, caress her face, and let her know how much he would always love her. He watched the slow rise and fall of her chest and listened to her soft breathing and knew she was finally sleeping after who knew how many nights of futile attempts to sleep through the night.

He always found peace he didn't know existed when he watched her sleep. Coincidentally, the first time he watched her sleep was the first night he had taken a life. He did what was expected of him, and he did it without fail, when a foreman at the Port of Boston had been shorting the count of containers that came in each week by five each shipment, taking the contents and selling them to another Family from New Jersey. Each shorted container cost Matthew thousands of dollars, and even though Matthew paid well, the foreman apparently felt that

New Jersey paid him better. Cornering the man behind a building, Tucker pushed the barrel of his pistol into the man's forehead while Christopher wrapped an electrical cord around his neck and held it there until the man stopped breathing. Afterward, Christopher appointed another dockworker as foreman, making the replacement prove his silence and loyalty by dropping a container on top of the body, thereby explaining his death as the fault of a malfunctioning crane.

After the unfortunate incident, riddled with remorse and self-loathing, Christopher went to her that night. Even though she didn't know what happened, she held him and comforted him with no words. He felt like a lost soul looking for his way home. She felt no pity for him, just the overwhelming need to make his pain go away. He kissed her with a passion she never thought possible and carried her to her bed, making love to her for the first time, softly caressing her body and making her flesh prickle from head to toe. He showed her what it meant to be enveloped in complete euphoria, taught her how to touch him to the brink of uncontrollable pleasure until his hand found its way between her legs, feeling the heat coming off her, begging him to take her as his fingers massaged, while at the same time his mouth enveloping her breast and listening to her moans of pleasure and her begging him not to stop. He felt her muscles contract around his fingers as her body shuddered with a spasm of pleasure and he buried himself inside her, moving her with his rhythm until his last powerful thrust when his world seemed to stop and explode at the same time.

Afterward, he wrapped her in his arms while they softly spoke to each other in the dark, each of their hands caressing and exploring each other for as long as they could keep their eyes open. Eventually, Renee had fallen asleep and he watched her, wishing he could feel as innocent as she looked at that moment.

He couldn't stop himself when he began to gently stroke her hair and whispered, "Hey, we're here."

She took a minute to wake up, stretching as best she could in the cramped quarters. He felt an urge he didn't want to control. He had never stopped loving her and never thought he'd see her again. He missed her with an ache he could never quite define. As she began to sit up, Christopher leaned forward and gently kissed her. He had taken her by surprise, but then she kissed him back and every nerve in his body began to tingle and both of their breathing deepened as the ache of the kiss began to take over. Sadly, it only lasted a minute.

She forcefully pushed him away with shame on her face. "I can't do this, Christopher."

It was at that moment Christopher understood he would never have her again as anything but a friend, and he could swear he felt a crack in his heart as he pulled away from Chloe. "He has no idea how lucky he is."

She lifted her hand and lightly caressed his face, apology in her eyes. "I love him."

"And what happens if you can't have him? Are you willing to put yourself through that pain all over again?"

"That's not fair. The pain I have gone through for the past eight years wasn't my fault. If it turns out that Hunter and I can't ever be together, then the fault is my own and I'll deserve the consequences that go with it, but I'd rather try and fail than run and never know."

Christopher nodded in painful understanding. He was jealous of a man he'd never even met and realized that she was right. He opened the car door. "Grab the box. David's waiting for us."

***

Chloe's jaw almost hit the floor when she walked into her apartment and saw Hunter and David in the living room, laughing heartily over who knew what. Both turned to her, stifling their laughter. She stood in silence, waiting for some kind of explanation, but knew she wouldn't get one. While David's eyes went directly to the box in her hands, Chloe knew exactly who Hunter was looking at with utter disbelief in his eyes.

Chloe brushed off her surprise and approached David, handing him the box. When a grunt of shock escaped Hunter's chest, David turned to him. "I was going to tell you but thought it best for you to see for yourself."

Christopher approached Hunter with his hand extended. Hunter looked between Chloe and Christopher in disbelief and stared at Christopher's hand, deciding against shaking it. "What the hell?"

"It's a long story," David said, "and we'll get to

the explanation in a little while. Until then, we have some things to take care of."

"Excuse me?" Hunter asked.

Chloe slowly approached Hunter, not knowing what kind of reaction to expect. "Hunter, I can explain."

"What the hell is going on, Chloe? Am I finally going to get the truth? All of it?"

"It's not her fault," David interjected. "She just got the explanation herself in the past forty-eight hours. If you would be willing to give us a few minutes, you'll get your explanation as well."

Hunter had no choice; he was going to have to wait. He sat back down and suspiciously watched Christopher take a seat next to David. Chloe didn't know what to do so she stayed where she was as David set the box on the coffee table and took the key out of his pocket.

"What's in the box?" Hunter asked curiously.

"That's what we're about to find out," David said as he opened the lock box to remove a disc. David and Christopher shared a questioning look and all Hunter could do was stare at Christopher, looking like he was trying to burn a hole right through him.

"So," David said, looking around the living room, "we need something to play this on."

"There's a player in the bedroom," Christopher said, and Hunter's head snapped up, glaring at him in concentrated aggression.

David looked at Hunter. "You deserve an explanation, but for now it will be the abridged version." David turned to Chloe. "Do you trust this man?"

Without a second thought, Chloe answered, "Implicitly."

Chloe knew what Hunter was being told was in confidence, and while he could use this information against Matthew and his associates, he couldn't tell anybody where the information came from. Hunter listened to David with intense concentration, every once in a while glancing in Chloe's direction for verification. When David was done with his story, he gave Hunter a few precious minutes to process the information he had just received. The abridged version turned out to be more information than he thought.

All Hunter could do was shake his head. "Unbelievable." He looked at Christopher, speaking in a hard, flat, distrustful tone. "And you?"

Christopher let out a heavy sign and spread his hands apart in resignation. "She loves you."

Chloe shifted uncomfortably in her chair, restraining the rainbow of emotions, preparing herself for the hurt, afraid to meet Hunter's gaze. When she finally was able to look him in the eye, he gave her a soft smile to let her know he wasn't going anywhere anytime soon.

"Now," David said, holding up the disc. "I understand we can watch this in your bedroom."

Chloe nodded and David went into the bedroom with Christopher behind him. Chloe stood and turned to Hunter. "Are you coming?"

"Why was he in your bedroom?"

"We stopped here this morning so I could shower and change clothes before driving up to

Alabama. He apparently took it upon himself to look around while I was in the shower."

She took his hand and led him into the bedroom, stopping in their tracks at the murderous rage on David's face as they watched what Sasha died to protect.

***

Hunter's mind still couldn't process what he had seen on that video and the way the others all reacted to it, like it was behavior that was expected and unsurprising. They had watched the video four times, all in stunned silence, before David and Christopher left the apartment with the promise to see Chloe again in a few days.

"What happens now?" Hunter asked as he watched Chloe pack her bags.

"Now, I go to Boston."

Hunter took hold of Chloe's hands and tightly wrapped them in his own. He wasn't sure how to tell her, but he had no other choice than the truth. The look of uncertainty she gave him almost broke his heart. "I need to talk to you. Sit down."

She looked at him with curiosity while Hunter moved her bags off the bed and sat beside her. "I know that look, Hunter."

He took a breath to steady himself. "Have you watched or listened to the news at all today?"

"No, I was on the road," she said, understanding instantly dawning on her. "Another one?"

Hunter's voice was steady as he remembered David's advice. *"What you have to tell her will shatter her. If you love her—and I believe you do—after you tell her, be there for her."* Unless she threw him out, he wasn't going anywhere. "Two, actually. Alice…" Chloe gasped in disbelief, shock gripping her, her muscles tightening, her breathing ragged. Hunter grasped her hands tighter. "…and her son, Samuel."

Dumbstruck, Chloe stared at Hunter. "I don't understand."

But he knew that she did. Hunter knew they were thinking the same thing. If David was in Louisiana, it was possible Matthew could be here too.

"How?"

Hunter closed his eyes, trying to find the strength to tell her. *Direct, to the point, and every detail.* He told her the facts as he knew them, all the while Chloe stared at the wall in shock, occasionally nodding her head and knowing the more she heard, the more Matthew was behind it.

"Reggie and Charlie," she said softly. "I have to go…"

"That's not a good idea. They're not in a good place right now. You should wait."

"I don't have time to wait! This is my fault. I have to go talk to them."

Hunter wrapped his arms tightly around Chloe and held her to him, her head resting on his chest. "Later. Right now, you need to take care of you."

"It's my fault," she repeated. "All of it. Every single one of the women who has been killed. Samuel. Everything is my fault."

He began to stroke her hair the same way Christopher had in the car. She violently pulled away and stood before him in anger, her hands shaking at her side. He could see the revenge burning in her eyes and stood to face her, his hands gripping her shoulders to keep her from running out the door. He knew exactly what she was thinking.

"Chloe, you have had a bitch of a week. You have been slammed with your past suddenly charging back into your life and you have been running on little to no sleep for days. Everything you are feeling is justified, but if you run off right now and try to find him somewhere in the city, he will win because you aren't in the right state of mind. And none of this is your fault. It's his."

The involuntary shaking began to ascend in every muscle in her body and Hunter knew no matter how hard she tried, she was about to crack. He sat her back down on the bed and gently held her face in his hands, watching as her eyes glistened with tears and waiting for the inevitable.

"It's okay," he told her, "I'm not going anywhere."

Chloe could barely speak. "He was only six years old."

A single tear managed to escape her grasp and she had no choice but to give in. She fell into Hunter's arms and sobbed until she couldn't cry anymore.

***

As the sun was coming up, Hunter stood in the bedroom doorway with a cup of coffee in hand, watching Chloe sleep. He could tell it wasn't a restful sleep, but it was much needed sleep just the same. Chloe had let go and exposed her vulnerability to Hunter, a part of her that she had never shared with anybody else, and he knew, without a doubt, that included Christopher. As Chloe slowly stirred awake, Hunter crawled into bed with her, wrapping his arms around her and pulling her close. She tightly pressed her body against his.

"You stayed."

He kissed the back of her head. "I told you I would."

"I dreamed about Matthew. I confronted him and he laughed at me. I can't be scared when I face him again."

"What are you going to do?"

She let out a heavy sigh. "I don't know. Even if I did, you carry a badge and a gun. I wouldn't be able to tell you anyway."

She's not a killer. He knew it deep in his gut. "You'll do what you have to do and you'll be strong and confident. You won't let him get the best of you."

"I made a promise to you, but I don't know if I will be able to keep it." She sounded ashamed.

Hunter squeezed her tighter. "Like I said, you'll do what you have to do. I just need you to remember that I'm here if you need me."

She rolled over to face him. He could see her fighting back tears again. "I don't want to—I can't—hurt you anymore or lie to you. Breaking my promise to you, it would be the same as lying."

"Chloe, you can't predict or control what is or

isn't going to happen when you see him. It wouldn't be lying if circumstances turn out differently than you hope they will."

"I kissed Christopher."

Hunter jerked his head back in surprise at both the confession and sudden change of subject, then realized he couldn't blame her. He couldn't deny that he would do the same thing if Amy suddenly came back to him. He leaned in and kissed her softly. "But my kisses are better, right?"

For the first time in what seemed like days, she smiled and said jokingly, "I'll let you know."

He kissed her again, this time to let her know he wanted to stay like this for as long as he could. She kissed him back, pulling herself closer to him as the kiss got longer and deeper. When the kiss broke, he rested his forehead against hers.

"Stay one more day," he pleaded.

"One more day," she said with both a smile and regret, "and then I have to go."

Chapter 48

Chloe woke the next morning warm, naked, and wrapped up in Hunter's arms with his legs entwining hers. She took a deep breath and felt, somehow, at peace. She had accepted everything that had been thrown at her over the past few days and knew what needed to be done. She didn't want to leave Hunter, but she accepted it and would never forget her time with him.

They had spent the day before getting to know each other as best as they could in the short time they had together. They talked and laughed, smiled and shared secrets. He would ask her questions and she would answer as truthfully as she could with no shame. She wanted to share as much of her life with him as possible so that he could try to understand the choices she made and the consequences that came with those choices. Neither one of them said it, but neither one of them expected her to come back from Boston.

They gave themselves completely to each other until exhaustion took them both. It was the first time since Christopher that she had given herself completely, mind, body, and soul, and she let him know it as she shuddered against him and held him tighter, thankful he was the one she had chosen to trust with her true self.

A few hours later, Hunter helped her load her car with what little possessions she had and followed her to the funeral home where Alice and Samuel were awaiting burial the following day. Samuel's casket open and Alice's closed, she studied the two, reminding herself that she would do everything she could to make sure Matthew would soon reap the consequences of *his* choices.

Chloe spent time with Reggie and Charlie, sharing stories about the Alice she once knew, stories they might never know otherwise. She made a promise to Reggie that he and Charlie would never have to hurt again at the hands of Matthew Parnell if things in Boston went as she hoped. She said one last silent goodbye to Alice and Samuel and left the funeral home without a glance back at the survivors.

Hunter walked her to her car, took her face in his hands, and kissed her solidly. This final kiss was enough to evoke memories of their passions, both good and bad, over the past weeks they had known each other.

"I love you," she whispered.

"I love you too. Don't ever forget that."

She left him on the sidewalk as she drove away from the safety of her new life and into the flames of despair that made up her old one.

Chapter 49

"Do you know if my father is here?" Chloe asked the valet, a twenty-something kid with tightly cut black hair and a sharp smile.

"Ma'am?"

Removing her sunglasses, she smiled, allowing herself to take on the behavior of her former self as the daughter of one of the most powerful men in Boston. It surprised her how easily it came back to her even though she had never really lost it. "Allow me to introduce myself. My name is Renee Parnell."

She thought the young man might pass out considering how quickly the blood seemed to drain from his face as he took in the sight of the woman before him. Her blue eyes glowered into his, almost offended that he didn't know who she was. He pulled it together rather quickly, taking the keys from her, and watched in awe as she walked toward the hotel, her back bearing the tattoo clearly confirming whom she was. As she rounded the corner, she turned her head and watched him leave her car where it was and run to the nearest phone.

She sat on the plush leather couch in the lobby of the Grand Hotel, deciding to give herself time to be seen. She surveyed the surroundings and found, aside from a few modern upgrades, nothing had really changed. The crystal chandeliers that lined the ceilings of the lobby, the second floor ballroom area, and the third floor conference rooms gleamed in the sunlight. The freshly waxed marble floors shown like glass, and the clicking of shoes made her think of her days when she worked the hotel operations from the offices behind the reception area. The flowers throughout the public areas, replaced with fresh arrangements every morning before the sun came up, filled the space with a soft and extremely pleasant aroma. She noted that he still used lilies and wondered if that was habit or an ulterior motive.

She knew she was being watched with curious eyes. She made eye contact with the concierge and cracked a smile at the corner of her mouth. The young man reached for the telephone, ultimately deciding not to make a call while she was watching him. She wasn't uncomfortable or afraid; however, the longer she sat there, the more she seethed for the pleasure of going toe to toe with Matthew.

She turned her eyes to the third floor balcony and exchanged a repulsive glare with Evan Crescent. The malicious smirk she gave him said she had no intention of moving until she was ready. She could almost see what he was thinking just from the distrust on his face and knew when Crescent got on the elevator a few moments later, he quickly and quietly informed Matthew that his daughter was home and waiting in the lobby.

***

Matthew was in his office with Crescent standing behind him. Chloe had disdain in her eyes as she approached him, stopping just a foot away. She flashed a hard and vengeful look at Crescent, then turned her attention back to Matthew, who warmly smiled and opened his arms to embrace her.

She gave a sharp shake of her head and said to him in a flat, contemptuous tone, "You are out of your mind if you think I'm going to run into your arms for a happy reunion."

Matthew's smile was gone in an instant as he dropped his arms and gazed at her from head to toe, finally meeting her detestable stare. Obviously, there was no point in trying to make this reconciliation cordial.

"Is that any way to greet your father?"

She studied him as well. He didn't look sick, but then again, Dr. Michaelson said Matthew had been doing everything he could not to let anyone know he had a heart condition. She decided to get down to business. "Let's just drop the pretense and get this reunion over with."

Matthew waved his arm toward the conference room. "After you."

"Without him," Chloe said, glaring at Crescent.

Crescent stayed where he was as Matthew followed Chloe into the conference room, closing the door behind him. Chloe took a seat and steeled herself, letting her inhibited anger motivate her. She

313

had many hours of driving to think about what she wanted to say and do, and she was determined not to let him get the best of her. She knew she had the advantage of knowing more than he wanted her to. All she had to do was make sure she didn't give that knowledge away.

"So," Matthew said, sitting across from her, "it's good to see you again."

"Cut the bullshit." Her breathing was even and her temper was in check. "Why am I here?"

He smirked in his self-righteous way. "You were homesick?"

Bastard, she thought, and instead said, "Hardly. You obviously want something from me. You've been leaving clues at morgues all over the country."

His smile disappeared and his hard, malicious face appeared. "You always did like getting straight to the point."

"Why have you been murdering all those women?"

"*I*," Matthew emphasized, "have not taken anyone's life."

"How very Catholic of you," Chloe said contemptuously. Matthew quickly tensed, scowling at Chloe with a burning hatred stronger than he had ever felt for her before. "You may not have pulled the trigger, but you ordered it and I want to know why."

"I wanted you home."

"You killed a six-year-old child."

"And here you are." He let out a satisfied breath and continued, raising his eyebrows in slight amusement. "If you recall, I told you, once upon a

314

time, that I would do everything in my power to hurt you. To make you suffer for ruining my life from the day you were conceived. Just because you were gone didn't mean I wouldn't follow through on my promise."

"When did you become so cruel? You put yourself above everybody else, you have no problem holding a gun to your daughter's head and threatening her life because children were never a part of your life plan, you have no compunction for handing out punishments to those you believe betrayed you even if they haven't, and everything you want in life you want for you."

"How I became who I am is none of your concern."

"It is my concern. I'm your daughter, and like it or not, what we do and who we are reflect on each other. The point is, *Father*," she said with disdain, "I don't ever want to become you."

"And what makes you think you'd ever be the person that I am?"

"Because," she raised an eyebrow at him, cocking her head with a semi-victorious grin, "you and I both know that, inevitably, one day your throne will be mine and I will rule the kingdom."

Matthew scowled. "I wouldn't be so quick to try to assume the throne if I were you."

"Then it's a good thing you're not me," Chloe replied as she turned and looked out the window, knowing he would be furious at the fact that she was purposely showing no interest in who he was or what he had to say.

Chloe didn't flinch as Matthew slammed his

hand on the table. "Look at me!"

She slowly turned her head toward him, regarding him as the shit on the bottom of her shoe, which only made him more uncompromising.

"Now that you're back, I have plans and nothing has changed. You are still, and will always be, a reminder of what I never wanted."

"These plans that you have, what would those be?"

"You'll find out soon enough. In the meantime, you'll do as you're told and behave as you should. Don't think for a minute that I won't be watching your every move. One step out of line and there will be consequences. I demand obedience from you."

She narrowed her eyes at him and leaned forward. "Actually, it won't be exactly like that at all. Here are *my* demands that you will agree to or I will do everything in *my* power to make you as miserable as you have made me, and don't think for one second that I don't have the ability or won't be willing to follow through with that promise. I'll play your game so far as going out in public and staying away from you as much as possible. However, if I'm going to be staying here for an indefinite amount of time, I will not be made to feel, or be treated like, a prisoner. You can try to continue to emotionally murder me, but there's a good chance a few of your plans will fall through if you do that. I will come and go as I please, and whether or not you want to have me babysat is your choice. If, at any time, I feel my life is being threatened or in danger, I'll be gone as quick as I was before. Count on it."

She sat back in her chair, an unreadable expression on her face as Matthew considered her words. "One more thing. I'll be taking my old job back; the girls and everything I had before with no restrictions."

"I have Patricia for that," Matthew replied. She could tell it was something he hadn't been prepared for.

"Not anymore. Find another use for her or get rid of her."

"And why would you think that I would do that?"

"As you said, nothing has changed with the exception that the girls you currently employ *will* live to see a full and happy life. They won't be afraid of death or punishment by hearing horror stories and watching the news. You will make sure to inform Mr. Crescent that I won't tolerate any mistreatment of them at any time, in any form. Should he decide to test my resolve once again, he will want to think twice. There will be no more deaths or pain inflicted on innocent—"

"Innocent?" Matthew raised his voice in anger. "Those other women stole from me, they betrayed me, and you gave them the means to do it. You encouraged them—"

"What about Sasha?"

Matthew abruptly stood, violently slamming his hands on the table. Chloe jerked back and her eyes widened in shock. "You know *nothing* of Sasha! She betrayed me in ways you will never understand! I gave her *everything*!" Matthew leaned forward, wagging his index finger at Chloe, speaking through clenched teeth. "*You* would do well to never speak of her again or Mr. Crescent will have the leisure of indulging any sadistic fantasy he wishes with whichever of your girls he chooses. And mark my words, you will be there to watch, if not participate in, every gruesome and ugly detail so that it will be burned into your memory for the rest of your days."

Chloe didn't know what to think as Matthew took a deep breath and slowly sat back down to pull himself together. There was a part of her that was frightened; she couldn't remember the last time she had seen him lose his temper, much less explode the way he just had. This outburst was the last thing she had expected and was utterly dumbfounded at his reaction at the mention of Sasha's name. And then the realization dawned on her. *He's getting worked up and doesn't want to have a heart attack in front of me, he knows about the video, and he was in love with Sasha.*

Matthew looked up at the ceiling and let out a deep breath, speaking calmly. "Fine. Your employment here is yours once more with all of the privileges and benefits previously bestowed upon you."

She would be able to go wherever she wanted and do whatever she wanted once again with one unspoken exception: she would be watched and her every move would be reported to her father. It was a risk she was willing to take if she was able to bring peace to Reggie and Charlie, and keep her promise to Hunter. She cocked a curious eyebrow at him. "And the murders? Will they stop?"

He gave her hard stare, certain and unmovable.

"That will be up to you, won't it?"

***

Much to Matthew's annoyance, and without stepping foot in the room she had once called her own, Chloe found an empty room two doors away from her old one and called that one home. She didn't trust Matthew and had to try to stay ahead of him. She was smarter than he was—a more logical thinker without his temper—and she had to do everything she could to use that knowledge to her advantage.

Within her first week back, she was getting increasingly frustrated because not one of the girls would speak to her about anything other than business, and when it came to Matthew, it was obvious they were terrified to even mention his name or say anything cross against him. She quickly realized that keeping her promise to Hunter was going to be more difficult than she hoped.

Chapter 50

Chloe used to sit in her room with her door open when clients were on the floor, but now she wandered the hall, briefly stopping at each door and listening for anything that sounded out of the ordinary or in need of immediate attention. The rules had changed over the years to the point that if the girls felt like they were in danger, or felt forced to do something they didn't want to do, they would have to deal with it themselves. Rarely did anybody have their back to protect the income these sexual fantasies brought in. Chloe had learned on her first day that the clientele requirement had changed. Now any regular Joe off the street was welcome as long as they could pay the price and keep their mouths shut.

Her frustration was beginning to get the best of her and she had to figure out a way to show the girls she was on their side even though she had to be a cold-hearted bitch every once in a while. Her opportunity came sooner than expected.

Chloe heard a door open and saw nineteen-year-old Violet Cummings standing at the doorway with one hand covering the left side of her face. Chloe watched as Violet's client, Mr. Myers, exited the room with a satisfied smile while straightening his jacket. When she met with Mr. Myers earlier in the evening to sign contracts and review the rules of engagement, her internal alarm told her his six-foot, broad shouldered stature might also have an ego worth worrying about. Unfortunately, she had been proven right.

Mr. Myers walked toward the elevators, ignoring Chloe as he passed. Chloe quickly scanned Violet and saw shame and pain on her face, and then she noticed a light trickle of blood running down Violet's right leg. The look in Chloe's eye changed to fury in seconds as she approached the man, calling his name as he stopped to wait for the elevator. As he turned to face Chloe, her fist met his face with all the strength she never knew she had, dazing him enough to make him lose his balance, bounce off the wall behind him, and fall to the floor. Violet watched in stunned amazement as Chloe stood over Mr. Myers, holding him to the floor with a foot on his chest.

"What the hell?" He was completely dumbfounded, trying to get off the floor, but the more he tried, the more weight Chloe put on his chest. She knew she couldn't hold him for long, but she could hold him long enough to make her point. While staring directly into his confused eyes, Chloe snapped her fingers to call Violet to her. Another door opened and quiet goodbyes between client and companion were abruptly cut off to watch the scene in front of them.

Violet cast an uneasy glance at the interested couple in the doorway as she nervously approached Chloe, unsure what to do.

"You did this to her?" Chloe asked Mr. Myers, who stopped struggling enough in an attempt to stare Chloe down. "I recommend you answer the question."

"So what if I did?" he answered defiantly.

Chloe glared at him with eyes that could burn a hole down to the lobby. "What part of 'by signing this agreement I will cause no harm to my companion, physically or otherwise, for the duration of my time allowed services' do you not understand, Mr. Myers?"

"Patricia never had a problem with it," he answered flatly.

Chloe lowered her face so close to his that he could probably smell what she had for dinner. She glared at him with dangerous eyes. "I'm not Patricia and it's a problem now."

"And what are *you* going to do about it? Get off me!"

"Firstly, you will apologize for your behavior." When he scoffed, Chloe took advantage of his vulnerable position and her knee met his groin, then she stood and allowed him the courtesy to stand up and collect himself, but not before shoving him against the wall. "Second, medical bills are expensive and you will pay for said bills before exiting this building." She grabbed his chin, forcing him to look her in the eye. "Lastly, you will not be coming back. Ever."

Mr. Myers cast a venomous eye at Violet. "All you're good for is ten minutes on your knees, and that's not even worth the money."

Just as the sound of another door opened and silent faces peered out to see what was going on, Chloe's fist connected with Mr. Myers's face again. Violet ran to one of the other girls who was holding onto her client's arms to keep them from trying to intercede in the confrontation. Chloe was too slow moving out of the way as Mr. Myers's fist connected with her jaw, but she was quick enough to catch herself and rake the heel of her shoe down his shin and put her fist in his groin as he bent over from the pain. He fell to his knees in pain and Chloe went to Violet, who had tears streaming down her face and was shaking in fear. Even though Chloe's rush of adrenaline helped some of her anger and frustration temporarily subside, she let out a soft sigh and put her hand on Violet's arm in an effort to let her know everything would be okay.

***

After Mr. Myers had been escorted off the floor and Dr. Michaelson had attended to Violet, Chloe sat in her room contemplating her options. Her thoughts were interrupted by a knock on the door, only to be further frustrated by the sight of Evan Crescent casually standing across the threshold, hands clasped behind his back and a look of indifference on his face. Chloe raised an irritated eyebrow at him.

"Am I interrupting?" Crescent asked.

"What do you want, Mr. Crescent?" She knew he wasn't there out of concern for her girls.

"Just simple curiosity. Why did you come back, Renee?"

The icy stare never left her face when she asked a question of her own. "How did it feel to murder a six-year-old boy, Evan?"

The corner of Crescent's mouth turned up in a smile. "I don't know. You'll have to ask Mr. Wilson. Good night." He bowed at her from the waist, turned, and walked away.

Chloe's chest began to tighten with anger and her breathing got deeper as one thought stirred in her mind: one way or another, Tucker Wilson would die.

Chapter 51

Madeline walked out of her Atlantic City casino and onto the boardwalk, intending to walk barefoot through the sand on such a beautiful day, when her phone rang.

"Good afternoon," she said cheerfully. "How are things in the South?"

"I feel terrible, Ms. Madeline," Willetta said on the other end. "We didn't think anybody was gonna die because of us."

Madeline gave a *tsk* before saying, "Don't you worry. It wasn't because of you. I promise."

"But a child…"

Madeline could hear the shaking in Willetta's voice and didn't really care. All she cared about was enjoying the peace of her day. Madeline tried for a sweet and consoling tone, but couldn't quite master it. "I know it's sad, but you can put your mind at ease knowing that nothing was your fault. In fact, you should be happy to hear that the friend went back home. She's safe with her father again."

"What about that man she been dating?"

Very interesting, Madeline thought, and it showed in the tone of her voice. "I don't know if he came with her or not, but I hope she's very happy with him. Do you have any idea who he is?"

"All I know is that he's from New Orleans. He come up here when Ms. Allison died and talked to people at work. He work for the FBI, he do."

Madeline couldn't contain the grin emerging on her face. "Really? Well, if he didn't come with her, then hopefully they can be together soon."

"But that don't change the fact that Bennie and I are still upset about those two dying. We sure do feel bad."

"Well, like I said, it wasn't either of your fault. Sometimes bad things just happen, but don't the two of you lose any sleep over it. Things happen for reasons that we aren't supposed to understand."

"Ain't that the truth."

***

Matthew sat at his usual table in the back of the hotel restaurant, quietly attempting to enjoy his dinner, while at the same time trying to come up with new and different ways to make his daughter's life just a little more unbearable every day. He didn't care about the altercation with Mr. Myers; she had handled it the way she should in addition to forcing him to pay for Violet's non-existent medical bills. Unfortunately, Mr. Myers still hadn't followed through with his promise to pay, so Matthew had sent Tucker to eliminate the debtor.

At the same time the waiter came to Matthew's

table to pour him another glass of wine, Matthew's posture stiffened and he gritted his teeth in annoyance as he heard a familiar flirtatious voice. "Matthew, it's so good to see you."

Taking a seat across from him, Madeline had a smile on her face and hunger in eyes. Matthew gave her a glare that showed he was clearly annoyed and had no interest in seeing her.

"You know, Madeline, you could call instead of dropping by."

She laughed. "As if you would take my call."

Matthew let go a resigned sigh. "How are things in Atlantic City?"

"How are things with Renee? Of course, with Patricia coming back to work for me, I heard all about her homecoming. It's too bad her boyfriend couldn't come with her. I'm sure she misses him terribly." Madeline's smile deepened at Matthew's stunned reaction. "I have to say, Matthew, that you surprise me. You should know by now that when I come to you, it's usually with information that is valuable to you."

"And what do you want in exchange for this information?" he asked.

"You know, I haven't decided yet," she gave her shoulders a happy shrug, "but I'm sure I will let you know."

Chapter 52

Chloe embraced David with the strength of a bear, listening to him repeatedly tell her how happy he was to see her again and how much he had missed her. Matthew impatiently stood against the wall of windows in the conference room, waiting for the reunion to come to an end. When David and Chloe broke their hug and took their seats, Matthew moved to his seat at the head of the table.

Beaming a smile, David turned to Matthew. "It's so good to have her back, isn't it, Matthew?" When Matthew didn't answer, David smiled and turned to Chloe. "You and I will go out to lunch and catch up."

"That would be lovely."

Matthew's scowl turned to indifference as David addressed him. "Now, let's get down to business. I would like to arrange a meeting with all of the underbosses of the Family. We will hold the meeting here, in Boston. There is business to discuss and announcements to be made."

This news was unexpected and Chloe could see

the wheels turning in Matthew's head. She also saw intrigue.

"Is there anything in particular you would like them to know about this meeting so they can prepare?" Matthew asked.

"Nothing that can't wait," David replied with the wave of his hand. To Chloe, he said, "You'll make the arrangements?"

"I would be happy to," Chloe said with a smile. "It's so good to see you, David. How have you been?"

"Better than I thought I would be at this age. Maybe I should retire." David let out a hearty laugh while Chloe watched Matthew's wheels spin faster.

"All I know for sure," David continued, "is that I'm getting older, I'm widowed six years now, my son is gone, and people I love are leaving me. Even Sasha. I haven't heard from her in months."

At the mention of Sasha, Matthew's body tensed and his eyes burned with hate, but Chloe ignored him.

"Really?" Chloe asked, a slight pang of loss for her friend kept to herself. "Did she finally meet a strange and mysterious man who swept her off her feet?"

"Ha!" David exclaimed, playing along. "I think it would be wonderful if she did; however, she went to California to see her sickly mother and I haven't heard from her."

"Speaking of strange and mysterious men," Matthew chimed in, "it has recently been brought to my attention that the Family has caught the government's eye. Specifically, the FBI."

Chloe's features didn't give away the surprise and fear she was actually feeling, which meant Matthew wasn't getting the reaction he wanted. She knew that no matter what she heard going forward, she had to react as if she wasn't already aware of the truth. David's reaction was exactly as expected when the Boss of the Lundy Family found out that the government was keeping tabs on him—inquiring, furious, and determined to shut any investigation down.

"What do you know?" David asked.

"There is an agent in New Orleans—two agents actually—who have taken an interest in our Family."

"Would their interest have anything at all to do with our former employees showing up on the news every other week?" Chloe asked.

Matthew shot a malicious look at Chloe then turned his attention back to David. "Jack called to let me know that a former associate by the name of Mack Finley was willing to turn against us in exchange for government protection. Because Finley was in his jurisdiction, and these two agents are subordinates of Jack's, he has been keeping an eye on the situation. I was informed that Mr. Finley was prepared to talk, then suddenly changed his mind, deciding to stay in jail instead of facing the consequences of speaking out against the Family. Mr. Finley went back to his cell, fell asleep, and never woke up."

David stated the obvious. "You have been in this business far too long not to consider the fact that if they are able to connect Finley to this Family, and the fact that he worked for you, you will become the target of their investigation."

"I'm not that naïve, David," Matthew said as he nodded in Chloe's direction, "but, on the other hand, it's possible they could suspect Renee."

Chloe's head snapped up. "Me?"

"You have the tattoo and you have recently been in Louisiana," Matthew stated. "If you were careless, it's possible someone has been watching you, which brings about a bigger problem. If they are watching you or looking for you, once you come out of hiding in Boston, they could easily find you and connect you to the Family. That would be a problem we would want to resolve *before* it becomes a reality."

Chloe and David exchanged a look that said they were both thinking the same thing—Matthew would use this as an excuse to either eliminate Chloe or use her to get David's position of power.

"What are you suggesting, Matthew?" David asked.

"Like I said, I talked to Jack and he and I are both in agreement that these two agents of his need to be quietly and quickly eliminated in order to prevent any kind of investigation against Renee, or the Family, from becoming a reality. I have already sent Tucker to New Orleans."

There was no way she could warn Hunter. Chloe tried to keep shock out of her voice. "He's already there?"

"If these two agents aren't stopped, they could ruin me and everything I have worked for in a matter of weeks," Matthew said sternly. The fact that he was talking only about his own ruination did not go unnoticed. "Tucker needs to be there on my behalf to make sure their death is imminent."

Reading between the lines, Chloe knew Matthew was more than worried. Her father had finally realized the enormity of the mistakes he had been making, all the while David had been sitting back and letting Matthew braid his own hanging rope. How he obtained Hunter and Judd's names wasn't important at the moment. What was important was that over the years, Matthew had ignored David's golden rule of staying out of the spotlight and not drawing attention to the Family through the media, and was now facing the possibility of irreparable consequences. Matthew's arrogance had finally gotten the best of him and he realized that he was not invincible. Even though he tried to justify and rationalize placing the focus of the blame on Finley or Chloe, he knew all evidence would lead back to him if Hunter and Judd weren't killed first.

Finally, David gave a curt nod. "You'll keep me posted, I assume?"

"Of course," Matthew said. Then to Chloe said, "In the meantime, we have a meeting to set up. I'll leave the details to you."

Chapter 53

Jack sat in the car across the street from Ma and Pop's Java, with Tucker in the passenger seat, watching Hunter, Judd, and Dennis at their table, apparently engrossed in a serious discussion. Accompanying Jack and Tucker were four of Jack's associates and two of his captains, strategically located around the coffee shop to ensure their targets wouldn't be missed. Jack was careful in his planning, knowing that the morning's events would be a public event and had given specific instructions to make sure there were no unnecessary losses.

Tucker turned to Jack with an impatient look. "How much longer do we have to wait? He's right there."

"What's the rush? You got a hot date?"

"I don't like waiting."

"Waiting is part of the game. We don't spend time planning for no reason. We have to be precise and get it done right the first time. You've been with Parnell long enough to know that."

Tucker let out an exasperated sigh. "Yeah, well,

Mr. Parnell gave me exact instructions for the boyfriend and I'm not going to fuck it up."

"What were his instructions?"

Tucker stared out the window, ignoring Jack's question. Jack dealt Tucker a slap to the side of his head with so much force that Tucker's forehead hit the window. As Tucker tried to rub the pain off his scalp, his irritation turned to confused panic as Jack pressed the barrel of his gun under Tucker's jaw.

"I asked you a question, boy, and I expect an answer, or my first bullet of the day will exit the back of your skull. What were his instructions?"

"He wants his heart!" Tucker cried out, and Jack's eyes widened in disbelief. "He wants to give it to his daughter so she'll know he will make sure nobody will ever be able to love her as long as he draws breath! That's what he told me, word for word! I swear!"

Jack slowly drew his gun back and sat back in his seat, contemplating. David had told him how Matthew felt about Renee, and knew that Matthew was an asshole, but never would have imagined he could be so sadistic.

***

Hunter was cornered by Mrs. Davidson and grateful that Dennis decided to save him. She was still hell-bent on finding him the perfect woman even though he had already told her he met somebody else.

"I won't believe you until I meet her," Mrs. Davidson told him.

Thankful for the rescue, Hunter cordially said goodbye to Mrs. Davidson and joined his friends at the table in front of the window facing the street. Hunter opened a file and started scanning the documents inside.

"All this is new?" Hunter asked.

"Everything I could find last night," Judd said. "Unfortunately, there isn't much more than there was a few days ago."

Hunter thought about telling Dennis and Judd about the recorded confession regarding the murder of Wyatt Lundy all those years ago, but he had promised David and Chloe that he wouldn't pursue it. Hunter had to respect the fact that David had the right to deal with Matthew concerning the death of his son and the father of his granddaughter.

Hunter went back to focusing on the papers in front of him and, finding nothing new, tossed them on the table in frustration. "She talked about these two guys, Crescent and Tucker. Have you been able to find *anything* on either of them?"

"If I could, you would have it in front of you, man," Judd said, then took a bite of his pastry. "So far, the only one I can find anything on is the doctor, and even that isn't much. It's like the second he retired, he fell off the map."

Surprised when they saw who entered the shop, the three men turned to watch as Jack walked in, greeted them with a wave of his hand, and went to the counter to order a coffee.

"What the hell is he doing here?" Judd asked.

"Good question. I'll be right back," Hunter told the others, and then joined Jack at the counter.

"I understand you met Mr. Lundy." That was all Jack had to say to let Hunter know he knew what was going on.

"I got quite the education. Are you here to tell me more secrets?"

"Have you told them?" Jack asked, indicating Judd and Dennis, who had turned their attention back to the work in front of them.

"No. They know what they know, but the fewer people who know, the better."

Jack took a photo out of his jacket and handed it to Hunter. "Do you know who this man is?"

It was a man in his mid-thirties, with broad shoulders and sandy blond hair, standing on a sidewalk outside of a restaurant, looking to be waiting for somebody or something. Just from the look in the man's eyes, Hunter instinctively knew everything about this man was dangerous, but he didn't know who he was.

"Did Chloe ever mention a man who works for Parnell by the name of Tucker Wilson?"

Every muscle in Hunter's body seemed to atrophy as he remembered everything Chloe had told him.

"I see you've heard of him," Jack observed.

"This is him?" Hunter asked.

Jack nodded. "It is. He's sitting outside in the black SUV waiting for you and Fowler. Parnell has issued a contract on you both. Sanctioned, of course."

Hunter tried to maintain a casual demeanor, but to say he was speechless with disbelief was an understatement. Hunter had too many questions running through his head and knew with this revelation time wasn't a luxury for getting answers. Giving Jack a skeptical look, Hunter asked, "Why are you here, Jack?"

Finally getting his order, Jack took a drink of his coffee. "I will explain only what I can as quickly as I can. There is a schedule in place, and if we are to make Matthew believe his orders have been followed, it is my job to get the two of you outside. Make no mistake, I *will* get you outside if I have to drag you both out by your balls."

***

Hunter had no choice. He had to get Judd outside without telling them what he knew and hope that following Jack's orders would succeed. Once Jack left, Hunter squared his shoulders and mentally prepared himself for what was coming.

"We should get back," Hunter said to Judd and Dennis.

"I need to hit the head," Dennis said. "I'll meet you at the car in a few minutes."

Take as long as you want, Hunter thought as Dennis excused himself and Judd gathered the clutter from the table.

Hunter and Judd exited the coffee shop and walked toward Judd's car. Hunter's eyes quickly scanned his immediate surroundings and, just as he was told, he saw Jack standing on the passenger side of the SUV talking to Tucker as he exited the vehicle. Hunter quickly assessed his options for the inevitable and realized he couldn't formulate a plan fast enough as a shot rang out and a bullet lodged itself in the grille of Judd's car. Traffic stopped and pedestrians scattered at the sound. As three more shots were fired from different directions, Hunter pushed Judd, who was completely caught off guard, behind the car, where they both drew their guns.

Judd was in his first fire fight and Hunter was confident he would be able to handle himself. He had no other choice than to trust Judd would do the right thing and hope for the best. Judd didn't let him down as he took cover and returned fire, even though Hunter wasn't completely sure if Jack's plan included them being able to hit anything they weren't supposed to. Hunter had to trust Jack knew what he was doing when he told him the plan.

Jack and Tucker broke their cover from behind the SUV long enough to fire shots in Hunter and Judd's direction. Both Judd and Hunter returned fire, but Tucker got off three shots; two missing his target and one going through the window of Ma and Pop's Java. The world seemed to move in slow motion as Hunter turned to look through the window just in time to watch as Mrs. Davidson fell into Dennis's arms with a gunshot through her neck. Infuriated and without any concern for his own wellbeing, and completely ignoring Jack's instructions, Hunter broke his cover and ran for the SUV.

"What the hell are you doing?" Judd yelled, but Hunter ignored him.

Hunter ran toward Tucker and Jack, firing every bullet he had in Tucker's direction as fast as he could. He crouched in front of the SUV and was able to take quick cover to reload his weapon. He caught a glimpse of one of Jack's associates standing on a corner the next block over, standing down, his gun at his side, and another of Jack's associates randomly firing his gun into the air. Hunter could only hope Tucker hadn't taken notice of these two men and figured out what Jack was up to.

The play of gunfire continued as Tucker turned back to get to his cover when Hunter rounded the SUV and pulled the trigger, firing four rounds before Tucker could think about getting another shot off, all rounds hitting their mark. It took about two seconds for Tucker to hit the ground with one bullet taking him in the forehead, one in his right eye, one in his right thigh, and one in his neck. Gunfire ceased and all Hunter could hear were sirens in the distance and his heart pounding in his ears. Both stunned and furious, Hunter watched Jack smile down at Tucker's corpse, then give Hunter a satisfied nod.

Hunter knew Jack's associates had quietly and discretely concealed their weapons and left their positions by now. Judd ran over to make sure Hunter and Jack were okay and, once convinced, ran back to the coffee shop to help Dennis try to control the panicked people hiding under tables.

Hunter looked toward the coffee shop, then back to Jack, shaking with anger. "Goddammit, Jack."

There was true remorse on Jack's face. "I'm sorry, Hunter."

Hunter spoke through clenched teeth. "She was a good, innocent woman. You tell your boss that I made the choice to play along with his game and did what I was told, but if he doesn't kill Matthew Parnell, then I will."

Jack spoke low and hard. "You do realize that the only reason you and your partner are still alive is because my boss ordered it, don't you? Matthew wants you dead, and it's only because of Mr. Lundy that you aren't. Trying to stare me down doesn't change anything, Agent Lawton. An innocent woman is dead because of Matthew Parnell and I can promise you that Mr. Lundy will not forget that fact or let it go unpunished."

With no other outlet for his mixture of sorrow and anger, Hunter turned and punched the window out of the SUV, leaving shards of glass embedded in his now broken hand.

As the paramedics rounded the corner, Jack started to walk toward the coffee shop, then stopped and turned to Hunter. "Get your hand taken care of, then go home."

Chapter 54

Chloe had heard about the shootout between federal agents and a suspected member of an organized crime family, as well as the death of an innocent woman and an unnamed gunman. It had been all over the news for the past few days and she did everything she could to keep busy and keep her mind from the worry. She instinctively knew one of the agents was Hunter. She tried to call Jack for confirmation, but couldn't get through. She had tried to contact David several times, but couldn't get a hold of him either. She felt like she was dying inside with each passing minute. If she could just find out if Hunter was okay, she could breathe easier.

Chloe decided to occupy herself in the conference room, reviewing various papers, when Matthew and Crescent entered. She ignored them as Matthew took a seat across from her, while Crescent stood behind him. Matthew had a cigar in one hand and a small metal box in the other, placing the box on the table in front of him. Chloe knew what that cigar meant and suddenly felt nauseous as she glanced at the box. She raised an eyebrow at him, waiting for him to talk first.

"What's all this?" Matthew asked, waving his hand at the papers on the table.

"Most of this is the scheduling and notes for the meeting, which will be held Tuesday after next, but I'm still waiting to hear back from Kansas City and Albuquerque. I have a block of rooms reserved for everybody and—"

"Tuesday after next?" Matthew asked. "Why so long?"

Trying not to look at the box, Chloe answered, "Because David won't be available until then. I also chose that day because it's your birthday. By planning a birthday party to coincide with the meeting, the visiting Family members and all of your admirers will be here. Afterward, the meeting can be held."

Matthew tried, and failed, to maintain a graceful tone. "I'm surprised you even considered planning a birthday party for me."

"Don't read too much into it. I know how much you love to celebrate yourself," Chloe said, disgusted, as Matthew's eyes began to crease in loathing. "It's just a coincidence."

Matthew cast a glance at Crescent, then turned back to Chloe. "You heard about what happened in New Orleans a few days ago?"

Chloe casually shifted in her chair in an effort to give the impression that she didn't care when, really, her heart was heavy with a worry she desperately tried not to show. "Of course I've heard about it. It's been all over the news."

Matthew leaned forward, wrapping his hands around the box as he spoke quietly. "Renee, I don't think you have been completely honest with me."

Right back atcha, she thought.

"This agent that was killed in New Orleans…" Matthew didn't bother suppressing a smile as Chloe's entire posture froze in horror, "…you knew him, didn't you?"

Did she hear him right? An agent was killed? How did he know that and why was she just now hearing about it? Most of all, was it true? Her thoughts were beginning to blur, but her response was cool. "I know that New Orleans was your doing, but there has been no word of an agent, or agents, being killed. If that were the case, it would be breaking national news."

"Sometimes the news isn't always the best source for information. Yes, an agent was killed in the fight. The news isn't reporting it because Jack Lawrence is very good at his job and isn't overly happy that one of his best men was a possible liability to the Family."

Chloe kept her breathing even and her composure still as her chest tightened and terror began to flow through her. The feeling of loss she swore she would never experience again was happening and it scared the hell out of her.

"As a matter of fact," Matthew continued, "I have it on good authority that not only do you know him, you fell in love with him." Matthew took a long pull off his cigar as he leaned back in his chair with a sinister look on his face and said, "*Chloe.*"

She froze, horror replaced by genuine fear for her life. Finally, she was able to speak, but only in a whisper. "How…"

"How isn't important. What is important is the fact that I have you exactly where I want you and nothing you do or say will change that."

"Why don't you just kill me and get it over with?"

"Because I'm not done with you," he answered as he pushed the metal box across the table to rest in front of Chloe. "I am far from done with you."

She swallowed a lump in her throat the size of a boulder and stared at the box, terrified of what she would find inside. "What's this?"

"A reminder that I always follow through on any promise or threat I make."

Chloe inadvertently glanced in Crescent's direction. He was watching her carefully and giving her a threatening look to let her know that if she didn't open the box, he would be the one doling out the consequences. She slowly reached for the box with trembling hands and pulled it closer to her, breathing deeply to steady herself and taking a few seconds to try to prepare for what she would find inside.

Matthew gave her a forceful glare and in a demanding tone said, "Open the box."

Chloe jumped out of her chair in revulsion as she saw a human heart resting inside. She covered her mouth in an attempt to keep the bile from rising, but failed as she found the nearest garbage can and released all of the contents in her stomach.

Matthew stood and turned to Chloe, who was

now bracing herself against the wall, shaking, gasping for air, and tears gushing from her eyes. "Nobody will ever be able to love you again. Do you understand that now?"

Matthew opened the door to leave and she couldn't help herself. She took the box off the table and threw it at Matthew with all of her strength, hitting him in the back.

"You sadistic son of a bitch!" she screamed. "How can you be so evil?"

She ran toward him with the intent of doing whatever she could to make him bleed, but Crescent was faster. He grabbed Chloe's arm, forcibly yanking her away from Matthew, and when she fought him and tried to pull free, Crescent flung her across the table like a rag doll, her body slamming into the wall, where she fell unconscious.

Chapter 55

Chloe opened her eyes to find herself face to face with Dr. Michaelson, who was taking her blood pressure and giving her a sympathetic smile. Her entire body pounded with pain as she turned her head and saw David sitting in a chair beside the bed, eager for her to wake up.

"Stay down," the doctor said when she tried to sit up. "Nothing is broken, but you hit that wall pretty hard."

She turned to David. "Do you know what he did?"

David nodded, fury on his face. "Yes."

"How could you let that happen?"

"It's not what you think," David said. "I'll explain—"

"Not what I think?" Chloe screamed, hysteria taking over. "He gave me a box with his fucking heart in it!"

Chloe couldn't stop sobbing. David and Elias gave her a few minutes before David rested a hand on her arm in an effort to comfort her.

Like flipping a switch, she stopped crying and jerked her arm away from David. "Don't touch me," she hissed.

"I'm sorry, Renee. I'm sorry for everything that has happened over the years—for everything that I have allowed to happen—but this situation is not what you think. Hunter is alive."

Chloe slowly gained control over herself and listened carefully as David explained what had transpired before, during, and after Tucker went to New Orleans. When David finished, Chloe sat up in bed, batting away the doctor's hands as he tried to keep her down.

"Is everything you just told me true?"

David tried not to take offense to her question. "You can ask Jack if you'd like, or Elias, but you have to keep in mind how imperative it is that Matthew think he's won."

"He has won. He has done to me exactly what he said he would do. I can't do this anymore."

"You can't mean that. You're stronger than that. You're better than him."

"Why can't that bastard have a heart attack and die already?" David and the doctor exchanged a knowing glance that did not go unnoticed by Chloe. "What aren't you telling me?"

David smiled. "It turns out that Matthew's heart condition is worse than he thinks it is."

Chloe's eyebrows creased. "What do you mean?"

"I told you that he takes medication to help control it," Elias stated, "but the truth is that Matthew hasn't taken his medication in almost nine months."

"But I've seen him take his medication."

"He's been taking a medication," David said, "just not *his* medication. I think it would be in everybody's best interest if a heart attack in the near future was a very real possibility for Matthew."

"And there is the possibility the attack could be induced," Elias added.

"There are just some details that we will need to discuss so that we are all clear about how to accomplish our end goal," David said. "Unfortunately, you are still the key."

"Hunter is alive," she said to nobody in particular, "and Jack is with him."

"That's right," David confirmed while he patted her arm with a smile. "But right now, you need to get some rest. We have a party next week and it's vital that as many of Matthew's people are there *and* at the meeting afterward."

She carefully slid back under the covers and stared at the ceiling. Then something crossed her mind that she should have thought of weeks ago. She looked suspiciously between the two men before they could leave the room. "Where is Christopher?"

Chapter 56

Hunter sat across from Christopher in Jack's hotel suite, analyzing him in silence, desperately wanting to find anything about him that would make Hunter hate him. He could see why Chloe fell for him in the first place all those years ago. He was good looking, quiet, respectful, and considerate of everyone around him. Despite what Christopher did for a living, Hunter had to admit that Christopher was a good guy.

Christopher leaned forward, resting his elbows on his knees, giving Hunter a hard stare. "Do you really think the two of you can be together? You are a federal officer and she lives in the world of organized crime. She'll never be able to leave it."

"I don't think—"

"What if Matthew kills her? Then what?"

"He won't."

"How do you know?"

"He won't," Hunter repeated with an unrelenting tone. "He needs her. As long as David Lundy is still breathing, he won't touch her."

"You seem awfully sure of that."

"It's all I have to hold on to," Hunter replied.

"You need to know that Matthew Parnell is not like other made men in organized crime that you know about, read about, or see on television. He's unpredictable and dangerous. If evil incarnate had a twin brother, Matthew would be it. I mean, Jesus, he cut off a woman's head; a woman, I might add, who worked for him and was loyal to him for over ten years."

"What did you do for him?"

Christopher sat back on the couch. "I'm not proud of what I've done, but I did what I did for Renee. It wasn't what I thought I signed up for when David sent me to Boston, but I had to do what I was told or risk losing everything."

"Including Chloe," Hunter stated.

"I guess what I'm trying to tell you is that you can hold onto whatever hope you want, but you have to prepare yourself for what might happen." Christopher gave Hunter a hard, serious look. "Everything she has done over the past eight years has been to protect herself, and now she's back, she's alone, and whether or not she wants to admit it, she's scared. She had to build this impenetrable titanium wall around her heart so she would never have to feel the loss of love ever again. Then she met you. She loves you and wants nothing more than to be with you, but in her mind, she has lost you forever. I will always love her, but know I can never have her again. You are the only one who can give her what her heart desires. If all of this turns out to have a happy ending, you'd better be good to her and treat her right, make sure she never cries and always smiles. I've already broken her heart once, and I know she couldn't live with it happening again."

Defeated, Christopher walked out of the room, leaving Hunter to stare out the window with an unexpected smile on his face.

***

"That's all I know," Jack said when he finished his story. "Matthew has eyes wherever she goes and nobody will talk to her unless they have to."

Hunter saw the raised eyebrow look from Christopher that said, *Told ya,* and turned to Jack. "We have to get her out of there whether or not she can get us the evidence we need."

"Christopher and I are going to Boston next week. I don't know all the details, I'm just doing as I'm told," Jack said.

"Wait," Hunter said, trying to understand, "*he's* going to Boston? He's supposed to be dead. What if he's spotted?"

"As I said, I don't know all the details," Jack replied. "I was told to bring him and that's what I'm doing."

Frustrated, Hunter asked, "And what do I do in the meantime? I can't do anything until this asshole is either dead or in jail. I'm being babysat while he—"

Jack cut him off with a terse tone of voice. "You are being 'babysat' for your own protection. You should be grateful that you're being extended the courtesy instead of being six feet in the ground."

"What do Judd and Dennis know?"

"What I told them." Jack pointed to the cast on Hunter's hand. "Medical leave until further notice."

Feeling frustrated and trapped, Hunter desperately wanted something heavy to throw or, if Jack would let him, which was doubtful, go to the shooting range to release his anger. "I'm a federal officer who has been chasing a ghost for years, and now that we finally know who this ghost is and where to find him, there's nothing I can do. I'm sworn to secrecy and caught in the middle of the mob and possible murder of the boss himself. How am I going to do my job from now on? Every time I get a file on my desk that could be or is related to organized crime, I'll have to ignore it."

"You have options. You just don't know it yet," Jack said. "Look, this obviously isn't the way things were supposed to happen, but it's out there now and you now have a choice to do something about it."

Hunter stood and faced Jack. "You'll let me know what you find out?"

"I'll tell you what I can."

"You mean whatever you're allowed to tell me," Hunter stated, and walked out of the room.

Chapter 57

Chloe had put together a grand birthday party for Matthew. Since nobody would tell her who was friend or foe, she simply invited everybody she could think of.

All twelve regional underbosses from were in attendance, sporadically arriving at the hotel over the past two days and enjoying any and all amenities that Matthew had to offer. Maybe two out of the twelve men actually liked Matthew, while the rest of them simply tolerated him, but they were there for David, and David alone. The thought of celebrating anything having to do with Matthew made her nauseous, and after a meeting with David, Elias, and Christopher earlier that afternoon, her nausea wasn't improving.

"I cannot guarantee success," the doctor said, "but given the right circumstance and timing, it very well could work."

"Whether or not we succeed makes no difference," David said sternly. "It will happen tonight either way. The outcome we want, however, is preferable. He is much too admired by the public. It's better to have a medical tragedy than a heinous murder."

"What about Crescent?" Christopher asked. "He's going to be watching very closely. He's a suspicious fucker."

"You can count on the fact that his fate won't be far behind Matthew's," David answered. "You understand your role?"

"Absolutely," Christopher replied. "I'm more than happy to play it."

"Then there is nothing left to do until the party." David turned to Chloe. "You'll be fine."

David gave her a brief kiss on her forehead and left the room, followed by Dr. Michaelson. Chloe and Christopher gave each other a skeptical yet slightly confident look.

"It will be okay, you know," Christopher told her.

"I don't know, but I have to believe it will. It's all I have to hold on to." Chloe could see the hurt in Christopher and tried to ease some of his pain. "I purposely haven't asked you because I know this whole thing isn't easy for you."

Christopher gave Chloe a defeated smile. "He's okay. Frustrated, angry, confused, afraid…"

"Afraid?" Chloe asked, surprised.

"He's afraid he's never going to see you again. He loves you. He's a good man, just a little uncertain at the moment. He's definitely a man who doesn't like it when he doesn't have the answers to his questions, but whatever you decide to do, do it knowing he would pull the moon out of the sky if you asked him to."

Christopher sighed and stood to leave the room when Chloe grabbed his hand and held it tightly. "Thank you, Christopher."

He squeezed her hand and nodded. "I'll be in the other room if you need me."

The only thing Chloe could think about was the way Hunter made her feel, and how she would give anything in the world to have that feeling back.

Jennifer Bates

Chapter 58

Matthew was in a heightened mood, elated with the knowledge that his plan to use his daughter to force David to step down and appoint him boss could be expedited and completed in a matter of days. Happiness was finally just around the corner.

Mr. Crescent answered a knock at Matthew's door and followed David into the suite as Matthew came out of his bedroom, adjusting his bowtie. "David. Come in. Can I get you anything?"

"Just a few moments of your time before the party," David said, dismissing Crescent with a definitive look. Once Crescent was gone, David said, "I understand Renee is healing well."

"The doctor assures me that she will be just fine. I had a conversation with Mr. Crescent about what happened and you can rest assured it won't be an issue again."

"He still breathes, and that tells me the conversation didn't end as it should have."

Matthew knew now was not the time to lose his temper when he was so close to getting what he

356

wanted. "It will not happen again."

"I know Mr. Crescent has been a devoted and trusted man with the Family for many years, and you wouldn't be where you are right now if it weren't for his enthusiasm. However, twenty-eight years ago, you and I made an arrangement whereby she would be forever protected and not unduly touched by anybody. This is not the first time Mr. Crescent has crossed that line, yet there has been nothing done."

Matthew could see where this conversation was going. "David…"

"We have rules and expectations that we must follow; a conduct of behavior that is pivotal to our way of life. So I have to ask myself, why do I allow you be an exception to that rule? I'm sure that if I really think about it, the answer is simple: our relationship changed when Renee was born. She is the one thing in this world that has been a common interest for us, and always will be. I love her more than you know, Matthew, and she's done being punished without consequences to the offender."

"Meaning?"

"Changes are coming, Matthew, and I need to make sure you are ready for those changes. The first of which will be to extinguish the problem between Renee and Mr. Crescent. Since you have done nothing about it, it appears I will have to take it into my own hands. I expect to see Mr. Crescent in your office after the meeting, and just so there is no misunderstanding, we will be meeting behind closed doors."

Matthew knew David would be expecting

Crescent to be waiting in the Red Room after the meeting, and if he wasn't there, a contract would be issued to hunt him down. Until Matthew had been officially sworn in as the boss of the Family, there was nothing he could do to stop it.

Matthew nodded with one thought in mind: *You pompous, arrogant son of a bitch.* "He'll be there."

"Now, I have something else for you." David motioned for Matthew to take a seat in the living room while he inserted a disc into the laptop on the coffee table. "Please sit."

A feeling of unease was steadily creeping over Matthew as he sat down and watched David poise his finger above the keyboard to play the disc. "David, we really don't have time for any of this right now. The party starts in thirty minutes and Renee and I have to be downstairs to greet our guests. Can this wait until later?"

"No," David said with a hard and deliberate stare, "it cannot. I've been doing quite a bit of thinking over the past few months, Matthew. I think about how I got started in the business and everything I have gained, while, at the same time, I think about how much I have lost. It's the losses that are weighing heavy on my heart. I have lost close and dear friends. My beautiful wife of forty years, who, to be honest, was the love of my life. Not a day goes by that I don't miss her. We had such a beautiful life together, and she gave me a son." David turned on Matthew and faced him with hatred. "God decided it was time to take my wife, but my son was taken too soon. Now all that matters is what he left behind and the truth."

Matthew could feel his heart beat a little faster and his eyes widened in horror as the picture came to life and he heard a voice from the past ringing in his ears.

"Your boss didn't like this guy he was partners with. I mean, he *really* didn't like him. Apparently, he had been stuck with him because he's the son of someone important, and your boss was sick of his friend fucking everything up. So, your boss paid us a little extra—two hundred and fifty thousand each—to take this guy out to the desert and make him disappear. We roughed him up a little bit but I got bored, so I put two shots in him. Afterward, we went to the casino and I won a grand at the blackjack table."

It was the video Sasha died for, and finally he knew why. Matthew couldn't concentrate on one single thought in his head; there was too much chaos to sort through. The only thing he knew with complete certainty was that his fate was sealed. Matthew placed his hand over his chest, willing his heart to stop racing.

"I expect now I know why Sasha never came home," David said calmly. "I'll see you at the party."

David left Matthew alone, giving him very little precious time to think about what just happened. As if in a dream, Matthew slid his jacket over his shoulders and reached for the doorknob, when a thought suddenly hit him. He could save himself, but he would have to act fast.

Chloe. Renee. Whatever her name is. He smiled at the irony; the last person on the planet he would have expected to be his savior was someone he was hell-bent on destroying.

Chapter 59

Matthew stepped off the elevator on the second floor with only Mr. Crescent to greet him. Crescent could instantly tell something was wrong simply by the paleness of Matthew's face.

"Everything okay?" Crescent asked.

"No," Matthew replied, looking around him. "Where is my daughter?"

Crescent inclined his head toward the lobby where guests filed in as quickly as they could to be greeted by Chloe. She stood at the bottom of the stairs, exchanging hugs, handshakes, and greetings, all with a smile of jubilation on her face. She was the picture of elegance in her floor-length, shimmering violet dress and the soft curls of her hair falling down her back. While shaking hands with politicians, judges, doctors, and any other acquaintance Matthew could squeeze in here, nobody would ever have been able to tell that her relationship with her father, and her life, had drastically changed.

While greeting the newly appointed district

attorney with a warm hug, she followed the gaze of another guest and locked eyes with Matthew, giving him a hard, defiant look and a grin that asked him what he was going to do about her brazen disregard for Parnell party etiquette. Matthew had to step back from the view of the guests, fists clenched in a tight ball, trying to get his anger in control.

"Our plans for this evening have been altered, Mr. Crescent. Come find me in one hour."

Crescent gave an obedient nod. "Yes, sir."

Matthew straightened his jacket and turned toward the stairs. Through clenched teeth he said, "Now, if you'll excuse me, I have to go join my daughter."

***

"Governor," Matthew excitedly said, extending his hand as he walked forward. "So glad you could make it."

Shaking hands with Matthew, the governor replied, "I wouldn't have missed it. Happy birthday, my friend."

"Thank you," Matthew said with as much humility as he could muster as he kissed the hand of the governor's wife. To her, he said, "Always a pleasure to see you, Eleanor. You look radiant tonight."

Eleanor tried to hide a bashful grin as the blood began to rise in her cheeks. "You are so sweet, Matthew. Thank you."

"Not just a birthday party," the governor said with a jovial smile, "but a celebration. It must be wonderful to have your family back together again."

Chloe stifled an amused grin while she watched Matthew keep himself composed. "You have no idea. The food smells intoxicating and the music is inviting. Please help yourself and I'll see you inside."

As the governor and his wife began ascending the stairs to the ballroom, Matthew turned to face Chloe, but she kept her eyes on the guests and spoke to him quietly while faking a happy smile. "Now is not the time, Father. We have guests."

Infuriated with her insolence and smugness, Matthew composed himself as more guests approached and received the same welcoming greeting from father and daughter. Matthew's agitation quickly accelerated as Madeline approached them with a victorious smile on her face. Chloe's behavior, however, didn't change at all.

"Matthew!" Madeline cried as she gave him a kiss on his cheek. "Happy birthday, darling."

Matthew solemnly nodded as he pulled back from her embrace. "Thank you, Madeline."

She turned to Chloe, who stood poised and gracious, taking a small step back as Madeline leaned in to hug her.

"Madeline," Chloe said coolly.

Madeline gave a nervous laugh. "Well, it certainly is good to see you again. It is so wonderful to have you home."

"Yes," Chloe replied. "I understand you profited well from it."

Like a rat caught in a trap, Madeline froze for a

few seconds and gave Matthew a questioning look, but Matthew either didn't hear the comment or was pretending he didn't.

"Well," Madeline said, "I will see you inside."

"You most certainly will. We have quite a bit of catching up to do," Chloe said as Madeline gave her a wary look and began climbing the stairs.

It took another twenty minutes for the arriving guests to thin out before Matthew was able to gracefully pull Chloe aside, out of view and earshot of other guests. He turned on her with fire in his eyes while she stared back at him with indifference.

"What the hell do you think you're doing? How dare you—"

"How dare *I*? What? Defy you? Disrespect you? Disobey you? Embarrass you? Let's get one thing straight, *Father*. You have done everything in your power to destroy me and have made it painfully clear what your intentions are and what you expect from me, but I haven't needed you to tell me what to do for the past eight years and I don't need it now. I am no longer a child you can order around. I will do what I want, when I want, no matter what you have done to me in the past or plan on doing to me in the future. It's been too long since I've danced, laughed, and had a good time. I'm going to enjoy myself tonight. Rest assured, I will be pretending, but then again, I was raised to pretend I was somebody I'm not. That's not going to change tonight simply because you order it. Now, if you'll excuse me, we have guests."

Matthew watched her walk away in complete shock, vowing that after he got what he wanted from David, this would be her last social gathering ever.

Chapter 60

Chloe couldn't help but smile as she watched how festive the guests were as they mingled and danced without a care in the world. The band she had chosen played an array of music, alternating every few songs and encouraging different cliques of people to enjoy their own tastes in music. After a few hours, she found that this was the first party she had ever attended where she was genuinely having a good time despite the fact that it would not be ending on a cheerful note, but would be a damn good story for all who wanted to hear it.

Chloe happily mingled with the guests while keeping her eyes on everything from Matthew's location to what food the caterer was serving at specific times. Crescent and a few of Matthew's associates were cleverly placed for security purposes and each visiting underboss had an associate with them at all times. Mr. Tempest brought Mr. Schedler with him, and when Chloe was able to acknowledge them both from across the room, she and Mr. Tempest shared a smile.

As far as Madeline was concerned, Chloe was keeping a close eye on her and found it amusing that she had a certain amount of nervousness about her that kept her from leaving her table, preferring to have others approach her. Chloe also didn't miss the fact that Madeline was doing everything in her control not to look in Chloe's direction.

Dr. Michaelson seemed to be having a good time visiting with old friends and colleagues, seeming to be finally at peace with the torturous nature of his past and the uncertainty of his future. He was enjoying himself and allowing himself the pleasure of company and laughter. It had been far too long since she had seen a genuine smile on his face.

She spotted David at a table with some of his guests in deep and discrete discussion. While she didn't know each of his underbosses personally, as a child it had become habit to refer to them by the city they represented unless she knew their name. None of them ever seemed to mind, and David, for some reason, thought it humorous. She knew that habit would need to be broken sooner rather than later.

Chloe's eyes swept the room and found Matthew in a discrete conversation with Mr. Crescent, and noticed Matthew's tense body language and carefully controlled animation. She wasn't particularly worried about Matthew and Crescent at the moment, there was somebody more important she was concerned about as the five men at David's table stood to greet her as she approached to say hello.

"Gentlemen," she said with a smile as she

hugged each one of them in turn. "Thank you for being here. I'm sorry I haven't gotten a chance to visit with any of you until now."

"Not to worry," said Kansas City, "we understand how busy you've been."

"You've done wonders with this party," said Detroit, who Chloe only knew as Paddy, but had no idea if that was his name or just a nickname.

"Thank you," she said while casting a questioning glance at Jack. "I hope you all enjoy yourselves. Is there anything I can get you?"

"Would you care to dance with an old man?" Jack asked as he stood from the table.

"Find me an old man first," she replied, and got a hearty laugh from the others at the table.

The band switched tempo from swing to slow as Jack took her hand to lead her to the dance floor. "Tony Bennett. Say what you will, but nobody can make romance dance with words like Tony Bennett."

"I don't know how much longer I can fake this smile, Jack," Chloe said once they started moving to the music.

"Not much longer, I'm sure." Jack smiled as they danced to the slow rhythm and couldn't help but see the despair on Chloe's face. "He's fine. Cabin fever is taking over, but he's fine. Mostly, he's frustrated because he feels like a caged animal."

"Can you blame him?"

"No."

"What about the others?"

"I put Fowler back to work, and Dennis…" Jack said with a smile, "…lucky bastard got a retirement offer he couldn't refuse."

"When you go back, could you tell him…"

"I'll tell him," Jack said as he let out a soft sigh. "I'm not going to pretend like I know everything. David is keeping whatever plans he has close to the vest, but I can tell you that everything will be okay. You are in no danger."

Chloe cast a glance at Matthew as he played host and laughed with guests. "He looks worried."

"He should be."

She searched Jack's eyes for some kind of deception but found none. "Thank you for everything you've done."

Jack smiled and gently kissed her forehead. "No thanks necessary."

Chapter 61

Matthew's eye caught sight of Chloe and Jack moving toward the dance floor and it made him scowl. He glanced toward the table and saw David staring at him, unable to read his thoughts, which made him nervous.

"You need to find out everything you can," Matthew spat at Crescent. "I need to know exactly what's going on so I can plan accordingly. I'll be damned if I'm going to go down. I have worked too hard to get this far."

"I'll let you know as soon as I know something," Crescent replied.

"You will also eliminate anything you deem a threat to me. Go take care of this and let me know when everything is in place."

As Crescent walked away, Matthew tried to keep his composure despite his quickly rising adrenaline and anxiety. While he tried to focus on the party, he couldn't stop thinking about the video. He knew his heart was beating faster than it should, and he also knew there was a chance his plans could fail.

Paranoia began to sneak up on him while watching Jack and Chloe dance together. What were they talking about? And what was David so intently talking to the others about over at his table? Matthew decided not to give in to his own irrationality and stopped short when he caught a shadow moving across the back wall of the room. As he watched the figure glide along the way, his eyes slightly widened when he caught a glimpse of the owner of that shadow; the man stopped, pausing for only a second before disappearing back into the crowd. Just for a moment, Matthew thought he knew that man, but his brain told him it was impossible.

Matthew turned to scan the crowd. His blood froze as he saw James and Lawrence Garafola enter the ballroom, each with a Parnell girl on their arm and laughing at something apparently hilarious.

There was no letting go of his paranoia at the sight of the Garafola brothers. If Matthew was going to get what he wanted, it had to be before the brothers caught David's eye. Matthew searched the room for Crescent and saw him standing in the opposite doorway, watching him. Matthew casually nodded to the brothers as they continued to move through the room, and made it known to Crescent these two needed to be removed immediately.

"Hey! There he is!" James shouted as they made their way to Matthew.

Shit! Matthew thought as he watched James and Lawrence approach him with their escorts in tow, Lawrence kissing Matthew soundly on the cheek.

Lawrence gave a raucous laugh. "This is quite a

party you throw."

Matthew turned to the girls. "Why don't you get your dates another drink, ladies?"

Disappointed as the girls silently and obediently walked away, Lawrence said, "Aww. You didn't have to do that."

Matthew's teeth clenched and he leaned close to the brothers. "What are you doing here?"

Confused by the question, the brothers exchanged a look, and James asked, "What do you mean? We were invited."

"Do you have any idea..." Matthew started, but his body tensed as he was cut off by a voice behind him.

"Gentlemen," David said as he shook the brothers' hands. "Welcome. You look familiar, but I'll be damned if I can remember from where."

"Vegas, maybe?" Lawrence asked, and David's eyes lit up.

"Garafola, is that right?" David gave Matthew a casual but knowing look, then turned back to the brothers. "You work for my savior in Sin City."

Matthew took a minute to scan the room again, looking for Crescent and making sure his men were where they should be. Instead of locking eyes with Crescent, however, he locked eyes with someone else for only an instant, but in that instant, Matthew's heart started beating faster and panic was just about to set in. *I'm seeing things that aren't there. I'm letting fear get the best of me.* Just as quickly as the emerald eyes appeared, they were gone. Matthew shook off the eerie feeling and turned back to David and the brothers.

"That's right, Mr. Lundy," Lawrence said. "It's an honor to see you again, sir."

Raising his glass, David said, "I just wanted to come over and say hello. I'm sure we will have an opportunity to talk later."

"Anytime, Mr. Lundy," James said. "Anytime. Just let us know."

"Enjoy your evening." David gave a short bow from the waist and, without taking a second look at Matthew, walked back to his table to resume his conversation.

Matthew hurriedly snapped his fingers to get the brothers' attention. "It would behoove the both of you to keep a low profile this evening. Better yet, leaving the hotel would probably be best."

"What are you talking about?" James asked. "We just got—"

"Matthew!" Madeline called as she approached with open arms. "I have been waiting all night for the opportunity to speak with you, but you haven't come to see me."

The Garafola brothers took Madeline's appearance to excuse themselves to look for their dates.

"Madeline," Matthew said, "I really don't have time right now."

"Make time," she said sternly. "What is going on?"

Before Matthew could respond, the music changed to "Happy Birthday" and the lights in the ballroom came down, only to be replaced by one spotlight on Matthew and another on the cake being rolled into the center of the room. Guests started singing as Chloe approached Matthew with open arms to lead him to the center of the room where the enormous six-tiered cake was waiting for him. Ever the picture of sophistication and modesty, Matthew played his part as he casually scanned the room again.

"Is there a problem?" Chloe asked.

"I know you know something," Matthew said, "and I intend to bleed every last piece of information out of you before this night is over." When she didn't reply, he said, "I notice you've been dancing with quite a few people tonight, particularly Family members."

"I can dance with whomever I please."

"Enjoy it while you can, because it will be the last fun you will ever have."

The birthday song ended and guests started clapping and cheering on Matthew. Chloe let go of Matthew's arm and, as expected of a daughter, gave him a kiss on his cheek. Unaffected by his words, she whispered in his ear, "So you've said."

Chapter 62

Matthew stood by the cake, sharing quick banter with friends. Standing next to him, Chloe turned to speak with another guest while Matthew casually surveyed the crowed, once more catching sight of the stranger in the shadows watching him with his sandy blond hair, green eyes, and a chivalrous grin. He almost dropped his plate when he realized he wasn't seeing things, even though he knew it wasn't possible.

Chloe turned to Matthew. "Is there a problem?"

Matthew spoke roughly through a plastic smile. "What is going on, Renee?"

Chloe casually glanced around the room. "Is there something wrong?"

Matthew looked at David, surrounded by eight of his twelve underbosses, together with their associates, all laughing, smoking cigars, and having a good time, completely ignoring Matthew and, thankfully, oblivious to Matthew's suspicion.

"Are you feeling okay?"

"I'm fine," Matthew snapped. "Where is Mr.

Crescent?"

"Probably off torturing small children."

Before Matthew could respond, the band started playing soft and low as guests resumed eating or visiting as they were before. Matthew graciously excused himself to look for Crescent, his eyes cautiously scanning the room, but David caught up with him and followed him into the hallway.

"Matthew, I've been giving our predicament some thought. You and I need to talk."

"This is ridiculous," Matthew spat. "If it weren't for this party, you would have already put a bullet in my head and been done with it."

"True, but that doesn't change facts. Look around you, Matthew. In the end, you can die knowing that everything you ever wanted in life came to you because you earned it. After talking with some of these people who actually believe they are your friends, it sounds like you will be missed very much."

A sudden confidence rose in Matthew as he leaned in close to David. "You aren't going to do anything to me. After our little movie earlier, I took pains to make sure your precious granddaughter doesn't breathe without me knowing, and if I'm taken by you, I can guarantee you that she will be next. Wouldn't it be tragic if an accident would happen to befall her this evening?"

David's features hardened and he moved in on Matthew. "Are you threatening me? Are you threatening my granddaughter?"

"It's no threat, David. I will have what I want or I will kill her getting it. I can have a bullet in her forehead with the nod of my head."

"And what is it you want exactly?"

"Tonight, at the meeting when you announce your retirement, you will appoint me your successor with all of the privileges and benefits thereof."

Matthew never knew the speed or strength David had in him until Matthew was slammed against the wall, David clutching Matthew's lapels with white knuckles and breathing like a dragon waiting to spew fire. "Do you have any idea why you're still here? Here in Boston, working for me, and alive? Do you? It's because I have allowed it. I have allowed many things to happen over the years for reasons of my own, but now one of those reasons has come home. And you dare threaten me? This is *my* Family, and I too can accomplish anything I want with the nod of *my* head."

Kansas City and Albuquerque stepped into the hallway to find Matthew pinned against the wall. There was no confusion, they only saw business and were ready to step in.

"Mr. Lundy?" Kansas City asked. "Can we help with anything?"

David inhaled a deep breath and released Matthew, allowing him to straighten his jacket before speaking. "Would they do the same for you?"

Matthew's eyes threw fire and daggers as David walked away, leaving Kansas City and Albuquerque to lead Matthew back into the party. Dr. Michaelson spotted Matthew sitting at a table furthest from the dance floor and approached him with grave concern on his face. "Matthew? You don't look good. How are you feeling? You've taken your medication?"

"Yes!" Matthew spat with irritability, then, like a deer in headlights, watched the mystery guest weave in and out of party guests, either keeping his back to Matthew or allowing a simple peek at his profile. *If I say it out loud, he'll think I'm crazy. If I say it out loud, I'll think I'm crazy.*

Dr. Michaelson watched Matthew follow the mystery guest as Chloe approached.

"Bad news. Unfortunately…"

Matthew's head snapped to attention. "Unfortunately, what?"

"Unfortunately, for the both of us, some of the guests feel that a father-daughter dance would be the perfect ending to the evening."

Matthew let out a grunt of disgust.

"Believe me," Chloe said, "I don't like it any more than you do, but we must keep up appearances, right? Let's get it over with."

***

Chloe found herself enjoying the moment as she and Matthew approached the dance floor, somehow finding graceful satisfaction in the applause and whispers from the guests wholeheartedly approving the sight of their beloved city savior and his daughter reunited once again. Tension ran high between Matthew and Chloe as they moved their feet to a slow melody. Chloe knew his heart was beating fast, and the sheen of sweat forming on his forehead was hard to ignore.

"What are you looking for?" Chloe asked as she

watched him scan the crowd of guests.

"Nothing of your concern," he answered.

"I know your plans for me and I also know you want to execute those plans as soon as possible. So, for once, why don't we try something we've never done—let's tell each other the truth."

Chloe held back a smile as Matthew tensed up again, catching sight of the green-eyed, blond-haired man weaving through the crowds.

"If you hated me so much, why did you raise me?"

Matthew gritted his teeth. "I didn't have a choice. Your mother was dead."

"Yes, but if you didn't want me and didn't want to raise me, why did you have her killed?"

Matthew's feet briefly stopped moving and his grip tightened on her hand, but Chloe continued dancing like he never missed a step.

"When you informed me that you would make sure nobody would ever love me again, that wasn't the first time you had taken away somebody who not only loved me, but somebody I could love in return."

Matthew's breathing was becoming rapid and Chloe could see some of the color leaving his face. "Renee…"

"You killed my mother, you killed Dr. Michaelson's wife as punishment for not killing me at the same time, you killed my friends simply because they wanted a better life away from you and I'm the one who gave them the means to do it. After all this, after everything you have done to make me miserable, what kind of sick pleasure do you get? What is your final reward for all of the evil you have done?"

"Renee," Matthew said, his breath short. "I don't have to explain myself to you. What I have done, I have done for the betterment of—"

"Ugh," she said, disgusted, "if you finish that sentence with anything other than 'myself,' I'll want to reach into your chest and pull out that twisted, diseased heart of yours."

...rare heart condition...

Matthew stopped dancing, his breathing ragged. His knees started to tremble and Chloe actually had to help him stay standing. Concerned gasps and whispers emanated from the crowd. Chloe followed Matthew's line of sight and watched as David stood and embraced Christopher like it was an unexpected homecoming. Which it was.

...surges of adrenaline that trigger episodes...

The music stopped when Matthew stopped dancing. Chloe, having to feign concern in front of a crowd of concerned friends, acquaintances, and media, turned to Matthew with a smile. "What's the matter? You look like you've seen a ghost."

...irregular heartbeats...which could lead to palpitations, fainting, or even death...

Matthew turned to face Chloe, nothing but haunting terror in his eyes. "How?"

She took his face in her hands and spoke with wickedness in her voice. "I know that the man I should have been calling my father died in a Las Vegas desert before I was born."

Matthew could barely breathe and tried to keep his footing. "Who...told..."

"My grandfather told me, you son of a bitch."

...sudden and loud noise taking him by surprise...

The vibrating echo of balloons being popped all around them sounded like gunshots in Matthew's ears. His eyes widened in shock. Matthew clutched his chest, his body went slack, and he fell to the floor. Chaos quickly ensued with Chloe pretending to become hysterical over her sickly father. Guests, as well as cameras and reporters, rushed toward them to offer assistance in any way they could. Dr. Michaelson pushed people out of the way to get to Matthew while a few of the wives took Chloe by the arm and escorted her away from the scene. Chloe was so convincing in her grief that the local magistrate's wife handed her a tissue to wipe the tears off her face while the governor's wife embraced her in an attempt to be comforting.

Chloe chanced a glance in the direction of David's table, where David and the other underbosses watched with unreadable expressions on their faces. David slightly inclined his head to let Chloe know he was pleased thus far with the events of the evening, and she reciprocated the feeling with her eyes. Christopher turned to smile at her and she couldn't help but smile back as the chatter and noise in the room suddenly went silent as Dr. Michaelson stood and faced Chloe with a look that told her their plan was a success. The crowd surrounding the body consisted mostly of women silently crying and cameras flashing. Chloe stared down at the lifeless body of the man she once called her father and held back every impulse to kick him as hard as she could while giving the impression of loss and disbelief.

In front of a crowd of party guests, the media, and loved ones, Matthew Parnell officially died of a massive heart attack at 10:23 p.m.

Literally, however, he had been scared to death.

Chapter 63

Through all the chaos, Chloe wished she could read lips as Crescent confidently entered the room and approached David's table. She watched the seemingly casual conversation as he and Christopher stood across from each other, the other Family members looking on with a mixture of awe and confusion on their faces—they, too, believing Christopher was long dead. She quickly shook off the women trying to give her comfort for the death of who they believed to be her father and stood next to Jack to listen to the exchange.

"I'm no coward," Crescent said. "I have been nothing but loyal to this Family."

"You were only loyal to him," Christopher replied.

"I have never done anything for this Family that wasn't expected of me."

"Does that include nearly beating an innocent woman to death?"

Crescent gave a malicious smile and cast a sideways glance at Chloe, ignoring Christopher's question.

"We have much to discuss, and this is not the time or place. We will meet upstairs in thirty minutes," David said as he stood. "This will be a private meeting. Your men will not accompany you."

Crescent nodded in assent and left the ballroom.

"Christopher should leave before someone actually recognizes him," Chloe said. "Eyes are lingering too long."

David turned to his Family. "Gentlemen, with the exception of those I have given previous instruction to, please make your way to the conference room upstairs. I'll meet you shortly."

Christopher turned to David. "I'll wait for you upstairs."

"With Crescent? Alone?" Chloe asked, trying to mask the concern in her voice.

Christopher gave Chloe his not-to-worry smile. "I'll play nice if he will."

Chloe watched him walk away, surrounded by the other men of the Family, knowing that Crescent had never played nice in his life.

***

When Chloe entered the Red Room a little while later, she expected to find blood flooding the floor. Instead, Christopher and Crescent leaned against opposite walls, silently scrutinizing each other and what the situation had become. Chloe took a seat near Christopher and tried to envision what the future of the Family would be now that Matthew was dead, Christopher was not, and she was in charge of New England.

She studied Crescent, but his demeanor gave no hint as to what he was thinking, except revulsion as he stared into the eyes of what should have been a dead man. Chloe knew Crescent well enough to know that, should the opportunity present itself, Christopher would be just that once again. Crescent was a killer and enjoyed it immensely. Chloe was more like David in that she would consider all angles of a dilemma before doling out any consequences. She had to wonder, however, if the circumstances called for it, if she would be able to be a killer as well.

"Why do you hate her so much?" Christopher asked Crescent.

"She is a stain on this Family. Everything she is, and everything she represents, has been a lie since the day she was born."

"Aside from a scar, which you deserved, she hasn't done anything to you."

"That's not the point."

"Then what is the point?"

There was nothing but loathing and anger in Crescent's eyes. "The doctor made a mistake in his decision and we have all been made to suffer because of it."

"You all have been made to suffer?" David asked from behind Crescent. Nobody had heard him enter the room.

Crescent turned and faced him, glaring. "There were poor decisions and mistakes made on Mr. Parnell's part because of her. Business would have run more efficiently but for the fact that every time he made a decision, she was figured into the equation. Everything Mr. Parnell did, every decision he made, revolved around her."

"And me leaving just made life more difficult for the Family, Mr. Crescent?" Chloe asked.

"Not as much as your obvious ascension will."

Chloe stood next to Christopher and put a gentle hand on his arm as he pushed himself off the wall, ready to defend Chloe's place in the Family. Her touch told him to keep his cool.

"Now that she is back," Christopher said, "you're going to have to get over it. She is in charge and you will give her the respect she has earned."

Crescent laughed. "Earned? She hasn't earned anything. Everything she has, and everything she is, she has because she is the bastard child of—"

"Don't finish that thought, Mr. Crescent," David said in a warning tone. "No matter your place in this Family, you will not slander my son or her mother. You're forgetting that Matthew made the choice—"

Crescent wheeled on David, his eyes as black as night. "He had no choice. The doctor made the choice for him and you reinforced it."

Chloe's grip on Christopher's arm slowly tightened the more Crescent spoke. She wanted nothing more than to reach over to the weapons table to find a way to stop him talking for good.

David circled in front of Crescent. "I run this Family as I see fit. Are you questioning my judgment and decisions?"

"I have been questioning them since the day her slut mother got pregnant by your whore mongering son."

Chloe gasped. David's fist connected with Crescent's jaw, making Crescent plant his foot behind him to keep from losing his balance.

Too late, Christopher broke the grip Chloe had on his arm when he saw Crescent raise his arm to reciprocate David's punch. In the two steps it took Christopher to reach him, David had been hit so hard that he lost his balance and stumbled into the weapons table, knocking its contents to the floor.

Mr. Crescent's fate was sealed.

As Chloe tended to a dazed David, Christopher exchanged blows with Crescent, who was determined to put Christopher back in his grave for good. As David slowly came to, Chloe moved him to a chair.

Christopher ducked Crescent's arm and delivered a blow to his ribs, then grabbed him around the waist to throw him to the ground. Crescent's head hit the floor with a crack and Christopher leaned over him, fist poised above his head.

Crescent began to laugh. "Do you really think my death will matter?"

"It will matter to her," Christopher said.

"Yours will mean more than mine."

Christopher cast a quick glance at Chloe, his eyes almost asking her permission. Chloe simply gave a short nod. But in those few precious seconds, Crescent reached above his head, grabbing a knife that had fallen from the weapons table. Christopher brought his fist down to stop him, but Crescent was faster, burying the knife in Christopher's neck, only to pull it out and do it again until Christopher collapsed, lifeless, on the floor.

Blinded by rage, Chloe grabbed the first thing she could reach. She threw it as hard as she could and heard a low grunt escape Crescent as he began to stand up. The handle of the hatchet was almost flush with his arm while the head was buried in his shoulder, pooling with blood, and set just below the scar Chloe had left him years earlier.

Unaffected, Crescent took the knife from Christopher's neck and began to approach Chloe. The gunshot almost deafened her as it echoed in the room. Her eyes still focused on Crescent, she saw a small hole in the middle of his forehead begin to slowly seep blood and brain matter, then watched him fall to the floor. David sat in his chair, the barrel of his gun smoking, and gave Chloe a mixed look of relief and despair. It was then that the events of the last few minutes came to reality in her mind and she made her way over the Christopher, once again holding him as she laid his head in her lap and stroked his hair. This time, however, there were no words of apology or goodbye, just an overwhelming feeling of loss knowing he would not be coming back from the dead. There were no tears, only certainty and shock.

David put a hand on Chloe's shoulder. Knowing they still had business to attend so, Chloe gently laid Christopher's head on the floor and followed David out of the room.

Chapter 64

Outside the conference room doors, Chloe had a strange and unexpected confidence regarding the certainty of where her life would go from here. She would grieve Christopher, once again, in her own way and in her own time, but her new life would be falling into place.

"Are you ready?" David asked.

"They won't accept a woman in the role."

"They will," David assured her. "They have always known you would be Matthew's successor because you're his daughter."

"But I'm not his daughter," Chloe said harshly.

"They don't know that," David pointed out.

"They should," Chloe said. "They deserve to know the truth."

David smiled, obviously not wanting to broach that subject just yet. "I have complete faith in your abilities and they will too. You may have to prove yourself for a little while, but you have already demonstrated that you are willing to do whatever it takes to protect yourself and your Family. Right now, you just have to believe in yourself."

Chloe thought back to the reunion conversation where she reminded Matthew that one day his throne would be hers and she would take power with more grace and tolerance than he ever had. She nodded her head and squared her shoulders.

The chatter in the conference room turned to greeting as David and Chloe entered. The visiting underbosses had welcoming smiles on their faces, some genuine and some forced, but as handshakes and hugs were exchanged, curiosity most likely filled more than one mind as eyes wandered to the patches of blood adorning her evening gown.

"Gentlemen, thank you all for being here," David said as he took his seat, Chloe sitting on his right and the others returning to their respective seats.

David began the meeting with a detailed account of what had happened in the Red Room, no apology or sense of loss over Matthew. More than a few of the men were surprised when they heard about Crescent and Christopher. David requested they all be present for Christopher's burial, but as for Matthew, his overwhelmed and grieving public would be all he would need. Chloe knew not one of the men in the room cared that Matthew was no longer among the living.

"As you have all already deduced, as his daughter, Renee will succeed to his position and take over where he left off. Let me assure each and every one of you that I have the utmost confidence that she will turn New England around and right his wrongs. I welcome any comments, questions, or objections any of you may have."

Denver stood and addressed Chloe. "First, let me say that I have no objections to the appointment. I do, however, have a question. You have been gone for many years, and before you left, you were simply a madam. Are you sure you're ready?"

There was a confidence in her that was different than she had ever felt before. "It's true that before I left I was simply a madam, but look at what I accomplished in all those years. The companions were bringing in hundreds of thousands of dollars weekly. With the exception of one unfortunate incident, none of them were unhappy or mistreated under my command. During that time, I made it my business to learn all I could. Before I left, I knew all of the inner workings of the business, including books, management, collections, construction, and loans."

"For reasons that I simply cannot even begin to understand, he gave away a casino in Atlantic City to Madeline Frost," said Paddy.

"Madeline used her knowledge of where to find me to get the casino. Make no mistake, gentlemen, I will get that casino back and I will get it back tonight."

The tone of her voice and the sternness of her look told all that she was steadfast in her resolve and she would prove to them that she would be a respected and successful colleague.

As Denver sat down, Chloe stood up. "Gentlemen, I will be the first to admit that I don't have the experience you do, but it is important for you to know that I am not my father. This business is a business, and it will be treated as such. I do not seek to solely benefit myself; we do what we do for the benefit of the Family that has provided for us all these years. I ask that you don't judge me based on my father's actions, judge me based on mine."

Salt Lake City stood. "We have all heard rumors and stories about the reasons for your disappearance, and, to be honest, were more than surprised when we saw your dead fiancé at the party tonight. While I am not seeking specific answers, I feel the need to ask if there is a chance you will disappear again."

"That's not even a worry to lose sleep over," Tempest said as he stood and extended his hand to Chloe. "You will be a pleasant and welcome addition to the administration of this Family."

Chloe smiled at him and took his hand as the other men in the room stood to applaud Chloe's succession. David could do nothing but smile. Chloe knew David now had his Family exactly as he wanted it and nothing would be changing that fact in the near future.

Chloe looked to Jack and he gave her a knowing smile. "There is one thing I would like to make clear. The circumstances of my disappearance are my own and I appreciate you all allowing me to keep that private. While I was gone, I had a new life and was finally my own person. For the past eight years I have been known as Chloe Riggs, and from this moment on, that distinctiveness remains. I have no problem with any of you remembering me as Renee, but I ask that you try to remember that I now go by a different name."

"May I ask why?" Denver asked.

"Because I want as little personal connection to Matthew Parnell as possible. I don't want the name any more than I want to admit he was my father."

Understanding crossed all of their faces as a quick knock came at the door and a young man poked his head in, nodded at David, and closed the door.

"Gentlemen, please excuse us," David said, and turned to Chloe. "We have a task to attend to."

Chloe stopped at the door and turned back to her colleagues. "If anyone would like to watch me get the casino back, you are welcome to join us. Mr. Parsons, you may find our errand of particular interest."

Chapter 65

After leaving the conference room, Chloe stepped into Matthew's office to take a few minutes for herself before she joined David and the others for the next leg of their journey. Her eyes scanned the office and hovered on the chair in the corner, remembering all of the times as a child she would sit and pretend not to listen to Matthew conduct business as if she were invisible. But now that chair was hers, along with everything else in the office.

She gently ran her fingers along the edge of the desk, staring at his plush leather chair, wondering if she should, or even wanted to, sit in it. She decided she didn't. The desk was neatly organized with everything in its place the way he always liked it—his brandy glass empty and clean next to his telephone and his humidor in the top left corner, full of his favorite cigars. She stared at the humidor with uncontrollable resentment and felt a fire beginning to burn in her gut. She slowly lifted the lid and removed a cigar, running it under her nose, inhaling the sweet scent that reminded her of her childhood, and wondered if she truly was ready for this awesome responsibility she had inherited. She put the cigar in her bag and turned off the lights before she left. She would soon find out.

***

The vacant warehouse her father used to store products upon import and preparation for export was located six blocks from the crematorium. The warehouse was remote enough and, for all intents and purposes, more convenient than the Red Room.

Chloe's senses were heightened and she was keenly aware of her surroundings. Every sensation she could possibly feel was driving through her body and she found she was no longer numb—she was now determined. Chloe waited until David, Denver, Mr. Parsons from Las Vegas, and Miami entered the warehouse, stopping and exchanging silent greetings with the four associates standing guard, then silently observing what was being guarded. Staring back with pleading in their eyes, both Garafola brothers and Madeline Frost sat before them, tied to their chairs, and each of them with terror in their eyes. It wasn't until a few heartbeats later that Madeline gasped at the sound of heels clicking slowly toward them on the cement floor.

The three guests watched as Chloe crossed the room with complete indifference and approached the large metal table against the wall that held various weapons. Chloe carefully considered which would suit her immediate needs until she spotted exactly what she wanted. She smiled as she picked up the Louisville Slugger and took her place in front of the confused and nervous guests.

After taking a minute to assess her victims, Chloe moved to stand in front of Lawrence Garafola, the man she knew to be the one who put two bullets in her biological father's head and liked it. She wasn't sure if either brother knew why they were brought here, but they remained quiet and still as their eyes pleaded with their boss for some kind of reprieve from their punishment. Mr. Parsons hadn't been told why his two best captains were being held tonight, but it was no secret there was nothing he could say or do to help them. If David Lundy brought them there to be on the wrong side of punishment, they more than likely deserved it.

Chloe spun the bat in her hand and cocked an inquisitive eyebrow at Lawrence. "I know you and your brother are usually on this side of the room during these situations, and just like the people in your current position, I'm sure you'll want to get this over with as quickly as possible."

She turned to James and asked if he knew who she was and why he was brought here. When James shook his head, she turned to Lawrence and asked him. While Lawrence emphatically shook his head in answer, Madeline let out a whimper of fear, then a muffled scream of pain when Chloe swung the bat as hard as she could, connecting with her right tibia.

Chloe leaned into Madeline and hissed, "You will suffer in silence. I don't want to hear another sound out of you. Am I understood?"

Wide-eyed and breathing heavily through her

nose, Madeline nodded vigorously, tears streaming down her face as she desperately tried not to make a sound.

From behind her, David said, "One of the reasons women are feared by men is because they are unpredictable, especially when they are pissed."

The others gave muffled laughs at David's accurate explanation.

Chloe internally smiled as she turned her deadly stare from Madeline to the brothers. "Twenty-eight years ago, Matthew Parnell hired you to do a job, a job you had no right to accept or carry out without the explicit consent from your boss. I know you were paid well to ignore protocol. By deciding to take this job, you irreparably affected many, but none more so than Mr. Lundy. You have no idea the pain, anguish, and sickness you not only brought down on yourselves, but the entire Family. Your actions broke a chain in this Family. Now, I'll give you the benefit of the doubt and assume you didn't know this at the time, but Mr. Parnell knew and asked you to do it anyway. I can see from the look on your faces that you know exactly what I'm talking about. At this time, I will ask if you have anything to say in your defense."

"Mr. Parsons, Mr. Lundy, please," James pleaded. "We were young and stupid. He was offering a lot of money and we were greedy."

"Do you have any idea who it was you murdered for Mr. Parnell?" Chloe asked.

James and Lawrence exchanged uncertain looks and it was obvious they had no idea who their victim had been.

James looked back at Chloe, begging for forgiveness. "You gotta understand, we didn't—"

A sudden and explosive report echoed through the room as David fired one round into the center of James's forehead. Lawrence let out his first panicked cry as he watched his brother's head go limp, and Madeline couldn't keep herself from screaming. Chloe threw the Slugger on the ground, walked over to the table, and picked up the first knife she could lay a hand on. She looked Madeline dead in the eye as she drove the knife into the top of her thigh.

"I said not another sound," Chloe spat through clenched teeth, and turned from Madeline, this time letting her wail and cry in pain.

David approached Lawrence, resting the barrel of his gun against the side of his head, and Chloe continued. "Mr. Lundy fits into this story twofold. One, you and your brother executed a job from somebody other than your boss. Two, the man you so willingly killed for Mr. Parnell, apparently enjoying every minute of it, was Mr. Lundy's son, Wyatt."

Mr. Parsons, Denver, and Miami were shocked by this revelation. This had to have been the last thing any of them were expecting to hear, especially Mr. Parsons, who had given everything he could to David for years, trying to find the person responsible for his son's death.

Lawrence desperately tried to save his own life. "I swear! We didn't know who it was! He never told us! You've gotta believe—"

"Two in the head," David said as he pulled the

trigger twice, the force of the blow knocking Lawrence to the floor, the blood quickly pooling underneath him.

Chloe turned to a terrified, hysterical, and pain riddled Madeline as David stepped back. This one belonged to Chloe, and Chloe alone.

"You and I need to talk, and I won't tolerate crying or screaming."

Somehow, Madeline was able to calm her hysteria somewhat, but squeezed her eyes tightly at the immense pain and terror running through her body.

"Renee, please!"

"Madeline, you know very well that isn't my name anymore. In fact, you know more than anybody could have imagined. Then you thought about what you could get from my father when you decided to turn my life upside down and destroy it again in a matter of weeks."

"Renee..." Madeline's words were replaced with a cry of pain as Chloe pulled the blade from Madeline's thigh and forced it into her arm.

"You told him who I was, you told him where I was, you told him who I was dating, and you told him where to find me. I lost a love, the closest friend I ever had, and a six-year-old child died because of you."

"I'm so sorry. I had no idea—"

"You knew exactly what you were doing."

Chloe could see Madeline was desperately trying to think of the right thing to say, while simultaneously trying to fight the pain and stay alive. Chloe turned to look at her colleagues, who each silently told her if she was going to do something, she had to make sure she was doing it for the right reasons. Being partly responsible for the death of a six-year-old child was reason enough for all of them. Chloe reached a hand out to David and he gently set his gun in her hand.

Chloe turned back to Madeline, whose hysteria had grown from fear to certainty. "As of an hour ago, the casino is no longer yours. Your people are gone and management is back in our hands."

"Please!" Madeline screamed. "Let me work for you! Let me help you like I helped him!"

Chloe raised the gun and looked at Madeline with incredulity, but couldn't blame her for trying. "A lot of people who know me used to say that I'm a lot like my father, but I'm not. My father was weak and a coward. I am neither."

"Renee, please!"

"He was six years old!"

Madeline tried to cry out to save herself one last time, but Chloe was faster at squeezing the trigger, putting one bullet in Madeline's chest and another in her head, her body instantly going limp in the chair. Chloe stared at the lifeless bodies, knowing she had made the choice to accept her succession in the Family and had unquestionably proven to three of her equals that she was more than willing to follow through with that job. More importantly, all of her friends, and six-year-old Samuel Morris, could finally rest in peace.

After a few heartbeats she removed the cigar from her bag and turned it in her fingers, feeling neither remorse nor pride for what had happened today. She felt relief despite the sacrifices she had to make in her own life once more. She broke the cigar in half and threw it at Madeline's corpse, then faced all of the men in the room with a stoic look that asked if they would be willing to accept her into the Family.

Their smiles welcomed her home.

Chapter 66

Boston Herald

Tragedy struck early this morning when a fire broke out in the Grand Hotel downtown. Renee Parnell, twenty-eight years old, the only daughter of Matthew Parnell, was trapped on the twenty-seventh floor and died from smoke inhalation before rescuers could get to her.

Fire Marshall Shane Tomack confirmed the fire started due to faulty wiring in one of the guest rooms and estimates the fire started around 1:00 a.m. The only floors of the hotel affected by the fire were twenty-five through thirty. Renovations were being conducted from the twenty-third to twenty-fifth floors, and no hotel guests were injured.

Matthew Parnell, who passed away two weeks ago from a heart attack, purchased the Grand over thirty years ago and was one of Boston's, and most of the surrounding communities', largest contributor and support for children and the homeless. After his passing, his daughter, Renee, took over operations of the hotel and announced that she would be passionately continuing her father's legacy with plans to branch out in surrounding states so that more people could be positively touched by the generosity and caring Matthew Parnell had shown to so many throughout the years.

"I will be taking over operations of the hotel effective immediately," said Reginald Morris, long-time friend and former business associate of Ms. Parnell. "Matthew Parnell set up a trust for the operations of the hotel in the event of his passing, which would transfer ownership of the hotel to his daughter, and Ms. Parnell designated me to succeed her. I promise that I will do everything in my power to make sure the Parnell legacy, and the hotel, will flourish and never be forgotten."

Matthew and Renee Parnell have no surviving heirs or family, and Mr. Morris confirmed it was Ms. Parnell's wishes there be no services for her passing, but instead, a donation made in the Parnell family name to be equally divided among all after-school programs in the state.

***

The newspaper article had not moved from the corner of Chloe's desk in almost four months. She kept it there to remind herself of the sacrifices she had made, the grief and pain her choices had caused to so many, the gift she had been able to bestow upon her best friend's widower and surviving son, and that she would never be the person Matthew had been.

Her new responsibilities demanded she maintain stability in one central location and she chose to settle down in Lafayette, thereby transferring Jack to the Bureau in Boston to take over the New England territory. Chloe opened a business consulting office that would allow her not only to monitor both business entities closely, but also to begin living her life rather than running from or avoiding it. Thanks to her many years of experience, her business seemed to explode nationwide overnight. She had convinced her Family counterparts that combining their resources by having various associates working with her firm would profit every region. It took less than six months to prove she was better than Matthew would ever have been.

"It doesn't sound like that big of an issue," Chloe said into the telephone as she watched the rain outside her window. "They either want it or they don't. Have you talked to Stephen? What did he say? Did he actually read the contract? I would, but I cannot stress the importance that you step up. I can only bail you out when there is the necessity for me to step in."

She suddenly got the eerie feeling that she was being watched and swiveled her chair around to face the door. Her heart stopped for what seemed like days as her eyes locked with Hunter, casually leaning against the doorjamb of her office, one foot crossed over the other, arms folded in front of him with his head slightly cocked to the side as he quietly observed her with a trace of curiosity in his expression.

The second she saw him standing in her doorway, she wanted to slam the receiver on the phone cradle, jump out of her chair, and run into his arms. She wanted to feel his arms tighten around her as he held her to him, wanted him to want her. Her expression, however, gave nothing away as she held the receiver to her ear, trying to pay attention to the conversation.

Not taking her eyes off Hunter, she pulled herself closer to her desk and brought the conversation to an end. "Resolve the issue and I'll see you when you come back at the end of the week. In the meantime, give Stephen another copy of his contract and tell him to read it closely. Call me if he still has a problem comprehending the fine print."

She gave Hunter a guarded expression and the tautness of her body language implied their reunion wouldn't start easily. What he didn't know was that her heart was racing and her head swimming; her tongue was thick and felt like a bag of cotton, terrified that for the second time in her life she would be facing the brutal consequences of falling in love. For the first time in a long time, she didn't know how to react except with surprise.

"Quite a place you've got here," Hunter said.

"Hunter," she almost stammered. "How did you…"

He ignored her question as he advanced into the office. "So, which business is this? I'm assuming you inherited the Family business, that's why I ask. I was more than a little surprised when I found out you were not only alive, but back in Louisiana. This explains why Jack quietly left New Orleans with hardly a goodbye to anybody. I wish I had the words to explain to you how angry and frustrated I was when Jack came back from Boston. He either couldn't or wouldn't tell me anything that could even remotely put my mind at ease. I'm sure he told me what he could, but it wasn't much. I honestly couldn't tell if it was the truth or not, but I've been living the past six months of my life in hell, Chloe, and I want out."

It wasn't until now that she realized just how much her past had hurt him. "I know I'm sorry doesn't mean much, but..."

His gaze fell to the newspaper article about the fire. "Did you kill him?"

"No."

"Were you responsible for his death?"

She decided to answer honestly. "In part."

"Was his death planned?"

"His death was desired and hoped for, but, then again, nobody can predict when someone is going to die. Well, most of the time." At Hunter's look, Chloe gave him the short version of the story. "You can't tell me you missed every article and news story that quoted the cause of death as being massive heart failure due to a congenital heart defect. Did we know it would happen? No. Did we hope it would? Yes."

"*We* being?"

"You already know the answer to that question."

"I'm assuming since Jack transferred to Boston that he's running New England now."

"The fire was necessary, Hunter. Renee had to die in order for Chloe to live."

"So how—" Hunter started, but Chloe cut him off.

"What do you want from me, Hunter?" This unexpected reunion tore at her more than she wanted to admit.

"Answers."

"Then ask me questions I can answer. You are a federal agent who knows what kind of world I live in. If this weren't the last time we were going to see each other, I would give you every detail, but we're past that now. There are too many truths I want to tell you but can't and you know it."

"Have you forgotten that there isn't anything I can do? The day I was sworn to secrecy the deal was sealed. You could tell me absolutely anything right now—even if there were a body buried under your floor—and there's nothing I can do. There's not a body under your floor, is there?"

She gave a small laugh and realized she had been putting all of her focus on trying to fall out of love with him that she actually had forgotten about that fact.

"No," she answered with a smile. "No bodies under the floor."

"If you're really not comfortable saying anything because of who I work for, there is another way for me to get the answers I need and protect yourself at the same time."

She let out a disbelieving scoff and asked, "How?"

"I quit the Bureau."

Her jaw dropped in disbelief. "Why would you do that?"

"When you left, I never expected to see you again, convinced Matthew would kill you. When I heard he died, I was relieved, and the thought of your death never crossed my mind again. Then I heard about the fire and it was like a gut punch. But that wasn't the worst of it because I already know what it's like to lose someone I love and I thought I would be able to get through it the same way I did when Amy died. But I couldn't because I didn't feel the same about your death than I did about Amy's. It was worse."

If she had any feelings about how he reacted to the news of her death, they didn't show, but her breathing had become shallow and she was having a difficult time trying to control the slight tremor in her hands.

Hunter produced a folded piece of paper from his pocket and handed it to Chloe. "And then I got this in an overnight package with no return address a few weeks ago."

It was a simple typewritten note with one short sentence.

Go back to where you met and love her as much as she loves you.

A knowing smile crossed her face. "David." She

408

let out a soft sigh. "I'm sorry, Hunter. I know it doesn't mean much but I'm so sorry I hurt you and caused you so much pain. I regret every lie I told you when I should have seen that you were trying to help me, but I knew everything between us was over from the second you saw my tattoo. For reasons and explanations far beyond my comprehension, it took less than a day for me for fall in love with you and I don't have any right to love you. It could never work between us. Knowing what you know, would you really be willing and able to set aside everything you believe in to go from fighting crime to participating in organized crime? In the past few months, I have done things that I won't apologize for, but that you wouldn't be able to forgive."

"Don't you think you should let me be the judge of that?"

He was right and she knew it, but she still didn't think he would be able to forgive her once he found out she had personally taken a life out of duty and vengeance. "I run things differently than he did, but there are times when it's necessary to do what I have to when circumstance calls for it. I have a devoted Family that I have earned the trust and respect of in a short period of time, and once they find out you're FBI—"

"Former FBI," Hunter pointed out, then said with a smile, "and don't forget that Jack and I are buddies."

"It will take time for them to trust you and, I'm sorry, but I selfishly don't want to give up what I have. Would you be able to look the other way simply because you love me?"

"If it means we can be together, yes." He held up his hands to keep Chloe from interrupting. "Chloe, this is something that has crossed my mind more than once since I found out who you were, and if this is the only way for us to be together, I'll do whatever it takes. Who knows? My background could come in handy every once in a while. From the second I got that note, I knew there was nothing I wouldn't do to be with you. I love you and I'm not letting you get away again."

There was a thick silence between them as they both considered their situation. She wanted him more than she had ever wanted anybody or anything before, but if she lost him like she had once thought she had, she knew she wouldn't be able to live with heartache like that again.

"There are a lot of secrets and many explanations that you may not be prepared for, and there are more than a few that you might hate me for."

"So enlighten me," he said, spreading his hands, inviting her to shock him. "Right now, tell me one secret you think I may hate you for."

She let out a deep breath and pushed herself back from her desk, exposing the secret with the most truth and vulnerability—the large, round swell of her belly. She could see the shock and surprise on Hunter's face and she watched him quickly do the math in his head.

"Six months," she said as she ran her hands across her stomach, tracing the curve of their child, closing her eyes and sucking in a breath as a hard kick hit her ribs, making her wonder not for the first time if any of her ribs weren't broken. She watched Hunter's reaction go from stunned to wonderment as he approached her, silently asking permission to touch her stomach. She nodded and let him take in the shock, expecting his reaction to be the complete opposite of what he was expressing now.

He leaned into her, awestruck, whispering, "You weren't going to tell me."

"I wanted to, but…"

"I thought you were dead," Hunter said, and kissed her, letting her know he wasn't going anywhere. And she returned that kiss, letting him know she wanted him to stay. Chloe's phone rang, forcing them to break their passion.

She cleared her throat and reached for the phone, watching Hunter's curious face. "There's a fifty-fifty chance this call might be your test, Hunter."

"For better or worse, we're in this together now," Hunter promised as he took a seat.

She watched his face carefully as she answered the phone on speaker. "Good afternoon, Mr. Staton."

The voice on the other end of the phone was deep and clear. "Good afternoon, ma'am."

"How are things on the West Coast?"

"I'm sorry to say that I'm calling with bad news, ma'am. We lost Mr. Leonard last night."

Anger immediately took over Chloe's features, yet she was able to keep her voice even. "What happened?"

"There was apparently a disagreement between Mr. Leonard and Marco Silva…"

"Silva?" Chloe asked. "Silva, as in one of Mr.

Yates's captains?"

"Yes, ma'am."

She and Mr. Yates of Kansas City had an amicable relationship, and what Staton was saying made no sense. "A disagreement about what?"

"I wasn't there, but Mr. Collins told me the argument was over who the product collection belonged to. Silva said the contract was issued in K.C."

"A contract Mr. Yates and I previously discussed since the product was initially coming through my territory. Where is Silva now?"

"Unknown, ma'am, but we are in the process of looking for him. I think you should know that, by Mr. Collins's account, Silva didn't seem to be acting on behalf of Mr. Yates."

Curious, she thought, and then asked, "The body?"

"Cleaned up and cleared out. We said a few words before the fire."

Cremation, Chloe mouthed to Hunter, and he nodded in cautious understanding.

"Please ask Mr. Collins to call me," she ordered. "Find Mr. Silva and keep him under surveillance until you receive further orders from me. If termination is necessary, it had better be for a damn good reason. I will contact Mr. Yates regarding the behavior of his captain."

"Yes, ma'am."

Chloe disconnected the call and turned to Hunter, waiting for either acceptance or arrest. Finally, he asked, "This is normal?"

"This would actually be considered a good day."

"I'd hate to see a bad day."

"Yes," she said, "you would."

"So, what's next?"

Chloe let out a sigh. "I call Mr. Yates and then I call David. Because Mr. Silva is a captain, David will have to authorize the contract. However, since Silva works for Mr. Yates, there is the chance that he may be able to take care of the problem himself."

"And then?"

"Then nothing. Business as usual."

Hunter approached Chloe, wrapping his arms around her with a smile. "You'll have to be patient with me. This will be an entirely new lifestyle and a lot of rules for me to learn. I swear I could see him saluting you with every *ma'am* he said."

She smiled back at him, and asked for clarification, "You'll be okay with all of this?"

He lightly kissed her, then pressed his forehead to hers. "I do have one question. What are the rules and requirements for a wedding in the Lundy Family?"

Chloe pulled her head back and produced the happiest smile she had in too many years. "The first is that you keep the promises you make to one another. The others you'll learn along the way."

ACKNOWLEDGEMENTS

I want to thank everyone who made it possible for me to not only follow my dream, but to achieve it. It wasn't always easy, but in the end completely worth it.

I have to thank my mom and dad, because without them I obviously wouldn't be here to write this story.

Lucky, Bugsy, Meyer, Al, Vito, and so many others, thank you for allowing me to be swept away in your world.

Thanks must be given to my husband, Ryan, for your love, support, guidance, and making sure I ate when I spent more time with my computer than I did with you. To Ethan, thank you for convincing me to stop talking about the story and just write it. In all honesty, this story wouldn't even exist if you hadn't come over to change your oil that day. Stacey, I cannot thank you enough for always knowing exactly what to say when my muse would take a temporary leave of absence. And Shelby, thank you for being the first to read the completed first draft, your excitement for the story, and encouraging me to never give up.

A special thanks to Lori, Jennifer, Gillian, and everybody at Limitless Publishing for believing in the power of the written word.

ABOUT THE AUTHOR

Jennifer Bates was born in Spokane, Washington and grew up in Burien, Washington. Craving an adventurous change in her life, she packed up her son and moved to Idaho. A year later she met the man who would forever change her life and went to Ontario, Oregon where she stayed until another adventure came calling and she found her home in Louisiana.

Jennifer started writing at a young age, always filling spiral notebooks with ideas and stories. When she was in 4th grade, she wrote a short story for a young writers conference and placed second. She always had a story of some kind in her head, and it wasn't until 2015 that her son finally talked her into putting her favorite story to paper and a new adventure was born.

Jennifer enjoys fiction novels of many genres, but her favorite book series (she reads it every year) is the Wilderness series by Sara Donati. Fascinated by anything organized crime related, she finds inspiration for her writing.

Among a few of Jennifer's favorite things (not necessarily in this order) are cheesecake, hockey, video games, and spending time with her family. By day, she is a legal secretary in Lafayette, Louisiana where she resides with her husband, kids, and grandchildren.

Facebook:
https://www.facebook.com/authorjenniferbates/

Twitter:
https://twitter.com/BranomJ

Goodreads:
https://www.goodreads.com/user/show/4980902-jennifer-bates

Instagram:
https://www.instagram.com/jennifer_bates_author/